WHERE WE BELONG
STONE RIDERS MC BOOK 2

ASHLEY MUÑOZ

Where We Belong Copyright © 2024
by Ashley Munoz & ZetaLife LLC
ISBN: 9798878652957
ISBN: 9798878656658
ISBN: 979-8-9874862-7-6
ISBN:979-8-9874862-8-3

ALL RIGHTS RESERVED

No part of this book whether in electronic form or physical book form, may be reproduced, copied, sold or distributed in any way. That includes electronic, mechanical, photocopying, recording, or any other form of information sharing, storage or retrieval system without the clear, lawful permission of the author.

This book is a work of total and complete fiction. **No AI tools, programs or apps were used in any part of creating this work.** The story was thought up from the authors curious and thoughtful brain.

Any names, places, characters, businesses, events, brands, media, situations or incidents are all made up. Anything resemblances to a real, similar, or duplicated persons or situations is purely coincidental.

The author acknowledges that while it was not her intent to use trademarked products, it is possible that a few slipped through. The publication or use of these trademarks is not authorized, associated with, or sponsored by the trademark owners.

NO AI TRAINING: Without in any way limiting Ashley Munoz (the author) and (and Zetalife LLC) exclusive rights under copyright, any use of this publication to "train" generative artificial intelligence (AI) technologies to generate text is expressly prohibited. Ashley Muñoz reserves all rights to license uses of this work for generative AI training and development of machine learning language models.

Cover Design: Wildheart Graphics
Photographer: Regina Wamba
Models: Colby Hartz- IG: @colby_hartz,
Summer Anderson IG: @okoksummer
Editor: Rebecca Fairest Reviews
Proofread: Tiffany Hernandez
Beta Dev Editing: Memos in the Margins

❦ Created with Vellum

MOTORCYCLE CLUB TERMS:

Cut: Usually a leather or denim vest with the club insignia referenced as patches, or colors. It identifies which club you ride with, and show loyalty to.

Sweetbutt: A term used for girls who aren't in a committed relationship of any kind but have been given permission to be in the club and spend time with its members.

Old Lady: A female inside the club that is either married to or in a committed relationship with one of its members, age is not a factor when referencing this term.

Prospect: The lowest ranking member, as in their membership is still being decided. They will do chores and extra things to prove their dedication to the club.

Property Patch: An honor amongst clubs as it's a way for women to show which member they're committed to, this is an elevated status that shows you belong with someone from the club, however, this does not mean someone wearing a property patch is a member of the club.

House Mouse: Someone who is given status in the club by doing chores, and cleaning, it can often attach protection and ownership if this service is given by a member.

Church: a meeting place for the highest-ranking club members where decisions are made and private club matters are discussed.

One Percent Patch: 99% of all motorcycle clubs are law-abiding clubs that gather for more of a brotherhood, hobby, or sense of community. However, one percent of these clubs wear this patch indicating they do not abide by the laws outside of the ones set by their clubs. This may include violent actions for protection, illegal means of earning money, and more.

President: In terms of the motorcycle club this person is the highest-ranking member, making all final calls and decisions.

CONTENT ADVISORY

While this book will follow a completely different couple from book one, it is highly encouraged to read Where We Started first. I have tried my best to conclude things so you won't have to, however, club dynamics will make it easier to understand the world if you read book one first. You can read it free with Kindle Unlimited, right here. It is also in audio or paperback.

This is not considered a dark romance, however, there are themes to be aware of such as:

Violence found common in MC books.
 Being held hostage, at gunpoint (this is a brief scene and while a gun is used to hold the character in place, the character is unharmed completely)
 Graphic sexual scenes including cum play.
 <u>All sexual scenes are consensual.</u>
 Reference to gore from a photo but not detailed.
 Murder.
 Parental Verbal Abuse

There is a scene in which a memory is recalled involving a graphic murder- it is brief.

Pregnancy- discussing baby names, rubbing the stomach, and picking out nursery decor.

Going into labor.

VIRGINIA 1% RIVAL MOTORCYCLE CLUBS

Stone Riders: President - Killian Quinn

Chaos Kings: President- Jameson King

Death Raiders: President- Silas Silva

Sons of Speed: President- Alec Veda

Mayhem Riot: President-Archer Green

<u>Rose Ridge is a fictional town inspired by Fredericksburg, Virginia.
All towns mentioned in the book are made up while being inspired by true locations.</u>

To those who feel fragile.
To the ones who have apologized for being soft.
The ones who feel like they cry too often.
There's a dark prince out there somewhere searching for you.... They're the ones who secretly plucked flowers and wished on stars.
Hoping that one day their harsh world would hold beauty.

Spotify Playlist
Pinterest Board

WHERE WE BELONG

ONE
LAURA

The bathtub had rust in it.

For some reason that tiny detail kept running through my mind as Callie continued to talk about the location, the spacious living room, and the lack of mold. Apparently, these apartments off Main Street were highly sought after, and the fact that we had snagged an appointment to see one was a miracle. I decoded the words and realized what she was really saying:

Her husband, who happened to run a motorcycle club, had called in a favor.

It was why I had agreed to see the apartment, and why I was currently keeping my mouth shut about the rust. Callie was my best friend, and ever since I had randomly decided to pack up my life and follow her to Rose Ridge, she had done nothing but help me. She let me live with her for two weeks when I arrived, and then her husband gave me the chance to live in his old apartment for free. It was a good deal, an amazing and perfect deal considering the apartment was brand new and had all top-of-the-line appliances.

Not a single stain, ring, or particle of rust to be found.

The only downside was the space would eventually be shared with the only person on this planet that got under my skin.

Killian Quinn.

The Wolf.

"I feel like I've been talking your ear off, Laur. What do you think of the place?" Callie turned, near the front door, to inspect my reaction. Her long dark hair was tied half up into an edgy updo, with wisps framing her face. Her arms were covered in a long-sleeve shirt, and she was wearing jeans, now that the weather had turned a bit colder. Something had changed in her since she arrived back home. Her shell had cracked, and her confidence had found a way back. She stood taller, her smile was wider, and her eyes seemed brighter.

I loved it for her.

I smiled while trailing a nail along the cracked Formica countertop. "I like it."

Not enough to want to live here, not when I had all the luxuries the club apartment provided. I knew I couldn't stay there forever, and I knew eventually Killian would actually step foot inside, and when he did, we'd probably kill each other.

Callie's countenance fell. "You don't though, I can tell you don't."

"Callie, it's great. I just don't know that I can afford it yet. It's sort of expensive, and just being real, the club apartment is much nicer."

Heaving a sigh, my best friend tucked her arms over her chest. "But you seem so miserable living there. I hate that and, deep down, I'm worried you'll move back to DC."

My heart squeezed tight at the apprehension in her voice. Callie and I had met in DC nearly four years ago, and when her father passed three months ago, and she had to come down here to sort out his funeral and will, it led to a whole shitstorm. Ultimately, she ended up back with her ex, and I was happy for her, but this tiny town was never on my radar, or in my plans. Still…

"I chose to move here, Callie. I want to live next to you. You're about to pop out a baby in nine months, who do you think is going to be that kid's aunt?" I pointed at myself because Callie had no siblings.

"Yes, I'm sure my kid is going to love their Aunt Laura and Uncle Killian trying to murder one another every five seconds." She rolled her eyes.

I winced, while lowering my gaze. Sometimes I forgot that Killian was like a brother to her; they'd grown up together in the club and her father had taken the idiot man child under his wing.

"We would never do that around the peanut. We can be civil when we need to be." I stood tall, trying to sound as reassuring as possible.

The thing was, Killian had sent me some mixed messages from the moment we met three months ago. Occasionally, it didn't seem like he hated me, but any time I softened toward him, he'd only prove that he was testing me for weakness. Still, I was mature enough to keep my mouth shut around Callie's kid. I already did that plenty around her husband. He didn't appreciate me shit-talking his best friend, and I understood it. This whole motorcycle club lifestyle bred loyalty and brotherhood, and they'd all known each other for a lifetime. I was new to this, and I had to be cautious with how I spoke.

Callie watched me with a worried expression when suddenly there was a horrible screeching sound coming from upstairs.

At the same time, our eyes flew up to the ceiling. There were two people loudly arguing. Their footsteps creaked and echoed overhead, and the walls were so thin, we could make out every word.

After we realized the couple was fighting over bills, and forgetting the goddamn beer again, our eyes slowly slid back down and collided.

With a burst of laughter, Callie shook her head. "You can't live here."

I snorted with her, grabbing my purse.

"Abso—fucking—lutley not. I'd end up strangling them both by week's end."

"Your temper, Laur. You need yoga or something." Callie exited, then let me pass before shutting the door. The super had left us to look at it alone, seeing as he was a friend of the Stone Riders motorcycle club, and didn't want to disrespect Callie by being in the same space as her without her husband being present. Something to that effect; the rules of being in the club were confusing.

"Yeah, I'll get right on that," I joked, following her out.

We exited the apartment building, still hearing the couple above us screaming at one another. Once the cool Virginia air hit my face, I closed my eyes and inhaled deeply.

The thing was, I actually loved this tiny town.

I hadn't found my place in it yet, but I enjoyed the little nuances and character that made up the smaller city. It was quiet here, everything moved slower, like I could finally catch my breath. It was so different than where I had lived as a kid, a small suburb outside of Richland. Chapel Grove was an entirely different sort of small-town. One that was built with old money and polluted with rich pricks who hadn't ever shown an ounce of loyalty or kindness a day in their lives.

"So, are you coming to the bonfire tonight?" Callie asked, while we walked down the street, toward her tattoo studio. Her husband owned it, but she had a chair inside, where she worked, and had started building up her own clientele. She was damn good too, the only person I trusted to ink my skin.

Staring at the ground, I shrugged. "Don't know. I guess, if I get hungry."

"You should come, at least to let loose for a bit. I know you're still trying to figure out the club dynamics, but Wes is starting to transition things over to Killian, and we're a little nervous about how the newer prospects are going to respond since they're used to how Wes does things. You're like eye candy to them, maybe you could flit around and flirt for a bit. Talk up the new club president?"

Gross. I nearly barfed in my mouth.

Her husband, Wes, was stepping down from leading the club, handing the reins over to my mortal enemy, and she wanted me to schmooze the club members? I'd rather stick a fork in my hand than talk up the asshole who made my life a living hell as often as he possibly could.

"I can make an appearance, Cal, but I have nothing good to say about him."

Callie stopped mid step, turning toward me.

"I'm so confused by you two. Aren't you guys living together? I remember when he said goodbye to you on that bus platform, he looked at you like…" She trailed off, as if she were nervous to voice what she was actually thinking.

"Looked at me like what?"

Her lips pursed, before she shook her head. "He gave you something."

She ignored my comment and decided to just go for the kill.

I knew I should have been more careful with my words. She had a difficult time understanding just how cruel her pseudo big brother could be, at least to me.

"So he gave me something." I shrugged, feeling agitated.

Callie searched my face. "So what did he give you?"

Why was she suddenly so curious?

Pushing on farther down the street, I shook my head. "It's stupid."

She was right at my shoulder, gently squeezing my arm. "Tell me anyway."

"Fine, but you can't ask follow-up questions."

"Okay, I won't," she swore.

With a heavy sigh, I stopped once more and looked around. "He gave me a pebble."

Callie's mouth parted slightly, her brows dipping as she tried to work it out.

"As in a rock?"

I nodded. "I need coffee."

I knew she wanted to know why he gave it to me, and months later, I was still curious about it too. I knew the significance of it. I just couldn't quite understand why he'd given it to me, except that he likely assumed he'd never see me again. It was why I had never brought it up to him, and why I would die a thousand times over before confessing it was still in my suitcase, tucked away where no one would ever find it.

Because admitting that Killian Quinn gave me a metaphorical piece of his heart, was something I would never admit to anyone, not even myself.

TWO
LAURA
THREE MONTHS AGO

I was working really hard not to sing along with the tune playing obnoxiously loud over the speaker system. I loved Hozier, and whenever "Take Me to Church" came on, I took it as my imaginary opportunity to try out for *The Voice*.

My best friend Callie was a few feet ahead of me, talking to some woman with white hair, looking like she had just stepped out of some pin-up magazine from the forties. Pretty sure Callie had said her name was Red.

As in the color.

We'd arrived today to settle her father's estate, which was all left to my girl in the will. But when we got here, the local, and apparently only motel, turned us away, saying a private party had booked the whole thing. Turned out, according to Callie—her ex had called and told the owner not to help us.

And what sort of batshit crazy was that?

I'd never heard of such antics outside of a television show.

We were now standing inside her childhood home, which I guess had been converted into some sleek garage club, surrounded by men and women wearing denim and black leather. There were pool tables to the left, motorcycles being worked on off to the right and all sorts of mayhem happening in the middle.

More people came over and started hugging Callie. It made my heart melt a tiny bit because in DC she was all alone. She had her dog Max, and her chair in the tattoo studio that treated her like shit, but otherwise, that was it. She had me, and she'd become the most important person in my life.

I was busy people-watching, silently mouthing the lyrics to a David Kushner song when Callie's ex walked up. Callie had told me he was the president of the club, and his leather vest had that title sewn in white along the left of his breast. The man next to him shifted, then suddenly pulled my best friend into a tight hug, and something in my chest seemed to perk up like a sleepy flower finding the sun.

My eyes landed on his ink first, considering it stretched up from his chest and covered most of his neck. Then his jaw because it was one of those clichés that belonged in one of my smutty romance books, with its jagged edge—sharp enough to cut glass. I was ogling the man, no question about it, and my staring only intensified when I settled on the twin emeralds he had for eyes, which were crowded by thick, dark lashes.

Callie had called him Killian, and he had called her Little Fox.

When his cold stare seemed to soak me up like a sponge, I nearly stopped breathing.

His gaze held weight, as if he were sizing me up, and something itched inside my veins to prove that I was worthy.

Internally, I scolded myself, this sort of thinking was stupid. Archaic. I didn't attempt to get men's attention, or strive for their affection, but my fingers skimmed the tattoo along my rib cage that Callie had given me, all on their own. Her work had come up in their conversation, and suddenly, I was a walking canvas, showing this gorgeous man all the ink I owned by lifting my shirt.

Killian's finger traced the mermaid scales, and my stupid fucking hormones perked up.

It had been so long since there was anyone who had the power to make me act like a girl with a crush. Silly and ridiculous, showing off, and standing taller. I practically begged him to look at me.

Then he opened his mouth, and it all went to hell.

Because while Killian was gorgeous in a way that made my thighs slick, and my heart race. He was mean.

The sort of mean that carried venom; he'd lure you in with a smile and take you out with whispered cruelty. Once Callie had walked away, I was thrust into the spotlight, and Killian Quinn took full advantage of making sure I knew where I stood inside his world.

"You ever been told you look like a cartoon character?"

Confused, I stupidly tipped my head back to catch the glint of those green eyes. Surely this was his way of flirting. Drawing closer to me, I nearly melted into his broad chest, but I certainly didn't step back or move. His presence was like air. Everywhere, and as though I'd need it to survive in this town.

His lips curved upward as he watched me squirm.

"Not the cute kind," his eyes moved from my face to my chest, "the kind of cartoon you'd find on a dirty picture crumpled up in some teen's garbage can. One you draw on the cusp of puberty when you're still too chicken shit to look up porn. So one of your good friends in art class takes his colored pencils and draws a woman with big tits, nice rosy nipples, makes sure she's got a tiny waist with over—the—top thick thighs, and of course, that ass. It's round and mouthwatering…but completely fake."

How was it possible that ice had slicked over my veins, all while heat engulfed my face? Anger surged through my chest like a battering ram, needing to get out and show this person, whoever he was, that he couldn't speak to me like that. No one had ever spoken to me like that.

"You know what? Fuck you."

Clicking his tongue, his eyes wandered over my shoulder. "Nah, I'm not into cartoon characters, never knew what everyone saw in Jessica Rabbit. You got all that plastic shit keeping your tits up, and it ain't attractive. Now, that girl," he pointed and gently turned my shoulder, so I could track who he was talking about, "see the one eyeing me right now with tits that don't look like a fucking AI generator popped 'em out? I think I'll go fuck *her*."

With one last smirk in my direction, he sauntered off, and I hated the fact that my eyes followed. The woman he went for had short black hair, with tattoos, and she was tall. So freaking tall, *and the complete opposite of me.*

Trying to come back to myself, I attempted to shake off his comments, but it wasn't easy. Confidence was my favorite accessory, and there hadn't been a single person to make me feel like folding in on myself since I moved away from home.

But he had.

Like a goddamn accordion.

He was wrong though, I didn't have the sort of money to enhance any part of my body. Not even whitening strips for my teeth. I ran my tongue over the canine that was twisted just enough to make me insecure, hating that this asshole had already got inside my head.

The sound of someone entering and causing a stir had people moving, and that was enough to get my mind back on Callie and her trying to find us a place to stay. Fuck that guy and his stupid assumptions, he could keep his tattooed girlfriend and this stupid motorcycle club. I wasn't sticking around long enough for it to matter.

THREE
KILLIAN
PRESENT DAY

It wasn't even winter yet, and there were double the number of trucks in front of the club, taking up all the fuckin' spaces. November, and everyone acted like their dicks would freeze off if they rode. Shouldn't even bother me, seeing as I had a reserved spot right in front, but it did. Or maybe I was just agitated over the impending transition.

Could also be that with the weather turning colder, I was getting tired of driving the longer route to and from the club. The duplex I rented in town was getting fucking old. I wanted the apartment that was owed to me as President. I'd given Laura free rein of the place, not wanting to make her feel uncomfortable by moving in…not wanting to stir shit up. Wes had asked me to let her stay, and while he was president, I followed his request.

But now that role had fallen to me, and I was ready to kick the pretty blonde out on her ass.

"You're here too early," someone called from inside the club, stealing my attention.

I was still straddling my bike, but swinging my leg over, I cleared it. Removing my bucket helmet, I ditched it on the seat before climbing the steps. I cut a quick glance to the side where the entrance to the apartment was; there was no real reason why my head snapped to the left every time I climbed these steps, it just did. I could tell myself it was because it was my apartment, and I was eager to move in, but truthfully, it had more to do with who was currently living inside it.

Nothing usually filled the empty space in front of the apartment, especially because for whatever reason, Laura didn't have a car. So I expected the same today as I entered the club; except today, there was a motorcycle parked out front.

My steps faltered for two seconds before I swung my gaze forward.

Wes, my best friend and the current president of the Stone Riders Motorcycle Club was standing there, leather cut over a long-sleeved shirt, glaring at me like I just pissed in his cereal. Like he could read my thoughts about kicking his wife's best friend out of the apartment.

"That a problem to be early to my own fucking club?" I snapped, pushing past him.

Things between us were strained. On the surface and in front of everyone else, we were the same as always. Best friends, brothers. I'd kill for him, I'd die for him, but I was also fucking pissed at him. Not only had he been chosen to lead the club over me, but he'd kept me in the dark about his new house, and Simon being there—which nearly got him killed.

"No, but we had plans," Wes muttered, following on my heels.

The club was murky without the sun out. The November sky was overcast, making the interior all shadows. The smell of beer and some fragrant air freshener tickled my nose. Red, our club mom for all intent and purposes, added something woodsy to the clubhouse to offset the smell of so many bodies being in here all the time.

This morning, the floors were freshly mopped, the bar organized and cleaned, which meant the prospects had already been in here doing chores. Unless someone got themselves a house mouse without me knowing it. The only other person to clean in here was Natty, but she usually did that in the afternoons after helping at a local coffee shop.

Wes strode toward the kitchen and I followed. There in the back were Natty, Red, Callie and the last person who had my feet nearly faltering again.

Laura fucking White.

Her blue eyes were up, locked on mine as if they were magnets, looking for their paired piece to connect to. I hated how she stared at me, always like she knew what I was thinking and what I was about to do. It made me angry because...I'd made it a point to avoid her these past few months. By this point, we should be completely indifferent toward one another, and yet one look and I felt like I was being pulled into her thrall.

Darting my eyes away, I focused on the cake they were all crowded around.

"He's early." Red clicked her tongue disapprovingly.

I smiled at the woman who was more like a mother to me than anyone else on this planet. Her white hair was thick and wrapped up in her infamous updo, still looking like a pinup girl with a black bandana wrapped around the back and knotted in front. Even at barely seven in the morning, she had on perfect makeup, thick, fake lashes and her signature red lip color. She was pushing sixty-seven, but still just as snappy and ornery as ever.

Pulling Red by her shoulders, I placed a kiss on top of her head. "Excuse me for not realizing I wasn't welcome in my own club, event isn't even happening for a few more days."

"Yeah, but you can't see any of the preparations," Callie said, holding a piping bag to finish off a few of the last swirls around the cake. There were likely four or five sheet cakes to feed everyone, but this one would be for show. Someone had drawn, in great detail, a motorcycle and the skull and roses insignia for our club. My money was on Callie, the tattoo artist, who gave me another glance and prodded with more questions.

"Are you ready for the big transition?"

I hated myself for letting my gaze slide back toward the tiny blonde at Callie's side, but it did so without permission. I noticed her long, thick hair first, and how even it being messily thrown on top of her head, made her look like a goddess. Tiny curls framed her face, and even though she wasn't watching me, I noticed how her pale skin reddened the smallest bit, as if she was fully aware I was observing her. I may not like Laura, but it didn't mean I wasn't attracted to her. Three months of studying her, and I had memorized her flushes, when her brows would dip or rise, how a genuine laugh sounded bursting from her chest.

I saw how she bit her lip when she had something to say but wouldn't. Or how they thinned into a firm line when she was upset. I had learned every small movement of hers, unconsciously, and absolutely unwillingly.

Focusing on Callie, who was like my little sister, I smiled. "Ready as I'll ever be."

Callie flicked a quick gaze to Laura, who hadn't looked up yet, then focused back on the cake. Laura was smoothing out the frosting along the sides, and Natty was busy with another piping bag, decorating the opposite side Callie was working on.

"Laura, you should get going, we need those extra ingredients and the meat picked up," Red said, grabbing a box of paper plates and cups.

"Laura doesn't have a car, so how is she getting around to get these ingredients?" I asked, hating that I even cared.

My proposed roommate still wouldn't look up, and it bothered me. I wanted her to tell me face to face why another member's bike was parked in front of my apartment. I couldn't care less who she spread those milky thighs for but having those fuckers in my house was not happening. Ever.

"Same as always, she can take my car," Red replied, keeping her focus on the paper plates.

A rasping voice shrilled up from the bar, "No she can't, did you forget I need it today." Red's old man, Brooks, walked up behind her and placed a kiss on her neck. Seeing them still in love after all these years was still a punch to the gut. I had only ever dreamed of finding someone like that, but growing up in this club, all I ever witnessed was a revolving door of sweetbutts who wanted to fuck, suck or score. A few men found permanent partners, even going as far as to fall in love, but it was rare. Even our previous prez, Simon, didn't find love until he was older, nearly in the grave.

Maybe that would be me. A long, hard life, and in my old age, I'd have someone to care and love me.

"Well shit, I forgot you're heading out to Richland." Red hugged Brooks' neck, then pulled away with a sigh.

"I have a client coming into Dead Roses in thirty minutes; otherwise, I'd take her," Callie piped up next.

I knew Natty didn't drive, not sure why but the girl walked nearly everywhere, or took her scooter.

Laura's face was practically crimson, but she kept her focus on the cake, so no one was really looking at her.

"Killian, take her for me, please. You're not supposed to be here yet anyway, so it's perfect," Red suggested, sorting through the box of paper plates and napkins.

Laura's face flew up lightning fast. "That's okay, I can ask Kip."

I fucking knew that was his bike in front of my apartment, I had a feeling. Asshole knew better than to fuck in my house.

"I don't have shit to do this morning, so I don't mind," I bit out coldly.

Laura looked around as if someone would help. "But your bike...I have a lot of things I need to get."

"I have a truck." God damn, fucking trucks. Besides, what did she think her precious Kip was going to cart her around in?

She wiped her hands on the tiny apron around her narrow hips and hesitated. "Well, what if I just borrow your truck then? You can go back home and rest until it's time to show up."

Tilting my head the slightest bit, I bit out, "Funny thing about that word, home. Why don't I just go and crash right now in the apartment I'm supposed to live in?"

I wanted her in the corner, without any choice but to confess in front of everyone here.

"I've never stopped you from moving in." Laura held her head high.

I wanted to press her, embarrass her, punish her. She knew it was unacceptable for a lower ranking member like Kip to stay in the president's house, regardless of whether he was home or not. She may not have grown up in this life, but after three months, she'd acclimated to it.

"I'm not letting you borrow my shit. You're already *borrowing* my fucking apartment, and you're not showing any signs of leaving. Wouldn't want you to get the idea that you could take my truck anytime you wanted. Fuck knows you'll never give it back."

Hurt flashed in her eyes, and it felt like a knife had slid between my ribs.

Callie slammed her piping bag down. "That was fucking rude, Kil. What is wrong with you? Laura and I went apartment hunting just a few days ago, she *is* trying, and she—"

"It's okay, Cal," Laura interrupted, untying her apron.

Callie's glare was a silent threat to be nicer to her friend. This was what needed to change. I didn't owe her or anyone else shit. I didn't need to be nice or do favors. Only reason I was willing to take her to run errands was because she was prepping for my party.

"We'll be back." I exhaled, locking eyes with Wes for a moment. His gaze was hard, but he remained silent.

Laura grabbed a zip-up hoodie and pulled it on, then snatched her purse before storming past me. I watched her ass sway in the tight jeans she wore. Her loose bun bobbed while she stomped, and more pieces began to fall around her shoulders, coming undone. She seemed completely unbothered by it.

"Where is your truck?" she snapped, folding her arms over her chest.

My eyes traveled there next, ogling her tits. She had the best rack of anyone I'd ever seen, but I wasn't a tit man, nor was I an ass man. I was usually drawn to women who were a bit edgier, covered in tattoos, leather and piercings. Nothing like the blonde-haired, blue-eyed pixie fuming in front of me.

"Garage," I clipped, jogging down the steps and striding across the gravel. I gave a long look toward my bike while Laura trailed after me.

Her face was down, and that was good. The less we interacted the better.

When we entered the large garage off the side of the clubhouse, I unlocked the doors and Laura quickly cut toward the passenger side. The gunmetal gray F150 sat taller with the lift I'd just had added to it, but with the foot bar, she shouldn't have an issue.

Once we were both inside, and she shut her door, I tried to ignore the subtle hints of citrus coming from her. It was orange and lemon, something spicy and addicting.

"You want to brush that mop out of your eyes, or you good?" I started the truck, knowing I was being a prick, but her beauty got under my skin. She was too pretty, and it made me aware of her in a way that bordered on obsessive, which I didn't like.

She slid her hands into her hair and let the weight fall as she pulled the elastic free. The citrus aroma amplified, and the way her hair looked, long and shiny, while being curled on the ends, fuck, it was perfect.

"Are we going to drive, or did you forget how?" Her blue eyes finally slid over, narrowing on me.

I hated that she was able to verbally spar with me. I cleared my throat and started the truck.

The overcast sky stretched overhead as we made our way toward the city. She began looking through her purse, pausing briefly on a list in her hand, before swapping over to her cell. She was focused, ignoring me, and I didn't like it.

"So, you're apartment hunting?"

Her eyes stayed on her lap. "Yeah."

I looked over quickly before refocusing on the road. "Find anything good?"

She made a small humming sound but didn't reply.

Fuck, I hated how we always seemed to fall into this role right here. I would be a prick, she would fight back, I'd get hard and want her to lower her walls, but she'd just throw up a middle finger, and we'd be in a fight. I'd never met anyone like her; most women wanted me. Or some aspect at least, my position in the club, or just a chance to suck my dick; either way, they were agreeable.

"So where do you need to stop first?"

She finally looked over at me. "The Dollar General."

Flipping my blinker, I turned down the street for the butcher. "They don't open for another hour or so."

"Shit," she breathed, crossing something out on her list.

"You need to grab some meat from the butcher, right?" I pulled into one of the open spaces in front of the shop. The smoke house had a raised porch, and an old, battered door that was abused by the weather, and hadn't been repaired in years.

Laura pulled her list closer to her face. "Yeah, I need to get patties and brats."

I jumped out and rounded the truck, not really thinking about opening the door for her but doing it regardless.

"I used to be the one who had to hunt all this stuff down back when we had big events."

Laura tilted her face to the side, keeping in step with me as we scaled the steps.

"The last one would have been for Wes, right?"

Her remark hit painfully hard. Months later, and it still felt like a rough rock being scraped over exposed flesh. Going back to that moment when Simon had announced to everyone that Wes would be the new president after his passing. Regardless that I had been acting vice president for over six years. He'd selected Wes, and not me and I simply had to accept it. Wes had tried to assuage my shame by explaining that he'd only been selected because Simon knew it was temporary.

Still fucking hurt. I was the backup plan, no other way to spin it in my head.

"Yep."

"I still don't understand why he's stepping down. I feel like he's been leading just fine while being with Callie."

She didn't seem to know her friend very well. She obviously had no idea how badly Callie hated this life, or why it was such a big deal that the man she was with would not lead a motorcycle club.

"Guess you wouldn't really understand it, outsiders rarely do."

Her gaze skimmed over me, her lips parting the smallest bit as if she were surprised by my answer.

"Can I help y—" The butcher's words died on his tongue the second he spotted me.

"Killian...I wasn't expecting you to be the one to grab the order." John ducked his head, wincing the smallest bit.

The butcher and I had a bit of a past. A bloody one, where the fucker tried to fight me for my spot in the club. When I beat him, he had to leave. I had told Simon getting our meat from someone who had an ax to grind with us wasn't a good idea, but he said we didn't need to worry about it. Still wasn't sure what that meant, but now that things were transferring to me, maybe it was time I found someone else.

"John." I nodded toward him.

Laura cleared her throat and stepped closer to the counter. "Can I add something to this order, or is it too late?"

John flicked a quick look my way before settling on the blonde in front of him. The way his eyes dipped to her cleavage didn't escape me, nor did the way his lips twisted into something salacious.

"You can add just about any sort of meat you'd like to that order, honey, and I'd be happy to oblige."

Laura's pouty lips slid into an easy smile, but I didn't miss the crinkle near her eyes. "Chicken...I need to add a few thighs and breasts to the order."

John's gaze flicked down her frame again. "Breasts?"

Something inside me bristled at how he was staring at her.

I cleared my throat, but John didn't seem to notice.

"I have some juicy breasts in the back, wanna come take a look? I think my meat will exceed your expectations."

Fuck. This. Guy. "Say one more disgusting thing to her, just one fucking more, and I will knock your teeth into your throat."

John's face paled as his eyes snapped away from Laura's chest.

"I wasn't saying anything inappropriate. I'm sorry if she took it wrong," John argued, but Laura cut him off.

"*She* didn't take it wrong. She understood perfectly what you were doing and saying. She is right fucking here, and if he didn't say something first, I would have. I'm a customer, not a poster for you to stare at. Meet my eye level and stop watching my chest. I want chicken added to the order, and because you're so unprofessional, I'd like you to add them at no extra cost."

John regarded me, as if he needed approval, but I merely stared back. I was mildly impressed with the way the tiny pixie handled that, but irritation over how unfazed she seemed to be by someone making lewd and suggestive comments to her, seemed to burn in my chest. While John went into the back to grab our order, I walked behind Laura's back, skimming her shoulder.

"Why do we need chicken exactly?"

Laura tipped her head back, nailing me with a severe eye roll. "Well, if you took two seconds away from getting your dick sucked, or fucking your way through the club, you'd notice that Hamish has been having some health issues. He's supposed to cut back on red meat. So are Pops and Brooks."

Shit, I had missed that about the old timers. Poor Hamish was getting up there in years. His limp had become more pronounced, and he'd been coughing a lot more. He was one of the only old timers who knew my dad, and watched out for me when he'd gone to prison. He was a good guy, and Laura's summarization of me was annoyingly accurate. Except of course for the reason behind why I came across as *distracted*. She thought I was getting sucked off and fucking my way through the club, and that's exactly what I wanted her to think.

"You seem rather bothered by the fact that I've been distracted lately."

She shrugged, pulling on a piece of plastic resting on the lip of the counter. "I'm actually impressed. Now that some time has passed and I've had a chance to get to know a few of the members, I plan on indulging in a little distraction myself."

"Is that why there was a bike outside of—"

"Here you go," John came out from the back with a cardboard box, "and the chicken is at no extra charge…sorry about earlier." His expression softened while glancing briefly in Laura's direction. I had the strange urge to stand in front of her, even with his apology. Dude gave off all kinds of bad vibes and red flags.

I grabbed the box while Laura handed over the club credit card. Once we'd been rung up, I held the door open until she stepped through, giving one last glare over my shoulder at John. We needed to get a new butcher, plain and simple. I was going to have to put a prospect on searching out a new one.

"Where to next?" I hauled the box of meat into the bed of the truck as Laura walked around, settling back into the passenger seat.

Once I was inside, I watched as she scanned her list.

"The Dollar General and the Market for a few groceries. Now that you've got the meat, I can walk to the store and head back when I'm done."

"Why do you keep trying to do this shit on your own?" I asked, angrily pulling out of the lot. Didn't bother me, but it was just more efficient to have someone drive her around. Especially since she was part of the club, but not patched in with anyone. If a rival member was close and saw her hanging around us without a patch, it could become dangerous.

Laura continued examining the list. "Why do you care?"

"I care because you'll just become a problem for me if something happens to you."

Her eyes were on the side of my face while I continued to drive.

"Okay, fine. Next time I'm just going to drive Callie to work so I can borrow her car."

"Why not just buy your own?" The store was coming up on the side of the road, so I flicked the blinker and slowed the truck.

Laura let out a small laugh. "If I wasn't trying to find a new apartment, I would, but it's sort of one or the other. Once I get the new place, I won't have to come to the club anymore. I'll get a job in town and walk everywhere."

My eyes were on her again; at this point, it was unsafe how distracted I was. Why was she saying this shit? Sure, she annoyed me from time to time, but leaving? She'd seen too much; she knew too many secrets. She couldn't leave the club. But shit, it was more than any of that...

I just didn't want her to go.

"Killian, watch the road!"

I swung my gaze in time to see a red Subaru swerve out of my lane, just barely in time.

"What the fuck?" I yelled, briskly looking over my shoulder to see where it had gone.

Laura did the same, holding onto the strap of her seat belt. "That was weird. It was like they were aiming for you."

That was unusual. Very fucking unusual.

"You know what? Fuck it, I need coffee."

We ventured toward The Drip, a coffee shop on Main Street. Usually, I'd pull up on my bike, and the crowd in front would part for me. Most of Rose Ridge understood what the club represented, and they respected it. We did a lot for this town, and with four other malicious clubs in the surrounding area, it went far to have a capable club at your back and in your pocket.

We parked in an open space, the weird encounter with the car still rattling around in my head, making me over analyze it. Didn't make any sense for a car that small to try and play chicken with a truck my size. Rose Ridge had some different characters, but we didn't get a ton of tourists or visitors, especially not in November. Besides, the plate read Virginia.

"That car coming into our lane, there was something to that, wasn't there?" Laura asked, hopping out of the truck.

"Just an asshole who doesn't know how to drive," I mused, striding up the sidewalk. I didn't need Laura to know more shit about the club if she wasn't even planning on staying. My gut said that car was a warning, and the situation would warrant pulling up a few of the surrounding cams to see what we could find on who was driving.

Laura lowered her face, tucking close to my side.

Something she had learned since being a part of the club is to stay close to us when we ventured into public. As usual, there was a line practically out the door. Rose Ridge was a small town, which meant a lack of variety. Not to mention, The Drip was a favorite for locals because of their baked goods. I knew Natty was one of the people who helped with that, but she kept a low profile here.

Laura tugged the sleeve of my jacket. "There's nowhere to sit."

Searching the space, I noticed one of the guys that had been hanging around the club, trying to decide if he wanted to join. His brown eyes flicked up to mine, his face blanched, but he kept talking to his date, while his gaze locked on mine. I nearly laughed at his shitty show of dominance. He didn't want to play coward in front of his date, but that's exactly what he'd be doing.

He just secured his role in not becoming a member, but he needed to vacate his seat, if for no other reason than he'd been wasting the club's time by hanging around and licking our club's available pussy.

"Grab us some coffees and food, I'll get us a spot."

Laura didn't even glance over to where I was headed; she just walked to the front of the long line and politely cut in front of the person who was about to order. I shifted so she wouldn't see my smile. She wasn't my woman, but fuck if she didn't carry herself like she was. As president of the Stone Riders, I had no time for anyone who didn't understand the role I held, and how that extended to them if they were with me.

I edged around a few people until I was in front of the kid who'd wasted my time.

"Up."

His eyes found mine again, that ugly as fuck red staining his cheeks. "Killian…uh, hey."

I eyed his date, smiled with all my teeth then swung my head back over to the kid.

"Get the fuck up. You hung around the club, drank our beer, tasted our women, and now you're going to pretend like you don't see me needing a seat?"

He shoved his chair backward, awkwardly. His date furrowed her brows, shoving up on her palms.

"Who the fuck do you think you are?"

I didn't hit women. Never laid a finger on one unless it was in pleasure, but the way this woman was speaking to me was striking a nerve. She could see my jacket, and all the patches, including the brand new, stark white patch that read *President*. Who the fuck did she think I was?

"Brit, it's okay, just chill."

"No." She swung her face to the kid. "And what does he mean you tasted women?"

People were staring now, including Laura, who was handing over a twenty for our food.

"Up. Move. Now," I barked.

Brit stood, sliding her chair back. Apparently, she wanted even more of a show. She pushed me, or tried, but she wasn't anything against my six-foot-three stature.

I saw in her eyes that she was going to go for my face, possibly my eyes. Her mouth twisted into something ugly, and right before she darted forward, a hand snatched her hair from behind.

"Don't think so, babe. Trust me when I say you don't want on this side of things. Leave while you can." Laura pulled on Brit's ponytail until her head was at an awkward angle. She tried to spin on Laura, but Laura's boot kicked between Brit's legs, forcing the girl's knee to buckle and her to land face down on the table.

"You don't want this. Now, I'm going to let go and you're going to walk out of here. Do you understand?" Laura murmured close to Brit's ear.

Brit was seething, the side of her face hard against the table while her date just watched in horror.

"Do you?" Laura pulled Brit's brunette hair tighter, forcing the woman to cry out in pain.

"Okay, okay."

Laura released her immediately then heard her name called for our order and pranced through the crowd, grabbing our drinks and food.

I watched her go, musing to myself, "I need to get her a fucking cut."

"She yours then?"

My face swung in the kid's direction and whatever he saw on my face spurred him into action. Bussing the table, he used a napkin to finish wiping it down before grabbing his wallet and darting out of the cafe.

I pulled out my chair right as Laura returned with our scones and drinks.

"You got me a scone?" My eyebrow rose almost on its own because I didn't eat this shit.

She smiled. "Yeah, it's a white chocolate raspberry, really good. Natty makes them."

"Fine."

I slid into the chair across from Laura and began tearing into the baked good.

"So..." I started, sipping my coffee to clear my throat, "you fucking Kip then?"

Laura's blue eyes flew up to mine in surprise.

"What?"

"Saw his bike in front of the place this morning." I tore off another piece of scone and stuffed it in my mouth. I wasn't particularly pleased with how my stomach seemed to flip, awaiting her answer.

She waited. Eating, drinking, taking her fucking time.

Until finally, she wiped her mouth and said, "would it be a problem if I was?"

I scoffed, keeping my eyes on the table as if she wasn't enough to keep my interest.

"My apartment." I shrugged. "If you're going to spread your legs for every member of the club, I'd rather it not be in my house."

Pink lips parted as a tiny sound came out, something like shock. Her eyes widened and a tiny flush entered her cheeks and neck.

I liked it.

Because, like usual, the only entry available through her locked-up emotions and forbidden heart was by sliding under her skin. Insulting her as frequently as possible and ensuring I was a mark of pain upon her conscience.

"You haven't stepped foot inside the apartment in three months. What I do there is my business, and I won't stop simply because you don't want me to fuck club members there."

"So, you are fucking then?"

Why wasn't she just giving me a straight answer?

She searched my face before smiling, toying with the cup.

"I wouldn't classify it as fucking per se…it's not like a girl could get pregnant by what we're doing."

She had to know what she was doing by saying that. She knew what I'd implied three months ago…it was the entire reason she left. There was some bullshit story she gave to Callie, and then there was the real reason she wanted out of here.

The phone conversation we had, where I was an ass. The one I regretted immediately after.

"Killian?" Laura reached forward with a smile in place, but I moved my arm so she couldn't touch me.

"I can make sure Kip has his own room, instead of sharing with Austin. That way you can be together there."

The words came out clipped and cold, and I hated the way Laura's face transformed into a painful frown as I said them.

"Are you kicking me out?"

I shrugged.

"Thought you were already looking at places."

Her pink lips twisted to the side. "I am…"

"I'm not kicking you out, but you can't be fucking club members in my house."

She rolled her eyes and slid her thumb over her phone. Her device was being turned in my direction, and I was suddenly watching video footage from inside the apartment.

"Wes had these set up but I'm the only person who has access to the footage. He said it's easier to keep them going for when you move in. I guess you'll need them active or something."

My gaze flicked back to the phone screen. The camera was angled at the front door, which was situated through the dining room, next to the kitchen. The doorbell had rung, and Laura lightly jogged into view, wearing a pair of tiny shorts and an off-the-shoulder sweater, showing her midriff. My stomach twisted into knots as I watched her open the door and smile at Kip.

Kip entered, lifting a box of tools. "Prez said I needed to come fix the garbage disposal."

Laura moved, giving him a wide berth.

He gave her a crooked smile before starting on his task. "When you gonna ride with me, Beautiful?"

For some fucked-up reason, I held my breath.

"Maybe when it's warmer, Kip. I'm terrified of the cold." Laura sounded sweet, but the screen was too pixelated to catch her expression. Regardless, she didn't seem interested in him, and I hated how that simple reaction calmed the wild animal scratching to be released from my chest. The rest of the time Kip was there, he spent under the sink, or hovering over it until Laura finally slipped out through the front door.

She had effectively put me in my place for commenting on her spreading her legs. I wasn't about to apologize for what I said. If the idea of fucking members of my club made her uneasy, then good. It should. Because if I saw one of those fuckers touch her, or kiss her, I didn't even know what I would do, and that honestly terrified me.

Laura pulled her phone in front of her once more, when it pinged with a text. I watched her dark brows furrow as she read over the message.

"Callie's free. Her client had to leave early. There was some sort of complication. She told me to walk over, and she'd finish taking me around."

I lifted my chin, hiding any hint of disappointment that might leak through.

"I'll walk you over." I slid back in the chair and stood.

Glancing over her shoulder revealed more than a few pair of eyes on us. The thought of having Laura protected with a patch thrummed through me once more.

But she wasn't mine. *She never would be.*

FOUR
KILLIAN
THREE MONTHS AGO

THE NOISE STILL GOT TO ME.

Two thousand angry and bitter prisoners trying to make the best of the sentences they'd been given. Some of these men might not have earned it, but there was no question at all that my pops had.

He was a mean motherfucker, and while I would never normally come here on my own or because I wanted to, he was still a Stone Rider, and we didn't leave our men behind. Regardless of what they'd done to get themselves put behind bars.

I entered the visiting room without my cut on because seeing the patches might incite violence with the other visitors. This part of Virginia was home to five dangerous clubs that carried the one percent patch, so it wasn't merely bloody or dangerous: it was a death wish.

I wasn't allowed to take anything with me inside the visiting room, but Carl, the guard, knew me and didn't mind letting me through with my paper and eraser. It wasn't like either could do any harm. Seated at a small table large enough for two chairs, I unfolded the paper I had shaded the night prior; it was completely covered in graphite. I took out my eraser and began tracing. I didn't consider myself an artist but drawing, or rather the opposite of drawing, had always worked to calm me down. Even now at thirty-two years old, it worked.

I had no idea how much time had passed, but before long, there was a loud buzzing sound that went off, which meant my father was being led inside. The eraser dropped from my fingers right as he folded into the chair across from me.

"You still doing that shit?"

I kept my eyes on the page, carefully folding it.

"That a fuckin flower?" my dad barked loudly, followed by a raspy laugh.

My jaw tensed, but I wouldn't show him. Once I had control over my words and my temper, I finally set my gaze on the man who sired me.

Green eyes, darker than mine, glowered. He had circles under his dark lashes, and his skin looked paler than normal.

"You stop getting outside time?"

His wince was slight, but I caught it.

"Had to be in the box for a while." His shoulders lifted while he briefly glanced over his left side. The guard by the door locked a hard gaze on him.

"Solitary sounds more your speed. What you do to earn it?" I was careful not to ask what happened or allow him to become a victim in any way. He was a narcissist and would take any opportunity he was given.

My dad shrugged once more, this time the mean glare on his face twisted into something sinister. "Gutted a Raider."

Normally I wouldn't mind that he'd killed a Death Raider, but Wes was worried about things escalating after hearing from Callie that a few had been staying in town. We weren't sure what they were up to but now that she was back, we needed to be careful.

"Came here to deliver some news." I sat forward, so our conversation would stay quiet.

This chat was overdue, but I had been dragging my feet. Fuck, he likely already knew, but if he had then he would have already said something. Maybe there was a reason I had stalled on telling him that his best friend of thirty years had died. Perhaps regardless of how mean he was, or the fact that he left me all alone when I was just ten years old, there was a part of me that hesitated telling him our president had passed.

Swallowing past my nerves, I blinked and spilled it. "Simon's dead."

My father's eyes narrowed as if he were trying to work out what I'd said then his jaw tightened.

He didn't reply for several seconds. Possibly minutes. His eyes finally left my face, wandering to the table as he relaxed in the chair.

"So, you're the new president then?" His dull eyes peered up at me with hope.

My gut churned with shame. This was the other reason I was holding off on telling him.

I shook my head.

"What the fuck do you mean, no?" My dad looked around briskly, before leaning forward once more. "You were Vice President last I heard when Simon came to visit…what, two months ago?"

Two months ago, Simon had lost nearly twenty pounds and looked like he was sick. Had my dad asked him? Did he even care that his best friend had died?

"Wes Ryan."

I could see the wheels churning in my father's head as he tried to remember who Wes was. Dad was put away before Wes first came over to the house when he was that gangly fifteen-year-old. I had met him when he was younger, only thirteen and starry-eyed in love with Callie. I had been patched into the Stone Riders by then, doing deliveries. Dad had already been in prison for a few years.

"Wes who?"

I shook my head again, scuffing my blunt thumbnail over the surface of the table. "Been around for a few years. Simon picked him."

That searing pain in my gut returned. I was embarrassed that Simon hadn't chosen me; there wasn't even a conversation about it. He was dying and just said in his last church meeting that it would be Wes and there would be no questions.

Fucking hurt like hell, but who was I to complain? Obviously, I was fucking no one if I had been passed over, and I was the goddamn Vice President.

Dad's scoff brought my eyes back up, his lips twisted into a sneer.

"Fucking useless. Can't even secure becoming president when you're the VP. No wonder Simon skipped over you. You always were too weak for this life; you don't belong in the club. You belong behind a desk, drawing rabbits and fuckin' flowers."

My heart burned in my chest. A familiar fire that raged on behalf of the monster my father had always been to me. The abusive words, the physical marks he'd left on my face that Simon noticed but never called him out for. He did offer me a place near his family block of the clubhouse, where Callie lived. But he didn't banish my dad from the club.

Shortly after my mom left, my father went and killed a Sweetbutt. A girl who was nice to me, and honestly not much older than me, barely eighteen as far as I could remember. It was unforgivable, not only because hurting women in our club was outlawed, but Sweetbutts were especially offered special protection. Which was why Simon refused to offer his connections to help my dad get out earlier. He assumed I would help him if I'd been given the role.

"You're loose gravel, Killian. Stone always needed someone like him, solid and formidable. You're nothing but a tiny pebble in the shoe of a great leader."

My heart rate spiked as I remembered back to my mother talking to me about pebbles and their power. How important they were, and I remembered my father slapping her for instilling such a weak thought into my head.

Shaking my head, I stood and peered down at my dad.

"Just owed you the truth about your president. Your new one is Wes Ryan, be faithful to him or leave. Choice is yours."

I heard him screaming at my back about loyalty and me being a pussy, but the guard came and grabbed him. The last words I heard before the door clicked shut was, "Take Wes down, claim your spot in the club or so help me, I will do it for you."

I shook off the remark, but something had dug under my skin after the visit.

I wasn't done fighting for my place in the club; it might take longer, but I knew one day it would be mine. I knew this because Wes had a weakness, and she'd just reappeared after seven years.

I had none.

I'd made sure when it was time to step into my role and claim it, I'd be ready.

No person or situation would ever change that.

FIVE
LAURA

THE FILE CABINET WAS JAMMED AGAIN.

The thing was nearly as tall as me, and just as old. It got stuck nearly every single day. Considering the majority of my job included keeping up the books for the club and filing enough legal documentation that it would pass with state auditors, I was in the cabinets all the time. I also helped file receipts and ensured the various club owned businesses were organized, up to date and regulated with the state offices.

There was an older cabinet squeezed along the back wall that was locked, and only Red and now, I assumed, Killian would have a key. No one ever asked me to open it, and no one ever told me what was inside, which I was perfectly fine with, considering I was eager to find a new job soon.

I only had this one because Wes pulled a few strings for me. Him deciding to marry my best friend basically meant she got whatever she wanted, and at the time, she wanted me to stay in Rose Ridge. Not that I hated being here, or even working here, but I needed space from the club. Especially after my confusing outing with Killian yesterday.

His big night was looming over our heads, and I was getting antsy with the timing of it all. With it being Thursday, I assumed his initiation or ceremony would have taken place last night. Give him a new patch, or whatever, and they'd throw a party. One, I'd decidedly miss if at all possible, and then we'd move on. But no.

They were dragging this thing out. First, we spent yesterday, prepping and purchasing all the goods. Today would be spent cooking and doing food prep, and then tomorrow would be the first party thrown, but Red had made it clear, they'd be partying all weekend.

Honestly, I was considering a quick trip back to Richland so I could skip the whole thing.

My mom had become a little desperate for me to return home, and while part of me wanted to pretend it was merely because she missed me. I knew better.

"Come on," I grumbled, tugging on the cabinet door once more with effort.

Stupid. Fucking. Thing.

My thumb was raw from trying to slide it into place and pull at the same time.

"That one sticks."

I spun around, surprised by the smooth, familiar voice. Sometimes Brooks would hang around because Red was, but she was at home today, and the only other person milling about was Natty...so my heart was pounding fast at the unexpected intrusion.

Killian stood in the doorway, staring down at his phone like he hadn't been talking to me. A piece of his thick hair fell into his eyes, and my stomach clenched at the sight of it. I loved his hair, hated myself for loving it, but loved it just the same. I constantly fought the urge to run my fingers through it. Feeling that familiar flush creep into my face, I returned my focus to the cabinet. I hadn't seen Killian since I left him at the coffee shop, after he accused me of sleeping with Kip.

Giving the drawer another tug, I froze when I saw Killian move around in my peripheral.

"Here." He stepped closer, and I moved completely, allowing him access to the cabinet.

His dark brow rose in question. "I'm not going to bite you, Daisy."

That nickname made my neck warm for some reason. Maybe because we'd had to interact yesterday, and now we were again. It was the most I had seen him in three months, and he hadn't called me Daisy since that night three months ago, before he started avoiding me.

"Let me show you how to do it." He coaxed, green eyes steady and solid until I was moving back in front of him.

He was at my back, and his hand eclipsed my smaller one. His thumb hovered over mine, and then, for some reason, his free hand moved to my hip.

I inhaled a sharp breath right as he pushed his thumb down, his hand over mine tugged on the handle and then kicked the bottom of the cabinet all at the same time. The drawer slid open and I fell back into him, so much so that he had to move his hand from my hip to hold me up.

"See, you got it now." He laughed and helped me stand up.

I knew better than to expect any kindness from him, so I put distance between us and smoothed out my shirt. He watched me move and then let out a small scoff.

"You think I'm gonna hurt you, Daisy?"

His leather cut was over a white long-sleeve today, one that gaped at the neck, revealing more of his ink than usual. His hair cut into his eye, forcing his hand up to push it back.

"Not physically."

His eyes narrowed, then his mouth opened like he was going to say something, but Giles walked in.

"Good, you're here. Did you explain to Laura what we'll need her to do?"

My eyes snapped back over to the new president. He had a small flush working into his wide jaw.

"Just about to."

Killian pulled out a key and went to the cabinet I never touched. Bending down, he slid the metal inside and then tugged the top drawer open.

"We need you to go through these, see what's here. No one has touched them for years, at least that's what Red says. I tried to talk to Wes about it, but he wasn't president long enough to know."

"Why not just ask Simon?" My gaze flicked between Giles and Killian, but they both froze.

Giles peered over his shoulder and let out an odd sound. Killian began pulling files and lining them up inside of a clear container.

"The club doesn't know he's alive." Killian finally explained once he was closer.

Well that was a rather big piece of information I wasn't aware was secret. I felt another flush working up my chest. How come no one told me? I blamed Callie, if she were actually a part of the club like Red was, she would have said something.

Did Red even know?

"Oh."

"You'll carry this key from now on, but no one else can use it. You can't loan it to Callie or Wes, not even Giles. I'm going to have you start working on these files now, so whatever you're doing for Red, it'll get bumped."

Peeking over the tote, I began thumbing through a few.

"What exactly am I looking for?"

"You're shredding anything that's in the files with red marks along the front." He showed me one that had a large red marker slashed in the form of an x.

"Okay, but why?" I folded my arms, glaring between the two Stone Riders.

Giles flipped his key chain over his thumb and finger, keeping watch by the door while Killian remained on the floor.

"It doesn't matter why. It matters that it's done, and that you don't talk about what you see in these folders. Everything in here is illegal, so you'll have to learn to keep your mouth shut."

That wouldn't be a problem, but I wouldn't dignify his comment with a response.

"And the folders without the red mark?"

His green eyes bounced up, landing on me briefly before sliding the key off the ring and placing it on a new one.

"They'll need to be relabeled and set aside for me to review."

The tote was nearly full when he finally stood and handed me the key.

"Is there a time frame you need this done by?"

"Next week."

"Well—" I started, but he just moved past me, lightly bumping my shoulder on his way.

With one last look over his shoulder, Killian lifted his lip in a sneer.

"Now, maybe you'll actually be pulling your weight in the club instead of having a free pass for being Callie's best friend."

Asshole.

"Oh, and you might want to rethink your little plan regarding leaving the club. Once you see these files, you won't be able to."

He was gone and I was left standing in the wake of Killian's wrath. I had nearly forgotten how mean he could be. What a fool I'd been to assume he'd treat me like anything other than his plaything.

My phone suddenly chimed with an incoming text, pulling my attention from the empty doorway. I'd push this interaction with Killian down, just like I always did.

Reaching for my phone, I saw the text was from my mom.

> Mom: There's going to be a reporter emailing you for a quote on the piece they're printing about your father. Please respond and remember to smile big even through text.

My eye roll was severe.

Smile big was my mothers way of reminding me not to do anything to make the family look bad. At least no more than I had already done.

In DC I had worked minimum wage jobs, sometimes two or three at a time while renting a room in an apartment shared with various people. My mother loathed my idea of freedom, and while I knew I was on a leash, at least she'd given me the option to leave. My father had thrown a fit, in private of course but mom understood that I needed this time away from home.

The only problem was mom assumed it was merely a faze.

She couldn't quite grasp that I had no intention of ever returning to their world full of politics and games. I would if it was merely to be their daughter and not a game piece to be moved around.

> Me: Thanks for the heads up, I will reply. How are you mom? I miss you.

Her response didn't come right away, which allowed me some time to start sorting folders.

> Mom: The political season is off to a great start. We'd like your attendance at a few functions this holiday season if you can swing it.

My heart plummeted with her response. It felt like texting one of those political campaigns that texted around voting season, letting me know my vote counted. Every now and then glimpses of my mom would come through, but during an election season it was always buried beneath her wide, beaming smile and perfectly tailored pant suits.

I decided not to reply.

She knew I had moved to Rose Ridge, I'd told her as much when I moved here on a whim. But no follow up questions were ever asked. Not about my job, or why I'd selected such a small town when I'd vowed never to live in one again.

It was like I'd become invisible, and with a sad chuckle, I focused on the folders realizing that's all I had ever been.

Three Months Ago

"Okay, so we are walking to the clubhouse...am I understanding you correctly?" I asked, swiping under my arms with a stick of deodorant. God, it was hot. I was used to a decent level of humidity living in DC, but this town was something different.

My best friend stood in the doorway with her arms crossed, likely still thinking through her plan. Since arriving, she was full of plans, ideas, and strategy. My girl had turned into a little battle commander, and I loved her for it. She was all glossy dark hair, tattoos and lip gloss. We were here in Rose Ridge, her hometown. Her pops had died and left her a ton of land, except her ex-boyfriend took issue with her claiming it because his club house was on the property. The jerk was messing with her, so I was here to help her in any way possible.

"Yeah...we need to start showing up and digging for information," she mused, while stepping closer to the bed.

"No, wear the one that shows more cleavage." Callie pointed, while shaking her head. I'd just slid on a tattered crop top that showed my midriff, so I looked down at it and frowned.

"My stomach is way more attractive than my boobs. Let me keep this one on."

"Your boobs are fantastic." Callie smiled.

I gently caressed the mermaid scales on my rib cage. "But this shirt shows my tattoo."

Letting out a sigh, Callie gave in. I knew she would; she loved this tattoo. It had taken her weeks to finish it, in between both our jobs and other clients. Since she was trading help with pet-sitting her gladiator dog, Max, and ensuring he didn't eat her couch while she worked, she was doing my mermaid tail for free.

"What about you, aren't you going to dress up even a little bit?" I asked, pulling on a pair of high-heeled boots.

Callie shook her head. "Wear the flat boots on the way over, then change once we get there. It's a good half-mile up to the clubhouse."

"Right, shoot." I tore off the kicks, noticing my best friend scrutinize her own outfit. She was in a cropped black tank top and a pair of ripped jeans.

"This outfit works, doesn't it?" she asked nervously.

I stood and tossed a pair of shorts at her, teasing.

"Show off your best *ass*et, Callie."

We continued getting ready, trying to lighten the mood, but I could sense the unease in my best friend. Finally, when we were ready to go, I assessed the behemoth Great Dane lounging on the two-seater sofa. He was probably going to eat it. The creature ate everything. Callie was just in denial about it.

"Will Max be okay while we're gone?"

With his chin on his paws, his eyes moved back and forth between us with a little huff.

"He's fine for a few hours, as long as he's fed and has water. He actually knows how to twist door knobs to let himself out, did you know that?" Callie applied some lip gloss, then winced like she hadn't meant to apply it.

I scoffed, "Oh I remember. He did that when I took him with me to a friend's house. Scared the shit out of me."

Callie checked Max's water bowl and then pressed a kiss to the top of his head before walking out the front door. We looked good, and I felt amazing. I kept thinking about how I'd agreed to only tag along on her little adventure for a few days. Callie didn't know this because I had never told her, but I had been fired from one of my jobs just last week, and the second job I had kept cutting my hours back, so I was going to have to quit. It was the same story, repeated over and over. Didn't matter, but it meant I would be sticking things out with her for as long as she needed me. I had left home in search of that one place in life that would feel like home and settled for DC. Mostly because I had found Callie, and she had become like a life raft for me.

No, more like an island. We were both stranded on it, but we had each other. So, while this mess of her past was in fact terrifying, at least we were together. I had nothing waiting for me back home except three pissed off roommates and a check that was left for rent but would most certainly bounce.

I followed my best friend through the glade. Nearing the massive stretch of house these bikers called a clubhouse. I was still trying to figure this place out, but after my less than stellar introduction with that Killian guy, I wasn't eager to spend any time around them. Callie had told me tiny pieces here and there, especially since coming back and staying in the cabin together, but it was all stilted and disjointed, almost as if it was hurting her to share. So I made quick work of changing the subject.

The sound of revving engines echoed as we came upon the back entrance to the club. I eyed the large patch of grass with cornhole and yard darts, trying to imagine this rough group playing outdoor games while wearing all that leather and denim, and chuckled to myself.

The stairs led to the club, and my stomach flipped as Callie pulled on the door. This place was dangerous, and the members seemed uneasy around newcomers. Callie was accepted, practically royalty from the sounds of it, but I was a stranger. Worse, I was a stranger with tits and an ass, so when the club members' eyes landed on me, it was like catching the gaze of fifty predators at once.

We walked down a dim hallway until we could see the kitchen where the woman with white hair and a red wrap stood, sorting food. Another woman my age stood next to her, smiling sweetly while sorting veggies from a large white box. Several of the older members were scattered around a jumbled mess of tables all pushed together, playing cards, while the younger ones seemed busy around the garage area.

"This round there's no cheating," one of the older guys hollered around the cigarette dangling from his mouth. I thought I remembered Callie calling him Hamish the other night when we were here. The elderly men across from him laughed, staring at the cards in their hands, while the overhead speakers played something older, drowning out the sounds from the garage across the building. I sidled up next to Callie, giving her an incredulous look.

There was no one here.

Only older members playing poker. How were we supposed to flirt and garner information?

Callie's eyebrows were arched too, likely just as confused as to how exactly we'd timed this so poorly.

"Looks like you're up." I pushed at my friend's waist, forcing her to move.

She walked forward and I decided to look around and see if I could find a different member to flirt with. There were a few guys working on bikes in the garage area that I might be able to sway into conversation.

The clubhouse was crazy big. I tilted my head back, taking in the massive three stories and large windows letting in natural light. Callie had mentioned that the place was once much older, more meager. Apparently, her ex had poured a ton of money into the place to spruce it up. No wonder he was so pissed at the idea of Callie selling this place.

Curiosity got the better of me, and I ended up scaling the steps made from glossed wood. The railing was made from some beautiful metal work, nearly black, and solid as steel. My fingers skimmed over the surface as I focused on the walls and images scattered along the forest green wallpaper, in black and white. A smile crept up my face as I stared at one too many photos of men stark naked, covered in mud, wearing nothing but their cuts, a pair of boots and wide smiles.

I had always wondered what it would feel like to be that free. To not care in the least bit about clothing or what society would think if you stopped wearing them. To strip and straddle the back of a machine powerful enough to carry me to a new place. I had never been on the back of a motorcycle, but one day when I found a way to do it, I'd close my eyes and I'd think of this picture. This crazy, odd picture.

Farther up the stairs there were a few images of younger members.

So young, they looked almost like siblings. A little girl with dark hair, and a boy, his dark hair slicked to the side, but cutting into his eyes, too long and in need of a trim. The girl had her arms crossed, the boy had a doll in his hand, trying to hand it back to her. There was a man in the background smiling at them both.

I drew closer, nearly placing my nose against the picture.

This was Callie and Killian. It had to be.

She'd told me he was like her brother, growing up together in this place. I had to ask after he called her Little Fox and the familiarity between them. I was confused by their interaction when her ex was still acting so fucking possessive over her. When she said sibling, it made sense.

There he was, a few years older than her. By the image, he looked about ten or so. He was smiling, surrounded by chrome and leather, like he'd been born to be here.

My brow furrowed as I thought over the place he had in the club.

Why wasn't he the next person to run things if he'd been a part of it for so long?

"Jessica Rabbit."

I spun around, nearly falling off one of the steps, searching out the rough voice that had slid up my spine like a trail of ice.

"Killian," I breathed, scanning his face for the mirth I was expecting.

I'd only had one other encounter with him, but it wasn't a good one. My nerves were still rattled from what he'd said to me.

"What are you doing up here?" Killian's dark brows pulled together. He wore a white t-shirt under his soft leather vest. Callie called it a cut. It had a myriad of patches on it, under his name was the title, Vice President, which meant he was important here. His right arm had tattoos that traveled down the expanse of it, all the way up to his neck. His left arm didn't. It was an odd contrast, considering how many members were completely covered in them.

My greedy gaze tried to memorize as much of him as possible, just in case I left tomorrow, and I never saw him again. I hated him, completely and thoroughly, but I also wanted to trace the sharp line along his jaw, feel the light scruff along that cheek under my nails. I wanted to taste his lips, and then I wanted to walk away.

I'd tuck the feel of him away in a tiny mental box, locked away where only I could access it. He'd be a treasure, my very own emerald wrapped in leather.

Remembering that I was in his clubhouse, and I was sort of intruding, I blinked and ducked my face.

"I was looking for Callie."

Killian's gaze hardened, but within an instant, it went playful, almost like it did that night he had called me an over-sexualized caricature.

"She isn't up here, and the only girls who do come up those steps are the ones who plan to fuck or clean. Which one will you be doing this fine afternoon?"

He crossed his arms and widened his legs, as if I were actually going to answer that.

Instead, I huffed an irritated breath and started back down the stairs.

A firm grip landed on my upper arm, halting me. My head swung around, glaring at the glint of excitement in his determined gaze.

"You're trespassing. I can't let that go unpunished." His lips slung to the side in a devilish grin. "Not in this club."

It wasn't usually easy for someone to rattle me. I had made sure of that after leaving my life behind, after what my parents put me through. My insides were built from stone and steel, or so I thought. Two interactions with Killian, and it seemed as though he'd dug his fingers inside my rib cage and wrapped his fingers around wood and straw. He was the big bad wolf, blowing down my proverbial stone house.

And deep down, I knew I was completely fucked because of it.

There was no walking away from him unmarked.

When he released my arm, I felt like I could breathe. With a thick swallow, I kept eye contact and lowered myself another step. Retreating.

His calculating gaze tracked the movement, and that grin became feral. His tattooed hand shot out, returning his grip to my arm, and this time, hauling me up the stairs. My arm flailed behind me as he pulled me to the second floor and then pushed me into a small alcove off the side of the stairs. We were tucked far enough back that whatever Killian was about to do to me, no one would see.

My breathing came in and out, painfully fast.

One of his hands moved to my hip, the other framed my face. His eyes were focused on mine, almost like we'd silently entered into a staring contest.

"I won't hurt you, Daisy," Killian whispered, his lips a breath away from mine.

He wasn't hurting me, but his body had essentially eclipsed mine and there was an odd feeling coming from it. I wasn't afraid...I felt.

Fuck, I felt safe. How messed up was that?

"Daisy?" I tilted my head back, still unsure of what he meant by punishment.

Killian smiled, and it was hard to tell with the shadows, but it almost seemed like he was blushing. "Decided you're not Jessica Rabbit. She would have pushed me up the stairs and tried to fuck me. No, you're a different creature entirely."

The reminder of what he'd called me that first day began staining the moment as effectively as an ink spilling over clean linen.

I lowered my face, but a tattooed finger lifted my chin, stopping me.

Green eyes glimmered in the gloom of the stairs. There was a good deal of natural light, but the sun had slipped behind a mass of clouds. Shadows emerged and settled around the floor, clinging to door frames, and those black and white photos littering the walls.

"Your punishment, Daisy, I've decided will come later when you least expect it. But let's be clear about something. When you're in my club, you're my plaything. No one else's. If anyone else approaches you, you find me. Do you understand?"

No, I fucking didn't. I wasn't about to fall into some toxic motorcycle club bullshit. Callie had sort of explained it, about the property patches and term Old Ladies and Sweetbutts…The old women were the married ones, or permanent partners…the Sweetbutts were just here to fuck…it was confusing for someone who hadn't grown up in it.

I pushed at his chest and slid out from under his arm, quickly walking away.

"I'm not yours."

Behind me, I heard him scoff, "you have it twisted. I don't *want* you, but if you're here in this club, then I own you."

I cleared the last step and spun. "No, the fuck you don't, and it's not your club!"

Killian's eyes blazed, his mouth opened right as Callie found me.

"There you are, we have to go." She pulled on my hand, looking upset. My heart lurched, wondering what had upset her. I gave the man at my back one last glance before following my friend.

SIX
KILLIAN

Wes wanted to go over a few last-minute things with me before the big transition.

After the ruse of our previous leader's demise, he continued to hold family dinners with the only people who knew he still lived. It was a tad awkward because he had decided to settle down with Sasha, an ex-Death Raider, and the mother of one of my enemies, Silas. Our dinners consisted of family, but somehow Laura and I were tossed in there too. A few weeks ago, during one of these family dinners, Simon had mentioned the files and how I needed to have someone go through them. Now that a new, and more permanent president would be taking over, inventory of our allies needed to be accounted for before we started taking meetings with rival clubs, such as The Chaos Kings.

And fuck me, but I saw an opportunity. Laura was already doing the books, and in the office. Laura who had mentioned wanting out of the club. I'd found a way to remove that possibility, and she might hate me for it, and for what she'd be forced to see in those documents but frankly, I didn't care. I was tired of her avoidance, the distance and bullshit dance we kept tiptoeing to. She wasn't leaving, plain and fucking simple.

Wes slapped a folder in front of me, drawing my attention back. "The property behind the club. It's been purchased using club funds."

I picked it up, then paused at the sound of feminine laughter echoing up from the bottom floor. Wes's office was on the top floor of his house, so everything echoed. He was going to have a hard time with things once their kid came into the world and started crying and teething and shit.

"Laura is over, helping with some party things—or something. I can't keep up with what they're doing all the time," Wes mumbled while clicking his mouse, staring at the computer screen.

Suddenly, and very stupidly, I had the urge to move our meeting downstairs. Just so I could look at Laura. I may have made an effort to avoid her for three months, but it didn't mean I ever stopped watching her. Examining every little thing she did was one of my favorite past times.

"This your old place?" I asked to get my focus back on our meeting. The folder had a picture of his old house, which sat on the back end of the club property. Technically, it was all left to Callie, his wife but when it was discovered that her father, Simon wasn't actually dead, the property was signed over to the trust, which was owned by the club.

Wes nodded. "Figured it would be an extra spot to put people if needed."

"The cabin still out there?" Simon had owned a small one-bedroom cabin that Callie and Laura had stayed in when they had first arrived. I hadn't been out there to see if anyone used it. Not after it was clear they weren't forcing Laura to live in it. Which was fine, I didn't need the apartment, and I could have taken the cabin—I just didn't know what the fuck was going on with any of it, which was partially why we were having this meeting.

"Yeah, keys are being handed over to the club as well. It'll go in as part of the trust that holds the deeds."

That made sense.

"All this will need to go into that new filing system."

Hearing another lilt of laughter, I peered over my shoulder because it sounded like they were closer. Wes likely caught the movement because when I returned to my position, a smirk tugged up his lips.

"You give the job over to Laura?"

"You wanted it updated, not digitized, right?" I avoided his very obvious change in conversation. He wanted to discuss his wife's best friend in regard to me. He knew I was starting to fall for her three months ago, but never said anything once she officially moved back, and I'd started avoiding her.

He paused for a few moments before responding.

"Right."

Keeping my eyes on the folder in front of me, I spoke easily. "Then it's getting done."

"Dinner is ready!" Callie called from downstairs.

Wes moved first, clicking out of a few things on his computer. I closed the folder and tucked it into the backpack I'd brought. I'd driven my truck tonight because the forecast called for black ice.

"You staying?" Wes asked, taking the stairs.

My stomach flipped. I should leave, but the prospect of being around Laura for an evening felt too appealing. For three months, I had denied myself the opportunity to be around her, always leaving first. Never staying where she was. I did it because I was afraid of falling too far and too fast with her. I was afraid of losing myself before I ever had the chance to do the one thing I'd always wanted to do, which was becoming president of this club. Simon had warned me not to allow myself anything that would pull me away from the club. It was a sacrifice, but in the end, this was what I wanted above all else.

But my mind flung the image of Kip's bike at me, forcing my jaw to clench. Regardless of what Laura said, there was still another man in that house with her. Still someone who was talking sweet, building enough of a relationship that she considered having him take her over me.

"I'll stay."

Wes paused mid step, laughing to himself while shaking his head. I kicked him in the back of the kneecap, making his next step falter.

"Fucker."

He was still chuckling when we cleared the stairs. The first floor of Wesley's house was massive. The far wall, facing the front yard, was all glass windows, and during the day, you could see the whole valley from them. Three leather couches framed the living room, along with two armchairs and a coffee table. The kitchen was all hardwood floors and quartz counters, top of the line fixtures and lighting features.

My socks padded over the floors, sliding slightly as I entered the kitchen. Laura was sitting atop a barstool, tucked into the island with a bowl of salad in front of her and a cutting board, littered with carrots.

"Hey guys, we're having million-dollar spaghetti with salad and breadsticks."

Callie finished explaining then her arms went around Wesley's neck, and he pulled her in for a kiss.

Laura's eyes remained on the carrots she was shredding in front of her.

"Can I help?" I pulled out the stool next to her.

She had on some kind of dress or jumpsuit that left her shoulders bare. Her golden skin drew my attention, but so did the soft waves of sunlight falling against her back, and the way her pink lips pursed while she attempted to ignore me.

"I got it," she murmured, keeping her focus on the mess in front of her.

Callie glanced over briefly but resumed hugging her husband.

Folding myself onto the barstool, I spread my legs, pushing my left kneecap into Laura's, but I acted like I didn't realize I'd done it.

A spark of humor lit my chest when she pushed right back, almost as if she were trying to get me out of her space. With Callie and Wes on the other side of the counter, they couldn't see us. Laura's face tilted, until she was glaring at me. I pressed my leg firmer into hers and gave her the same expression. She wanted to challenge me.

This was the wrong fucking way to do it. She was basically waving a green flag to touch her.

Keeping her attention, I lowered the hand closest to her body and gripped her thigh, while reaching over to grab a carrot with my other hand.

Her lips parted when my fingers moved farther north, feeling her heat against the backs of my fingers suddenly had her scrambling off her stool and grabbing the salad bowl.

I bit back a smile as I crunched a carrot and followed her toward the table with four plates.

Laura took a seat first, which allowed me the chance to pull out the chair next to her.

Except one second after sitting, she was sliding her chair away from me, which Wes caught because he raised his brow at me in question.

I leaned in close before Callie got to the table and whispered in Laura's ear, "Keep moving away from me and I'm going to keep my hand on your thigh for the rest of the night."

She exhaled through her nose, making her nostrils flare.

Before her best friend could come back in, I gripped the bottom of Laura's chair and slid it back into place, right next to me, so close our shoulders nearly touched.

"Doesn't this smell delicious?" Callie beamed, carrying in the casserole dish of pasta.

She'd made this dish exactly eighteen times in the past three months, and now the smell and sight of it was starting to make my stomach curdle, but we all still told her yes, and that we couldn't wait to eat it.

"Can you please pass the salad?" I asked Laura.

She gave the couple across from us a fake smile while reaching for the bowl, then slid it over to me.

"Thank you."

Callie watched our exchange with a puzzled expression.

"So, Kil. You ready for everything this weekend?"

I took a bite of salad, while nodding. I didn't want to talk about this again. Every time she asked me about this, it only reminded me that her husband took my role. All for some fucking game Simon wanted to play.

And he left me out of it.

Hurt was still a barbed wire wound tightly around my pride.

"Laura has been prepping all the members by sending invites via email, text and making calls." Callie smiled at her friend, as if that would make me happy.

It was just another reminder.

Wes said something to Callie, forcing her attention off us, which Laura took advantage of.

Tilting her face so her words were hushed, she asked, "Reminds me, how exactly would you like me to personalize your friend's invitation?"

Her lips spread into a sly smile. "Should I just put, 'girl with real tits,' or 'Killian's fuck buddy?'"

Who was she—

Fuck, she was referring to that first night we met, when I joked about fucking another woman instead of her because she didn't look fake, like an AI filter had popped her out. I nearly laughed, but the sound would draw Wes and Callie's attention back over to us. As it was, their heads were bent together as Callie showed him something on her phone.

I took the opportunity to whisper back, "Want to know something, Daisy?" I used that nickname again with her, and it thrilled me to no end.

"That night, I couldn't fuck her. Wanna know why?"

She kept her face down, but her chest was rising and falling so fast, I knew she wanted to know.

My hand returned to her thigh, pulling it toward me, which only spread her legs apart but her dress was floor length, so all I felt was heat and fabric.

She flicked her gaze up to the couple across from us but didn't respond.

I leaned in close and whispered, "Because it was your tits in my head that I wanted to touch. Your pussy I wanted to taste, and your cunt I wanted to fuck. You ruined me from one simple encounter, and yet you seem to wonder why I can't stand being around you."

With that I released her and took a large bite of my food.

I could sense her next to me, struggling to compose herself, but I ignored her and focused on the mind-numbing conversation Callie started regarding the different members coming and how worried she was about trouble being riled up. I knew most of her concern was likely for the delicate creature next to me who had never been to an initiation ceremony. Things did get wild, and likely would.

I wasn't worried though, not when I already knew there wasn't a chance Laura would escape my constant attention.

The meal was finished nearly an hour later, and Laura had indulged in four glasses of wine. Callie was tired, and Wes looked…eager to fuck his wife.

So, I offered, "I can take you back, Laura."

She glanced over at me from her spot on the couch, her nose scrunching.

"I might just stay the night."

My best friend winced from behind where Laura sat, then gave me a look that practically begged me to get her out of there. They were definitely going to be fucking tonight.

"Come on, I'm sure they're tired. I'll take you." I moved over to the front where my shoes were.

Laura was about to protest again when Callie bent over and whispered something in her ear. Considering how pink Laura's face flushed, I assumed Callie's filter was gone, and she told her best friend what I already knew.

Sure enough, Laura got up, depositing her empty wine glass on the coffee table and then wavered the slightest bit before heading over to where her shoes and jacket were.

"Thank you, guys, for a lovely evening."

"Bye!" Callie waved and then mouthed thank you to me.

I smirked and then held Laura's arm as she descended the steps one by one. The moon was shining over us, and the cold air clouded in front of our faces.

"Did you already know they planned to fuck?" she asked bluntly while walking toward my truck.

"Yep. Wes had been rubbing her shoulders for a good twenty minutes while you talked about that book you started reading."

"So that's it, he rubs her shoulders and that means he wants to fuck?"

Opening the passenger door for her, I laughed. "Yeah. Doesn't take much for us, but getting to touch and have you in our laps, feel you. That'll about do it every single time."

She held my hand as I helped her into the truck. Once I shut it, I ran around to the other side and got in.

"So..." Laura started, and I was already smiling because I liked a buzzed Laura.

"Is it that simple for all guys? Like if I were to ask you for a back massage, and I was near you in any capacity, you'd..."

"Wanna fuck?" I glanced over with a smirk.

She blushed and tucked a few strands of her hair behind her ears. "Yeah."

"It depends on the person. I've had my dick sucked while another girl rode my face, and I still wasn't in the mood to fuck. But there's other times, the person could be wearing a potato sack, with eye holes cut out, and one glimpse at their eyes would have me hard within minutes."

I watched the road, but I knew I'd gotten her attention. That is, if she recalled what I had once mentioned about her eyes.

"I find that hard to believe."

I glanced over. "Which part?"

"The riding your face, having your dick sucked part. You obviously had to have a hard cock in order for her to suck it, which meant you were ready to fuck."

"You think so?" I scoffed, while adjusting in my seat because hearing her say fuck and cock had me hard as shit.

"You'd be surprised what Sweetbutts are willing to put in their mouths, regardless of pleasure or reaction. I was flaccid as fuck, and that girl still went to town. What about you? Obviously, Callie was turned on by the rubbing of her shoulders. That sort of thing turn you on?"

This was dangerous, it's what got us into trouble last time.

She shrugged, that much I caught between driving and watching the road. "Maybe. I mean, truth be told this conversation has me turned on."

"But you're also drunk...or buzzed."

She smiled at the windshield. "True."

I hated that she was, seemed like this whole conversation wasn't really happening because of it. It meant perhaps she didn't mean anything she was saying.

"Do you remember how last time we played Truth or Dare, and—"

I pulled the truck over, which resulted in her grabbing her seat belt and letting out a surprised squeal.

"What...why did you—"

I punched the gear up into park and unbuckled.

My hips twisted as I faced her. "Whatever you're about to say..." I leaned closer. "Just know I won't lay a finger on you while you're drunk, or remotely close to it."

Her blue eyes seemed to glisten in the light of the moon and nearby streetlamp.

She blinked and then whispered, "what if I touch you?"

"Fuck, you *are* drunk." I lowered my head with an agonizing laugh.

"Well, maybe, but I'm also wet and really worked up."

"Laura." I shook my head.

She gripped my jaw, holding it still. "Just let me be Daisy tonight. Just for right now and then tomorrow, you can go back to hating and ignoring me."

My heart constricted. "You think I hate you?"

"You said as much at dinner, now can I take advantage of you or not?"

My eyes were anxiously searching her face for any trace of humor, any chance at all that this could be a joke.

"I won't touch you," I vowed again.

She nodded, then slowly advanced toward me as I retreated. My legs were spread, and she found her way atop my right thigh, straddling it.

I wanted to grip her hips, hold her in place while she rode my leg, but instead, I just tucked them behind my head.

"Close your eyes, pretend like I'm the girl you want."

If she only fucking knew.

I didn't close my eyes, and after a few seconds, she seemed to take it as a challenge, and then she was lifting her dress until she was showing me the piece of black fabric between her legs.

"Need more friction," she explained as if she needed to justify it.

But then the top part of her dress was being pulled down and her tits were falling free, and my fucking heart nearly stopped.

"What are you—" I whispered, but she merely palmed her breast and then rolled her hips.

"You have no idea what you're doing, and I think you're going to regret this tomorrow."

She laughed, rolling a hard nipple in between her fingers.

"You'll be a gentleman and not remind me."

"I am no gentleman, Daisy. A fact you are well aware of."

She continued to roll her hips, letting out tiny gasps, and then her pace increased, which forced friction against her cunt.

"Wish you were touching me," she rasped, placing her hands on my chest.

I nearly groaned when I felt her wetness begin to seep through my jeans. "Me too."

"Talk to me," she ordered, "what else do you wish?"

"I wish you were riding my cock for starters."

Her tits bounced as she fucked my leg. I couldn't stop watching the way her nipples pebbled from the cold air.

"I wish I could grip your ass and fuck you properly. I wish that soaked pussy would drip for me, I wish I could fuck you bare, and watch my cum slowly leak out of you—I wish I could pull it up with my fingers and feed it to you, shove my fingers into your mouth, make you choke."

"Oh god." She moaned, rotating her hips. I knew her release would be soon.

"Wish you were in my bed, where I could flip you over and fuck you from behind."

"Killian, I can feel you under me, you're getting hard."

"I've been hard, Daisy."

She smiled, trying to catch my eyes in between fucking my leg. "Since when?"

"Since you laughed that first time."

She shattered putting her hands on my neck, holding on tight as she slowly rode out her climax. "I'm ruining your jeans."

"Feel free to ruin me anytime you want, Daisy."

"Pull out your cock, let me see you finish," Laura rasped close to my ear.

Fuck. *Fuck.*

I made sure she was off my leg; a creamy white stain likely would be there once I saw it in the light. Only made me ache at the thought of it.

I pulled myself free and stroked up and down, watching her smile down at me, a hungry look entering her eyes.

I was already on the cusp when she said, "on my tongue."

I shook my head.

"You're not touching me."

"Daisy." I let out another groan.

"Please, Killian." The desperate way she said my name had me. With her tongue out, hovering over my exposed flesh, I did as she said and finished over her waiting taste buds.

She licked her lips with some of the pleasure still dripping along the edge, and it was the hottest fucking thing I'd ever seen.

I wanted to kiss her.

But I knew come tomorrow, if she remembered any of this, she'd surely regret all of it.

SEVEN
LAURA

Rose Ridge had a few perks.

And I really do mean few, not that I'm complaining. I didn't regret moving to this tiny slice of Virginia. I meant it with my whole heart when I came here, even if part of my reason for coming had to do with a man who had a penchant for breaking my heart.

I'd hitched a ride with Red into town after spending six agonizing hours poring over the files. All of which made my stomach churn and left me nauseous. One, I had the hangover from hell, and no amount of greasy food or coffee had helped, but two, the content of the files should have come with trigger warnings—because holy shit.

Blood. Body parts. Gunshot wounds. And other things I couldn't bring myself to name.

The only solace I had was knowing the red mark meant the club was no longer working with that person or club. It wasn't just varying clubs listed in those files. There were politicians, gang leaders, cops, and CEOs for reputable companies.

Disgusting, all of it. And I still had several piles of folders to go.

But, I desperately needed a break, which was why I was now walking away from the market where Red dropped me, and veering for a nearby neighborhood. She wouldn't have minded taking me all the way to my destination, but I liked keeping my secrets.

Not even Callie knew about my little hobby, and it wasn't like I expected anyone to keep their mouths shut. It was just that for six weeks, for whatever reason, no one had spilled the beans yet. So I was riding this tiny thrill of secrecy until someone did.

Cutting around the corner and down a side street, I tucked my arms closer, thinking over what had happened last night. My face burned with the suspicion that I had done something truly regrettable. While I knew Killian had driven me home, I was fuzzy on what took place in between. I had these flashes of being in his lap, and possibly lowering my dress, but I inspected my skin and there wasn't a single mark, bruise or any other identifier that Killian would have left behind. If I had offered myself up like a meal to the wolf, he would have taken a bite.

With his fingers, teeth and nails. I'd never fucked him, but I knew him.

I knew how he made me feel that one time we nearly went too far.

A brief lilt of laughter spilled from the open doorway ahead of me, forcing my face up and a smile to spread across my face.

The Hollow was a simple house at one point. It was tucked in between other residential homes with a wide porch and a chain-linked fence. During the day, you'd mistake it for another random house, but during the night—not a chance.

The trees were lit up with glowing lights, stretching to the porch, where vines intertwined over the gaping arch and roof. Entering The Hollow, you'd think you stepped inside a children's book. Once used as a library, there were artificial trees built inside the living room, archways built to make it feel like a kingdom, with transitioning rooms, and even fake stone making up most of the inner walls. Oversized chairs and couches were scattered around the top floor, along with a few misplaced trays and tables.

A feisty woman named Heidi, and her two sisters served coffee upstairs, while running a used bookstore.

But downstairs, the sound of a stringed guitar danced on the air, beckoning me deeper into the house. The metal, winding staircase led to cement floors and more stringed lights, with various tables and chairs littering the open space in front of a raised platform.

A lone musician sat atop the wooden stage, holding his guitar while he sang a moody melody into the microphone. There were at least thirty people squeezed in between tables, while at least fifteen others were hanging out at the bar, which stretched along the back wall.

I took my coat off and hung it on a hook reserved for participating artists and wandered to the bar.

"Hey, Jack!" I waved at my favorite bartender. He was old and cranky, but I loved him.

The best part, he had no club affiliations whatsoever. At least that's what he told me while we bonded over organizing a huge shipment that came in, half of which busted all over the floors. It took us hours to clean up all the glass and liquor. He vowed to never charge me for a drink for the rest of my life after that night five weeks ago.

I left him tips instead.

"I'll get your usual ready, but you better go set up." Jack called over the noise of people clapping for the singer who had just wrapped up his set.

I nodded, then ducked around a few people standing and drinking, walking along the wall until I was able to get into the back of the stage area. It wasn't large, at all, just big enough for two people to stand, but it helped me with my nerves before walking out on stage.

"Up next we have a local favorite, Daisy White!"

The crowd erupted with cheers and applause. I smirked at the stage name I gave myself and pushed through the curtains.

The house lights nearly blinded me as I waved and headed toward the Yamaha piano set up near the edge of the stage. It took me back to when I was a kid, and my mom had entered me into a thousand different beauty pageants, and how when I was old enough, I started singing, which was not what my mom had intended.

She had planned on me playing the violin or classic piano pieces, nothing contemporary and certainly, no singing. Not when it cast a spotlight on me instead of my father. Not when it stirred crowds, and clogged emotions, moved people in a way that had them straying from certain political platforms my father stood upon.

My life had been lived in a cage, and singing was the door I carved open to escape.

I sang for fun, never wanting to make an actual career out of it. I was too zealous for a life lived without parameters to ever chase singing professionally. It was just something I loved doing.

The piano gleamed under the house lights. Sometimes I sat in front of it, but tonight, I was feeling the need to stand. I adjusted the microphone until it was just the right height, and then I smiled at the audience.

"Hi everyone, thanks so much for coming out tonight. Be sure to order a drink and leave a fat tip for my man Jack back there."

A few people applauded, and I used the sound to help me focus.

"Tonight I had a special song I wanted to play for you, so I hope you enjoy it."

Closing my eyes and moving my hands over the keys, I slowly began to play "Can't Help Falling in Love" by Elvis. It was one of my favorite songs, and it always managed to soothe me whenever I started feeling stressed out or worried.

Sure enough, as I allowed the emotion of the song to cut into me, and the lyrics to swell along with the keys on the piano, my stress from the day began to wane. My worries over Killian, the files, the apartment. It all just melted into every single word I sang into the microphone.

Once I was finished, I sang two more songs and ended with the crowd begging for another. I had sung "Paint it Black," and Sia's "Chandelier," both of which always felt heavy to deliver, especially when I allowed myself to get lost in the music. So I thanked everyone, soaked in the cheers and shouts, then exited back through the curtain where I came from.

I was practically floating on a cloud when my eyes caught on a familiar face.

"Hey!" I walked over to Natty and threw my arms around her.

She squealed. "Laura, you are so incredible! I can't believe this is the first time I'm seeing you perform."

Untangling from her, a tiny tendril of worry worked itself into my stomach.

"Do you come here often?"

She shrugged, turning toward the bar with me. "Not as much as I'd like, but tonight I was over at the coffee shop, prepping some ingredients for tomorrow, and decided I'd stop in."

"What are you drinking?" Jack asked Natty, flicking a concerned gaze at me as though he was silently asking if I was okay. I didn't make friends here, and I never usually talked to people, so he was probably worried I'd had an aneurysm or something.

"Just a shot of crown and a diet coke, please."

Jack turned away, and Natty tucked a piece of hair behind her hair.

"Kinda nice that no one from the club is here, huh?"

I laughed, my eyes wide. "I know, right?!"

She crowded closer to me. "It's part of why I like to leave the club so often…sometimes I just need a break from them."

Jack slid a Moscow mule in front of me, and an amber liquid shot in front of Natty, followed by a can of Diet Coke.

"Honestly, I assumed you didn't mind it." I sipped my drink, loving the bubbly feel of the ginger beer against my tongue.

Natty tipped her head back and swallowed the shot with a hiss. "I don't…I mean, honestly, I really don't. But every now and then, it just feels too repetitive. I think it's why they ride."

I watched her sip her Diet Coke and we fell into easy conversation, learning new things about each other.

"You knit?" I asked, my brows hitting my hairline. A new singer had taken the stage, and this time, everyone was clapping as he belted a Matt Maeson ballad in a deep, melodic voice.

Natty nodded. "I do, but for some reason I can only knit these tiny squids. It was the tutorial I had initially used to learn how to do it, and I know I can simply try a new one, but for whatever reason, it always ends up resembling a squid."

"I have to see these for myself."

Natty suddenly slid off her stool. "Let's go back to the club, I'll show you."

We were laughing again when Jack came back over with a small envelope in his hand.

"For tonight."

The cash was likely close to one hundred dollars, which is about what I made out in tips every time I did a set here. I flipped open the white tab on the envelope and pulled out half the cash and tucked it into Jack's tip jar.

He clicked his tongue, but I ignored him, shoving the rest of the money into my pocket.

The cash would help me save up for a new place. I flicked a hesitant gaze at Natty as we wandered to the coat rack.

"I won't say anything about you singing here." Natty vowed as we pulled on our coats and began ascending the staircase up to the first floor.

"I'm shocked more people don't already know I sing here." We walked through the bookstore and then pushed outside. The fog was cold against our faces, and off to the side of the house was Natty's one-seater, motorized moped, which I knew she'd be driving home. It wasn't big enough for the two of us.

"I don't mind if people do, but I don't want them to think I need to focus on the club job. It's a good job; I just like the extra money." I talked to keep my teeth from chattering. I was also determined to cut ties with the club once I was able. I didn't care what Killian thought.

Natty unhooked her moped and walked back over to me.

"You okay to get back?"

I waved her off. "Of course, I am."

She turned toward her transportation. "We could try to both fit."

I snorted first, then Natty followed with a full bellied laugh.

"How do you ride that and live in a motorcycle club?"

She shrugged, then began stroking the pastel yellow handlebars. "They would never make fun of me. At least not to my face."

We both began laughing again, and then she finally grabbed her helmet, bid me goodbye and zoomed off.

I inspected my cell and saw the time.

Shit, it was nearly eleven at night. While I didn't mind walking, and I knew Natty would have walked with me, I didn't want her to because I knew how early she had to get up for work.

The fog thickened, and I realized I didn't want to walk back. My thumb hovered over Killian's name, the text thread with him was still untouched from three months ago. His last text still unanswered.

Because I'd shown up in person.

Regret from last night flushed through my chest, forcing my thumb to click out of his thread, and open another.

One that was less complicated, less frustrating and altogether less.

Exactly how I wanted it.

EIGHT
KILLIAN

FOR THREE MONTHS, I'D AVOIDED LATE NIGHTS AT THE CLUB.

Or at least, that's how I made it seem. If Laura were there, I'd make it seem like I was taking off with a girl, or otherwise acting engaged with someone. She was always around, sipping a beer, smiling and chatting with Natty, Red and the various Sweetbutts around.

How she made friends so easily I had no idea.

Couldn't they all see her for the threat she was? She was more gorgeous than any girl in this club and had more of a chance at getting patched in by a member. I kept expecting a Sweetbutt to fight with her, or get catty, but they never did. Laura was sweet, considerate and never flirted.

Well, with the exception of Kip.

She flirted with him, and I noticed every small smile she offered him freely, every touch on his arm, and every single hungry expression he had for her. He wasn't the only one either. Laura had a fan club, and she didn't even know it. Which was why I tried to make my presence here scarce, but that was going to have to change with me becoming president.

They'd expect me here, so I was going to have to get over her and my little issues with being around her. Tonight was my first attempt.

The image of her riding my thigh, asking me to tell her what I wished for was stuck on repeat in my head. The way she'd licked her lips and that tiny bit of cum had dripped down. Fuck, I wanted to be around her, especially to ensure she *wasn't* around other members.

Except, she didn't seem to be present. I watched for a few hours, letting it go, but now I was starting to get restless.

My presence by the bar and near Red was probably exhausting to all the members crowding in, trying to get a drink, but I wanted a chance to look in the kitchen.

No Laura.

I made an excuse to head out back, but she wasn't there either. I didn't want to look inside the apartment. I hadn't set foot inside it for three months, and I had a fear that being inside with her would thrust me back to where I was when she first arrived.

Obsessed and addicted.

She was probably in there, in bed, reading or asleep. She had an actual day of work, so she was probably tired. Was I an asshole for wanting her to face me and talk about last night?

Grabbing another beer, hoping this one would at least create a buzz, I was about to head back into the central part of the club when I saw Kip stand up from the sunken leather couch he and his friends were settled in. He swayed as he stared down at his phone.

"She finally lettin' you between those fine legs?" Royce, his best friend, joked loudly.

Kip leaned to the side, still holding his beer.

"Fuck I hope so. She's been playing the long game with me, but she just texted that she needs a ride. So—" He tipped his head back, finishing off his beer.

"Knight in fucking shining armor." Royce laughed, while Kip took a bow.

That was enough of that. I approached the group, patting Kip on the back, even though I really wanted to wrap my hand around his fucking neck.

"Let me see that." I grabbed his phone, and the screen was still lit up with her text.

She sent a pin with her location, and I forwarded it to my phone.

"I'll get her." I shut down the irritation over the fact that she hadn't asked me to begin with.

"Prez, it's not necessary," Kip argued, taking his phone back, "besides, it's the first night of your big weekend. You need to be here."

Pushing him back into the couch where Royce was already sitting, I pulled my own cell out. "You're drunk. So, yeah, it's fucking necessary."

Without another glance back, I headed out through the front door and hesitated.

I could grab her with my bike but that would mean she couldn't tell me why she was in town to begin with, and I needed to know what the hell she was up to. It was nearing midnight, and I made myself pretty clear about her not leaving the club, so I knew she wasn't trying to apartment hunt. So what *was* she doing?

Letting out a heavy sigh, I turned for the garage, pulling my keys from the reserved spot on the wall. Minutes later, I was hauling down the road, heading toward her location. The dashboard said it was nearly thirty degrees out, which with the wind chill and fog was practically freezing. We didn't normally get harsh winters here, but every now and then the season would throw us a curveball. I flipped the temperature gauge up and pressed the heated seat button for the passenger side.

Within five miles, I was approaching her location. I began to slow down and then hit my blinker, turning onto a residential street. What the hell was she doing here?

Seeing her standing out on the curb, I pulled up directly next to her and idled the truck.

Her eyes snapped down to her phone while she took a step back, which had me shoving my door open and getting out.

"What the fuck are you doing out here alone?" I asked, rounding the hood. I searched the street, my nerves suddenly raw as I had to picture her just standing here, waiting for fucking Kip.

Her blue eyes locked onto mine; it wasn't fear but something else reflected back in them. Hesitancy or nerves.

She narrowed her focus on the phone again. "Kip's coming."

"Kip is drunk as shit." I opened her door and held it for her. I wanted to add that tonight was a special night for me. I wanted to know why she wasn't there. I wanted to explain how badly it burned that she'd decided to leave.

Her shoulder sagged, but it got her moving. I didn't wait for her to ask for help, my hand went to her ass on its own, lifting her into the truck before she could turn me away. "Hey—"

I slammed the door on whatever she was about to say and stretched my hand out.

Touching her ass was absolutely one way of sliding back into obsession territory.

Once I was back in the truck, I took off, not even checking to see if she was buckled. I needed to get back to the club, and get her out of my truck, and out of my space.

The silence began to stretch, the radio was playing something moody and slightly perfect. Then it began to snow.

Laura gasped. I caught how she leaned closer in her seat, trying to see out the windshield.

"When's the last time you saw snow?"

She looked over at me with a small smile. "The better question is, when is the last time I saw it in Rose Ridge? That would be right now. Every place is different when it snows, and that very first one is always special."

I tried to hide my smile at her excitement.

"Why were you in that neighborhood so late at night?"

She shrugged. "No reason."

That fire she always seemed to have was burning again under my skin, and I hated how much I liked it.

"There had to be some reason?"

With a tiny tug at the hem of her jacket, she finally released a sigh.

"There's a bar I like to go to from time to time. Red dropped me earlier, but she already went home."

I looked over at her then refocused on the road. "And how do you normally get home?"

My stomach twisted, waiting for her to say that Kip was the one who picked her up. If they had a weekly routine where he'd come and get her, fuck I'd probably end up breaking his legs or something.

"I walk."

That made me laugh.

Her head swung over as I did. "I do."

"All the way back to the club?"

She better fucking no—

"Yeah, all the way back."

"Even in the dark?" I don't know why I asked that; it was a stupid, very obvious question.

She smirked, facing the windshield again. "In the dark."

"Why ask for a ride tonight then?"

Her fingers spread out over her thighs as she continued to watch the snow.

"Something happen?"

We were nearly to the club, and I knew I was running out of time.

Her smile only tilted the corner of her lips as she gestured toward the windshield. "Well for starters, it's snowing...and really freaking cold outside."

Right. Shit, why was I being so basic tonight? I flicked the blinker and slowed the truck. "And you called Kip to get you?"

"Who else would I call?"

I nearly flinched at her tone because she was right. Red was already home with Brooks, Callie was home with Wes, and I...well, I hadn't ever been an option.

But I was last night.

Pulling in front of the apartment, I said, "I'd want you to call me. If you ever need a ride again—"

She pulled on the handle for her door and pushed. "I'll call Kip."

Fuck.

I was out and rounding the truck with her.

"So you don't mind that he's here, drunk and that he was about to drive to come get you."

She spun around on the porch, her key to the apartment out and in her hand.

"Of course, I care, but you're insinuating he'll be drunk every time."

"I'm insinuating that you're leading him on. Unless you want him to give you a property patch?"

Her eyes searched mine, until she finally stepped closer. Her nose was nearly at my chin.

"What if I do? He's nice, treats me well, and a few of the Sweetbutts have talked, said he has an impressive dick."

My vision went red, and there was an odd sound filling my ears.

"You're fucking serious? He's who you want?"

"No!" she answered too quickly, and it made my gaze latch on to hers.

With a much softer tone, I stepped closer. Our bodies were nearly flush.

"Then what?"

She waited there, sharing the same frosted breath as me. The snow was still lightly falling, and I swear her glare drifted to my lips.

"Then nothing, Killian. You made sure there would always be absolutely nothing."

With that, she turned again, and this time, I let her unlock the door. I should allow her to slip away…I should be the gentleman she talked of…I just wasn't.

My hand shot out, stopping the door right as it was about to close.

She made a sound as I pushed, letting myself inside. Then I shut it, locked it and pushed her up against it by sliding my knee between her legs.

"Kil—"

I put my hand gently over her mouth.

"You really don't remember last night? Nothing you did…nothing you wanted?"

Her eyes searched mine; her nose flared as she breathed.

"You wanted to touch me, Daisy. You begged to touch me. Begged me to come on your tongue, and then when I did, you licked it all up, every fucking drop like it was the best thing you ever tasted."

She shook her head, slamming her eyes closed.

"You did. Now, I didn't lay a finger on you because you were drunk. But you're sober now, and I have this strange need to remind you what I'm capable of."

Her hot breath fanned my fingers, but her body began to relax. So much so, the apex of her thighs rested against my knee cap.

"That's it. You want a repeat of last night, where you fuck my thigh?"

She didn't shake her head or nod. She merely breathed and watched me. The apartment was illuminated only by a small light on under the microwave, but it offered enough light for me to do what I needed to.

"I'm going to fuck you with my hand, Daisy. If you want me to stop, you need to shake your head or use your arms to push me away."

I watched as her blue eyes heatedly searched my face, and tendrils of gold kissed her cheek.

But she didn't make a move to stop me.

Exhilaration barreled into me.

Removing my hand from her mouth, I flicked open the button to her jeans and then didn't give her a chance to say anything before spinning her around and pushing her chest up against the door. Her profile met me as her cheek was pressed against the wood.

"Stay right there, Daisy."

Digging my fingers into the waistband of her jeans, I swiftly pulled them down to just below her ass. She wore another thong, this time it was dark purple, and the way it slid through the crack of her perfect ass was nearly my undoing.

I gathered her wrists behind her back with one hand, and the other I skimmed down the purple fabric until I was dipping into her pussy.

"Are you just walking around perpetually wet, Daisy?"

She didn't respond, just remained against the door, heavily breathing. But her lips parted when I pried open her pussy with another digit.

"You're sucking me right in. So greedy."

She made an agonized sound when I added a third finger and tried to adjust her stance so her legs slid farther apart.

"Need me to fuck you with these fingers?"

Again, no answer. Which prompted me to pull my fingers out.

"I'm going to need you to reply, but if you can't then you might as well choke on the taste of your body telling me yes." I shoved my soaked fingers between her pillow soft lips until they were nearly touching the back of her throat, making her gag.

"Suck, Daisy."

Her eyes locked with mine in determination, but she didn't suck.

"Fine." I pulled them out, then shoved them back into her pussy and began to fuck her with them. I rubbed her clit in slow circles that had her sliding back in search of friction. I released her wrists in favor of pulling the string of her thong up, while keeping three fingers buried in her cunt.

"Fuck my hand, Daisy."

With a gasp, she rocked her hips back and forth. My fingers shifted to rub only her clit, and I had her writhing. The sound of her arousal and my fingers moving over her sex filled the room, then came her heavy breathing.

"I'm almost there," she panted, and I moved my fingers faster over her until her head tipped back, her spine arched and her palms found the surface of the door. Pushing her hips back, it was a fucking sight to see with my hand pulling her thong, her jeans around her thighs, and her perfectly round ass pushing against my arm as my hand was buried inside her pussy.

I could feel her tightening around my fingers, as her breathing came out in tiny bursts.

Then she ruptured.

"Killiannnnnn." She moaned, slowing her hips as she found her release.

I stood there, milking the orgasm out of her, every last ounce of pleasure she might find by moving my fingers inside her, feeling her release coat every single one of my fingers.

Once she sagged against the door, I pulled my fingers free and spun her around.

Then licked every single finger clean.

"You call me if you need a ride. Not Kip."

Pink lips parted again as she tried to lock on to my words, but before she could respond, I opened the door and walked past her.

She was right. I did make sure nothing would ever happen between us, and while I couldn't risk any emotions getting in the way, she wouldn't be riding with Kip again.

NINE
LAURA

THERE WERE TOO MANY PEOPLE FOR THE CLUBHOUSE TO HOLD.

Regretfully, I had not planned a trip home, mainly because I had no car. Which meant, I was stuck here during the celebration of the Stone Riders welcoming their new president. I managed to skip last night, but apparently it was only the preliminary celebration.

I'd kept a mostly low profile, just helping Natty and Red as they needed it, but the later it got, the more relaxed I became and the more curious.

It wasn't just the Stone Riders here; it looked like there were various other patches and colors clinging to leather and denim. I was behind the bar, watching the people fling back drink after drink, yelling, laughing and even singing. A few smiles slipped free as I tested the waters of joining in. A sense of belonging slowly crept into my chest, warming with a comfort I hadn't felt anywhere else.

I laughed, tossing my head back as I sang along with everyone else who was belting the words to "Sweet Home Alabama." I slapped Sadie's ass, one of the Sweetbutts who had become a rather familiar face around the club, as she jumped on the bar and began twerking. I was happy, and regardless of the day or the week I had, I would still cling to the tiny moments of joy and tuck them away for later when I needed a reason to stay in Rose Ridge.

I glanced around, trying to locate my best friend, when a flash of green stopped me. It was an instant thing, me slipping back into my shell as I registered the president's gaze. The feeling like I was an imposter smothered all the fire in my core.

Killian was watching, and I already knew he was waiting for me to mess up. The memory of last night was a string pulled tightly around my heart. As if he were merely creating these sudden encounters as a way to play me. As if he'd walk up and pluck at one, and the entire thing would just unravel.

The evening I was drunk had begun to come back to me, and that paired with the incident last night, was just too much to see him again so soon. He had ignored me for three months, only to now swoop in like a wildfire and consume every ounce of air in my lungs and every star in my sky.

I turned my back on him, hoping it would get his attention off me and maybe on Kaya, or one of the other girls around here who worshiped the very ground he walked on. Busying myself with refilling the beer and stocking more liquor. I completely missed when Killian had drawn closer, and now crowded the bar.

He was talking to Clive, one of the newer prospects who tried to attach himself to Killian's side every chance he got. Clive kept talking about something that was rather large by the way he kept expanding his hands. I couldn't hear, but Killian wasn't really paying attention.

His gaze kept gliding toward me, like we were two doors stuck on the same track, sliding back and forth toward one another.

Red came up behind me, startling me by patting my shoulder. "Okay, we're done serving for a bit. We're moving outside for the barbeque and bonfire."

I hid the way my shoulders tensed and gave her a wide smile. "Okay."

Red's red lips slid into a smirk as if she knew I was trying to save face. I had spent three months with the woman, working nearly hip to hip as we handled kitchen duties, finances, deliveries, club arguments and placing orders. She was the only other person I had gotten close to besides Callie and Natty. So when she curled her arm around me and tugged me farther into the kitchen, I went willingly.

"Be careful out there tonight, honey. You're not patched, which means you're free game—the men can get a little intense if you're not used to dealing with them. Try to stick close to Callie tonight if you can, okay?"

I nodded, appreciative of the warning. While I knew how to handle myself, I valued her concern. No one in the club knew of my background, or my parentage. I wanted it to remain that way, but I had been handling aggressive men, toxic women and overall shitty humans since I was old enough to speak. Bikers celebrating too hard wouldn't really faze me.

The crowd began to disperse from the bar, heading out back with a chorus of hollers and buoyant yells. I untied the apron and slid it over the back of a stool before turning to grab my jacket. Stupidly, I'd worn shorts because of how warm it was in the clubhouse. I hadn't really thought through how frigid it would be outside. At least there was a bonfire.

Right as I was about to slip out, warm fingers made contact with my lower back. A looming presence at my spine had me huddled against the wall, completely covered by a firm chest and intoxicating scent. Leather, soap, and something zesty that would make a billion dollars if it were selected as a candle scent. I closed my eyes and inhaled, while swallowing back the scream caught in my throat. Killian didn't just grab me by the belt loop, his entire hand was clutching the waistline of my shorts.

His warm lips brushed against my ear. "Need you to wear this tonight."

Leather was pressed under my fingers, as he pushed the item into my hand.

I looked down, seeing it was a cut. My brows furrowed.

"What—"

"Just put it on, we're making sure Natty has something too."

My heart was a zealous thing, waking up and winking at the warmth coming from Killian's presence. He'd given me his—

"It's Kip's." His tone was flat, his eyes betraying him. He didn't want me to wear Kip's cut, but he'd given it to me regardless.

Why would he do that after what he'd done last night?

I took the leather from him, and his hand found the back of his neck. "It's not a property patch, but he's wearing his jacket tonight, said you could slip this on so no one bothers you. There are other clubs here tonight, just don't want anyone getting any ideas."

Something painful and poisonous had lodged itself inside my chest. Why did I think he'd give me his cut? Why was I so stupid when it came to this man?

I lifted my face, setting my jaw, then slipped it on in front of him, so he could watch as Kip's name slid over my breast.

Killian's eyes narrowed and his jaw tensed as if he were biting back a reply. I pushed past him and briskly walked outside, feeling the cool air calm the fire caught in my face and neck.

Large rocks encompassed the massive bonfire, burning in the center of the yard. Members were drinking beers, eating from paper plates, or gathered around picnic tables, while others were relaxing in lawn chairs with their boots kicked up, the fire light brightening their faces. My gaze slid over to Callie, perched on Wesley's lap, and while I would normally make my way toward her, my feet continued forward. If Killian wanted me to wear Kip's cut, showing I belonged to him, then I'd physically ensure it was true.

Kip was a nice guy, and he made me smile with how cute his dimples would flash when he flirted or how he tried to impress me with talks of his bike and fights. He'd been trying to take me on a date for two months straight, although I had a feeling his version of date differed from mine. Most men in the club considered a date to be a blow job or a make-out session. If a girl got really lucky, they'd be taken to the local bar. Kip didn't seem like the type to do flowers and big acts of romance, but neither did Killian.

I hated that my mind even tried to compare the two. Not after Killian had just shoved me into Kip's arms, wearing his cut no less. Everyone who saw me knew what this would mean, and whether it was real or not, there'd be gossip over me belonging to Kip come tomorrow morning.

I saw his blond messy hair first as I approached the circle he was in. His dimples popped as he told a story, his blue eyes wide with surprise as he laughed and nursed the beer in his hand. Kip was handsome in a rugged way; I wasn't attracted to him, but he was objectively gorgeous. After tonight, things between us would shift, whether I wanted them to or not. It was out of my hands. Drawing closer to the small crowd, I caught his attention and slid under his arm.

"Hey."

His blue eyes clung to me; his mouth gaped in shock.

"Shit, baby, did you just walk up here wearing my patch?"

My face burned. It wasn't my choice, but I ducked my head as if I was shy.

His arm came around me; his palm landed on my ass with a quick squeeze.

"Well, fuck, you don't have to tell me twice." He tilted his head as he threw the rest of his beer back. I took the moment to peer over his shoulder.

Twin emeralds burning with hate burrowed into the man hugging me to his side.

It took all of my strength not to smirk at Killian as he focused on Kip, and the leather at my back. I had no idea why he seemed to have such a visceral reaction when this was what he'd intended all along.

Returning my focus to the fire in front of me, I sidled closer to Kip, trying my best to find comfort in this new role.

I played them all the time. The doting daughter, the perfect princess, the broken doll. I could play Kip like a fiddle, only it wasn't really him who would feel the deception; it would be Killian. I'd be careful to keep Kip's emotions intact since he was innocent in all this, but I would do nothing at all to spare whatever once existed within Killian Quinn for me.

I had to remember that Killian was stepping into his new role. Club President, it was best to stay on his good side, even if that meant finding sanctuary in one of his members. He'd offered to give Kip a bigger room, maybe this was the most logical move for me. I needed a place to stay until I could afford a new place, and it was clear that I'd be settling for rusted tubs and God only knew what else.

My time inside the president's apartment was over.

He'd just sent me into the arms of a different man. It wasn't like he'd ever asked me to be his, but I couldn't stop thinking about that fucking pebble sitting in my suitcase.

Why did he give it to me?

And why did it burn me so much that I wasn't handed a cut with his name on it? It would be stupid to give a random girl his cut, now with his power in the club...I knew it didn't make any sense, but I was still resentful that he'd chosen Kip.

The arm around me clenched, the hand on my ass squeezed again, and I smiled into the arm of the man I was paired with.

All I needed to know was that Killian hadn't chosen me, and Kip was potentially my ticket out of sharing the apartment with him.

Kip was drunk.

I wasn't usually bothered by inebriated people, especially after being in this club for three months, but Kip's drinking was so bad that he couldn't walk straight, and his hands kept roaming.

Speeches had been made by Wes, handing things over officially to the wolf, Killian Quinn. Everyone cheered, music blared and then the party really started. I had no idea what I was in for until someone started a car on fire, then another person drove that car through an old shed. It was madness, and so fucking loud. Eyes and hands were everywhere, which only made me want to stay next to Kip. Which, in turn, gave him the wrong impression of what I was okay with.

His hand kept sliding down to my ass, but now it was sliding under my shirt, hovering over my stomach and drifting toward my bra. Every time I pushed his hands away, I would glance around and it was never the various glassy-eyed expressions laced with hunger and lust that caught me. It was the president's gaze cutting through them that had my heart hammering against my breast, as if I were a rabbit caught in the snare of a wolf.

Killian watched me like I was wearing his name over my breast, like the patch on my back said I belonged to him. He watched me like I was an extension of his person, and he had to make sure no one tried to run away with me. People were walking up to him, slapping his back jovially. Sweetbutts had brought him food and sat in his lap. One whispered in his ear, and it looked like she might have kissed his neck, but with each girl, he would strategically push them off his lap. He smiled at them with that wide grin that likely made them wet between their legs and eager to be back in his lap.

I was a collector of those smiles.

I'd watch from afar as he handed them out so freely to everyone else, everyone but me.

He was careful too, aware of how far that smile stretched, and for how long and to whom received them. It must have been his calculated way of stepping into this new role. The one where everyone called him Prez.

It was something I had to get used to, or maybe I didn't. Not if I found a way to get out of the club. The reminder that I was trying to get free of The Stone Riders rushed back, and suddenly made me want to completely disengage with all the festivities. I didn't feel like faking being Kip's girl anymore. I didn't belong here.

Which was only hammered more fiercely into my heart when I saw Killian hug a familiar looking woman. She was the one he'd pointed out to me that first night I had met him. The tall woman with tattoos, dark hair and legs for days. The one he said had natural looking tits…the one he'd told me he couldn't fuck because he was thinking of me.

My breathing became shallow as I watched this woman steal his attention. She seemed to be the only one who had been able to distract him. It was a reminder that being here tonight was a mistake.

Sliding away from Kip, grateful he didn't even notice, I picked my way through groups of people. Callie was still in Wesley's lap, but she was laughing with Natty about something and Red was with them, along with her man, Brooks. They were in a little circle, and I didn't want to make it awkward by breaking it up. So I crept around the edge of the bonfire, until I was making my way toward the private gate that would lead back to the apartment.

I was yards away from the bonfire and partying, a few feet within the private fenced off yard that had been created for the studio. I wasn't sure what to expect with Killian finally becoming president and claiming his house back, but there were two rooms, we'd figure it out. I was tired, and I wanted to sleep.

On the fringes of the party, the darkness crept in around me, forcing me to pull my cell out and use the flashlight. It wasn't far to the entry gate that was protected by a keypad and access code. It was how Wes had ensured no one from the club would ever bother him back when he had lived here.

My steps felt heavy as exhaustion tugged at my body. I had been up since five in the morning, and with-it nearing midnight, I was done for. Finally, the gate came into view, and right as my hand went out for the pad, I felt an arm wrap around my middle.

"Fuck yeah." Kip's familiar voice crept up my neck, followed by whiskey-soaked breath. "Been ready for this all night."

His arms tightened around me, and panic began to burrow inside my gut.

"Kip, let me go." I tugged at his hands.

His nose grazed my neck again and then he placed open mouth kisses on my shoulder.

"So fucking sexy, been wanting this for so long."

"Kip!" I pushed back, tugging once more at his arms until my nails were digging into his skin.

"Fuck, baby, you want to play like that?" He tilted to the side, taking me with him.

Tears burned at the edges of my eyes as we tipped, and then Kip stumbled forward, and we hit the fence. My face slid against the wood, forcing me to cry out, especially as Kip's weight pressed heavily against me. Before I had a chance to push him away, his weight was suddenly gone.

"You motherfucker."

I spun around in time to see Killian holding Kip by the collar, while his other hand was fisted, pummeling into Kip's face.

"Prez, fuck. I didn't..." Kip pleaded, but his words were cut off with the sound of a sickening crunch.

Kip was on the ground, not even fighting back as Killian hit him repeatedly.

"You think you can touch her?" His fist flew again, and Kip's eyes suddenly rolled back into his head.

He was going to kill him.

"Killian, stop, please. He's just drunk."

Killian's wild gaze met mine and he let Kip drop to the ground.

"Just drunk? As if that excuses him for touching you?"

Why was he making it seem like Kip wasn't allowed to touch me period, even sober?

"Regardless, it's over. Let him go back to his friends and sleep it off."

Killian looked down again, seeing Kip roll to his stomach with a groan.

"Fucking prick thinks he can touch what doesn't belong to him. I should kill him."

A swift kick landed in Kip's ribs and I couldn't take anymore, I spun around and punched the code into the keypad. Tears lined my eyes and I heard Kip struggling to get to his feet behind me, murmuring apologies to his new president.

"You ever touch her again and—" Killian's voice trailed off as I pushed open the gate.

I was two steps inside the yard when I felt a presence at my back, and this time, I knew it was Killian. I didn't want to fight with him, but I also didn't want to be in the house with him tonight.

"I'll just get my things and go to Callie's house. I think they're still at the party."

Killian was next to me, gripping my elbow, pulling me into the apartment.

"What's the fucking code to get in?" he barked as we neared the back door.

Why didn't he know the code? I guess it made sense he hadn't stepped foot in the apartment in three months.

"Four, Four, Six, One."

The beeps from the keypad echoed around us until the lock gave and Killian was pushing into the house, still holding onto my elbow.

It was dark as he pulled me through the house.

"Which bathroom has medical shit inside?"

"Killian, I can handle it. Let me go."

He didn't. In fact, he only held me tighter.

"He fucked up your face, now walk."

"We can't both go up the stairs walking like this, let me go." I pulled at his hold, and he finally let me go, but seconds later, I was being lifted off the ground.

"Killian, what are you…"

In the pitch-black house, he started up the stairs with me pressed against his chest as he carried me bridal style.

"Just stop talking. You probably don't even know that you're fucking bleeding."

I gently prodded at my face. It was sore, but as I pulled my fingers away, I could feel something wet.

"Go left, the door is open," I muttered as Killian cleared the top of the stairs.

Light from the bonfire bled in through the back windows, shedding enough illumination that I could see us in the mirror as we walked into the bathroom. Killian used his elbow to hit the switch, dousing the darkness, and forcing me to wince at the bright intrusion.

"Set me down, I can walk."

He pulled me closer before finally situating me on the counter. The surface was chilled under my thighs as my shorts slid up, and a hiss left my mouth as he tilted my face and began inspecting the wound. His fingers were gentle, but his eyes held an ire inside that made me shudder.

Killian hissed, while inspecting my face. "What the fuck was he thinking?" He stepped back eyeing my shoulders. "And take this fucking thing off."

He peeled Kip's cut from my body with shocking gentleness and tossed it to the floor. My sweatshirt came next, leaving me in just my tank top. I waited as he dipped below the counter to dig for the medical supplies before speaking again, especially as his face became level with the apex of my thighs. I thought of last night, but also…my mind went back to that first time he snagged a piece of not just my heart, but my hope.

Your eyes are Cinderella blue.

I blinked to push away the memory and focused instead on the way he was applying ointment to my face in such a gentle way that it made me wonder who else he'd ever touched like this. Then I remembered the girl he was hugging tonight.

"Why were you following me anyway?"

Killian's gaze stayed on my wound, his fingers bracing my face as he gently cleaned it. I watched his dark brows and the way his thick lashes fanned the tops of his cheeks. The silence filled the room, but music and the revving of engines could be heard from outside. Orange flickered through the clouded window over the tub, making the room feel cozy and safe.

"I was headed back to the apartment, got tired."

He was lying, and for months I had been letting his little lies slide because I didn't want to confront the truth, but tonight, I wanted nothing but honesty between us.

"But you were with someone. I saw you."

His movements paused, his eyes drifting down to mine.

"You mean Jill?"

Fuck if I knew. I shrugged, hating that it made pain flare in my shoulder.

Killian dipped his head, resuming his gentle ministrations against my wound.

"I said hello to her, she's a good friend."

It irritated me that he wasn't telling me the whole story. He wasn't explaining why he'd been there to pull Kip off me or telling me why he'd been watching me all night as if I belonged to him, only to stop the second she showed up. I wanted to go back in time and erase the fact that I knew he'd done it at all. But saying anything more on the subject would lead him to believe that I cared, or that I was jealous. While I knew I was, there was no way I wanted him to catch on.

The silence grew again, and this time, I wasn't going to fill it with stupid questions that didn't matter. Regardless of why he was watching me, he had been there in time to save me.

Gripping his wrist, I forced him to pause and look at me.

"Thank you."

He searched my face, the intensity almost overwhelming. His rigid jaw was shadowed with a day's worth of growth, just barely. It seemed he could grow a very effective beard if given the chance. I had the strangest sensation to run my hand along his wide jaw to feel the harsh growth against my smooth palm. His dark eyes seemed to hold a question he was too stubborn to ask out loud.

Then he leaned in and pressed his lips near my ear, invading my space completely.

"Don't thank me, Daisy. Just don't ever put yourself in that position again. His hands ever go near your body again and I will cut them off. Do you understand me?"

Daisy.

That fucking nickname again. God damn him and that stupid nickname.

Feeling a fresh fire bristle in my chest, I pushed at his, feeling the smooth leather under my palms.

"Put *myself* in that position? You put me in that position."

I jumped down from the counter and tried to clear the bathroom, but he was on my heels, grabbing my wrist.

"Like fuck I did."

Spinning around, I glared up at him and pushed again.

Pushing him felt akin to pushing a large STOP button.

"You put his cut on me and sent me into his arms. That was your fault."

Towering over me, he caught my other wrist and pulled me closer.

"The cut was to protect you. I never told you to walk over and let him grope you all fucking night. Or to let him put his hands under your shirt and feel your tits. I never once said to do that."

"So you *were* watching."

His smirk landed somewhere in my stomach, but it was like a belly flop. All wrong and potentially lethal.

"Yes, and you were watching me, Daisy. Round and round we go in this fucked-up circle once again."

I hated this. I hated him. I hated that he was right.

"What do you want from me, Killian?"

His glare softened the smallest bit before hardening again.

"I want you to stop being a complication. You're a flicker in my peripheral vision, a glare, a goddamn floater that corrective lenses would fix. I want to erase you."

Oh…

I couldn't even—

Killian stepped closer. "But…I also want to wrap your soul around mine, feel the beat of your heart in my neck as I breathe, and carry you with me everywhere I go, all at the same fucking time."

Inhaling a silent breath, I stared up into his emerald gaze. Silence passed between us. What he'd said would be just another secret added to the pile. It would be another pebble added to the rubble that was our fucked-up dynamic. Whatever this was…it was impossible, irrelevant.

In the end, Killian would never be mine, and I would move on. I'd get an apartment outside of the club. I'd get a job somewhere else, and I would meet someone new. He'd become nothing but a memory, and I'd be better for it.

Speaking soft but stern, I muttered. "I'll be out of your life in a week."

We were in the bedroom now, and I couldn't stand the eerie way the firelight reflected in the room, so I clicked on the small lamp and began picking up the few random articles of clothing I had on the floor.

Killian stood silent near the door.

Ignoring him, I folded the small pile of clothes and set them back in my suitcases, which were in the walk-in closet. A few of my jackets and dresses were tossed over the bars because I didn't have hangers yet.

"What the fuck is this?"

I peered out of the closet, seeing Killian lifting the edge of my mattress with his boot.

"My bed, why?"

It was made, why was he looking at it weird?

His brows crinkled as he continued to inspect my sleeping space. "But why is it on the floor?"

"I don't have a frame for it yet. This is what people do who don't have bed frames."

He looked around the space as if seeing it for the first time.

"You have the lamp sitting on a cooler."

My face flushed the smallest bit, but I pushed it away. Wasn't like he'd never been poor; he'd shown me where he once lived.

"It serves dual purposes," I joked, lifting it to pull out a bottle of water. "See, it's like having a mini fridge up here."

He walked over to the window and picked up the sheet that had been hanging over it. I liked to unpin the side in the mornings after I dressed so I could have natural light in the room.

I watched him as his motorcycle boots pressed into the carpet, heading toward the closet.

"You're still living out of your suitcases?"

This was starting to feel a little redundant, so I didn't answer.

"You've been here for three months; how come you haven't moved in?"

His gaze was soft and curious. I shrugged, pulling on a sweater, desperately wanting out of my shorts and into some sweats. I wanted to take my bra off and get under my covers and prop my phone up so I could watch *Never Been Kissed*. I had been making my way through nineties and early two thousand rom coms.

"This was always going to be temporary. I wanted to stay ready to leave in case you came back and kicked me out."

Killian's jaw went slack for a moment before he recovered, clearing his throat. I thought he was going to say something else, but instead, he turned and started downstairs, flipping lights as he went.

The office space across from the room was empty, so were the linen closets. He took the stairs one at a time, until his heavy tread was echoing over the hardwood.

"You've got to be fuckin' kidding me." He scoffed.

I watched from my perch near the stairs, close to the room. I was beyond ready for bed and the sooner Killian let himself out, the better.

"No couch. No fucking television." His voice trailed as he transitioned to the kitchen. "Two plates, two spoons, two forks, one bowl, and a single coffee mug."

Rolling my eyes, I decided I'd heard enough. I'd never lived alone, and I came to Rose Ridge with exactly zero things to my name except my clothes. Callie took me to the thrift store, and I grabbed a few things, and of course she wanted to make me her pity project and buy me a whole apartment's worth of shit, but I refused.

I'd eventually build up my stuff, but why buy new stuff I'd have to move when I wasn't planning on being here for very long?

"You're living like you're not getting paid by the club. Why the fuck is that, Laura?" His arms went wide as he looked up at me and slowly slid his leather cut off his shoulders. He placed it gently on the counter, since there was no table or chairs for him to lay it over. Next, he slid his boots off, and my heart began raging in my chest. Why was he acting like he was staying?

"I get paid, I'm just saving up."

"This isn't living, this is squatting." Killian was in a pair of white socks, a pair of denim jeans and a plain white t-shirt. I could see his tattoos running down his right arm, and the way it dripped down his hand and fingers.

I loved the way it looked on him, and how his left arm didn't match. It was strangely perfect.

"I already told you that I'm moving out soon. I'm not sure why you're so bothered by how I'm living." My voice was starting to grow thin the later it became. I just wanted to sleep.

Killian muttered a curse as he replied, "you did say that didn't you."

His head dipped, like he was finally giving up, then with a weary expression he said, "Fine. Just get your ass in bed, you're exhausted."

I didn't need him to tell me twice. I shuffled back to the room, taking my sweatshirt and bra off, tossing them in the closet as I went. My shorts went next. I was in just my tank top and underwear when I clicked the light off and crawled into bed.

Sleep weighed down my eyelids, and I was nearly out when I felt the bed dip and a rather giant-like presence fill the opposite side of my mattress.

I let out a groan as I fought the overwhelming urge to ignore him and slumber.

"What are you doing?"

Killian stretched out next to me, his body heat immediately enveloping me as he claimed all available space on my full-sized mattress.

"I'm sleeping."

His hand grazed my ass before quickly moving to my hair, shifting a few pieces off my shoulder. Goosebumps trailed down my skin after his fingers lifted. I shifted closer to the edge to avoid him.

"Why here?"

"There's no couch, no extra bed. Nowhere else for me to sleep in my own apartment."

It wasn't like I could argue with him. It *was* his apartment, and I was starting to care less and less about his reasons for being here and more about how him being next to me made me feel…*safe*.

"Fine, but don't touch my ass."

I heard him laughing behind me then his fingers grazed my ass again.

"But it's one of my favorite things about you."

"You don't get to have a favorite thing about me, not when you said my ass was fake and not natural like Jill's."

Had I just thought that or said that out loud? I kept dreaming and feeling him touch me, and it was so soothing that it was making me even sleepier.

"No, she's nothing like you, Daisy. No one is. You're in a league all your own. That's what makes this so hard."

"Your dick?" I snorted and somehow shifted closer to the center. He was so warm.

"Yes, actually. Want to feel?"

I did want to feel, but I also didn't want to. Another secret between us would be too much.

"I don't want any more secrets between us."

He went quiet behind me, and I started to drift off, but right as sleep nearly claimed me, I heard him whisper, "Then maybe we should confess."

TEN
LAURA

LIGHT POURED INTO THE ROOM, PRACTICALLY PRYING MY EYELIDS OPEN because I forgot to pin the sheet above the window.

Groaning, I rolled off the mattress and stumbled to my feet, pawing at the edge of the sheet with one eye closed.

"You need real curtains." A deep voice echoed from behind me.

"Shit!" I yelled, spinning around. My heart was thundering as I backed into the wall, tripping over the cooler and knocking over the lamp.

I heard that same voice mutter, "Fuck."

I was flailing my arms, trying to get up when warm hands were suddenly on my wrists, tugging me up.

I pawed at the intruder's chest, trying to push.

"Shit. Stop. What are you doing?" he asked, but I kept pushing. I needed to get to the bathroom.

"It's me, what is your problem?"

His voice sounded like Killian's but shit, it was early, and I was still exhausted, so I wasn't sure.

"Move, let me get to the bathroom."

The person stepped back, leaving me on my own to figure out how to get where I needed to go.

I stepped on the mattress, falling forward, and then flailed my arms again before straightening. I was so mad at myself. I never forgot to grab my glasses before heading to bed, but last night was a mess and I was so tired, I literally collapsed into bed and gently pulled my contacts out, then just left them on the floor like a disgusting weirdo.

"Are you blind, Daisy?"

Definitely Killian then, his voice was cheery, and I could imagine a smile curling his lips.

I knew the layout of the room and no, I wasn't blind. I just had really terrible vision. I was considered legally blind without my corrective lenses in place, so if I didn't have my contacts, or my glasses, I was completely and utterly fucked. Everything was a blur, and I couldn't make out a single thing.

My hands landed on the counter, and I began feeling to get the layout.

Sink. Toothpaste. Electric toothbrush that fell over the second I touched it.

"Here, shit. You looking for glasses?" Killian asked, pulling on my elbow.

"Yes." I finally found my voice because, at this rate, I wasn't going to find them on my own and that terrified me. My contacts were in the cupboard and as long as no one moved them then I'd be able to make my way to them, but I still had eye makeup on. I usually wanted to wash my face and drink a cup of coffee before putting my contacts in.

I heard Killian moving something, glass clinking, and then he was gently guiding a pair of frames onto my face.

His defined jaw came into view first, then his sensual lips that were far too pillowy to be real. Then his nose, and his stormy green eyes that were framed by thick lashes. I suddenly wanted to know if he inherited them from his father or his mother. Then I remembered what he'd said about his father being a murderer and winced.

"There she is. Finally registered the wolf standing in front of her."

Gripping the edge of my glasses, I pushed them into place with a slight smile.

"Thank you."

He searched my face, and I assumed that gaze would travel like it usually did, but he just stayed fixated on my eyes, or rather the large black frames over them.

"You wear glasses." His smile widened.

A blush crept up my neck for some reason as his fingers traveled to the sides of my head.

"Thick ones, which means you're really blind…how come you didn't say anything?"

Scoffing, I pushed past him. "Why would I tell you that I can't legally drive or even eat cereal without a prescription?"

"So you wear contacts most of the time?" Killian caught up with me, seemingly engrossed in my eye condition.

"All the time. I never wear glasses unless I'm in bed, or early in the morning."

Where were my sweats? I usually had them by the bed at night because it was always so cold in the morning. I searched the area, now able to see, recalling everything that had happened last night and the fact that I was currently in front of Killian in just my underwear.

"Can you go downstairs or something?" I asked, quickly darting toward the closet to grab some clothes.

A dark laugh followed me. "Why would I?"

Ugh. He was being annoying this morning. The light in the closet came on with a flip of the switch, and I dipped down to dig through one of my larger suitcases.

"Because I'm currently occupying this room."

His shoulder found the doorframe, his eyes fixated on me as I scoured for clothes.

"My house. I can be anywhere I want."

"And what you want is to be standing here, watching me?" I knew I shouldn't have asked. Toying with him wasn't smart, and he'd already proven that I was the idiot, lost girl who kept falling in the large paw of the wolf, who very much liked to play with her.

His eyes gleamed.

"What I want is to finish what I started this morning."

My brows caved. "What are you talking about?"

He stalked closer, pulling me out of the closet. "Get on the bed, Daisy."

Heat slid up my chest, practically choking me. His command, the way he'd ordered me…it was fire in my core.

"What did you start?" Because I knew him, he'd never touch me while I was asleep or drunk. He was an asshole, but he'd never go that far. Deep down, I trusted him and while he was hot as fuck with that mouth, he was also very protective.

"I'll tell you in a second, but first, get on the bed."

He stalked forward, and I fell back on the mattress.

"Truth or Dare, Daisy?"

My heart raced indecently fast at his words. Tossing them out there as if that simple game wasn't the reason he'd first made me want him. Playing Truth or Dare with Killian was a dangerous activity and exactly how we got into trouble three months ago. It was the sole reason I left early. But also the reason I came back.

I tried to turn over. "Pass."

Killian had lowered to the bed, and his hand clamped down on my hip, stopping me from fleeing.

"You're in the president's bed. You owe me a game."

"This is my bed!" My voice came out as a shrill, my fists balled up as they pressed into his chest.

"Choose, Daisy. Truth or Dare."

I waited. Still not liking that he thought he could boss me around.

"What are you going to do if I don't pick?"

He laughed, his face lowering until he was mere inches from my lips. "For starters, I'm going to drink your coffee and eat your scone, and I'll do it while you watch me."

"You got me coffee and scones?" Was he bluffing?

How long had he been awake? I couldn't risk missing out on the scones, so I made a decision.

"Fine," I huffed, thinking over my decision. Truth had got us into the most trouble last time we played, and I knew Killian would respect whatever boundary I put in place if I said Dare…regardless if he might push it, it would still be the most harmless.

"Dare."

His smile could not be rivaled, especially as his eyes focused on my lips.

"I dare you to let me tie your hands above your head."

His wolfish smirk had unease sliding through my stomach, and unfortunately pooling between my legs.

"That's it, you're only going to tie my hands?"

He shrugged. "Sure."

I stared at him, trying to gauge his real intentions. Why else would he want to tie my hands together unless he planned on touching me?

"Okay." I surrendered. "But I'm getting under the blanket first."

I slid under the covers, pulled them to my chin, and then held my wrists out to him.

I should have known better.

He gently guided my hands above my head and then gave me a savage grin. "This part you're going to have to forgive me for." He laughed, and then with one hand on my wrists, the other gripped the edge of the blanket and ripped it down.

He stared at my chest, and I knew my nipples were poking the thin fabric of my tank top, revealing how cold I still was. His hands went to the hem and lifted it all the way above my head.

"Killian!" My yell came out muffled as the fabric passed over my face.

His hips were over mine, as he straddled me, and he began using my tank top to bind my wrists together.

"Are you fucking kidding me?" I yelled, trying to buck him off my waist, but it was a futile attempt. We both knew it.

He pulled his shirt off, then warned me not to move as he stood to shrug off his jeans, until he was in a pair of black boxer briefs. The fabric hugged his muscular thighs, raising as his knees bent, revealing twin tattoos on his upper thighs. They were nautical star maps, and they were completely beautiful. He was straddling me again, and I was so distracted by his beauty that I hadn't even fought him.

"Eyes up here, Daisy."

My hands couldn't move and were trapped above my head. My bare breasts were on full display, my nipples were hard and pointing at the ceiling. My stomach clenched as I tried to lift my hips, but all it did was help his erection to dig into me.

"Fuck, you need to stop moving or else we're going to have an even bigger secret between us."

I knew he meant we'd fuck, and I wasn't ready for that, but hearing that he wasn't either was disheartening for some insane reason.

"Why did you want to tie my wrists?" I couldn't help squirming the smallest bit again.

His smile returned as he leaned down and sucked one of my nipples into his mouth.

"So I could see you."

I lifted my hips, hating how good his erection felt against me. "You're doing more than seeing me."

His tongue slowly lapped at my right nipple, leaving a trail of goosebumps. "Realized seeing wouldn't be enough."

He left a wet trail along my skin as he continued to suck and lick my breast. "That's the problem with you, Daisy. It's never fucking enough for me. I always have to have one more look, a taste, something. It's why you're such a complication."

His kisses moved down to the underside of my breasts, while his finger toyed with the band at my hip. "If I feel under this fabric right now, are you going to be wet for me? What would you do if I fucked your tits right now?"

I had no words. As much as I knew I should be keeping him away, there was also a desperate part of me that wanted to see him lose control. I wanted his attention, his desire and his lust. I wanted the part of him that was raw and animalistic. I had seen his softer side. I wanted the primal side to come out and play, and I had no idea why. It should terrify me, I should tuck tail and surrender, let him know he's won whatever fucked-up game this was between us.

Instead, I locked my gaze with his and breathed, "Do it."

His eyes narrowed, but they hooded too. I knew I had him when he let my hands go and gripped my hips.

"I'm serious, Daisy. Don't say yes unless you understand what's going to happen. I'm going to stay straddled over you, pull out my cock and slide it between these fucking delicious tits. Then I'm going to—"

"I said do it," I snapped, lifting my hips.

I knew what I was saying yes to, and I hated myself for it.

His gaze lowered to his erection hidden under his boxers, and while he hadn't tied my wrists to anything, I continued to keep them bound and over my head.

The room was quiet, and all I could hear was my ragged breathing as I peered down the length of my body and finally caught a glimpse of that glorious appendage that surely aided this dominant male with all the absurd confidence he carried around. The head of his dick was a purplish hue mixed with a dark tan. He pulled from the left side of his boxers, popping free the entire fucking thing and robbing me of breath. He was huge...and as his thumb rubbed over the liquid beading at the tip, I realized with a shaky breath that he was pierced.

My eyes widened as I took in the silver loop connected to the tip of his cock. I'd never been with anyone who'd been pierced, well not on the dick. I was with a guy who had his nipples pierced, but it wasn't my thing. This, however, was absolutely my thing...or maybe it was simply because it was Killian.

"Must have missed this that night you begged me to come on your tongue." He smirked, slowly rubbing his thumb over the piercing.

I silently answered by stretching my arms higher to force my chest out. I still didn't remember that night in full detail, but apparently, I had turned into a greedy little slut for the guy who consistently broke my heart. Sounded typical for me.

His eyes gleamed as he lifted onto his knees and moved from my hips to bracing my ribs and then he was even closer, straddling just under my chest, but keeping enough distance that he wasn't crushing me.

"I'm going to need you to lower your arms and help push your tits together."

He reached forward and brought my wrists down, still bound together, and pressed my palms into his stomach, which forced my biceps to push the sides of my breasts together. He made a hissing sound as the head of his cock slipped between the silky skin of my cleavage.

Killian rasped a curse while tilting forward. He held onto the fabric around my wrists, which held me to him and kept my arms in place.

I loved the look in his eyes, the way his gaze hooded and the way his mouth parted as he watched where we connected. Increasing his pace, my tits began to bob as he slid back and forth. Every time he surged forward, cum would leak from the tip of his cock, and he would growl.

His reaction was making the ache between my legs insufferable. My hips raised, desperate for some sort of contact.

Killian realized this and reached the hand that wasn't holding my wrists in place, behind him, sinking three fingers into my throbbing center.

"Killian," I cried out in pleasure, his thick fingers moved slowly and perfectly as he continued to fuck my tits.

"Shit, fuck," he muttered, his eyes going wild, "not fucking yet."

The sounds of how wet I was filled the room, as did our heavy breathing and the animalistic, gruff sounds of losing all control. I watched his tattoos shift as his hips moved. I loved them, I wanted to inspect them closer, and see where else he had them.

"I might need more of you, Daisy. I can't—"

He moved faster, his dick completely slick with his arousal. I elevated my ass to encourage his fingers deeper.

"Don't stop, don't stop," I begged, and right as my climax came, his did as well.

With a loud groan, Killian let go of my wrists and held his shaft as his release covered me.

Our chests were still heaving when Killian slowly moved his still hard cock through the strands of cum sticking between my breasts. He'd made a mess of me. Green eyes glossed over as he focused on the sticky chaos he'd created. With a hiss, he slid the fabric off my wrists, then with a concentrated furrow to his brow, he dipped his thumb into his thick release, coating my skin.

"Fuck, what have I done?" He brought his thumb to my lips where he smeared his cum, and then I opened my mouth and sucked. His eyes homed in on my lips, his own parted as though he were about to say something.

"Prez!" someone suddenly shouted from downstairs.

My eyes went wide as I froze in place, and Killian's hand rested protectively on my stomach.

Killian peered over his shoulder with a low curse.

"Why the fuck is he here already?"

Giles yelled up and his voice echoed every word for us to hear perfectly. "I don't know if you want me to come up, but after seeing what you did to Kip last night, I don't want to. My eyes are closed right now just in case she walks out in her pajamas."

I narrowed my eyes at him.

"Why would he be worried about coming up?" Kip had attacked me, which was why Killian had reacted the way he did last night. It wasn't like he was going to manhandle everyone who came near me.

Killian locked his jaw, letting it pulse a few times before letting out a sigh.

"It's nothing. Can you stay up here until he leaves?"

"No. Unless you're kicking me out?" I raised an eyebrow, my pulse thundering.

I could afford the apartment with rust and the arguing couple above it. Worst case scenario, I could do it.

"I'm not. I am, however, moving in."

With that, he got off me, and began pulling on his clothes. I did the same, grabbing my twisted tank to wipe off the remnants of what Killian had done to me. I pulled on a hoodie, and shorts, keeping my focus on the president.

"You're moving in? Does that mean you're taking this room?"

We scaled the steps briskly; Killian's broad back was all I could see until we turned the corner. Giles was waiting by the kitchen counter with a brown bag and a drink carrier holding two coffees.

"Hi Giles," I said kindly, attempting to quell my frustration with his president.

His gaze flicked to Killian in front of me before cautiously landing on me.

"Hey Laura. I like your glasses."

Oh shit. I had completely forgotten I was wearing them. I risked a quick glance at Killian while I pushed the frames higher. His jaw was locked, glaring at his vice president.

"You brought food and coffee?" I asked, moving closer to the counter and hoping to break the tension in the room.

Giles stepped back, eyeing the man at my back once more as if he were worried Killian had adopted some strange superpowers to maim anyone who talked to me.

I sipped the coffee, moaning delightedly. "You are the best; you have no idea how badly I needed this."

His smile crept in, lighting up his roguish features. He had thick golden hair the color of wheat that was always styled in a way that made him look like he was about to start a photo shoot; it was messy and chaotic but still gorgeous. He was shorter than Killian, just barely taller than me, but he was built like a truck with defined muscles and a smattering of ink to cover them. Currently, he wore his black leather jacket with his patches, with a brown t-shirt underneath and distressed jeans.

He honestly gave me big brother vibes more than anyone else in the club.

His warm brown eyes landed on me in a sisterly way, as though he were happy that I was caffeinated and wanted to see if we could go find some trouble now that I could function.

With a sweet laugh, he muttered, "Prez bought it."

I spun on my heel, giving Killian a quizzical raised brow.

"Keep looking at me like you're not sure if you want to fuck or slap me, and I'll take you back upstairs to settle it, Daisy."

My face erupted in flames, and thankfully, Giles was at my back so he couldn't see.

"Thank you for the coffee," I deadpanned.

He reached around me, his long arm brushing mine. "Got you those scones you like too."

Ohmygosh. I dug into the bag like a badger.

I loved Natty's scones.

I bit into it and was about to let out another delighted moan when Killian stepped around me and covered my mouth.

"You gotta stop that shit when other members are here, unless you want me to kick Giles out."

I licked his palm to get him to release me and then shoved away from him.

"You're so insanely rude, Killian."

"And you're so insanely hot, which causes a lot of fucking problems.

So if you could just take your food and go upstairs, I would really appreciate it."

He was an asshole, but I was hungry, and he'd fed me.

"Fine." I grabbed the bag, and my coffee, and started back toward my room, but right before I hit the top of the stairs, I heard Giles ask, "Does Wes know how bad this has gotten?"

Killian grumbled in response, "Wes can go fuck himself. He doesn't call the shots anymore."

Giles let out a sigh. "Not going to comment on that, but you were two seconds from grabbing my throat. It needs to be handled, Kil. And soon."

Killian didn't respond.

I tried to make sense of what they were saying, but the only thing that kept coming back to my mind was the idea of him moving in. If he was moving in then I needed to move out, simple as that. He'd already said I was a complication for him, maybe there was an attraction there he just didn't like. Who knew, but he didn't want me here.

I needed to figure something out because I knew as much as I hated Killian Quinn, I hated the idea of hearing or seeing him with anyone else even more.

Three Months Ago

I had never been on the back of a motorcycle before.

There was no way I was going to tell Killian that, especially after telling me I didn't really have a choice. Callie had asked me to do some recon at the local bar, but Killian had shown up half way into my sleuthing attempts and demanded I go with him. Saying my best friend had been picked up by Wes, and I needed to be kept safe until further notice.

I put up a fight, but in the end, I crawled on to the back of his bike and hung on tight, but now, as he took a tight curve, I withheld a scream.

This was terrifying, but I also sort of loved the thrill.

The wind blew the hair not trapped by the helmet away from my face, and there was something so soothing about that with how humid and hot the air was. I also loved that when I hugged him tighter, he seemed to go faster.

I was smiling against his back, and I knew we'd fall back into our roles of bickering and fighting when he parked, but I was enjoying this peace for as long as I could. I felt free and alive and like that picture I had seen in the club house. If I could let go of Killian's waist and throw my arms wide, I would.

Killian pulled off on a small road and slowed his speed considerably. I lifted my head, looking around. There were large trees spaced out along a vast property that had dying grass planted in patches. A small house sat in the middle of the property: it was old and weathered with chipped white paint and a few broken windows.

When he parked off to the side of the house, there was a detached garage with an old brown station wagon parked inside.

He set his feet down and unbuckled his helmet before turning his head.

"Watch the exhaust, you'll burn the fuck out of your leg."

I peered down, cautious with how I hopped off the bike. I ignored how he muffled a small laugh at my theatrics.

"What is this place, did you bring me here to murder me?"

Because this place gave serious murder vibes.

Killian hesitated by scratching the back of his neck.

I took advantage and pushed toward the station wagon. There was something about it...why keep something so old?

"What is this?" My voice was quiet as I tried to look inside the clouded windows. For some reason, my heart pinched, and my chest pulled tight like a string about to snap.

With a sigh, Killian placed a hand on the top of the rusted roof.

"My first home."

My eyes snapped up, completely unprepared for the emotions swirling in his.

He gestured toward the house behind him. "And that's my second home...come on."

Killian moved toward the back door, bypassing a laundry line that was loose and blowing in the wind. The steps were faded, chipped and barely holding.

"Careful." Killian held the back door open for me and gestured me inside.

The interior of the house actually looked livable. The linoleum floors were intact, outdated but clean. The sink was white and stained but had been cleaned recently. There was a green couch that looked fairly new sitting inside the living room, an older television was set up, along with a card table, two chairs and an armchair that had seen better days.

"Do you live here?" I gently touched the back of the chair, eyeing the rest of the space.

Killian let out a sigh that held a mixture of uncertainty.

"It's my pop's house...he's in prison. I don't live here, but it's a safe house used by the club. We'll come here if we need to lay low because of cops, or just to have a meeting off the books."

That made sense, but why did he bring me to a place that seemed so important to the club?

"Why am I here?" I finally asked, holding my arms in close.

Killian dipped down to where a small fridge sat, which I had missed, and pulled out two beers. "Figured we could chill here for a bit. Until Wes is done talking with Callie. He's got something planned and just needed you safe until he tells me what's next."

Club stuff confused me. I was trying to gather what I could and use what I had learned from a few tv shows that I had seen, but this was crazy. Seemed like this club wasn't entirely legal, which didn't exactly bother me. I knew there was a code they lived by, or I assumed there was.

Realizing I was going to be here for a while, I slumped onto the couch and held out my hand for the beer he'd pulled out.

Killian handed it over, lifting his dark brow at me.

"What?"

"You don't seem fazed by what I said."

I shrugged. "Seems to make sense. Callie and Wes definitely have some things to talk about, and it makes sense that he'd want to keep an eye on the friend who came with her. I get it."

Killian sat on the coffee table across from me, his knees invading my space.

"But the idea that this is essentially a hide out, that doesn't scare you? You seem to be going along with club shit pretty easily. This patch doesn't scare you?" He pointed at the white patch on his leather vest...or cut, whatever it was called. It was the number one with a percent sign next to it.

I shook my head.

"Interesting. You seem like you'd be on the proper side of the law."

A laugh escaped me as I tipped the beer back. "I grew up in politics, the way they skirt laws and don't adhere to them scares me. There's no code, no loyalty. It's cutthroat and a bunch of bullshit. Your club seems like it has a code, and a sense of right and wrong, I can get behind that."

Killian seemed to be scrutinizing me as though he wasn't sure to believe me.

"Play a game with me."

I glared at him, sipping my beer. "What?"

"We're going to be here for a bit. Play a game with me."

He made me nervous. I thought back to how he'd made me feel so insecure the first time we met, and then yesterday when he caught me in the club...there was already an undertone to our acquaintance. I didn't want to add to it.

"You don't have to babysit me. I get it. I need to stay safe until it's time to go back. Good, cool. I'll be good and sit here until it's time to go back. I have a phone with lots of things to keep me occupied. We don't have to play games."

That wolfish grin of his face was so disarming. He leaned closer and stole my beer away. "But I like games, and I want to play one with you."

I swallowed, hoping he didn't see the way my pulse beat in my neck. "What kind of game?"

Green eyes glittered as he sat back and sipped from my drink.

"Truth or Dare."

ELEVEN
KILLIAN

Was it possible to fuck up literally every single thing within a twenty-four-hour span?

First fuck-up—Watching Laura with Kip last night.

Second fuck-up—following Laura. Although, I was glad I did because that idiot, Kip, was being rough with her. But seeing him rough with her was what caused me to do the next stupid thing.

Third fuck-up, and this one truly is the worst—Sleep next to her.

Then this morning, I had to touch her. She was just too fucking tempting...but it was more than that. It was watching the way the golden rays of morning had collided with the strands of her hair and the way her mouth parted as she slept.

Something in my chest shifted as I lay there, just watching her and wondering what it would be like...

The pondering of a domesticated life with her is what had me texting Giles to go and get us coffee and scones.

All because I knew she liked them.

This was becoming a problem, and I needed less problems in my life, not more.

Now she was in my house, and Giles was here and something in my chest was growing claws and teeth, desperate to tear through bone and skin. I thought I had fixed this issue with Laura when I had lowered my walls and let her inside. I had tried to kick her out just as fast, but then I'd fucked up and now she was like a stain on my conscience I couldn't seem to erase.

Three months of silence, of pushing her out of my mind and away from me, and now she was in my space. And another member was here, seeing her and I wanted him to stop seeing her. I wanted him gone, and I generally liked Giles. I liked him enough to make him my Vice President, but fuck, he couldn't be here with her. Not with those easy smiles she offered him, or the way he looked at her. I wanted to kill him.

The sound of motorcycles rumbling down the drive reverberated through the house, and that would lead us to fuck-up number four.

"He's early." Giles winced.

My gaze traveled back to where Laura had been standing. She was safe upstairs for now, and that was all that mattered. She'd been around the club long enough to know club affairs were private, and I didn't think she would wander down to check it out.

Giles' cousin wanted a meeting. Took us three months to finally get this set up, and it was supposed to be a peaceful one, so I shouldn't worry. But I'd been in this life long enough to know how quick things could turn to shit. I needed Wes here. I pulled my phone out and saw that he'd already texted.

> Wes: I'm on the way, try and stall him. I don't want you meeting with him without backup and Giles isn't enough.

He was right. I needed to think clearly on this.

I decided to go in through the back of the club, so I wouldn't draw attention to this place. The gate slammed shut behind me as I jogged over to the back door of the club and slipped inside.

Natty was already prepping breakfast in the kitchen; she gave me a warm smile as I passed.

I gave her a quick nod before moving upstairs, but at the last second, I paused.

"Natty," I called to her until she was walking over, "Chaos Kings are on their way in. Just in case you have past shit with them."

I didn't wait to hear her response. I had a room in the club, although I hardly used it. Once in my room, I closed the door. Dragging the top drawer of my dresser open, I pulled out the Glock. I ensured it was loaded then slammed the clip back into place before tucking it into the back of my jeans.

I heard some yelling from below. I turned for the stairs and hoped this meeting would go as well as I needed it to.

Wes stood on my left, with his arms crossed, and Giles was on my right in a similar stance. Hamish, Brooks and Rune were behind us.

In front of us, Jameson King stood next to his bike, while four of his members flanked him. I noticed his vice president, Luke, was absent, which was odd.

Giles glanced over to me first and after I nodded, he walked over and gave his cousin a quick hug. I was still surprised by what was revealed a few months back when we were looking for allies. Giles had exposed that his cousin was the leader of the Chaos Kings, and not only that, in a rare turn of events, the two of them actually got along and didn't have any bad blood. That almost never happened with two different club affiliations. Giles was the entire reason we were even able to set this up.

The two cousins smiled, exchanging greetings before Giles walked back over and Jameson walked with him. That made me feel a bit more at ease; it seemed their intent for a peaceful meeting was genuine. Next to each other, the two could be mistaken for brothers.

Jameson was a few inches taller, and I couldn't see his ink because of his leather jacket, but they shared the same sharp jaw, the same brown eyes, the same wheat colored hair, although Jameson's was longer and slicked to the side with product. He was young, about Wesley's age, but he'd been leading for a lot longer. He'd taken over his father's club when he was just nineteen, now at twenty-nine or thirty, he was feared by every club in Virginia. An alliance with him would be a powerful move.

"Killian." He gave me a nod, then looked over to my left. "Wes.

Wanted to say congrats on the transition, and I heard you got married to Stone's daughter."

Wes didn't move; he just glared at Jameson.

The leader of Chaos Kings laughed. "Just wanted to congratulate you...I'm here in good faith. I'm hoping we can become allies, especially now that leadership has shifted over with the Death Raiders, and now you. Shit is fluctuating, and if we're not ready, it's going to put us on our asses."

"Thanks." I put my hand out, seeing Wes still wasn't moving to do shit. I knew it was because Jameson brought up Callie. He didn't trust anyone knowing about her, especially now that she was pregnant.

"Let's head inside, I need some breakfast."

Jameson walked in behind me, while my men brought up the rear.

Red was behind the bar, and Natty must have decided it was safe to stay. Still, she settled behind Red, and tucked farther into the kitchen. Then I did a double take when I saw another head pop up from the back.

Laura.

My heart raced, but I cooled my expression to ensure no one saw my reaction to her being here.

"I have eggs, bacon and pancakes started," Red said, tossing a rag over her shoulder. She caught my eye. I nodded to ensure she knew I was okay with feeding them.

"Sounds good to me," Jameson said, sliding onto a stool.

I was extremely aware of Jameson's eyes and how he was inspecting who was in the kitchen behind us.

Natty came forward and started placing plates in front of everyone, one by one. When she got to Jameson, his eyes were trained on her and a smile slid into place.

"You're Natty, right?" he asked, and she completely froze.

"Or do you go by Natalie, I wasn't sure..."

Oh shit.

Natty's eyes stayed trained on his face, and she even smiled, but I could see how her nose flared and her grip on the plates tightened.

I caught Wes's glare and knew he was about to lose it. Turning off being president was likely just as difficult as turning it on.

"It's Na—"

"You don't get to speak to her," I cut in.

Jameson lowered his gaze to the counter. "Didn't mean any disrespect."

Natty cleared her throat. "It's okay…and yes, it's Natty, how did you um…how did you know about me?"

She glanced around the room, and I saw that Laura was making her way to the front, still behind Red, but watching what was going on, likely getting protective of Natty. I gave her a warning glare, but she wasn't looking at me.

"Actually, you're the reason I wanted this meeting."

Aw fuck.

Wes was going to lose his shit, and I was already on the cusp of losing it too. Then Red and Laura both walked forward and were suddenly at Natty's elbows in a protective stance. A sliver of pride surged in me because Laura instinctually was club, even if she didn't realize she was.

"This is something you should have run by me; you don't just come in and start saying shit to my members." I practically growled.

Jameson clenched his jaw. His men glanced back and forth at one another.

"I think every club has heard of the deal Simon Stone made for you, Natty. The one where he literally stole you from—"

The sound of the plate smashing at Natty's feet cut Jameson off. Natty's eyes were pinned shut, then her face flushed.

"Oh shoot. Sorry about that." She bent to pick up the pieces, when Laura moved to help her. Natty's grip hadn't been slack on that plate… she stopped him from continuing on purpose. I just wasn't sure why.

Laura stood with a few pieces of broken plate in her hand when Jameson suddenly seemed to notice her. She was pulling back, about to leave, when his gaze narrowed and one of his men cleared their throats, and the other leaned in to whisper something. I felt ice slide down my spine as they all stared, and it wasn't lust on their faces. It was curiosity…surprise as if they were shocked to see her here.

"You seem to have an interesting collection of members, Killian." Jameson shook his head and began eating the food Red started dishing out.

Laura and Natty slid back into the kitchen, and everyone seemed to move on from the conversation and even started talking shop about bikes and Wesley's repair show.

I didn't miss the way Wes kept glancing at me, or the tension in his jaw.

"King, we need to talk." I pushed off the counter, giving a nod to Wes and Giles.

The leader glanced once at his cousin, then his men, before following me in through the church doors. The double doors led to a spacious room: the walls covered in memories and memorabilia from over the years. There were photos with Simon and my pops, and the original crew, retired cuts, patches, conquests. There was a Raider cut pinned to the wall with a railroad spike after Wes used the spike to end the asshole's life who had helped kidnap Callie when she was eighteen.

Jameson pulled out a chair and dropped into it, propping his elbows on the table.

He was taking too long. "Cut the shit, just tell me why you're here."

His eyes dropped to the table before he let out a small sigh.

"I have a delicate scenario that requires discretion."

What the fuck did that mean?

I slid into the chair across from him and paused to let him continue.

His brown eyes found mine as he slouched.

"My vice president, Luke...fucked up. His old lady is in a hard way, and unlike here, where your men are protective of the women, Chaos Kings have sided with their brother. I feel responsible for what happened to her...but I don't know if she can stay there."

My stomach tilted. I did not need this shit right after becoming president.

With a sigh, I scratched at my chin.

"You asking for her to come here?"

King shook his head, staring at the table. "I'm not sure...I just need to feel it out. I need options. I was hoping I could talk to Natty without anyone else listening, you can watch from afar to make sure she's safe, but I need her to be able to speak freely. I need to know for sure she feels safe here. If she does, then I might continue this conversation and see what you think about harboring her for a time."

"This isn't a fucking homeless shelter, King. We don't just take in strays."

Even as I said it, I felt a tiny bit of shame because Stone Riders were made up of strays, misfits and people who had nowhere else to go. It's what made our people so loyal.

"It wouldn't be forever. I just need to deal with my men, and the situation without her being at risk."

I stood and began pacing, running a hand over my head. My mind kept going to Laura; for some strange reason I wished she were here, so I could ask what she thought of this.

"Is there some reason she can't leave on her own, give her money and shit. Have her take off."

Jameson let out a long sigh and sat back.

"She's knocked up. She's been Luke's old lady for two years, not married or anything but serious. He decided to go fuck around behind her back, then found out she was pregnant with his kid and he lost it. He dumped her, and now he's fucking other women in the club in front of her. It's messed up. There's a rift between the old ladies of the club, which is making it hard on the men. They're approaching me privately, asking me to get rid of Penelope, but...I was raised better than that. We don't treat our women like this."

Feeling anger surge in my gut, I sneered at him. "And yet your club is treating her like it. Just end it, throw Luke out. Make an example out of him."

King hung his head. "I tried. It's more complicated than that. When Wes took over the Stone Riders, the club was loyal to *you*. He was insecure about it, ask him if you don't believe me, but if this situation were to happen in this club, the Riders would stand by you. That's how it is in our club. They're loyal to him because of his legacy, who his dad was. How he lives by an older and more fucked-up code than I'm willing to live by."

That settled in my chest like concrete. His pops was likely cut from the same fucked-up cloth my dad was. Where women had no value and were disposable...especially in clubs like this. He likely had a much bigger problem on his hands if the majority of his club was itching to stray back to the old ways. He'd need a new VP, and strength behind him to instill the code he wanted for his club. Which made our alliance make more sense. It made me uneasy thinking his own club might not follow him if it ever came down to needing them.

Another problem for another day.

"Let me ask Natty if she's okay with it. If she is then you'll have your time but where you're visible. I want to be able to see you at all times."

King nodded. "Understood. Thank you, Killian."

"Just don't make me regret it." I walked toward the doors and was about to exit when King suddenly stopped me.

"Oh, and Killian?"

I turned toward him, seeing he'd moved around the table.

"You might want to keep it quiet that you have the senator's daughter here, that or place a patch on her back. She's completely exposed and it's like finding a random hundred-dollar bill on the side of the road. She's leverage. Powerful leverage. Especially with the shit coming from these activist bloggers, stirring up shit."

What...who was he talking about?

I tried to keep a straight face, but I couldn't help the way my brows dipped.

Jameson caught the look but was respectful enough not to push it. He'd caught me unaware, and I still didn't know who he was talking about. Was it Natty, or—

"Those fucking activists have been trying to sneak onto our compound. It's another reason I'm nervous about this whole scenario... Penelope is pregnant and vulnerable. We owe her our protection, but if it goes wrong, she could go to them and deliver secrets."

I winced but was silently grateful for him moving past the topic that I was so obviously ignorant about. "You think she'd do that?"

He stared at the ground, lost in thought. "Honestly, I have no idea. She's been through a lot over the past few months. Coming here is a bit of a last resort for me. Penelope has been part of that club since she was a teenager. It's her home. I can't simply tell her to leave while she's pregnant with one of our highest-ranking members' babies."

What a shitshow.

"We'll figure it out though, right. That's what we do as president. We handle it."

He stood, slapping me on the back before moving toward the door, but I had to stop him.

My gut was screaming at me that I was missing something, so I blurted.

"Your men...they won't say anything?"

Turning toward me, his expression softened.

"About Witt's daughter? You have my word."

Witt...*Witt.*

My mind flashed back to being seventeen, sitting in the office and seeing that name for the first time. *Then all the times after.*

"You good?" Jameson asked, and I waved him off.

"Good. Just thinking."

I followed him out, hoping I was wrong because if that name was surfacing again and it were somehow attached to who I thought it was, then I was more fucked than I realized.

Killian
Age 17

The club was quiet for once, which was unsettling. The noise had become like soothing background music in my mind. I liked the chaos, and the extra volume always made me feel less lonely.

Which was annoying, and frankly just bullshit.

I didn't want to rely on anyone to make me feel less lonely, let alone an entire club full of people.

Using more force than necessary, I pressed the tip of the pencil into the paper in front of me, shading until there wasn't a single space of white available. I knew the old timers would be coming in soon enough, and they'd play a game of cards, and their laughter would at least keep me company.

I'd leave the office, but a few prospects were cleaning in the main room, and I needed a break from mine. Simon's office had the best lighting anyway.

"You doing your homework?" A slap landed on the back of my head, making me duck down with a wince.

I hadn't even heard Red walking in, and she wore those impractical heels, so I always heard her. I glared over my shoulder at her flipping through files in one of the taller cabinets along the back wall. She was like a mother to me, but it didn't mean I appreciated the fact that she treated me like a child.

She caught me staring and raised one of her dark brows. "Well?"

I nodded, but she knew me better than that.

"That don't look like homework to me."

"Fine. It's not homework." The pink pearl eraser slid easily between my fingers until it was pressed into the paper.

Red clicked her tongue before sliding the drawer shut with a loud snap. "Killian, you have to graduate. I don't care what Simon says, you need your diploma."

I started with a circle, wiping the residue by blowing on it. I had to be careful with how hard I pressed and not to swipe with the side of my hand.

"You listening to me?" Red stepped closer and poked over my shoulder to peek at my creation.

"This again? Why are you always shading and erasing, it's the most backward form of art."

I needed to go pick up a new pack of erasers. Once the corner turned dull, it was nearly impossible to get straight lines.

My face was hovering just above the paper to ensure accuracy. This helped shut out the quiet. I could hear my favorite sound buzzing in my head, even without music playing, and it made me feel at peace.

"I'm going to have Simon chat with your teachers. If you're not passing, I'm going to make sure he doesn't let you ride with us this weekend. We're going to the capital for a big rally, you wanna join us, then you're going to need to ensure your grades are up."

My fingers froze.

I never missed a ride and going to the capital meant we'd be riding with members from all over the state. Not to mention I'd never been to the capital before.

"Red, leave the boy alone." Simon walked in, and out of habit, I looked up to give him a respectful nod.

I turned toward the two and let the eraser hang in my fingers.

"We're goin' on a ride up to Richland?"

Simon kept his focus on his phone. "Yeah."

"You can't come unless—"

"Give it a rest, Red. Boy's going to take over the club someday. Criminals don't really give a fuck if you have your diploma or not."

He moved around the space, and something in my chest seemed to expand at the idea of leading the club someday. It's what I wanted from the time Simon took me in at ten, after my pops landed in prison for murder.

Red was glaring at our president now, and I knew if she were anyone else, she'd get in trouble, but Red got away with more than anyone else.

"You will encourage this boy to graduate, Simon Stone."

My eyes pinged between them.

Simon finally met the woman's gaze. She could be his mother for how big of an age difference they had. Prez always treated Red with respect though, like she was in charge instead of him. I wondered if it was because of her old man, Brooks, or simply because she'd earned his respect. "Fine, he'll graduate, but he also needs to be on that ride. We're meeting with the mayor."

"The mayor?" Red spun with the prez as he moved around the office, tugging open drawers and sliding a cigarette between his lips.

He smirked, and it made me want to smile too. He was the only father figure I'd ever had, and being near him made me proud. He wasn't afraid of anything, and when I led some day, I knew I'd be just like him. Nothing and no one would ever get in my way, or make me lead from a place of fear.

"Yes, the mayor. Nothing as dirty as crooked politicians who want you on their payroll."

Red was glaring again, but this time, she muttered under her breath while leaving the room. I returned to my sketch, lightly perfecting another circle.

"You need to graduate. Don't care how you do it, but you're walking across that stage in five months."

Keeping my eyes down, I laughed, nearly snorting. "And what, my cap and gown will be made of leather and denim?"

Simon looked up from a paper, his cigarette going limp as his mouth turned down. "If you have to. Don't fucking care, and honestly, if you don't walk, I don't care, but it would be nice for Callie to see. She looks up to you."

That really made me laugh. "She does not."

His hands cupped his metal Zippo, until the bud of his cigarette was glowing.

"She does."

"She has that preppy kid from next door to look up to now."

Simon inhaled, his eyes landing on the circle I'd drawn on my paper. "Wes looks up to you too."

I rolled my eyes, sliding the sheet out from in front of me.

"Didn't ask to be a role model," I murmured low, aching for my own cigarette. I hadn't had one for a while and being around the smell was making me crave one.

Simon returned to the filing cabinet where Red was earlier.

"We never get to ask for those sorts of roles. They just get set in front of us, and we do it because we love the people who set it there."

I considered his words and already knew I'd graduate, even if it was simply because he'd asked me to. I didn't want to be a role model, but I wondered if Simon did either? He was my hero, and he probably didn't want to be. Yet, he continued showing up for me and I knew it was because in his own way, he saw me as his kid, just like Callie was his daughter.

"I'll graduate."

Simon paused, looking over while he exhaled a cloud of smoke, and after a few seconds his head gave a slight nod.

"What are we dealing for the mayor?" I asked, trying to change the subject. Because I'd have to hire someone to hack the system and change my grades or pay someone to do a shit ton of extra credit for me if I was, in fact, going to graduate.

Simon smiled, letting out a laugh. "Oh, mostly we're just offering him some padded protection at a few of his rallies. While also making a few disruptions happen for his competitors. He wants us on his payroll."

"And in exchange?" I'd learned a few things since shadowing our club president, but one of the biggest lessons was, no matter the status of the person, we offered nothing unless we got the better end of the deal.

Sure enough, Simon smiled again, this time pulling out a file labeled, *"Mayor Witt."*

"Clemency."

My face must have conveyed my confusion. I may be failing two of my current classes, but government was actually one of the ones I had a passing grade in. We would only need clemency if we'd done something wrong.

Simon rounded the desk, and gently took my paper. He lifted it up to see the design and then gently placed a new sheet in front of me with a fresh pencil.

"One day there will be someone who wants our club to atone for a sin or two. That or they will want us behind bars. Witt, who will no doubt eventually become the governor, fuck maybe even the senator of this state, will ensure that won't happen. He'll protect us from measures passed that might negatively impact us, and overall, he'll keep the powers that be away from us."

"You're putting a lot of trust in him…what if he isn't even reelected?"

With a dark chuckle and a new eraser handed over, he moved away from the desk with one last parting phrase.

"We'll just have to make sure he is."

TWELVE
LAURA

Buzzing from the shredder filled the room as I continued to feed the machine image after image.

I really didn't understand why the club, or any club for that matter, would want to hold on to this sort of information. It was morbid, and sort of felt dangerous to just have it all locked away in the office.

What sort of establishment wanted to hang onto evidence of their crimes?

Shaking my head, I slid another manila folder into the finished pile I'd created and then took a small swig of water before moving on to the next report. The office door was cracked in order to protect the images, in case anyone was walking past, but for some reason, I didn't want it to be closed completely. I was also slightly jarred by the arrival of the Chaos Kings and how they'd talked to Natty.

After bonding with her the other night, I was feeling protective and wanted to be sure she wasn't afraid of them calling her out by name. I was too far removed from everything in the club to understand anything that happened, but I still wanted to keep her safe.

Hopefully Killian would ensure she was.

Suddenly the door to the office pushed open and Killian was stalking in, wearing his cut over a plain white tee, black jeans and motorcycle boots. My heart leapt in my chest at seeing him. He had suddenly been touching me nearly every chance he got, and yet acted aloof and distant when we were in public.

His focus went to the stacks of files around me.

"As of right now you're pulled off these."

"What?" I was nearly finished; I was through the letter T as far as names went. I had a handful left.

Killian began stacking the remaining files into a heap.

"Club business. Just know you're officially relieved of your duties pertaining to these documents."

His green eyes quickly slid over my features before returning to the stack.

"Killian." My voice was soft, and my hand gentle as I placed it on his bicep. "What happened?"

Because why on earth would he give this to me days ago, only to rip me away from it out of the blue?

"Does it have something to do with the other club that showed up?"

That sharp jaw I obsessed over clenched tight, and then once he'd gathered the files, he stood.

"It's not for you to worry about. I'll have Giles finish shredding that, you can be done for the day."

Okay...his dismissal stung, but not more than the understanding I had that this man was essentially using me for sex, or sexual things, but he had no intention whatsoever of treating me like an equal.

My chest ached, but I pushed it down. Didn't matter.

This wasn't new, and more importantly, I knew from that day three months ago that this toxic thing between us would likely never last.

Three Months Ago

Killian was toying with me.

His eyes lit up whenever he was about to dare me to do something, but he'd ask for a truth instead. So far, I had only given three truths: my middle name—Jane—my favorite ice cream flavor—cookie dough—and my favorite color—pink.

I asked him the same in return.

His answers were easily given, even his middle name.

Russel. Mint Chocolate Chip, and Black.

I could have guessed the color, based on what he was wearing, but I was hoping he'd surprise me by saying purple or something.

"What do you mean by you grew up in politics?" he asked, sipping his second beer.

I had no idea how many he could handle but I was halfway through my second and starting to feel it.

I didn't want to talk about my upbringing, but it wasn't like I was staying here in Rose Ridge. Callie was selling, regardless of how fucked up her relationship was with her ex, seven years apart was unlikely something they could reconcile. Still, I knew better than to give anyone leverage over me, least of all a random biker I didn't trust.

"Nothing, just someone in my family was mayor of our tiny town a long time ago."

"What did you say your last name was again?" He tipped his bottle back, his gaze lingering for too long.

I hadn't given my last name to anyone yet. No one had asked. I knew if I gave him my real last name, he'd call me on my lie...then he'd have leverage.

The lie slid easily off my tongue. "White."

Killian's movements paused, his eyes focusing on me. His mouth parted right as his eyes narrowed, almost like he was going to call me on the lie, but I powered on.

"Truth or Dare, Killian?" I wanted to move past my life and hold him off on asking any more questions.

Killian smiled. "Truth."

"Have you ever been in love?" I sat up, setting the empty bottle on the table.

Killian focused on the bottle in his hand, his foot shifting the smallest bit.

"Nope, and I don't think I ever will be."

"Why?"

He shrugged, lifting the bottle. His biceps flexed, showing his ink, distracting me from my question.

"That's not how this works. I answered, now it's your turn."

I shook my head. "You asked me about my last name after I'd already answered."

"Nope that was all a part of the same question." Killian smiled.

"So is mine," I argued, feeling light and free as I grinned.

"Tell you what..." Killian sidled closer, sitting next to me on the couch. "Answer dare and I will answer your question about why I don't think I will ever love."

Now he'd made it too intriguing.

"Fine." I let out a sigh. "Dare."

His rough voice replied immediately, "I dare you to come here."

I was already shaking my head as I noticed his palm gently slap his thigh. He clicked his tongue with a roguish smile.

"I'm not asking you to strip, or to fuck me. I just want you in my lap...and if you prefer a different dare then I'll dare you to go into the attic."

I stood, making a show of not doing what he asked. "Point the way to the attic, I'm not afraid."

I didn't love the idea, but I wouldn't back down now.

Killian smiled but didn't move.

"You don't want to. Trust me. My pops murdered someone up there."

Okay, well, that changed things. I faltered, still standing, but gaping back at him.

"How old were you when that happened?"

His green eyes held mine, and I had a feeling he wouldn't answer because of the rules, but I still wanted to know.

"Ten. I was the one who discovered her. Blood was leaking down through the attic door. Pops was gone, so I pulled the string and lowered the stairs, so I could go up. Every step was already soaked in her blood, and when I crested the top, there she was."

"Oh my god." I walked back to the couch, holding my stomach.

His father had done that to someone...I tried but failed not to imagine a younger Killian, big green eyes, those thick dark lashes as he slowly walked up those steps. How horrible that must have been, how that pain and horror had to have curled inside him like a nightmare, never letting go.

He looked up at me, almost in a teasing fashion, which made me wonder if his story was even true. I found that I didn't really care.

"Climb on, Daisy."

I only hesitated for a second before reminding myself that I was out of here. I was only in town for a few more days, then I wouldn't ever have to see him again.

My left knee pressed down into the sofa; my right knee landed on the opposite side. Before I had a chance to lower myself down, his hands gripped my hips and pulled.

Our faces were so close now, I could see the tiny hairs that had already begun growing out after his shave. I could see the tan lines around his eyes, as if the sun had soaked his face, but spared the space where he wore sunglasses. I saw how his eyes reminded me of a meadow early in the morning when the sun kissed the grass. I hated how beautiful they were.

"A pebble," Killian whispered.

I quirked a brow at him as his hands stayed on my hips.

"You asked me why I would never fall in love."

"And your answer is because of a tiny rock?"

His chin dipped, and I took a moment to stare at his defined jawline.

"It's a metaphor. For the fall…the destruction, and yeah, I guess the heart. A pebble is small, hardly noticed, but with the potential to do untold damage. My mother used to tell me about strong leaders, kingdoms and empires and how all of those things could be brought down by such a small thing as insignificant as a pebble. A pebble in the shoe of a great leader is a distraction.

A loose pebble in the wall held in place by other stones could bring down an entire structure. A pebble thrown at the right velocity and speed could bring down a giant. A pebble may be small, but it's still made of stone. It can shift and change the tide in a war, it can bring down leaders. I know that if I were to ever love, that person, whoever it was, she'd only have to do something small, like that pebble, and it would bring me down. She'd walk into a room and if another man were in that room with us, I'd go insane. Because if I were to ever love, I would love with my entire being. All my fucked-up darkness, all my demons, they'd all bow to that love. Then, like the weak fucker that I am, I'd be brought down by jealousy and fear, I'd always be afraid of losing her. That pebble would be my downfall, and I'm too fucking prideful to fall, and I'm too goddamn afraid to love."

I watched him as he finished explaining, and the entire time, all I could think was how I'd never look at him the same again. His heart was such a fragile thing, beating under such a dangerous exterior. He was a wolf, and he'd just shown me that underneath his fur and teeth was a bleating, lost sheep.

"How about you?" he finally asked after the silence had stretched too long.

I shrugged. "I haven't been in love, but I hope I find it someday. I see what Callie still has for Wes, and if I could ever have even a portion of that, I'd be grateful."

Killian's grip tightened on me, and I felt a bulge underneath me grow.

"But I'm assuming you've fucked other people before...boyfriends?"

The way he said fuck was harsh and sultry; it stirred something in me.

"Yes." I moved my hips the smallest bit. "I have fucked. I've had boyfriends."

Killian caught my hips and then lifted his, the erection under his jeans was granite now.

"So what, you fuck them, date them to feel good, to let loose?"

My hands went to his shoulders, and I ground down against him.

"Sometimes I indulge to feel good."

"Wanna feel good right now?" His chest lifted, his hands slid up my back, pulling me closer.

"What did you have in mind?" Because I was not having sex with him, no matter what.

His hands moved until his fingers were dropping to the copper button of my shorts.

"Kiss me."

My breath stalled in my lungs. Kissing was intimate, and everything this man had done so far was the opposite of that. He didn't seem like the kissing type.

I tilted my head. "Why?"

He smiled, pulling me closer. "Because I want to taste you, and you're leaving anyway, what could it hurt?"

Wasn't that the justification I had been using this entire time?

I answered by leaning in and gently pressing my lips to his. They were soft, so much softer than I had expected, and warm. I moved my head to the side right as his tongue slipped inside my mouth and he emanated a groan. His hand came up, gripping the side of my face in a possessive hold. That mouth moved over mine in a desperate sort of way. He acted starved, like he'd been thinking of kissing me, as if it were the only thing on his mind. Moving with him, I pressed closer, his hold on my face drifted to my neck and then my hair. He was tugging on my locks, tipping my head back when he finally released my lips and began kissing down the column of my throat.

Open-mouthed kisses, sloppy and wet, had me writhing against him. I clutched at his shirt, desperate to have him closer when suddenly his lips returned to mine.

It was electric, dangerous and full of filthy promises. I wanted to strip, fuck and somehow gather every fiber of him and stuff it inside my veins. I didn't want to leave, and that…fuck, what was happening right now?

With a frantic flutter in my breast, I pulled away from him panting.

His eyes were wide, his chest heaving as well. We stared at one another as if we were silently asking the same question.

What the fuck was that and why did it feel so good?

His hips lifted, and mine rolled on instinct, loving the friction it provided. I said on a gasp. "You can unbutton your jeans, but stay in them."

As if he could read my mind and understood what I was trying to say, he murmured, "Deal, Daisy."

He lifted me from his lap then his hands were on my shorts again, flicking the button and dragging the zipper. My shorts slid down my legs, leaving me in just my black lace thong.

His eyes searched me, narrowing on the space between my thighs. His hands were on his own jeans now, flicking them open and sliding them down just an inch or so, until I could see his dark blue boxer briefs and his firm erection pressing through.

He pulled me down on top of him and the sensation of him under me, against my soft skin, felt so good.

"You feel me, Daisy? Feel my cock straining to slide into your wet cunt?"

I was breathing hard, hissing and rocking my hips.

Killian's hands were on my ass cheeks, hauling me against him.

"I can feel how wet you are. You're soaking this scrap of fabric." His mouth went to my breast, trying to bite it through the fabric of my shirt.

"Fuck." He spat as he lifted up, and I pressed down. We were fucking with our clothes on. I could feel the tip of his cock press through his boxers, and just enough of his long length was poking through that I was getting off. The pressure and hardness felt impossibly good.

I was close and then his lips landed on mine again and he kissed me like he wished I wasn't leaving. He kissed me like he wanted to press his lips to mine every day for the rest of his life. It was hot, and intense, and it left me breathless when suddenly his length felt more defined, he moved so brash that I didn't even realize something was different, not until he nearly parted the fabric between my legs and I felt his hot, silky skin against mine.

He'd pulled his cock out of his boxers.

I was coming. "Fuck, fuck, fuckkkkkk." He let me clamp down, a cry in my voice as I rode out my climax.

"Keep those pretty eyes on me, Daisy," he ordered, and for some reason, I obeyed. I didn't see his cock as he gripped it, but I felt his hot release land on my stomach and knew he'd come as he let out a painful groan.

We were both gasping, and our eyes were still locked on one another.

Suddenly his hand came up to cradle my face, his thumb resting directly next to my left eye.

"Your eyes..." He panted. "They're Cinderella blue. The unreal kind that baits princes into giving up their crowns and tossing kingdoms on their head, looking for a goddamned shoe. That dude was fucked the second he saw her, and I never understood it. Not until now."

My mouth parted on a silent gasp because that was the sweetest thing anyone had ever said to me and the juxtaposition that it came from a hardened criminal was making my head spin.

Those glimmering eyes suddenly dropped to my lips, and I wondered if he'd kiss me again. If he could sense how badly I wanted to feel his lips pressed against mine just one more time. I wondered if he could sense that I was starting to fall for him, that a severe—possibly the most severe—crush I had ever experienced was starting to develop.

His phone rang from inside his pocket, which had me glaring down, confused how he kept it in there with my legs crushed against his hips.

Pulling the phone up to his ear, he listened then said, "on our way."

He shifted, and it felt like I'd been plunged into an ice-cold lake. The hardness in his gaze returned, a mask falling into place as he easily discarded me on the seat next to him and began buttoning up.

I was at an awkward angle with his cum all over my stomach as he milled about the room as if I weren't there and he hadn't just nearly fucked me.

Realizing he wasn't going to find me a tissue of any kind, I dug around for something I could use, but there was nothing but beer, cans of spam, along with a few microwavable burritos.

"Here." Killian held out an old t-shirt to me while glancing at my stomach.

The fabric was pink, and very likely from another female he'd fucked.

"So is this where you bring women to hook up then?" I asked, cleaning up the mess on my abdomen, then pulled my shorts on, risking a quick glance at him. I wasn't entirely sure how we were supposed to interact with each other now. I wouldn't be here long, but while I was, it wouldn't be terrible to have someone to hang out with or have some casual fun with. Shit, if I was being honest, it wouldn't feel so casual to me. He didn't need to know that.

"Yeah, sometimes. I usually fuck at the club, but every now and then I'll come here. I'm not a fan of having women in my home or knowing where I live."

Right.

"Ready?" He walked into the kitchen and tossed the bottles we'd consumed into a plastic bin.

I nodded, while following him out through the back door. I felt dirty and annoyed. Why had I given in so easily to him? Something about it made me feel like I had given him the upper hand. Normally I wouldn't care, but he kissed me, and I hated that it was still wreaking havoc on my lips like invisible live wires sparking every five seconds.

"So after this, are we acting like it didn't happen or what's the plan?" I forced the question out, mostly to make him feel as uncomfortable as I did, but partially because I genuinely wanted to know.

He shrugged as a way of responding.

"Guess if we both find ourselves alone, and no one sees us, I'd be down to do this again. But not tonight. I have plans tonight with a pair of Sweetbutts that have been dying to double up with each other."

God, my face was on fire.

What an asshole. What an actual fucking prick.

"What?" he asked, pushing at my arm.

I shook my head and darted for the bike on quick feet.

"Daisy, what's with the face and the sudden glare of death?" His pace quickened, although I wasn't sure why. We were both headed the same place. I had to ride back with him, and there was nothing I could do about it.

Suddenly his arms came around my waist and he hoisted me up in the air. "You're not a fan of the adventure twins keeping me company tonight?"

I pushed at his hold. "I could care less who warms your bed, Killian, but it's fucking rude to talk about who's going to suck your dick next right after you—"

"Right after I what?" he challenged, pulling me around to face him, his hands still around my ass. "What we did was early high school shit… we didn't fuck, we didn't even do oral sex of any kind. You have no reason to be pissed."

I hated him. I hated him so much it was physically painful.

"It's not that I care, okay. It's just a matter of being polite or kind. I didn't tell you that I already had my eye on some guy in the club, hoping he could actually seal the deal and give me some real relief, did I?"

His grip tightened on my hips as his eyes became two pieces of stone. "I told you already that while you're here—"

Laughter bubbled up and out of me, forcing me to push hard enough for him to drop me.

"Go fuck off with that. I owe you nothing. You're no one to me just like I'm no one to you. Still, I wouldn't have said it in front of you."

I began walking again, nearly to his bike when he was suddenly next to me again.

"Fine. It sucked hearing that, I'm sorry for saying shit in front of you. Now, who are you trying to hook up with tonight?"

"None of your concern." I pulled the black bucket helmet on my head and buckled it. Killian studied me with his hands on his hips.

"You can't fuck any of the Stone Riders. I forbid it."

Shaking my head, I threw my leg over the bike, nervous that it would fall over. Killian's hand came out to steady my knee a second later.

"I don't want to talk about this anymore. I don't even know you…I really don't care."

His jaw flexed, and then he was straddling the bike and aggressively handling his helmet.

I hated that our time here had ended the way it did. I had actually enjoyed my time with him, before he became an asshole and lied about all of it.

Suddenly I had to know. "So all that stuff about my eyes, the way—" My face was going to catch fire. I dipped my head and stopped talking because this was so fucking embarrassing.

He peered from over his shoulder, his hand dropping to my knee to pull me closer. "Nah, I meant every word. You have the prettiest fucking eyes I've ever seen. The kind I could see someone throwing a kingdom away for. But I'm no prince, I'm the bastard who'd sneak in and usurp him, but you are most definitely a princess. Which means you're not my type, it's nothing personal."

I was about to reply with something quick witted when he shook his head as if he were sad. "Look, I already know I'm not your type either… trust me…I am well aware."

His bike roared to life, and before I could reply, he took off.

THIRTEEN
KILLIAN

"Your pops wants to see you," Brooks said around the toothpick tucked into the side of his mouth.

I glared up at the old man, confused as fuck as to why he randomly just approached me with that shit.

"I just got back from seeing a buddy at Cherrywood, had a missive passed through for me to see."

Fuck.

"They're passing messages now?" I released the wrench, tossing it back into the tool bag closest to my bike.

I knew there was a network of club members inside those walls, but shit, the fact that my father got a message to Brooks through one of his friends, and the message pertained to me, was just fucking insane.

"Seemed rather urgent."

I watched from my peripheral as Brooks gnawed away at his toothpick. I knew he did it because he had to stop smoking. Red made sure he didn't risk picking the habit back up.

Wiping the grease from my hands, I finally turned toward the old timer. "Things with Jefferson are always urgent."

Brooks toyed with the engine mount off to his left, his gray beard was untamed and bushy, nearly hiding his entire face. "So they are."

He wasn't leaving.

Heaving a sigh, I gave in. "You think I should go?"

"Doesn't matter what I think, but intel from inside has always proven useful."

I clicked my tongue. "Didn't you just return from seeing Paul, anything worth knowing—he would have shared."

Brooks laughed. "He doesn't traffic the same sort of intel as someone like Jefferson Quinn."

That was true. My dad had more loyalty than most, and he'd been in there for years establishing his place and the pecking order.

"Fine. I'll go." Didn't fucking have time for it, but it was practically winter, my bike could wait a while longer. I'd just have to take the truck.

Brooks slapped me on the back, then on his way out called, "Take Giles or Wes with you."

Yeah, wouldn't want this entire fucking thing to be a trap, and sadly, knowing my dad, it probably was.

Cherrywood Penitentiary was a sunny name for a place so devoid of joy. A joke, the real name was much duller and more lifeless, but those inside had given it a name, and it helped when creating their messages. The cherry blossom was a stamp for this prison. There were a few others in the state, and the network managed to eclipse them all.

The buzzer sounded, alerting me that they were leading in a prisoner.

My head lifted and caught on my dad. He hadn't changed much in the three months since I last saw him. Except for the way he was staring at me.

The guards secured him to the table and then walked back toward the wall, waiting.

"You came," my dad almost sounded relieved.

I nodded. "Brooks said it seemed urgent."

His eyes searched mine, taking in my ink, my plain white shirt, my clenched jaw.

"You're president now." His voice didn't tip with pride, or fluctuate with any emotion whatsoever. He was merely stating facts.

I dipped my head again, preferring to answer silently.

"You gonna pull some strings to get your old man out?" His smile made my stomach churn. He had to know that I wouldn't. I hadn't been back in three months. I was devastated when he'd murdered that girl. His sins spilled over into my life, staining my soul in a way that I felt perpetually fucked up.

So much so, I had a difficult time even picturing the possibility of having a long-term relationship.

"Time is running out, better spill what intel you have while you can."

His face fell, but he recovered faster than I had anticipated.

"You have the senator's daughter in the club. Rumor has it, she's club pussy."

Shit.

There was an invisible hand wrapped around my throat, choking the air from my lungs and burning it all to ash.

I had to be careful because if I lost my temper, it would tip him off that she meant something to me.

"What do you know of it?"

"I know a few clubs have been talking about it. Rumors are circling, and there's a pretty price tag being discussed."

"There's a lot of pussy in the club, you got a specific name?" Deep down I knew it was her, but I was still clinging to the hope that I was wrong.

I had ripped Laura off the files because of that feeling. Not only because a profile with Senator Witt existed in those documents, and with that, there was a strange need to shield her from what might be inside. I hadn't looked at the file in years, but I knew enough about his previous dealings that whatever it was, wouldn't be something she needed in her head.

"You got a fuckin' phone?" My dad laughed, making fun of me. "Or a computer? Just google him, and I'm sure you'll see who his daughter is."

I'd been too anxious to look it up. I didn't want it to be possible. She'd given the last name, White, and I wanted to believe that name had no association to the vile piece of trash I knew as Senator Witt.

I dipped my head, knowing I couldn't get through this acting like I didn't know who she was. "She's not club pussy, but she is under our club's protection. Need you to stop the rumors."

My dad's brows furrowed, his eyes searching my face as if he couldn't piece together what I was saying.

He waited too long, and I knew I'd given it away. I should have just kept my mouth shut.

"She's yours."

I shook my head faster than I could even think. Anything to get him off the trail.

"Not mine. Just protected by the club."

"She's also leverage. She may be protected, but she can also be an asset. You could use her to get me out of—"

"No, I wouldn't, and you know I wouldn't. You deserve to be here, every fucking day of your sentence, and you know it."

That angry menacing glare replaced his easy-going demeanor.

"You're a spineless piece of shit, Killian. Can't understand why Ryan handed the club to you. Rumors also circulating about that too that you're pussy-whipped, not thinking clearly. Some dame has your head all clouded. Now I know which one it is, and since you don't want to help me, perhaps I'll encourage the other clubs to take your precious jewel."

The storm slowly building within me was too much. I snapped.

My hand shot forward and gripped his throat as I swiftly stood and hovered over him.

"Say. Another. Fucking. Word." My grip tightened. The guard by the door watched on, which meant he likely wasn't one in my father's pocket. "I will end you."

His face turned red, a horrible sort of red that would become blue if I had my way and continued squeezing. The guard finally moved.

I released my dad and was already walking away when I heard him wheeze at my back.

"You're a coward, Killian. Use her to free me. You don't belong there. I'm going to have you ripped from that position, just watch."

I shook my head and clenched my jaw, fear clawing at my chest over what I was going to do with this new problem that landed in my lap.

Daisy wasn't safe in my club anymore.
Fuck, she might not even be safe in Rose Ridge.

FOURTEEN
LAURA

I stared at my reflection in the mirror and tried to wrangle my hair into something presentable. The bathroom downstairs wasn't nearly as large as the primary bedroom's, but I'd get used to it.

I moved my mattress, suitcases and singular lamp down to the guest room after Killian randomly relieved me of the files the other day. He hadn't been around much, and today would mark three days since I talked to him. I didn't know what his plans were for the apartment. He'd told me he was moving in, so the first chance I had to move my things downstairs, I took it.

The last thing I wanted to do was get in his way or be caught near his bed. Especially if he decided to bring someone back here. That would not only devastate me, but it would start shit because I was too petty not to say something, and too annoyed to let it go. I would have if he'd just left me alone, like he had for three months.

Now things had changed. He'd been touching me, creating a whirlwind of expectation inside me. If he showed up with another girl, I would a thousand percent make a scene because he didn't get to pin me to the door and tell me to fuck his hand one second and then bring someone else around the very next.

I understood it was common in motorcycle clubs, but I wouldn't tolerate it.

Ever.

Finally twisting the last piece of hair into place, I flipped the switch in the bathroom and walked back into the guest room. Pulling on my boots, jacket and hat, I exited the apartment. Red wanted me to go to The Drip to grab a box of donuts. Apparently, there was going to be a big meeting, church or whatever they called it, and Red wanted them to have some sustenance.

The sun had barely cleared the ridge, the fog from overnight still hung in the air and likely coated the roads. Most of Rose Ridge wasn't even awake yet, and I was heading out to pick up food for a club I wasn't sure I'd remain attached to.

Red was all smiles and warm humming when I found her in the kitchen of the clubhouse.

"Morning."

She peered over her shoulder. "Hey honey, you lookin' for the keys?"

I knew where she kept them, but my mind was all over the place.

"Yeah."

She wiped her hands on her apron. "In my purse, right—"

I grabbed them from the top of her massive black leather purse. "Got 'em."

"Thanks for making the run, I need to keep an eye on this bread."

I only smiled at her, unsure why she enjoyed making loaves so often. I came to work one morning and saw at least a dozen that had been baked, and while I had no idea what she did with it all, it seemed to keep her in good spirits.

With her keys tucked into my fist, I exited the kitchen, rounded the bar and veered for the front door. Right as I was cutting past the main room, feet pounded against the staircase to my left. My eyes flew up, right as Killian came into view.

He froze right as he saw me, and we both just stood there staring at one another. He wore a black hoodie, with his leather cut pulled over it. His hair was mussed from sleep or...sex. Dread curled inside my chest, like smoke.

I parted my lips to try and breathe through it, but it was so painful that tears burned the backs of my eyes. Not able to hold his gaze any longer, I dipped my face and thundered through the space until I was clearing the front door.

I heard him exiting a second later, jogging down the stairs as if the club was on fire.

"Laura."

I didn't stop. I just continued toward Red's truck, ignoring the man at my back.

I heard him curse again, then it sounded as though he'd picked up his pace and started running.

Right as I reached for the truck door, his hand eclipsed mine.

"Fucking stop."

I whirled on him, shoving at his chest. "No. You stop, I have somewhere to be."

I tried moving again, but this time, his arms came around my middle and he lifted, pulling me against his chest.

"I can see that you're upset."

"I'm not. I just have somewhere to go," I lied, heaving clouds of white as the frost laced my worries.

His lips came next to my ear. "Nothing happened. I slept alone."

"I. Don't. Care," I bit out, pulling at his hands.

Finally free, he released me. "You do care. I can see it in your eyes. You care the same way that I care."

I practically barked out the laugh caught in my chest. He was such a liar.

"You don't care."

He stepped closer, so close my back was pinned to the truck. "I care about every eye that lands on you. Every breath that's inhaled your scent. Every smile given to you, every hand that's ever touched you. I care, Daisy. Too fucking much if we're being honest."

Anger and hurt, along with longing, tangled in my chest. I tilted my chin in defiance.

"I care that you were rude to me about the files. Treated me like shit for no reason. That's what I care about, Killian. Who warms your bed, or sucks your flaccid cock doesn't bother me."

His smile was feral and lethal. "Flaccid, huh? Sounds like someone remembers our little trip home that night. If you remember me talking about that, then surely you recall how you begged to touch me, and how you straddled my—"

"Stop." I turned and reached for the handle again, and his hands locked onto my hips, right as someone called for him.

"Prez, we need to go over a few things before the meeting." Giles began running toward us.

Killian's jaw locked in place as he searched my features.

"This isn't over, Daisy."

I brushed his touch off and climbed into the truck and pulled away from the club. The rearview mirror provided a glimpse of his thundering expression, but I shifted it, so the reflection lowered.

My thoughts were messy as I drove.

He said he cared, but why was he so possessive of my body, while regarding my heart so apathetically? I did care about who he was with, which is why my feet carried me outside so swiftly. I couldn't bear the image of a girl traipsing down after him, wearing little to nothing, or worse, one of his shirts. My heart would crack in half, and the understanding of how much power he held over me angered me.

For months I was fine with seeing him flirt with other women. The minor sting to my pride, and dull ache in my heart was all manageable.

Then he went and crossed the line he'd drawn himself in the sand. He'd touched me repeatedly, said things that had wrangled the beast in my chest into submission, until my heart only wanted him. I'd been in denial and embarrassed by his dismissal three months ago, but now…it was unbearable.

There was no way to undo this feeling, and I loathed my lack of respect for myself. My standards might as well be lying on the floor with how much sense it made. He was a shadow within my own, a hammer in my pulse, a chord of music thrumming against my veins. He was all the things I was always so completely horrified to ever allow in.

I was in love with the wolf.

I knew he was dark, broody and mean. He handled me with sharp edges and claimed me with vicious intent, and yet, I craved him. I needed the piece he kept hidden, the beating heart under his thick exterior, his walls that he kept so secure. I wanted to sneak inside and destroy him the way he had ruined me.

The coffee shop arrived abruptly, and my navigation was all turned around, so I had to loop the block to park in the back. I sniffed and swiped at my eyes at a few random tears that had crept free.

Then I was swinging in through the back door of The Drip.

Natty was huddled over a butcher block, dusted with flour. Her hair was swept up into a top knot, a white apron was tied around her midsection. A few other employees were milling about but didn't pay me any mind.

"Hey, Natty," I said softly, coming to her elbow.

She turned a bright smile at me. "Laura!"

"You here for the donuts and coffee?" She wiped her hands on the apron and moved down the counter.

"Yeah, Red sent me."

A pink box was produced, still open so I could see inside.

"These look amazing."

Natty smiled and began shutting the top, so it was secure. "I have three dozen ready, and Red already paid."

I stood there watching as she set one box on top of the other, when I heard a loud round of applause coming from the front part of the coffee shop.

Natty's eyes thinned in the direction of the noise.

"I'm so sick of them having their meetings here."

Curious, I wandered closer to the opening and peeked my head out. There, near the front of the shop, were three tables shoved together, and several people sitting shoulder to shoulder, while they watched someone give a speech.

"That is why we need to move up legislation. The mayor of Rose Ridge won't be able to tell us no if we're parked right outside his house."

Natty was suddenly behind me, quietly speaking so only I could hear her.

"That's the group that is trying to ban motorcycle clubs from being able to meet or gather within city limits."

"Aren't the Stone Riders technically outside of the city limits?" Not that the answer lessened the effect legislation like that would have on us.

Natty shook her head. "No, technically we're within them. That whole property is. Which makes this extra frustrating. I overheard Rune talking about how they've caught a few of these members poking around the edge of the property with video cameras."

The group clapped again, but I had missed what they said.

A man with a red beanie and spiral curls stood up from the table. "I think we need to print pictures of some of their crimes, blow them up so everyone can see how dangerous this club is. People think they're peaceful, but there's too many questionable things that they've covered up."

"I think they could begin to react if we do that, none of it would be admissible in court...there's not even any way to prove they're guilty," a woman in a soft yellow coat countered.

Another person piped up, "I have a friend who's been inside their clubhouse, there's tons of proof in there. We just need to get inside."

My stomach tilted. Did they have any idea what would happen to them if they did?

"You can't break into a place to steal evidence, that's not how the law works," someone yelled, but then a man in a dark jacket yelled over them, "So what? It will piss them off enough that maybe it will create a reaction. That will be admissible in court."

Natty pulled my arm, and we were ducking back into the safety of the kitchen.

My chest was rising and falling too quickly.

"Natty, this is bad," I murmured, gripping her arm.

She nodded with her lips pursed.

"We need to tell Killian about this," I said, almost to myself, but I knew Natty was likely thinking it.

"I don't know if we should get involved, Laura. Yes, it's where we live, but neither of us really belong there, it's not our home. We're just outsiders living on the fringes of it all. It's not our fight."

I knew she was right, but the way my chest rioted at the notion told me I had become more attached to the club than I had initially thought.

Instead of replying, I squeezed her hand and picked up the order for the club.

I wasn't sure what to expect that night as I sat on the guest room floor and watched my laptop.

The delivery of treats for the church meeting went without a hitch, as I didn't see Killian again. Red had been the one to deliver the boxes into the meeting, and I tucked back into the kitchen and began cleaning and then moved to the office to do the books.

It was all very dull, and so when I finished early, I walked the ridge line along the back property and took my notebook. Walking out there always helped me think. While I loved singing cover songs, I occasionally featured my own work. So, as I walked, I jotted down lyrics and began to weave them into a song. I had sat out there until the sun dipped behind the hills, and then I finally sauntered back, relishing the way the ground had become frozen and so different from when I'd arrived in summer.

The apartment was empty again, just like it had been for several days. The sun had dipped behind the hills, bringing the day to an end. I had my headphones on, my notebook next to me, a small piece of toast as my dinner, and was now blocking out the world. The beats flowed in cadence as I jotted down ideas for lyrics and allowed pieces of my heart to exit my chest, and bleed into text. My fingers cramped; my back was sore from sitting on the floor, but I kept writing. I had no idea how much time had passed, but eventually, there was a tattooed hand that gripped the bedroom door and pushed it open.

I lifted my chin, catching a green, defeated gaze. Whatever had happened throughout the day, it had wrung Killian dry.

He practically collapsed next to me on the floor, all while plopping a greasy, paper bag in my lap. I pulled my headphones free and quirked a silent brow at him.

"Didn't think you ate, considering you don't keep any food here. Looks like I was right."

He gestured toward the toast.

I hadn't even touched it. But smelling whatever was in the bag had my stomach growling.

"Thank you." I opened the bag and pulled out a wrapped burger, then another. I handed one to him and then dumped the fries out of the containers and folded the bag down.

"Shake Shack has the best fries and fry sauce," he commented, while folding the wrapper back on his burger.

We ate in silence, dipping fries into the pinkish sauce, and at some point, I clicked on a funny television show on my laptop, and let it stream while we finished up. We didn't speak of what happened earlier in the day, or the files…or any of the other complicated bullshit that kept happening.

We just sat in each other's presence, and when we were finished, Killian took the laptop and placed it on the bed, then took off his cut, his hoodie, then his jeans.

I held my breath as I waited for what he'd do next.

When he crawled under my covers, and sat up against the wall, something in my chest cracked open.

It was the most docile I'd ever seen him. He looked exhausted, like he barely had the energy to hold his head up.

"You asked if for one night you could just be Daisy. I'm asking you the same. Give me one night where I can just be Killian, not the club leader, not the wolf, or any other monikers. Just let me be me."

Feeling a soft tug in my chest, I crumpled my wrapper, wiped my hands and then got up. I watched as his bare chest rose and fell, but his eyes remained on the screen. As though if I did reject him, he didn't want to witness it. I let out a silent sigh and pulled my side of the blankets back. I crawled in next to him, wearing just my sleep shorts and a tank top.

He clicked the lamp off and pulled me under his arm.

"Tell me something," he murmured quietly while the show played in front of us.

Nestling closer, I decided to share something I was terrified of. "I am deathly afraid of marshmallows and marshmallow fluff."

He snorted quietly. "Marshmallows?"

"And that fluff stuff."

His fingers toyed with the strap of my tank top. "Not spiders or sharks…"

I shook my head. "Nope. I can handle all that, but that fucking marshmallow fluff—Noppppppeee."

"Where did this fear come from, might I ask?" I could hear the laughter in his voice.

My hand trailed up over his abs. "The very first Ghostbuster movie. When I was little, I remember watching it while I was home alone…"

"Well, I think my nanny was there or something, but I was alone, and that freaking Marshmallow guy showed up, destroying the whole city." I shivered just thinking about that freaky scene.

"It scared you?"

I nodded. "I can't even enjoy smores."

That sent him laughing so hard, he had to tip his head back.

"My poor, poor Daisy. Brought down by a fluffy—"

I put my hand over his mouth.

"I don't even enjoy the word fluffy."

He gripped my wrist and then twisted us, so I was flat beneath him.

"Kiss me."

My lips parted as I searched his face. He'd asked me the same thing that day three months ago, and it felt like a firecracker had been shoved under my veins then, but now it was…worse so much worse.

I turned my face away from him.

"I don't think that's such a good idea."

His grip moved to catch my chin. "Why not?"

The words burned my lips, branded them as a silent vow. I didn't want to let them free.

"Tell me," he whispered, lowering his head to place a kiss on my stomach.

"Earlier when you said I cared…"

"And you lied." He interrupted with a smirk.

My lips spread into a smile. "Yes, I lied…but Killian, I think I care too much. I think I'm falling in—"

His mouth crashed against mine, cutting off my words. I knew he didn't want to hear them, that or he just simply couldn't.

My fingers came up, spearing a path through his hair, until I was holding the back of his head and pulling him impossibly closer.

He made a sound and moved his hands up my back. My tank top was lifted over my head, and then his hands moved to my shorts.

I was breathing so hard, merely from the idea of being with him. My fear was like a knife point against my heart, but with his lips moving against mine, I ignored it.

"We don't have to fuck. I just want to taste you." He pressed a kiss to my stomach again. "Feel you."

Frustration wound through me. I wanted to go all the way with him, to finally seal this and ruin whatever we were. The sooner we did it, the faster we could close the lid on this and end it. Distance would be the only way to fall out of love with him, and to get that, we need to do this. Just once and we'd both be cured.

"I'm clean," I whispered to the dark room, illuminated only by the laptop screen, "and on birth control."

His head slowly left my stomach, that green gaze on me, heavy and full of need.

"Think fucking you will only make me fall harder, Daisy. I'm barely hanging on the ledge as it is."

For some reason that punched at my pride, like letting the air out of a sail.

"So why are you in my bed, Killian? If you're so afraid of falling for me, then leave."

I tried to pull away, but he kept me exactly where I was, pinned underneath him.

"I'm not afraid of falling, Daisy. I'm afraid of who I'll become if I lose that part of myself to you. Because it's all or nothing. I'd keep nothing of myself for me. You'd own it all."

I was incredulous. "Why do you think I told you I didn't want to kiss? You just bypassed my boundaries, regardless of how I was afraid. Why should I care about yours?"

His stare was so intent, I nearly cried. I hated revealing that to him. Offering him a scrap of my fears, my worries that he'd just disregarded them.

"You want to bypass my boundaries and fuck me, Daisy?" He rolled over and shoved his boxers down, revealing his hard length. "Then come climb on."

This was too reminiscent of the night in that truck. I didn't have all the details back, but I knew I had made a fool of myself.

"Just get out." I turned away from him, a lone tear slipping down my face. "Please."

He didn't move.

A heavy sigh left his lungs, and then I heard fabric moving.

"Daisy, come here."

I didn't turn because more tears were falling, and I didn't want him to see. When I didn't move, he finally just pulled me back against his chest. I felt his length press against my ass, and his hand moved around my torso until he was cupping my breast.

"I haven't fucked anyone since I was nineteen."

My body stiffened. Words wouldn't come, so I just waited to see if he'd expand.

His forehead landed against my shoulder. "Oral, but not actual fucking…I have a rule. Doesn't really matter with you, but I wanted you to understand that it's not just being afraid of getting too attached, it's more than that."

My mind went back to when he'd carelessly talked about where he chose to fuck women. All the times he made it seem as though he was with people.

"But you'd talked about being with—"

His breath fanned my neck. "I lied."

I wasn't sure how to respond.

His arms tightened around me. "I'm not touching anyone else. I haven't since that first day I saw you, three months ago. I knew you hated me with how mean I was, but there's been no one else."

"Not even oral?" I practically yawned because exhaustion was tugging at me.

His laugh reverberated through my chest.

"No, not even oral. Nothing and no one but you, Daisy."

I didn't know what to say, so I didn't say anything at all. I just relaxed in his embrace, letting his warmth envelope me like a cocoon.

"Now, with that said, I do have an obsession with hearing you come apart at my touch, so I'm going to slide my hand between your thighs and make you come."

My eyes snapped open, my breathing ragged, as he didn't wait a single breath for me to ready myself.

With the hand cupping my breast, he tweaked my nipple, while his other hand moved down the expanse of my stomach until he was lightly caressing my clit.

With my legs closed, he let loose a growl while pulling my thigh over his hip, which gave him ample access to my spread center. His cock was also tucked into the crevice of my ass, the tip poking at my soaked entrance, which he acknowledged with a hiss.

"You're going to drench my cock, Daisy. Just because I'm not going to fuck you doesn't mean you won't feel me."

He jerked his hips back, and his length slid through my wetness, right as his hand returned to my clit, rubbing circles.

My moan was sultry and desperate.

"That feel good, Daisy?" His lips were right at my ear, as he continued to rub his cock through my arousal.

With one grunt, he shoved his hips forward, and his hand held his cock in place, pushing it, so it was sliding in-between the lips of my swollen slit.

"Move your ass, Daisy. Slide that pussy over my cock."

I did as he said, even at the awkward angle, but it must not have been enough for him because the next thing I knew, he was flipping us, so my back was on the mattress and he was hovering above me.

"Fuck. I need to see you." He reached behind him and moved the laptop so the screen lit up again, then made it play so it wouldn't time out again.

I heard laughter in the background from the show as Killian pushed my thighs apart, spreading me wide before him. He stared down at my slit and groaned.

Then he spit, and his engorged cock was sliding through my wetness once more.

"Feels so fucking good."

I lifted to meet his strokes, desperate for penetration, but still trying to respect what he wanted. His massive length slid in-between the edges of my pussy, and the ring on the tip of his cock kept brushing over my clit with each pass.

I was writhing, gasping and desperate for him to add more friction.

"When I fuck you, it's going to be bare," he demanded, his voice turning dark and breathy.

I nodded, my voice feeling lost on the impending orgasm that was building.

"Tell me yes, Daisy. Tell me I can fuck you as hard as I want, and fill you with my cum, over and over if I want."

"Yes." I moaned, and then suddenly something in him snapped, and the gliding through my cunt became more intense with more pressure. He slid back, and when his cock began gliding forward once more, the tip of his cock was suddenly sliding into me in a way that—

A gasp cut through my chest, forcing my head up.

Killian froze.

My eyes darted down to where his length was now partially inside me.

His eyes slowly rose to mine, and then he let out a pained groan as he pushed farther in, until he was fully sheathed. My mouth parted, as he stretched me, and I couldn't even breathe as he pulled out, and then his hand went to my hip, and he pulled me closer, which forced him deeper.

Suddenly he angled backward, pulling his cock out, which was coated in our joint arousal. He stared at his glistening length and muttered another curse before sliding all the way back in, which forced my head back against the pillow.

He was so much bigger than anyone I'd ever been with, the stretch was incredible.

"You ruin everything, look at what you do to me. I had to fuck you because it felt like my chest was caving in. Having you but not entirely claiming you." He moved his hips slowly, but each thrust was so intense, it made my tits bounce.

He pulled my leg up over his hip, which forced him even deeper, and as his hips rotated sensually slow, I came apart.

My nails dug into his arms, my head shoved into the pillow, a scream falling from my mouth as he groaned, holding me in place.

"Fuck, fuck, fuck."

I felt him spill inside me, and I would keep to myself that it was the first time I'd ever allowed someone to be inside me without a condom.

Our breaths were heaving, as we slowly came down from our high, and I didn't want him to say anything to ruin this moment. To take anything from this perfect slice of time that belonged to just us.

But then he slid out of me, and he stared down at what he'd done.

"Taste what you did, Daisy. You were so greedy that night for my come on your tongue, open those pretty lips and let me show you what you do to me."

With two fingers, he dipped into my core and then brought the mess he'd made to my lips. I opened for him, and when the warm salty mixture met my tongue, I grabbed his wrist and held him there while I slowly licked each finger. Our eyes connected, and his mouth slightly parted as he watched.

"More." I breathed, cupping my breast for him.

His eyes hooded as he returned his fingers to my dripping slit and gathered more of his release and shoved his digits back into my mouth, where I repeated the process of cleaning his fingers, slowly while moaning my pleasure.

"Fuck, why don't you crawl over here and lick it from my cock if you're so desperate."

He slid his still erect cock into me and pulled out and I moved onto my hands and knees and did exactly that. I lowered my mouth over him, letting his tip hit the back of my throat.

"That's it. Clean every drop."

I did and more. I sucked so hard, he became granite in my mouth, and then on a muttered curse, he began slowly fucking my throat.

"This how it's going to be then? We're just insatiable now?"

I smirked around his length and then felt a slap on my ass.

"As long as you understand—It can only ever be this between us. I refuse to give you anything more, not just for my sake but yours."

A fissure formed inside my chest, gaping and bleeding. I felt it with every ounce of my being.

It was later that night, while he was lazily fucking me from behind, that hope dissolved in my chest.

Any shred of it I dared to carry regarding him was gone.

FIFTEEN
LAURA

I was avoiding the clubhouse.

After the night in my bed, where Killian fucked me three times, then held me all night, the following morning, he was gone.

No explanation as to where he went, although Red said a few of the guys had gone on a ride up north.

It was frustrating because I wanted to text him.

I wanted to ask where he was, and when he'd be back, but he'd told me nothing more than a quick fuck could ever be between us. I'd gotten the message, loud and clear, and wouldn't be that girl who begged for more.

It was also infuriating because I had no idea where we landed with the apartment. I wasn't eager to share the space with him when he'd said nothing more than a physical relationship could ever be between us. It certainly didn't seem as though he would want to cuddle every night, as that was something couples did.

Even if he did want that, I wouldn't give it to him. I deserved more than that.

"What's with the expression?" Callie asked, pushing my leg with her toe.

We were in her house, both on our laptops working, while taking in the gorgeous view her house offered. Floor-to-ceiling windows in her living room allowed us to see the entire valley.

"Nothing. Just the apartment stuff—Killian is moving in."

Her dark brows rose. "Why can't you just stay there with him? I know you guys hate each other and all that, but I watch how he looks at you. There's no way there isn't something there."

I still hadn't told her what happened three months ago, or anything recent. I certainly hadn't shared that we'd had sex a few days ago, and it wasn't even intentional. I usually told Callie everything about my dates, all the good ones, bad ones and especially the toxic ones that provided exquisite orgasms. But when it came to Killian, words just died on my tongue.

I was worried she'd be mad that I was getting involved with him.

"Even if there was, I can't live with him and I doubt he'll let me." I knew he would, but for the sake of looking innocent and trying to put this complaint to rest, I added it.

"Wes already told him to let you stay there, so I know he won't kick you out."

Wait...*what?*

I sat up straight. Worry and a flicker of unease began to press in on my chest.

"What do you mean exactly?"

Callie's expression shifted as though she realized what she'd just said. Her eyes widened, and she reached forward to grab my hand as if she knew I was two seconds from darting away.

"I have no idea if Kil would have done it on his own, but Wes wanted to be sure you had somewhere to go."

I pushed onto my feet, needing space. "So this whole time I've just been this charity case among you three?"

"No, not at all." Callie got to her feet, and my eyes immediately went to her stomach; she wasn't showing yet, but I was dying for the day she did. I watched her relentlessly, making sure she was okay, safe, healthy. She wasn't just my best friend; she was like my sister. I loved her like a sister.

I tried to let that connection calm me down. Callie would never do anything to hurt me; she only ever cared about me and wanted to make sure I was okay.

"I'm sorry, I'm just…" I shook my head. "I don't like being at his mercy, or that he's had the upper hand this entire time. It makes me feel helpless and angry. He has probably loved the fact that he was helping me or doing me a favor for three months."

Tears were burning the backs of my eyes, and all I wanted to do was scream.

"I'm going to head into town, I need some fresh air," I said, about to grab my coat.

This not having a car thing sucked.

Callie rushed around the couch. "But I thought we were going to go shopping to look at baby décor for the nursery?"

Shit. That had me pausing. I really wanted to help her pick out the theme for the baby's room.

"Well then, let's get out of here. I just need to move. I feel like I'm coming out of my skin."

Callie grabbed her purse and coat before turning toward the front.

"Laur, I hate that you're upset. I only wanted you to feel confident that you can stay put and not have to move right before winter."

We walked outside and rounded her huge rig.

"How exactly do you think Killian took being told he had to let me stay there from Wes? I think the fact that he told me he was moving in the day after becoming president shows he didn't take it well. He was riding out Wes's order until he was in charge. Now, he doesn't give a shit what Wes said, and I wouldn't stay regardless. I just want my own place."

Callie started her car, a somber expression tugging her smile down into a frown. We drove in silence, and with each minute that passed, I faced the window fighting angry tears.

"Green would look good." I smiled, holding up the letter F. I had a name picked out that I wanted to try. I doubted Callie or Wes would take my suggestion, but I was going to slowly push my name into their minds until they thought they were the ones who had come up with it.

Callie smiled, touching the letter and grabbing a few others.

"Felicia?"

I laughed. "No, and your blood test said it was a boy, I thought."

She shrugged and turned. I inspected her cut. She had a hoodie on underneath it; the leather vest went over it, and her dark hair was braided to the side. I had never envied her for wearing a property patch, but something was squirming under my breast, as though the feeling wanted to reach through and grasp the leather for ourselves. Just to belong to someone. To have someone love me and claim me.

"What if it's wrong and it's a girl?"

I shook out of my thoughts and grabbed a rose gold L.

Callie's eyes widened before she laughed. "No, whatever you're thinking, the answer is no."

"Lauren is such a cute name for a girl." I batted my lashes at her, which made her laugh again.

She shifted to the side, and I noticed we had a few women in the store looking over at us. This was normal to me now; it took a while, but Callie's cut caught people's attention. It was like a cloak of danger that Callie wore with pride, along with the massive rock on her finger, boasting of her marriage to one of the most feared men in Rose Ridge. That or they were eyeing the bearded man standing by the exit with his hands across his chest.

Wes still had Callie tailed by members of the club, and I knew Killian would never challenge that. Not when Callie was pregnant.

"Excuse me."

A woman wearing a sheer scarf over a black turtleneck came over, gently putting her hand on my arm, while eyeing Callie furtively.

"Is there something I can help you find? Are you looking for a gift for someone…"

Callie gave me a quick glance before smiling at the woman.

"We're fine, thank you."

I pulled my arm away, annoyed that she felt comfortable enough to touch me. I wasn't a fan of people touching me.

"Well, it's just..." the woman started, stepping closer to Callie, which made Harris walk over.

The woman's eyes rounded. "He needs to leave; he's making the other customers uncomfortable."

I snorted, making a spectacle of her fear.

"Harris is a teddy bear; in fact, if you ask him nicely, I bet he'd even share his secret chicken and rice casserole recipe with you. He's a fantastic chef."

Not as talented in the baking area as Natty, but any chance Red could convince Harris to cook for us, we were all giddy and excited.

The store clerk paled as the beefy biker drew nearer.

"Please, you need to leave."

Callie's brows came together. "Are you serious? We haven't done anything wrong."

"We just don't need your sort of trouble in here."

I pointed between Callie and myself. "Our sort of trouble?"

The frail woman stood straighter. "Just the other week, there was an instance where one of you caught a journalist's car on fire. It was completely unprovoked and outright criminal."

My head was spinning. What was she talking about?

"There was nothing on the news about that," I argued, flicking a quick gaze to Harris.

His stern expression hadn't shifted, but my best friend's face was suddenly a light pink color.

With a wrinkled finger pointed at Harris, the woman yelled, "Because they terrorize people and make sure nothing gets reported! My son is a part of the movement trying to get your kind out of Rose Ridge. It starts with us banning you from our stores."

I started toward the woman, but Callie grabbed my arm.

"It's not worth it, Laura."

The clerk sucked in a sharp breath as she focused on me.

"I beg to differ. I think it would be totally worth it."

Harris made a sound from behind us, and the woman started backing up as if we were going to hit her. I would never hurt someone, but I might make a mess out of her store to show her just how worth it I found it.

Callie pulled my arm, and I gave the woman one last look.

We pushed through the exit, and I was livid.

"What the hell is she talking about?" I peered back at the glass window where the clerk and others were huddled together as if they'd just been harassed or assaulted. Total and complete bullshit.

"Uh...you know about the bloggers or activists that are trying to get the club kicked out of the city?"

I nodded. "I heard them holding court over at The Drip."

"Well, a few weeks back, Killian did a little demonstration for them in an effort to get their attention off Wes and me."

Harris stood close with his arms crossed, a small smirk skirting his mouth.

"What sort of demonstration?" I thought about the folders I had sorted before being removed from the job. The images of said 'demonstrations' from the past. The burning, the explosions, and the murder.

Callie glanced up at the biker, then winced.

"So it's true then. He caught the guy's car on fire?"

"You should see the photos this group has taken; there are kids involved, Laur. I know it sounds harsh, but they're a hate group, and they need to be stopped."

I already knew as much based on what I'd heard. "I'm not judging. I'm trying to understand, and if anything, be prepared."

Harris made a sound of agreement before moving toward his bike.

We began doing the same toward Callie's car when my heart pinched tight.

"Did you grow up with that sort of response from people because of your dad?"

She paused, staring at me with a surprised expression.

"Yeah, actually I did. It's not new to me and it doesn't bother me anymore. I would have liked to shop local, but it's her loss."

"Damn straight it is. Stupid, snobby bitch."

Harris laughed, shaking his head while he pulled on his helmet. His bike was parked directly behind Callie's rig.

"I'm hungry. Let's go eat."

We went to a soup and salad place with tall, deep booths and soft lighting. It was cozy and warm, thanks to a fire roaring in the hearth. It was early November, but a chill had definitely entered the air, and the clouds were heavy with an impending storm.

While we ate, I decided to fill Callie in on what small information I could share with her while not divulging everything. I landed on telling her what had happened with Kip that big initiation night.

My best friend's eyes were blown wide the second I finished.

"So that's what Wes was talking about?"

"What?" I moved my salad around with my fork.

Callie shrugged, ducking her head until she was focused on her meal. "Nothing, he was just on the phone asking questions to someone. I'm assuming it was Giles, because he kept saying things like, 'he did what, and how bad was it, is he going to be okay' those sorts of things."

"I have no clue why Killian lost it on him like that," I lied, already knowing full well he'd lost it like that because Killian considered me his plaything. Nothing more, or less, just a toy.

But his just the same.

Callie kept her face down and her tone low. "He doesn't like seeing women hurt…something to do with his dad, I'm sure. He's in prison for murdering a Sweetbutt. She was really young, like nineteen or something."

The memory of Killian's nonchalant threat of being dared to go in his attic slammed back into me, forcing my fork to drop. He was being serious…

"Don't worry, he's behind bars," Callie was quick to reassure me, swallowing her bite of food, "My dad never lifted a finger to help him get out, and I know Killian won't either as president. Jefferson is still loyal to the Stone Riders, even if he's in prison."

Jefferson, that was Killian's dad's name. His father, the murderer.

"Okay I have to know." I blinked, feeling untethered and confused. "Why would Killian take me to his dad's house and act so casual about it? He said he took hookups there. I mean…is something wrong with him? Doesn't it seem sort of strange that he's so comfortable being in the place where the murder happened?"

Callie's focus was completely on me now, her lips spreading into a smile.

"The murder didn't happen in that house. Poor Jenny was found in a dumpster behind Strings. She was a dancer in Pyle…"

I felt so stupid.

With my face blanching, I lowered it. "Oh. Well good then. I was worried Killian was a sociopath."

Callie started laughing.

"I don't doubt there were things he's seen in that house; regardless, it is odd that he took you there. That location is secret and no one outside of the club is allowed to know about it. I don't think he's taking his hook-ups out there though…Killian doesn't exactly go all the way with women…I mean as far as I know."

She had my full attention now. "What do you mean exactly?"

I was being greedy, knowing what Killian had told me himself, but ravenous for an extra perspective.

Her face flushed while her eyes flicked over to Harris, who was a few tables away. Then she lowered her voice and leaned in.

"Sweetbutts talk. I've been gone for seven years, so who knows if any of it's true, but I've heard a few call him the 'suck-off-king.' The girls have a bet going to see who can get him to cave first. I guess he talks about fucking and all that, but in the end, the girl just sucks him off, then he loses interest, or just doesn't want to go all the way. I have no idea, but back in the day, Kil would always stay in the club. Girls would try to kiss him; he'd dodge them, until eventually one would just settle for getting on her knees."

The image of girls kneeling in between his knees was like a knife in the chest, but somehow it was a thousand times better hearing that he didn't have as many oral hook-ups as he made it seem, and that he'd been telling the truth.

Callie waved her hand as though she was dismissing the whole thing off.

"The only thing I know for sure is that he doesn't kiss, the rest is all hearsay and a bunch of rumors."

"He doesn't kiss?" I scrunched my nose while my heart was thundering in my chest.

Kiss me.

He'd ordered me.

It wasn't something we'd fallen into; he wanted it. Demanded it. Twice.

My best friend's dark hair swayed as she shook her head. "That's a definite no. Even Wes commented on it a few months back when one of the Sweetbutts had a fit over his rejection. She snuck into his room in the club house and said all she wanted was a kiss. Kil didn't do it. Even as we were growing up, he never did. Always said kisses were like pebbles, you give one and suddenly you're being buried six feet deep because you're fucked in the head and in love."

My fork clattered to the plate.

Callie flinched at the sound.

"Sorry."

He'd shared an even deeper sentiment regarding pebbles…and *said he didn't want to lose himself to me…and yet he kissed me, and then he fucked me.*

Suddenly I needed more. I was desperate for details about him, and I needed to understand why he changed his rule for me, of all people.

I was about to prod further into Killian's life when there was a commotion happening outside. Turning in the booth, I watched through the glass as a familiar looking red car was flying down main street with its tires screeching as it took a turn onto our side street.

I watched in horror as the car stopped next to Callie's and the person in the passenger seat jumped out, wearing a mask. It was one of those harry wolf masks with the exaggerated jaw and fake teeth, but it covered the person's identity completely.

They took out a white bottle and began spraying it all over Callie's car.

"Oh my god." Callie gasped.

"Harris!" I screamed, jumping out of the booth.

The biker ran over and grabbed Callie, tugging her away from our table.

"Laura!" I heard Callie screaming as Harris lifted her off her feet and carried her out.

The fucker outside had a Zippo lighter.

I was at the door before I heard people screaming for someone to call 911.

It swung open for me with a whoosh, and I was running toward the car.

"What the fuck are you doing?!" I screamed, flying toward the guy.

"Carl!" I heard the driver yell; he was wearing a wolf mask as well.

The man, Carl I guess, looked up and locked eyes with me.

"Don't you dare!" I shouted, placing my left boot on the front tire of Callie's rig, and then vaulted up onto the hood. The lighter fluid made the surface slick and I nearly slid right off, but I gripped the opening near the windshield right at the last second.

"You fucking crazy?" the man screeched, the Zippo still open in his palm.

The rumble of engines echoed from down the street, indicating motorcycles were approaching.

The driver leaned his head out of the window. "Carl, get in the car now! Leave it, you're not about to light some random pedestrian on fire!"

Carl seemed to shake himself out of it; the Zippo dropped to the ground and then he dove into the back seat before the car took off down the road.

I was covered in lighter fluid, and my hand was nearly cramped from how hard I had gripped the edge of the hood, somehow my knee felt tweaked. Finally letting go, I slowly slid off the hood as people began filtering out of the restaurant.

I eyed the Zippo and looked around before taking a Kleenex from my pocket and ducking to grab it.

The woman in the store was right, the Stone Riders didn't do business with the police, except for the ones on their payroll. Whoever these guys were, they knew who Callie was and what car she drove. This was a direct attack on the club.

"Laura!"

I spun, seeing Callie on the back of Harris's bike.

Suddenly two more Stone Riders pulled up behind him. I ran toward the closest one, not even knowing who it was. I jumped on the back, and the rider took off down the road. I wrapped my arms around his waist and my head was tucked into his back as we made our way back to the club.

The cold air whipped at my back and my thin sweater. I could see why people wore leather while riding motorcycles. Within minutes of being plastered to the back of the man in front of me, I was shivering. Rain pelted us painfully hard as we hurried through the city and pushed toward the outskirts of Rose Ridge. Trying to hide my face in the leather of the rider, I briefly slipped my eyelids open when I heard the sound of several other engines edging in beside us, there were a dozen more members flanking us. I was still new to the club, but I assumed them gathering like this meant they all must have learned about the attack.

A sudden surge of pride and an odd warm feeling of peace thrummed through me. I knew at that moment that I was safe. For months I had felt like the tag along, a misfit in this club. I kept my head down and worked, earning a paycheck and soaking up the time I spent with my best friend, but the dynamics of the Stone Riders hadn't really clicked for me. I didn't really get the appeal for anyone to give up their weekends and pledge their loyalty to a band of like-minded people. Now I understood it.

This feeling of belonging to something bigger, to being a part of a family that would protect you and have your back no matter what. I was proud to be with them, and through this they had earned some of my loyalty in return. I wanted to protect them like they had just protected me.

Suddenly we were tilting to the right and I knew we were making our way to the dirt path leading down to the club. The bikes slowed, but not by much. I held on a little tighter as the gravel under the tires seemed to get a little loose, and then finally, we were slowing enough that I lifted my head.

Killian must have returned from his trip because he was jogging down the stairs in front of the club, fury etched into his face like stone. I swallowed thickly as his gaze landed on me and the rider in front of me. A vein seemed to throb in his forehead, and to protect himself in the pouring rain, he only had on his cut with a Henley underneath. His hair was soaked within seconds, but he didn't seem to care. He walked as though he couldn't see anything except for me. Suddenly Giles was in front of him saying something, but Killian pushed him out of the way and continued toward us.

The rider parked, and I scrambled off the back as quickly as possible.

"What the fuck?" Killian's voice snapped, his glacial glare landing like stone on the rider I'd ridden with.

"It was a safety situation, Prez," the rider clipped.

I recognized him now. It was Riley, a nice guy I'd flirted with a time or two.

"Thanks Riley." I patted his shoulder, but Killian had my wrist in his grip a second later and began pulling me away. We were headed to the apartment, even as Giles yelled at his back and Wes leveled us with a severe glare. Wes was holding my best friend to his chest, her head tucked under his chin, as rain pelted them, and the sky seemed to break open.

Meanwhile, Killian ventured up the steps and barged into the apartment, slamming the door behind us. Within a single breath, I was pushed up against the door with his strong arms caging me in. I could hear the rain slamming against the roof and his breathing, but that was it.

His panting was erratic, and his eyes searched as though they were frantically hunting for something. His fingers tangled in my hair a moment later, his gaze following a trail of water down my face.

Between breaths, I wet my lips and muttered, "It was just a ride."

A sharp laugh broke through his exterior, and that's when I realized he was shaking.

"I don't give a fuck about the ride. I care that you're soaking wet and rode in twenty-degree weather while the rain drenched the roads. I care that you didn't have a helmet, and when I heard what happened…" He faltered.

Those green eyes were unfocused as he worked to catch his breath, then his hands were on my arms, trailing down to my hands.

"Are you hurt?" He skimmed my stomach, and then as if he was certain there was a gunshot underneath, he pulled my sweater up over my head. "You smell like lighter fluid, tell me why the fuck you smell like lighter fluid."

His voice was shaking, and it seemed to untether something inside me. Something that wanted his arms to come around me and hold me. Something I'd be an idiot to crave.

Just as I was about to open my mouth, the thud from the lighter in my pocket hit the floor and had Killian raising a dark brow in question.

I dipped to retrieve it. The silver Zippo was still in the tissue, so I walked to set it on the counter.

"There were two men wearing wolf masks. The driver was in that red car that swerved into your lane that day we went to The Drip. The second jumped out and doused Callie's car with lighter fluid. He was about to torch it."

If I thought that explanation was going to calm anything inside Killian, I was completely wrong.

With barely controlled rage, he stalked toward me, coldly asking, "and how is it exactly that you now smell like that lighter fluid, Daisy?"

The nickname had my heart swelling, and I hated myself for it. It had become so familiar, and so safe, like coming home.

I kept my glare on him and refused to dip my chin, regardless of how intimidating he was.

"I intervened."

It was as though a spark had caught the fuse of a bomb. His eyes narrowed, his lips slid into a sneer, and he advanced.

"So, let me get this straight." He held up his finger. "Callie was taken to safety…"

I nodded. "By Harris."

He'd done his job, and I wanted to be sure everyone knew it. Dude was one of the best guys in the club, and I didn't want anything bad to happen to him.

"But you…" He raised that dark brow again, as if he couldn't bring himself to say the words.

"I ran outside and jumped on the hood to stop him. They were amateurs, Killian. I could tell, and I knew if they were confronted, they'd stop."

Killian grabbed a glass that was sitting on the counter and threw it across the room.

"It's a fucking car, Laura. Why wouldn't you go with Harris?"

I knew his anger was because he wasn't there, and some part of him worried for me. Or worried for his club, but I knew it wasn't *at* me.

Firming my resolve, I crossed my arms over my small tank top. My cleavage was pushed up, and I smelled like a fucking gas station at the moment, but I couldn't afford to care.

"Harris had one job and that was to protect Callie. He did it. He didn't have room for two on his bike. I knew I was on my own getting back, and I was fine with that, but I refused to let those shit bags start my best friend's car on fire when it was preventable. She just got that car, and she needs something safe to drive—"

"Stop," Killian yelled, bringing his hand to his face, and rubbing his forehead, "just fucking stop, please. You're standing here, smelling like lighter fluid, worried about Callie and her ability to get around when you nearly caught on fire today, Laura. On fucking fire!"

He stepped closer, and I retreated a step on instinct.

"You don't have a way to get around, and yet you're worried for her. *Fuck* Callie. She has a rich husband who will provide everything she could ever want. They have insurance, and within a single day, Wes would have a new rig in their driveway. You, however, just ruined one of the three sweaters I know you own. You hurt your leg; I can tell because you're leaning to avoid putting pressure on it. You're soaked to the bone, and you're standing here, not even officially a part of my club, telling me you put every one of its members before yourself."

He was breathing hard as he finished his sentence. His eyes were wild.

I stared, unsure what to do because he was right, and I hadn't even considered what he was saying. I loved Callie, and I wanted her to be safe, but it was more than that. An attack on her was an attack on this place that had somehow become my home over the past three months.

His eyes continued to search my face, as if I could provide more details, and then his head lowered, and his mouth was on mine. His hand slid into my hair, cradling my jaw as he moved sensually slow, sliding his mouth from the side and invading with his tongue.

My hands were up around his neck—my fears surrendered to the call of his touch.

I was an idiot, but I didn't know another way to exist where Killian was concerned.

He kissed, and I kissed him back until he finally broke away, pinning his forehead to mine.

"You need to get in the shower, change into something comfortable and wait for me upstairs. I need to go take care of this."

"I moved downstairs." I shouldn't have said it, but it just came out.

"Not anymore." He said with one last glance at my lips. Pushing his eyes closed, he turned away from me.

Right as he was about to exit, I called toward him.

"You should know they only stopped because they assumed I was a random civilian. Not having a patch may have saved my life today."

I turned and realized Killian was frozen at the door, his hand in midair as though he was about to open it.

I didn't wait around to see what he'd say or do next.

SIXTEEN
KILLIAN

The room was packed, and because it involved everyone in the club, we were in the spacious area where the couches and fireplace framed the room. A few people were perched at the bar, and Red was behind it, mixing up a few drinks. Likely just keeping busy. I knew these sorts of meetings had a tendency to make her nervous.

Wes had Callie in his lap, his jaw was rigid, like he was biting back words. My anger surged seeing them there, all safe and protected. Knowing what Laura had done to keep their stupid fucking car safe.

"You put Harris on Callie or both women?" I asked, loud enough that everyone heard.

Rage over how Simon had given the club to Wes flickered in my chest. A violence was humming inside me, and something told me some blood would be shed tonight over it. My best friend and I had some words to say to one another, and these would best be spoken with our fists.

Wes glared then dipped his head. "Just Callie."

Fuck. Him.

Callie turned in his lap and her jaw dropped. "What?"

Harris lowered his head as though he were ashamed.

"I will not apologize for this; you knew it was a part of the deal when you said you needed space while being out in town."

Callie rubbed her forehead, searching the floor as if it could provide some reason as to why her husband just shit all over the only other person who mattered to her.

"But Laura needs just as much protection."

Wes glared at me then focused back on his wife. "She doesn't. She's not a member, she's not patched to anyone, she helps in the kitchen. If anyone here wanted her protected, they'd offer her a patch."

I knew that comment was directed at me, but I only glared back.

Callie scoffed then stood from Wesley's lap, throwing her hand toward Natty. "So Natty isn't considered a member, or worth protecting?"

Natty flinched, looking down.

"She's not a member." Wes double-downed on his statement. "But she knows that, so does anyone who is patched in. We wouldn't leave her behind, and she is safe here. We offer her protection just by existing. Same goes for Laura. She's lived in the club apartment rent free for three months. We gave her a job here. She has a place, but she's not the same as you, and I'm not about to get into a fucking argument about wanting to keep my wife safe."

I crossed my arms over my chest, staring down my best friend.

"You may not want to get in an argument with her, but you will with me. You fucked Laura over today. She risked her life for the club, for your wife, and all you can do is sit here and talk about how she isn't owed protection?"

Wes stood while Giles looked on nervously.

"If you have a problem with how things went down then I suggest you do something about it."

I'd had enough.

Stalking forward, I gripped my best friend around the back of the neck and pushed him until he was ducking and trying to catch his balance. It allowed me to get both our asses outside.

The rain pelted us, but I didn't care. I let my fist fly as hard as I could into his jaw.

Callie was outside seconds later, screaming at us to stop.

Wes came back for me, pummeling me at the waist. It knocked the air out of my lungs as he pushed me backward and I lost my footing in the mud. A hard hit landed on my cheek, and then I threw my fist into his eye.

"Fuck." He bellowed then with a roar he was tripping me, until my back was on the ground and his boot was coming down. I rolled at the last second and then heard shuffling behind us.

"Let 'em fight it out. This is how things are done." I heard Brooks say, but Callie was still yelling.

My fist flew again into my best friend's mouth. He spit a wad of blood into the mud. The rain had his hair slicked and messily cutting into his eyes. One of which was already swelling while his lip was busted open. We stood apart, heaving chests, staring at each other.

"You need to fix this shit, Killian. I don't know why you're dragging it out, but you're putting the club at risk by doing so."

Hot rage spiked inside me at his words. I knew what he was talking about, so did everyone within hearing distance, at least they probably did. First, I fucked up Kip, now this.

I was a goddamn mess.

"I can't." Was all I could say through gritted teeth.

Wesley's eyes softened as he stared at me, as if he pitied me. He didn't know why, but what Laura had said only solidified my position.

"She'd be safer," Wes said quieter, so those on the porch wouldn't hear.

I swiped at my face and shook my head.

"Saved her life not having a patch today." I wanted to tell him what my father said, how that sick, perverted fuck had mentioned her to me. Wes would get pissed, and then even more people would know about her being the senator's daughter, and I didn't want that. I wasn't ready to lose her. A panicked part of me worried I'd lose her regardless because if she grew up in that world, there was no chance of her ever honestly settling for this one.

Wes sagged and walked over to me, gripping my shoulder. He was close enough now that whatever we said would just stay between us.

"You don't think I worry about that every day with Callie? The target it paints on her back? There's power in this club, brother. Power in us being together and a family. That patch will protect her, regardless of whatever happened today. You owe it to yourself not to keep stressing over this. She's here; she's not leaving. You need to realize she's going to move on soon enough, unless you give her a reason to stay."

With a pat on my back, he walked off, heading back toward his wife.

I stayed put, frustrated with myself. This feeling under my skin was burning, itching to shed itself, and be free. I had feelings for Laura. Strong ones, but I had just finally become president. The last thing I was about to do was let her mess with my head. She was already messing with my first week as acting president. If I gave her any more space in my life, she'd take it and own it, and deep down, I knew the chances she'd actually stick around were slim.

She was born to privilege, and whenever her mother or dad called and asked her to pick out a pretty diamond ring and marry some guy named Griffin from Yale, she would do it. She'd put on a pretty cocktail dress, apply fancy makeup worth more than my bike, and she'd smile. I'd be a memory to her, a dark, twisted memory.

I wasn't going to be her future, so why would I risk giving her mine?

Giles walked up to me, waving me off to the side.

Veering toward the garage, I followed my vice president until it was just the two of us.

His brown eyes searched my face, narrowing on the place where Wes hit my jaw.

"You good?"

I gave him a quick nod while digging into the loose gravel at my feet.

Giles waited a breath before pushing on. "Jameson asked if he could do a meet up. He knows it might stir shit if he comes here. Wants to know if you'll bring Natty somewhere neutral."

I needed to get the fuck out of here anyway, seemed like a good idea to me.

"Tell him to send the location, we'll meet him there in thirty."

Three Months Ago

• • •

Laura had gotten into my head.

The idea of her being with another member had gotten under my skin. I was just fucking with her about the twins. I didn't have anyone, just like I had messed with her about Jules that first time I had met her. Jules was an old friend, and she looked like the stereotypical pick for a member to fuck. Truth was, she was broken hearted over the woman she'd lost and usually just needed a drinking buddy.

She worked to piss off the only woman I had ever seen that had managed to crawl under my skin. She was a problem from day one, and now she was festering.

I had broken my one rule for her.

That fucking kiss.

I had to remind myself she was leaving and wouldn't be a problem for me anymore.

Still, the idea of her trying to see someone tonight wasn't happening. Just because I couldn't have her didn't mean anyone else could.

Turned out I didn't have to worry about it; the second we arrived back at the club, Wes ordered the girls to stay put. Then Wes put me on security, watching over both Callie and Laura.

Being in the apartment that was supposed to be mine was never as difficult as it was when occupied by a girl that I wanted for myself. She had decided to go outside the second I had walked in.

Fine by me.

I didn't need to talk through our little exchange from earlier. Didn't need to relive that kiss, or the fact that it was the worst and best thing I have ever experienced. I didn't need to relive her smiling at me while straddling my hips, or how it seemed to remove every doubt I'd ever had about letting someone inside this fucked up heart of mine.

I blinked, staring up at the seventy-five-inch screen. Wes had good taste. I liked how dark and masculine everything in his apartment looked. My mind drifted to what it would look like if I had it. A flash of blonde entered the image in my head, Laura smiling at me from her spot on the couch. Her laughing as I dove in for a kiss. Us planning meals, cooking together in the kitchen...me fucking her slowly against the counter.

Jesus.

Where did that come from?

My chest ached; this was bad. So fucking bad.

Suddenly the glass door from outside opened and the woman walked in. I stared at Laura as she walked past me as if I were invisible.

Under her shirt, she still had invisible ropes of pleasure smearing her skin. I had marked her, and she was just walking around as if I hadn't.

Callie walked out through the garage door, leaving Laura all alone in the kitchen. I took the opportunity to get up from the couch in search of a glass of water. I found her standing at the counter, her back to me as she wrestled with the top of a frozen dinner meal. She didn't turn or even acknowledge me, so I reached around her and grabbed the dinner meal from her and took my knife out to slice through it.

"I was perfectly capable of doing that."

Smirking at her, I caged her in against the counter. Her blue eyes lit up with the afternoon light, her face flushing just the slightest bit. My hand suddenly traveled to her stomach, just because I wanted to skim it, touch it. See if she would respond for me like she had before.

She responded alright, but it was with a push at my chest.

"You made yourself clear back at the house. I'm good."

She moved to the sink, and I grabbed her hand and spun her around.

"I'm not. I don't want you to see other members while you're here."

She didn't pull away, but her glare was enough to have my confidence waning.

Drawing closer, she was practically right in front of me when she whispered, "then maybe I need to leave."

That took the air out of my lungs, like a sucker punch to the stomach. I searched her face, a million words on the tip of my tongue, none of which I'd ever say out loud. Until finally one word cleared the fog, just one.

Stay.

And my mouth parted right as Callie came through the door. I moved away from Laura and walked back to my spot on the couch. She was leaving. Regardless of when, she wasn't staying here, it didn't matter if I wanted her to stay or not.

...*But why did my stupid heart kickstart at the idea of her abandonment?*

Later that night, I had stolen Laura's phone number.

I wasn't proud of it, but I also wasn't sorry. The entire night I thought over our encounter in the house, the only place I never took anyone. The place I was most ashamed of. Being with Laura was like having the chance to be the one thing I was afraid of being with anyone. I could be honest, vulnerable and it didn't matter because she wasn't staying.

But for some reason, she was stuck in my head.

So when Wes came back and carried Callie upstairs, I decided to text her. I knew she was asleep, but I had to make sure she had this on her phone the second she woke up.

> Me: what if I don't want you to go?

I did though. I knew I did. This thing I felt would pass. She was just a pair of tits, and a fucking fantastic piece of ass. It was just physical.

I set my phone down, and walked around my house. Made a sandwich and then returned to the couch where a new text waited for me.

> Laura: aren't you supposed to be with the twins tonight?

With a smile, I texted her a picture of my sandwich.

> Laura: My god that's a lot of mustard. Did you even add mayo?

> Me: Of course I did, on one side like a normal person, the other side is mustard.

> Laura: So you add mayo to only one side of the bread, and only mustard to the other?

Taking another big bite of my sandwich, I chewed while responding.

> Me: yes…that's perfectly normal.

There were a few minutes until she replied again, and a GIF of a monster came through.

I laughed, nearly choking on my food.

> Laura: Seriously though, you're so weird. That is not normal at all. What happened with the twins? Bet you at least one of them could have prepared you a better sandwich than that.

> Me: I was lying about the twins, okay?

Laura waited before responding again, forcing me to fidget, which resulted in me cleaning. Once the floor was spotless, and the kitchen was perfect, I tugged my shirt free, and settled back into the couch.

Suddenly a FaceTime request came in from Laura, making my stomach flip.

I answered, and the small side lamp illuminated her face. She was stunning.

"You have mustard on your face. That was the only reason I called, had to see…k goodnight."

"No, you don't, you better wait." I laughed, while swiping at my jaw.

She smiled while digging deeper into the covers.

"Can't sleep?"

She shook her head and then looked up at the ceiling.

"Sort of wish I had packed earplugs."

I gave her a sympathetic wince.

"They fucking or fighting?"

She let out a sigh and turned on her back, the camera going with her, but now the swells of her breasts were visible. I tried not to look, but fuck she was perfect and it was late, and I was hard.

"A little of both."

"Sounds hot," I joked, now stroking my cock.

Her brows dipped into the center of her forehead. "Why did you lie about the twins?"

I didn't want to explain it, but my mouth opened regardless.

"Things felt like they were getting serious…wanted to make sure you understood I just wanted some fun."

"Then why text me tonight?"

My face warmed, the flush invading my neck and chest. She had me there.

Hesitating the smallest bit, I explained, "Because what you said earlier messed with me."

Her pink lips slammed together; her blue eyes searched mine, but I was moving the screen to reach for something. It was nothing, but I didn't want her scrutinizing me.

"So you don't want me to leave?"

Bringing the camera back, I stared at her golden hair looking like a halo in the light. Sentimental words burned the edge of my tongue. Words that would describe her beauty, what it did to me. More shit like I had sputtered earlier about Cinderella. I'd probably break down and even explain why I called her Daisy. It made me weak, all of it.

And I refused to be weak.

Clearing my throat, I stroked up my shaft once more and said, "Just wanted the chance to fuck you at least once before you left. That's all."

Hurt flashed in her eyes, a gleam that I had witnessed earlier when I spoke of the twins and shut her down in pops's house. I knew I was being a bastard, but I couldn't figure out another way to keep her without becoming weak. Which meant I had to let her go.

Finally she seemed to understand that this was who I was and how I acted. She let out a sigh and muttered, "Fuck off, Killian."

Then the phone went dark.

SEVENTEEN
LAURA

The adrenaline from the day had finally worn off, leaving me exhausted and expectant.

I brought my knees up to my chest and looked around the room.

Everything had been upgraded, and I hadn't even noticed.

My eagerness to avoid the club had put me at Callie's house for longer than usual. While I was gone, the entire apartment had been furnished. Killian's bed was massive and set inside a gorgeous wood frame with a lavish headboard. There were matching side tables with lamps, and a dresser across the room with a television mounted on the wall.

The bathroom had rugs, and fluffy towels folded inside the small inlet closet.

The office space across the hall had a desk with drawing supplies, a bookshelf and a deep-set reading chair. The living room was now complete with a luxurious leather couch set, chair and a wood coffee table, along with the largest flat screen I had ever seen.

The biggest change that I was still trying to process was the fact that the guest room where I had been staying was emptied. My suitcases were in Killian's closet, my mattress was nowhere to be found, and the one lamp I owned was likely in the trash. But my glasses and skin care products, along with my shampoo and makeup, were all in his bathroom.

As if he was asking me to move in...

Now, after a shower and some time to process all of it, I was sitting in his bed, wearing an oversized t-shirt and a pair of boy short underwear, along with a pair of thick socks that went to my knees. After my shower, I braided my hair into two plaits and applied lotion to my whole body, waiting for the wolf.

Chills broke out along my skin every time I thought of how dark his gaze became, or the way his eyes lingered on my lips before turning away. It was as though the chapter we'd ended on three months ago was suddenly plopped open, ink spilling onto the proverbial pages, out of our control.

He'd said all we could have been was physical, but he was so tender today. The worry and fear, there was no way he wasn't just as into this as I was.

Just as I thought it, a restlessness had me jumping up from the bed, curious as to where Killian could be. He said he'd be back, and he was a man of his word...at least from what I had encountered so far.

Unless something was keeping him.

Briskly making my way downstairs, I slipped out the front door and tucked my arms to my chest, watching the front of the club. There were still people milling about, but over by the garage, I could make out a flash of honey blonde hair and that tall stature I had come to know so well.

Natty was standing next to Killian; he was saying something to her while handing her a bucket helmet. She smiled up at him, and then he handed her a jacket.

Confusion swept through me as I watched. She took the jacket while Killian explained something to her, a frown tipping her lips down. She shook her head and handed it back, which made me walk closer to get a better view.

Killian glared, pushing the jacket toward her once more.

Natty stepped back, glancing at Giles, and waved him over. She said something to him, resulting in him sliding out of his jacket and handing it over to her. She slid it on and then held her hands up toward Killian as if she were innocent of something. He shook his head and straddled his bike. Natty climbed on behind him, and then her arms went around his waist, and it felt like my heart was being strangled just as tightly.

Tension gathered in my chest, as I watched them leave. Honey hair flying in the cobalt sky, the remnants of the storm still lingering in the air.

Giles finally turned and caught me watching, a furrow to his brow when he took in my expression. I swallowed thickly as he seemed to register my reaction to Killian and Natty. His brows shot up as he started shaking his head, then he was veering toward me. I backed up and slipped into the apartment before the vice president could make his way over.

It wasn't like Killian owed me anything.

We weren't together.

I blinked, staring at the apartment and realizing Killian had moved in, and now he was with another woman. A woman he'd put on the back of his bike and handed his jacket. That was the equivalent of being given a property patch in the Stone Riders. A tiny voice in the back of my head reminded me she hadn't accepted it...*but he'd still offered it to her.*

Which meant...I needed to get the hell out of his house.

I made my way upstairs, numb and unfocused.

He was free to do whatever he wanted. The fact that hurt was swelling like a balloon in my chest only meant I'd been a fool. I had to remind myself that this was what I had expected to happen after we'd had sex. I knew it was merely an itch to be scratched.

Now he'd scratched, and he was moving on.

But why had he told me to shower and wait for him? Why kiss me?
Didn't matter.

Dressing quickly, I packed a small bag that I could use to store my things overnight, including my glasses and toiletries.

"Phone charger," I mused out loud, tugging mine from the side table outlet.

I gave the room one last look, feeling a strange sadness well within me. I'd have to come back for my suitcases, but I could do that later when Callie was with me.

Pushing past the doorframe, I flicked the light off and jogged downstairs.

I didn't want an audience for what I was going to do next, so I left through the back door and ventured down the patio and through the yard until I was exiting the gate. No one was outside hanging out in the backyard, which was a nice reprieve.

There was a side entry into the kitchen, that only Natty, Red and Killian knew about, and he only recently learned because he'd become president. Wes knew, but we'd changed the code since the shift in leadership. It wasn't like we didn't trust the rest of the club, but it was our little secret and a good way to load in groceries without everyone in the club seeing.

Peeling the panel back, I pushed in the code and opened the door. I could hear voices from the bar, which was toward the opening of the kitchen. The door I came in was back near the storage shelves. Tucking my bag closer to my side, I made my way past the large industrial oven, and stainless-steel tables, until I caught sight of Red.

She was pouring someone a drink, shootin' the shit. I waited until Red turned and waved her over.

Her white brows furrowed as she glanced back once more to the member at the bar.

"Hang on sweets, gotta check on somethin'."

She sauntered back, tossing a dish towel over her shoulder as she walked. Her eyes took in my appearance then dipped to the duffel at my side.

"What happened?" she asked as though she knew it was only a matter of time before I stood before her with a duffle bag in tow.

Smiling and acting as though nothing was wrong, I shook my head.

"Nothing is wrong, just need to ask if there's an open room I can snag until I can find a more permanent solution, which I can secure by tomorrow. I'm sure of it."

I had the money saved, and I had made a few calls. There was a one-bedroom apartment above The Drip that I could move into. There was no tub for rust to grow in, because all it had was a tiny shower, a toilet, enough room for a twin bed, and that was it. But I didn't care. It would work for now.

Red's hand came to her hip, fire engine red manicured nails shone under the lights in the kitchen. Her eyes focused on my face, her lips twisting to the side as though she were thinking it over.

"I put you near the men, Prez will come in here tearin' through every one of them until he finds you."

I forced a smile.

"See he won't because I saw him leave with Natty."

Red laughed, while keeping her focus on me. Laser sharp.

"Oh honey, you're pretty. Too pretty and too dangerous for that boy, but you're about as dumb as a box of rocks if you think there's anything to him taking Natty anywhere."

"He offered her his jacket and took her on the back of his bike." I bit out in return because those two things meant something in this club. Perhaps all clubs, but especially this one. You didn't ride on the back of another member's bike unless it was an emergency, or you were fucking him. You especially didn't ride on the back of that member's bike while wearing his colors, unless it meant you were his old lady.

Red's façade cracked. Her eyes took on a new luster of interest, her gaze searching my face as if I could explain what I'd done to lose the interest of the wolf.

"Basement. There's a room with a bed. It's a twin and there's no bathroom. You'll have to use the one down there, but the only other member who goes down there is Giles. He'll keep you safe, and I know you two get on okay."

This was better than I hoped.

"That's perfect." I beamed, gripping the strap of my duffle.

"Sheets will be in the linen closet down there. A pillow too. Check for a heater, it'll likely get cold as a witch's tit down there."

Red gave me one last glance, then reached out and gently gripped my shoulder before turning to leave. It was something I liked about her. She was stern and strong, not overly emotional but still fair. You knew she was thinking things, even if she didn't say them, and she was always protective of the girls here. Even the Sweetbutts.

The club was in mild upheaval tonight. Extra members had been called in from the looks of it; there were more people here than usual. It felt like it did the night of Killian's induction. I passed people, ducked and smiled. Avoiding men who tried to grab me or corner me to talk.

Soon, I was passing a group of guys who were talking near the entrance to the stairs. I'd need to skirt past them in order to head down to bed. It was still shamefully early, but I wasn't hungry, and anything else I needed would be downstairs.

I hedged close, hoping to go unnoticed when I heard the men talking.

"Now that the Roman has taken over, we're not allowed to move on the Death Raiders. It's complete and utter bullshit. I heard it was from some deal Ryan made back when he was president. Killian wouldn't stand for old bets and promises. One of the reasons he's going to turn this club around. The second he gives the green light; I'm gettin' one of them fuckers."

The man who was talking wasn't a regular member, not from what I could tell. He might show up for weekend rallies and a few parties, but I didn't recognize him.

A new voice piped up, this one from a man I did recognize. Riley from earlier, the biker who'd driven me here. His focus was on the floor while he sipped from a glass bottle of beer.

"Honestly, I like the peace. I'm tired of all the fucking fighting. I lost my brother to a war with those fuckers. Enough is enough."

Three of the men yelled, clapping shoulders, the other four yelled their dissent. I chose that moment to slip past them and down the stairs. A dark hallway greeted me, so I pulled out my phone and used the flashlight app to navigate.

The noise began to fade as I stepped off the last step and my feet sank into plush carpet. Finding the light switch on the side of the wall, the space illuminated, revealing a spacious room. Three leather arm chairs, in addition to a long leather couch, faced a massive flat screen television. A pool table sat off to the side. Behind it was a darkened bathroom, and next to it was a space for a simple top loader, washer and dryer. A closed door sat on the opposite end, and another tucked farther back, almost hidden away.

Making my way back in the direction of the hidden space, I relished the quiet. Down here was even better than Killian's space. Somehow the room seemed to completely muffle the party from upstairs. It was a wonder that no one was down here, unless the members just instinctively knew that this area was off-limits. This was the first time I had ever been down here, or even realized it was here, and I'd been here for three months.

Just as I suspected, the hidden room was the empty one that Red had mentioned for me to use. A single twin bed rested against the far wall, and a small side table and lamp were next to it. The rest of the space was sparse.

Setting my bag on the floor, I went searching for the linens Red had mentioned. They would likely be near the washer and dryer, or the bathroom, so that's where I headed. The silence wrapped around me, cocooning me in a way that I hadn't realized I needed. The chaos of the club and rage of the party couldn't reach me down here. It almost felt like I could just breathe for a second and forget where I was. Forget Killian and Natty, and the way their actions felt like a knife to my chest, digging into a place they had no business being.

I knew better, I knew falling for him would hurt. He'd warned me; from the first moment I met him, he was a walking, talking, red flag.

Yet, I wanted him.

I craved his destruction, the devastation I knew he promised. I had some sick and twisted desire to hurt. There was no other explanation as to why I let him under my defenses. It was the stupid nickname he called me, and the way he was so protective of me. It confused me, nothing more. It was a stark contrast to what I had grown up with. My father, being the mayor when I was little, made me feel like we were living in a glass snow globe. One wrong move and our world would upend, or even shatter.

When he became governor of the state, it only got worse. Then he became senator, and I couldn't stick around any longer.

Everyone was expendable, especially his only child.

I was a pretty face, but my wild nature was constantly getting me into trouble. The one constant I had, the one that always stuck, were the threats and promises from my father about ruining my life. Every time his arm came around me for a photo op, he'd pinch my side while whispering threats of behaving.

I grew up feeling like my peace and safety were on a thin line, every waking moment. I hated the wildness that lived within me. I hated how curious I was, and how I'd always needed to investigate, and how it inevitably would end with me getting into trouble.

Killian made me feel protected, and like I could unapologetically be myself for the first time in my life, while still being cherished.

Blinking past the burning in my eyes, I gripped a bundle of sheets and a pillow.

Perhaps if I had some space from him, some time away from seeing him or being near him, just like I did over the past three months, I could go back to being apathetic toward him.

I was still standing, staring at a closet with the linens in my arms when I heard the door to the top of the stairs open and close. Then feminine laughter.

Oh shit.

I quickly ducked as Giles made his way down the stairs, kissing a Sweetbutt. I couldn't recognize who she was from here, but it didn't matter. This was his space, and I had just invaded it, like I did to Killian.

Shame flared aggressively in my chest, as I got on all fours and began crawling out of sight.

The couple was kissing and heavily petting when they paused near the pool table, making me freeze.

"You ever fucked on one before?" the girl asked in a sultry voice.

I was within viewing distance of Giles, but he wasn't paying attention. Hopefully she'd strip or something and he'd be distracted.

"Why don't you just take those shorts off and show me exactly what you want me to fuck, and we'll start there," Giles muttered, all low and sexy.

Oh no. That was definitely Sadie. She was the only Sweetbutt that was still wearing shorts in November. I was still on the floor and I did not want to have to watch them, or hear them, have sex. Maybe if I—

"You mean these shorts?" Sadie asked, and I could see from my spot she'd tossed the denim at Giles's face. She stood in front of him in just a light blue thong. Her shirt went next, and of course, she wasn't even wearing a bra.

Giles smiled at her, his hands dropping to the copper button on his jeans.

"You gonna let me have your ass this time?" he asked all husky, and oh my god.

They were about to fuck, and I had a decision to make. I could scatter across the floor while they were going at it, but if they didn't move to the couch, or his room, then he was going to catch me. It wasn't that I cared that he did. I just didn't want to talk to him. I knew he was going to mention Killian, and I wasn't ready.

I was so stuck deliberating my choices, I missed that his phone had rung…and the idiot answered.

"Hey boss. Nope, not busy at all."

Poor Sadie was just perched on the edge of the pool table, watching Giles as he held the phone to his ear.

No girl wanted to hear that, but especially not while she was in front of a man naked.

"Yeah, I can go check on her, but I'm almost positive I saw her earlier mingling at the party." Giles placed a sweet kiss on the side of Sadie's face before tucking himself into his boxers.

Were they talking about me? Was I conceited to assume they were?

"She saw you two…no she saw *her* get on the back of *your* bike, and how you tried to hand her your jacket. She was hurt, Kil. No idea what she plans to do tonight, but whatever it is, it'll likely be with that image in mind."

Definitely me then.

I heard Killian's billowing "fuck" all the way from my place on the floor.

"I tried to explain it to her," Giles said, now walking back toward the stairs.

Sadie was scrolling through her phone, half naked on the pool table as if she were completely used to this. Maybe she was, but I'd eat a dead cockroach before this ever became my life. Where I just lay around, ready to be fucked only to be silenced and shelved a moment later.

I needed to get in my room before Giles found me.

Eyeing the open doorway once more, I dared another few paces on my hands and knees when I heard Giles continue.

"What exactly do you want me to do? If she is with another member tonight, there's nothing I can do about—"

He stopped, and I heard Killian yelling, but I couldn't make out what he was saying.

"No," Giles muttered.

This was so ridiculous; I wasn't going to fuck anyone tonight. I wanted to *read* about people fucking and get into my pajamas. Have a nice pity party, if these idiots would just let me.

"You got it. But..." Giles hesitated, rubbing the back of his neck, "Killian you need to fix this. It's getting past the point of anyone being able to deal with you. You were willing to give your patch to Natty for protection, but you won't give it to Laura? Doesn't make any sense to me."

His words landed painfully hard in my chest. My eyes burned with unshed tears, and the fear that I would never truly understand what had happened today threatened to choke me. Not with the way Killian reacted to me, the danger I was in, or the reason he'd taken Natty. Maybe it was all innocent, but the fact that Giles had just said Killian wasn't willing to give me his cut even for protection, spoke volumes.

In fact, it said absolutely everything I needed to hear.

Giles must have hung up because he resumed talking to Sadie.

"Let me make it up to you, but come upstairs with me real quick. Okay?"

He kissed her long and hard, feeling her up and then letting out a sigh as he pulled away.

"Okay, as long as you promise." She purred, and then she was hopping off the table and gathering her clothes.

I waited for them to hit the stairs, and then I reached back for the pile of bedding and shuffled the rest of the way into the room and shut the door.

I knew what Giles was doing. He was searching for me, and any signs of the guy I was hooking up with. All I could do was hope that Red didn't rat me out because if she didn't then I might just be successful for once in driving the new president of the Stone Riders a little crazy.

Flipping on the switch in my new room, I took my time stretching the fitted sheet over the mattress. Then I shook out the top sheet, and laid it flat, smoothing out any wrinkles. There was a threadbare blanket I found in the closet, but there wasn't anything else in there, so it would have to do.

Red was right, it was freezing in the basement, so I pulled on a hoodie and some sweats then crawled into bed. My phone was in one hand as I navigated my playlist, while my kindle was in the other, and I was two seconds from hitting play when I heard the sound of rumbling engines.

I paused, glancing up at the wall as if I could see through it to the yard. The sound of approaching motorcycles permeated the walls, and from the echo, it was a lot of bikes, which had my stomach churning.

Most of the Stone Riders had already pulled in, which meant these bikes weren't Stone Riders. Killian was gone, so was Wes, which meant the highest person in charge was Giles, and while I loved the guy, he was not ready to hold off whoever had just arrived.

The rest of the club was here though, he'd be fine.

But why did Killian leave, and by himself? That wasn't normal, was it...he was the president, which meant he should have had backup.

I could just ignore it; the club wasn't my business. I turned my phone back on, about to hit play once more, when suddenly someone screamed, and then a gun went off.

EIGHTEEN
KILLIAN

The president of the Chaos Kings was sitting two tables down from me while smiling at Natty. It wasn't the sort of smile he'd give a girl he wanted to fuck, it was warmer than that, as though he truly cared about what she was saying. He looked hopeful.

Which meant she must be giving him a good report regarding living with the Stone Riders.

I stared at my dark cell phone while the two across the room laughed. Natty had shed Giles jacket, and the reminder that I had offered her mine reverberated in my head like a fucking song that wouldn't end. I knew why in the moment that I had done it.

Natty hadn't been on the back of a bike with a member since she was transferred to the Stone Riders several years ago. She was having issues with even getting on the back of my bike. I nearly took my truck, just to calm her down, but she knew it would be faster if we took the bike, and she needed to get back to help Red with something.

Knowing Natty was nervous about leaving the club, and on the back of a bike no less, I assumed my jacket with my patches would put her at ease. I knew she trusted me, and I knew she understood how powerful the president patch was, and how untouchable it would make her.

That same logic wouldn't compute for Laura for some fucked up reason, and I had no idea why. When I thought of putting my patch on Laura, all I could think of was how it would put a target on her back, and how I couldn't live with myself if something ever happened to her. Especially since that meeting with my father.

Which brought me back to the entire reason I wanted a little space tonight.

Daisy had found a way inside my chest and stamped her initials all over my pathetically weary heart. Now she was there, and she wouldn't budge.

No matter what I fucking did.

Giles was right, this was becoming a problem.

Tapping my phone screen, I checked the time once more and my knee began bouncing under the table. Giles said he'd look for Laura, and I didn't think she'd do anything stupid, but what reason did I give her to remain loyal to me?

None.

If anything, she'd fuck someone just to make a point to me. I already knew how I'd handle it too, which meant I wasn't fit to be president.

Jameson walked over with Natty next to him. "Thanks Quinn."

She smiled and took the seat across from me.

"I'm going to go back and talk to Penelope and see what she thinks. But, I need to know, if you even have space for her?"

Natty eyed me then blurted before I could, "we'll make room."

Yeah, we were good at that.

"We will…there's a few options. A cabin on the back part of the property, and a house that the club just recently purchased. Needs some renovating, but it would work."

Jameson's expression grew distant as he nodded along.

"I just want her to be safe."

"She will be." I nodded, regardless that I was itching to leave. I didn't honestly give a fuck about this Penelope chick, or the fact that King's VP knocked her up. I knew offering her sanctuary was the right thing to do, and a good way to gain an alliance with the Chaos Kings, but I was ready to get back.

Jameson tipped his chin in understanding while staring off as though he still wasn't sure.

"I'll be in touch. Thanks."

Gripping Natty's shoulder, he gave her a solemn smile. "Thank you for sharing your story with me. I appreciate it."

She smiled back. "I'm glad you're helping her. I'll be a friend to her when she arrives."

The two gave each other another long look, and then Jameson was walking off, out through the front door.

I stood, pocketing my phone. "We need to get back."

"I knew you shouldn't have come. You could have sent Giles." Natty clicked her tongue disapprovingly.

"This type of situation, I had to oversee."

We moved outside, Natty pulled on Giles's jacket, zipping it, while letting out a sigh.

"If it gets back that you tried to give me your patch, she's going to hate me."

Handing her the spare bucket helmet, I ignored how worried her words made me. Tempted to play dumb, I nearly asked who she was talking about, but I didn't have the energy.

"Laura isn't my girl, I'm not her man. We're not—"

Natty made a sound, almost like she was about to puke, interrupting me. "She's not your girl, and yet you're practically bursting out of your skin because you're imagining her with another member right now. You can't see her with anyone else. Her eyes are always on you, even when you're not looking. She lived in your house for three months, Killian. Anyone else would have tucked tail after the first three weeks. She was waiting for you. I don't even know if she realizes that."

Confusion tugged my brows together; I was about to snap a rebuttal when my phone began to ring.

Giles.

Giving Natty my back, I turned to answer it.

"Yeah."

He was breathing hard, and I could hear chaos in the background. "The Roman is here, and he's pissed, Killian. He's going to shoot someone. I tried to talk him down…"

"What are you talking about, what happened?"

He was still trying to catch his breath. "Everyone was scared, and

Sadie screamed, which prompted Silas to give off a warning shot. Laura came running outside, and he saw her—it was like he immediately recognized her, but I don't know how that's possible."

Her father is the senator of Virginia.

My heart was thundering so hard, I was sure it was about to tear through my chest.

With a crack in my voice, I asked just barely above a whisper.

"What happened when he saw her?"

Giles hesitated, then cursed. "He called her Virginia royalty and then said she must belong to someone important…no one spoke up, but then…" he hesitated like he didn't want to say the rest.

"Giles!"

"Fuck. Sadie and a few other Sweetbutts shoved Laura forward, saying she was yours."

This wasn't happening.

"Are you telling me…" I swallowed the thick lump forming in my throat. I thought I'd asked the rest of my question, but then Giles spoke up again, and I guess I hadn't actually said it out loud.

"I'm telling you that Silas, the new leader of the Death Raiders, just took Laura from right under our fucking noses, they're here—keeping her at gunpoint until you arrive."

My phone dropped.

Then my fist flew and Natty screamed from the sickening crunch when my knuckles met the brick wall.

Natty was practically melded to my back as we flew down the road. We passed car after car, breaking the speed limit. My hand was throbbing, but the cold air against it felt good. I kept my gloves off, and my jacket off, needing to calm down. I hadn't even texted Wes before I left, seeing as Callie was the reason that fucking Death Raider wasn't dead yet. She'd made a deal with him after he helped save Wes a few months back.

All I could do was focus on getting there.

If they were keeping her hostage, that meant they wanted something.

I knew this asshole was going to pull something like this the second I became president.

Callie swore he wanted peace, but Wes and I knew better.

Within ten minutes, we were pulling off toward the driveway of the club. There were Death Raiders lining the road, forcing us to slow down. Natty's grip slackened until she let go completely. With quick movements, she was pulling Giles' jacket off and stuffing it in her lap.

The action seemed odd, considering the wind was still whipping at her hair, and the cold stinging our cheeks. *Unless she didn't want someone to see her wearing it.*

We drove down the path, eyes of Raiders on us the entire way until we were near the front of the club, where Giles, Brooks, Rune, Hamish, Pops, and several other Stone Riders were waiting. In the middle of the lot was Silas, and on his bike, sitting in front of him was Laura.

She was straddling his lap, facing him, with her back to the clubhouse. As we approached, her eyes trailed us. Her face was impassive, as though this didn't bother her in the least, and she was bored out of her mind. I knew she was hiding her reaction, and likely her fear.

I pulled off as close to the entrance as I possibly could.

Once I parked, Natty shocked me by standing and making eye contact with Silas.

The two stared at one another for a stretch of time, his pale eyes locked on hers. Finally, after her lips pursed and her fists clenched, Natty handed Giles his jacket back before giving Silas her back and going inside.

I left my bike, giving a glance to my VP, and then cut the distance to Silas.

Once I was within ten feet of him, he made a tsking sound, shoving the barrel of his gun into Laura's temple.

"That's far enough, Mr. President."

Seeing that gun against her head made me feel like my pulse was going to burst through my neck. I ground my molars together, staring and feeling helpless as this psycho held the girl, I was fairly certain I was in love with, at gunpoint. All I could think about was that day I had confessed what her eyes were like to me.

Cinderella Blue.

She had to be okay. He couldn't hurt her. If he did, I'd rip his throat out, and we'd have a war. Likely one we'd lose, but it wouldn't matter anyway because if those beautiful eyes stopped seeing the sky, then what was the point of any of this?

Understanding registered slow and painful. *She was more important than the club.*

"What the fuck is this, Silas?" I lifted my hands.

Tilting his head, his creepy eyes caught the light. His dark black hair was slicked back, his leather jacket on, his own President patch in place along with the death reaper and scythe. He looked every inch the monster I heard so many stories about.

His free hand went to Laura's hip, pulling her closer, so her chest was flush against his. Her head moved to the side, but her expression remained the same. I stepped forward again, fucker needed to stop touching her.

"You need to tell me why the leader of the Chaos Kings was seen speaking to one of your wards, not once but fucking two times in a row, Killian."

My fury was blinding me, making my brain go blank.

"What the fuck are you talking about?"

Silas glared at Laura, as though she was annoying him. "Is she important to you, Quinn?"

He pulled the black barrel down the length of her face again, this time slowly grazing her lips.

I faltered closer, my throat nearly closing. "Yes. Okay, that what you want to hear?" My voice was cracking again as I stepped even closer, but I couldn't bring myself to care. "Just let her go."

"See, it's strange. You seem unnerved at the idea of someone important to you having a meeting with the president of a rival club. Makes you uneasy seeing her in my lap, right?"

I had no idea who he was talking about...unless.

Fuck.

How could I have been so stupid, of course he was going to find out. Natty had some explaining to do. This was the second time he'd threatened our club on her behalf.

"She was never in any danger. I made sure of it, you have my fucking word, Silas."

His eyes finally left Laura, and they were wild, unhinged as they attached to me.

"I have your word that the most important person in my entire fucking existence was safe with the wolf, while he went and met with the King of Chaos? Do you even know who they're working with, do you know what his own club is doing to him?"

Silas suddenly lifted Laura, until she was standing on the gravel by the bike. He quickly followed, holding on to her elbow. Her blue-eyed glare finally met mine, and my knees threatened to give out.

Finding my voice, I asked him about Natty. "If she's so important to you then why is she here? How come she isn't with you?"

His ghost-like gaze pierced me with a look of absolute abandon. "Why isn't *she* wearing your patch?" His gun grazed Laura's shoulders, lifting the hood of her sweatshirt then letting it plop back down. She had her hair in two braids tonight, tiny curls were framing her face and kissing her skin. Even dressed down in sweats and a hoodie, she made my breath hitch.

All I could picture was her under me, writhing as I slowly fucked her.

"You know she came out here, charging forward with her fists clenched like she owned this entire fucking club. She heard one of the Sweetbutts scream, and suddenly she was trying to step toe to toe with me. She gave zero fucks as to who I was. Even now, she'd be mouthing off like she was earlier except we told her that Mason over there would shoot you in the back the second she opens her pretty little mouth."

"You're a coward, Silas. Let her go and come talk to me." I was close enough now that we were speaking in tones where the rest of the club couldn't hear us.

"This is a warning, Killian. What belongs to me stays safe under your protection, or I come back for what's yours. Even if you do decide to eventually claim her, I'll take her. I will be back for what's mine. In the meantime, I highly suggest you put a property patch between these delicate shoulders." He stroked down Laura's back, and I lunged.

He released her, pushing her toward me right as his other members started their bikes and began riding directly at us. I pulled Laura until she was cradled into my chest.

The bikes moved in such a way that made it impossible to go after Silas for what he'd just done. The rest of the members followed him out, until it was just the Stone Riders left.

Within a single breath, Laura pushed me back, and because I was still reeling from seeing her at fucking gunpoint, my arms came loose, and she briskly walked back toward the club.

Before she reached the door, I yelled for all the members still outside to hear.

"Sadie, and any other Sweetbutt who turned Laura over to Silas, your ass is out of here."

Laura spun on her heel, her face flushed, and then she stepped in front of Sadie and the other girls.

"You will not remove them from this club. Not a single person." Her voice carried, and I saw the looks on every single member's face. Silas said she'd stepped up for them, as a way to protect them while I was gone.

Laura stayed rooted by the porch as the rest of the girls looked scared.

"They aren't guilty of anything you didn't do to me yourself. You didn't want me thrown to a Death Raider, then you shouldn't have started shit with me, Killian. Especially shit you had no intention of following through with. These girls stay."

With one last glance at each Sweetbutt, Laura turned and went inside.

I knew without a second thought she'd just earned the loyalty of half my fucking club, if not more. The Sweetbutts would now do anything to protect her, regardless that they'd shoved her forward this time. They'd never do it again, not now that she'd stepped to me and demanded they stay.

The men watched me for what I might do next, likely expecting me to overrule what Laura had just said. I saw Sadie thread her fingers through Giles as she waited, fear stamped across her features. A lot of these women found clubs they could be in safely, and Stone Riders was one of the only that didn't hurt their unattached females. If I said they had to leave, then they'd just fall in with another club.

Dipping my chin to my chest, I decided to leave Laura's words hanging in the air and ran after her instead.

Why had she run into the club instead of the apartment?

Bursting through the club doors, I scanned the bar, seeing Red wiping her white rag across the surface with a glare fixed on her face. Since I couldn't place Laura anywhere, I walked over to the woman who knew everything that went on in this club.

"Where is she?"

Red let out a huff, almost like an incredulous chuckle.

"You give Natty your patch?"

Of course everyone in this fucking club knew about that, and if they all assumed Laura was mine, then I'd just embarrassed her by offering it to Natty.

"Natty hadn't been on the back of a bike in years, Red. She had to go meet with the Chaos Kings, and I needed my bike. I wanted her safe."

Red tilted her head to the side, humming to herself. "Yet you're too scared to extend the patch to Laura because you're afraid of what your name on her back will mean for her."

I had no response to that, because yes, if Laura wore my actual property patch, the one that said she was my property then she'd be a target. Callie's car was targeted because of her attachment to the club, I could only imagine what things they would do to Laura.

Red leaned in close, setting her dishrag between us. "That girl is your equal Killian Quinn. You'd be punching God straight in the mouth if you reject the gift he created in her for you. She's patient, a hard worker, loyal to the bone and the only other person that's as protective of this place as you are. She cares about the members here; she cares about *you*."

"I don't need a fucking lecture."

She huffed again and pointed toward the basement. "You do, you idiot, but I'll spare you. She's downstairs, took the spare room."

I pushed off the counter, giving her a glare. "With Giles?"

She shrugged. "Not my concern who warms her bed, I did tell her it gets mighty cold down there at night."

My rage reared and sputtered, but I had to remember that Giles would never do that. He was too nervous to even walk up the stairs when he thought she might be in pajamas.

Members started filtering back in, the music kicked on and I was headed for the basement. Giles tried to flag me down, but I only gave him a warning look before throwing the door open leading to the stairs.

Why was she down here? Didn't make any sense, when I told her to stay in the apartment.

Pounding down the steps, once I cleared the bottom, I veered toward the spare room, tucked away closer to the back and tried the handle. It wouldn't turn.

So I knocked, politely.

"Daisy, open up please."

Nothing.

Frustration gnawed at every nerve ending in my body, and I was still shaking from seeing her on Silas's lap, with that gun drifting across her bottom lip.

My fist curled and I pounded on the door. "Open. Now."

Still nothing, and my temper wasn't built for this shit. I stepped back, and thrust my boot into the wood, shattering the frame.

Inside the tiny space was a twin bed, and on the bed was Laura, curled onto her side, facing the wall. She had a pair of headphones on, which explained why she wasn't answering, but fuck. She had to have known I would come for her.

Walking to the edge of the bed, I placed my hand on her hip and finally saw her face. She was crying, swiping at her eyes with the sleeve of her sweatshirt, and my heart had officially hit its limit.

There was a sadness that tugged at me, burrowing into my sternum and solidifying this shaky, terrible feeling that had started growing three months ago. From the first time I ever laid eyes on Laura.

Love.

Instead of pulling her up, and throwing her over my shoulder, I slipped my boots off then my jacket, and lifted the threadbare blanket, slipping in behind her. Half my body was off the edge of the mattress, but Laura made room, scooting closer to the wall. I tucked one arm under her, pulling her into my chest, and wrapped my other arm around her. My knees bent, fitting behind the backs of her legs, until we were spooning.

Emotion clogged my throat as I inhaled her citrus scent, and the reality of the night really hit me. She could have been taken from me. She could have been kidnapped or hurt. She could have been shot when the girls pushed her forward. She could have been...

I couldn't even think about it. I needed to keep her safe, but the only way I could do that was if I sent her away or told her to leave.

Red's words came back to me, reminding me that Laura could handle this life, I just had to give her the chance.

NINETEEN
LAURA

THERE WAS A WARM HAND ON MY BARE STOMACH.

My shirt was lifted, and Killian's massive arm was twisted around me, his hand planted across my ribs as if he were worried I'd try to move in the middle of the night or something. I stared at the white wall, seeing the daylight pouring in. We fell asleep?

Not only that, we slept all night?

It was barely seven when I had run upstairs and burst outside, seeing the Death Raiders on our property. My rage had sputtered and flared when the leader pulled Sadie from the crowd and placed a gun near her temple. One shot had already gone off, but it might have just been a warning, as no one was down from what I could tell.

Killian thought they had given me up, but I was already in the leader's face, practically begging him to look at me and leave them alone. The fucking psychopath. All I wanted in that moment was Killian. I wanted the wolf, to see him tear through the Death Raiders and maim the man who dared step foot in his kingdom and threaten his people. But then Killian arrived with Natty on his bike and he looked…scared.

I'll never forget the way his features pinched, his dark brows dipped as if he couldn't figure out a way to get me out of his enemy's lap. As if there wasn't anything he could do to guard his heart from feeling the pain of losing me. It was in that moment that I realized why Killian was so terrified of falling in love.

The great wolf was afraid of a tiny rock, one that could bring his whole world down.

I didn't want him to regret me, and from what I knew of Killian, the very last thing he wanted was a weakness. And I'd become exactly that.

He stirred behind me, and I shifted forward, trying to break his hold on me. I'd taken my headphones off sometime during the night, or he had...but they were gone now. My hair was frizzy, my eyes were dry and cracked from crying and keeping my contacts in all night. I just needed a second to myself before I dealt with him.

"Where are you going?" he rumbled behind me.

Tucking a few stray strands of hair behind my ears, I moved to sit up. "Bathroom."

He seemed to accept that, drifting off to sleep. I moved to my knees so I could crawl over him to get free but right as my left leg swung over his hip, his hand came out and gripped my ass.

"Killian."

His grip turned into a soothing stroke, his fingers curling in until he was tracing a line down my crack.

"Daisy."

He was so gentle like this, all sleepy with his hair messy and his soft white t-shirt warm under my touch. I hadn't even realized my hands were braced on his bicep for support.

"I need to get up."

He made a sound, his eyes still closed as he held on to me.

"No, we need to have a conversation about why the fuck you're here instead of the apartment."

I wouldn't allow myself to hope he still wanted me there.

"I don't—"

A knock came from the door and Giles pushed in with his head down.

"Prez, I need to talk to you."

Killian made some kind of annoyed growling sound from under me, and then he twisted, pulling me back down to the bed while lifting on his elbow.

"What?"

Giles lifted his head, still hanging by the door. "Members want to go to Death Raiders club and make an example out of them for just showing up here."

Killian groaned, his hand still on my ass while I laid next to him.

"Tell them I'm taking care of it, but no one else rides."

My head snapped over, taking in Killian's face. His eyes were finally fluttering open, his green stare on the ceiling as the hand under me continued to stroke gently. My mind threw images from those folders at me. How many of those atrocities was he a part of? How many more would there be once there was new space in those file cabinets?

"I can tell them, but they haven't seen you since you took off last night. You came straight down here. They need to—"

I chose that moment to take my leave. Whatever was going on was not my business, and I really didn't need any more images in my head to haunt me at night.

Killian moved too, now sitting up, his head cradled in his hands.

I shoved down what it did to me to see him like that, exhausted from a night spent curled up on a twin bed with me. He had that new huge bed back in his apartment and he'd chosen to stay with me. Not only that but his men had to have been foaming at the mouth last night, desperate for an encouraging word from their president, but he'd come down here instead.

This wasn't good. Killian's focus was supposed to be the club, *not me*.

I grabbed my things and darted for the bathroom around the corner. Locking myself inside, I took out my contacts, showered, and then got dressed. Wearing blue jeans and a cropped sweater, I left my hair wet, laying against my back.

Checking the mirror, I winced at my reflection. My face was pale, and my eyes were puffy. Letting out a sigh, I crouched to the ground to dig through my duffel and pulled my cosmetic bag free. After doing a whole skin regiment and swiping some mascara onto my lashes, I felt better. Then I braided a piece of my hair, small and right at my hairline, letting it hang free while my ends began to curl. It was the most natural I'd been since arriving, and it felt good.

Finally done, I pulled open the door, only to stop short.

"Daisy." Killian bracketed the doorframe with his long arms, his intense stare fixated on me, taking in every detail of my appearance. When his eyes tracked the tiny braid, a small smile lifted his lips.

I tried to push past him, but he wouldn't move.

"Excuse me."

His fingers went to my neck, tipping my head back while he brought his body flush with mine. "We need to talk about last night."

"We don't." Because really there was nothing left to be said. I pushed at him again, but his hand tightened around my neck, possessively.

I looked up, and his gaze told me we would be discussing the Natty situation. I really didn't want to, so I blurted—

"You said everything that needed to be said when you handed Natty your jacket and left with her on your bike. I'm not playing these games anymore, Killian. Move."

Pulling myself free from his grip, I tried to shove him off again, but he moved with me.

"So that's it? You won't hear me out? You pretending not to care again, Daisy?"

My face was red, my chest flushed. A flash of hurt and pain was still laced around my heart, making patchwork out of my fears. He knew I cared for him, and now he was making jokes of it.

"Go deal with your club, Killian."

"Not until we talk. Now I can follow you and carry your things for you, like a gentleman. Or I can throw you over my shoulder and take you where I want to go. Choice is yours, either way we're talking."

I scowled up at him, and realized he wasn't moving and regardless of what was going on with his club, and all of its members, he was going to deal with this first. Some tiny thrill shot through me as the reality of his actions sank into my heart. It felt like quicksand, and this stupid feeling wasn't going to budge no matter what.

"Fine, lead the way." I crossed my arms, still feeling defiant.

With another smirk, he dipped to grab my duffel, pulling it up on his shoulder. Turning, he veered for the stairs, and I followed, taking the steps one at a time. Once we made it to the main level, sunlight crept in through the tall windows, stroking the hardwood bar top and floors. Red was in the kitchen somewhere, prepping food, so was Natty.

She saw me and paled.

I turned to leave, but she was rounding the bar, heading right for me. "Laura, wait."

I didn't want to. I couldn't stand there and hear from the two of them about something that might have been going on for far longer than I even realized.

I saw Sadie gathering her coat, still wearing those ridiculous shorts. Her friends Jasmine and Tess were with her.

Killian continued moving toward the front, and I knew we were headed to the apartment. I was a few feet behind him with the girls all gathered in a group and Sadie shot her arm out, gripping my wrist.

"Laura?"

I turned, which made Killian stop by the front door. I didn't catch his expression, but Sadie flicked a nervous glance his way.

Empathy had me peeking over my shoulder at Natty. Her face looked stricken as she searched my face. I didn't want to talk to her at the moment, but I knew I would eventually hear her out. She had rejected his jacket, that meant something, and she was important to me.

"Later, okay?" I said quietly before returning my attention to Sadie.

"We just wanted to thank you. No one has ever protected us like that…none of us have property patches, we know our role and where we rank. But we like this life, and we like this club. So, thank you for standing up for us."

Tess stepped up and threw her arms around me. "You're our girl, Laura. Whatever you need, we got you."

Jasmine was next, looking a little misty-eyed. "He could have killed us if he wanted to. Everyone seemed so scared of him…but not you. I've never seen anyone storm out there like they weren't afraid of anything. It was like, even if he shot you, you didn't care."

Killian made a sound from behind me, but I ignored him. This feeling in my gut, this exhilaration, it was the best feeling I'd ever had. It was as though those moments growing up in my parent's circles, with the vicious debutantes and upper class who always gossiped and made me feel less than, was all being covered in one proverbial bandage. One made of leather, denim and loyalty. This was where I fit. Where I wanted to fit. For the first time since arriving, I didn't feel like I was riding on

Callie's coattails, or just existing in the background. I felt seen. More than that, I felt wanted.

"Thank you," I whispered back, hoping each girl understood how much their gratitude meant to me, "I'll always have your backs too."

Pulling away, I saw them each smiling at me and then waving. "We gotta go get some rest before our shifts tonight, but we'll see you later."

I knew they all worked as dancers in the neighboring town, Pyle. I hated that Strings, the closest strip club, was so far away, and from what I understood, it was in Raider territory, which made it especially dangerous for them, knowing they chose to spend their time here with Stone Riders.

A warm hand suddenly found mine, fingers lacing through mine. Killian was gently tugging me behind him.

I tried to ignore how good his hand felt and how safe it made me feel with his imposing stature in front of me, and his broad back shielding me. He was a force of nature, and I was merely a dandelion, at risk of losing myself to him.

We exited the club, veering for the apartment. The early dawn stretched across the sky with streaks of gold and a lingering layer of fog. It was beautiful and made my breath hitch. I was curious about which members were already up, wanting to talk to Killian. I had yet to see anyone aside from Giles, the kitchen crew and Sweetbutts.

"Where is everyone?" I decided to ask out loud.

Killian grunted, then peered over his shoulder without letting me go, "Probably in the garage, there's a bunk house in there for the Riders from out of town. They're usually the ones who are thirsty for a fight, more so than the locals."

"Aren't you worried they'll go off on their own while you're talking to me?"

His eyes found mine again as we approached the steps to the apartment.

"If they do then they don't belong in this club. Silas will take care of them, and it will be one less job for me."

Damn that seemed cold. But I was starting to understand the dynamics of how this club and others worked.

Killian unlocked the door, and we moved inside, letting the quiet wash over us.

The apartment was exactly how I left it last night. Still fully furnished with Killian's things, and fresh with the feeling of betrayal.

"Okay we're here," I said with a loud, exaggerated sigh.

Killian ignored me and made his way upstairs, still carrying my duffel.

Frustrated, I followed him, unsure of what he was going to do with my stuff.

Once I cleared the top of the stairs and made my way into his room, I saw that he was in the closet.

I caught sight of him opening a drawer then letting it slide shut.

"Are you…" I began but paused at the sight of him emptying my bag. "I appreciate what you're doing, but I'm actually just going to have to pack it right back up. So, feel free to toss it on my suitcases."

He paused mid movement, then slowly turned toward me.

"Why are you going to have to pack it right back up?"

The wild expression on his face told me he already knew, but he was going to make me say it regardless.

Lifting my shoulder the slightest bit, I assessed the massive closet instead of his demanding stare. "Found a place in town. Guy said I can move in today."

His face dipped as a sardonic laugh left him. The duffel dropped to the ground, and then he faced me.

"Fuck it. This has gone far enough."

My brows crowded my forehead as I tried to work out his words. What had gone far enough?

His body shifted suddenly, prowling toward me like a predator.

"You aren't leaving. If you try, I'll just bring you back here, every fucking night if I have to. If you want to try sleeping downstairs again, I'll just show up and crawl into bed with you. And if I find out you ever tried to sleep in another member's room, I'll kill him then burn his bed for good measure."

I backed up, too confused to even realize I was retreating toward the bed.

"But…you took Natty—"

Killian tossed his jacket on the floor, then gripped the hem of his shirt and pulled it over his head, which made my brain short circuit.

I'd had this man inside me, and while I knew Killian had copious amounts of ink on his body, highlighting his washboard abs and broad chest. What drew me up short was the odd tattoo over his heart.

How had I missed that the other night?

"I took Natty because the leader of a rival club needed to speak to her. It couldn't be done at the club, and it had to be where I could watch their conversation from afar. I offered her my jacket, so she'd feel safe, considering she hadn't been on the back of a bike in several years. Her situation is unique and required a different set of rules. Natty has been in this club for years, and we've never had anything more than a platonic—almost sibling—like relationship. Me extending my jacket was similar to me offering it to my sister to make sure she felt secure. And as you saw, she's pretty much been claimed by Silas in some fucked-up way."

My breathing came in tiny sporadic spurts as understanding began to settle in my heart like a warm blanket.

Killian stepped closer, flicking the button of his jeans, which made them rest low on his hips. I could see the band of his black boxers, and the delicious muscles contracting as he walked.

I retreated a step until the backs of my legs hit the bed. My eyes went to that strange tattoo over his heart. I'd never been close enough to him on lake days, or anytime I saw him without his shirt to make out what this tattoo was. I tried to rack my brain for the last time I saw him shirtless, and whether or not he had it.

"I told you already...there wasn't anyone but you, Daisy. I meant it. I fucked you, thought maybe that would have cleared things up for you, but I guess not."

He was furious. I nearly winced at the way his voice shuddered and the hurt that leaked into his tone.

My gaze dipped again, my fingers aching to trace the figure on this chest.

Killian's eyes dipped to his chest. "What?"

"Is that a...flower?" I pointed at the tattoo.

It looked like...I didn't want to assume but it looked like a *daisy*.

Killian's face flushed, and I could see him hesitate. His heel retracted the smallest bit and his brows cinched in tight, as if he were reconsidering whatever he was about to do.

Panicked, I reached out and grabbed his wrist, eager to have him look at me again.

As soon as those green eyes landed on me, it was like something had fractured between us. I was desperate for him in a way that I hadn't ever been. It was as though I was seeing behind the ink and muscle, the bones and blood that made him up, down to the piece of his soul that was surprisingly good and whole.

Not wanting to talk myself out of it, I lifted on my toes and pressed my lips to his.

I chose to believe him, and more so...trust him.

He responded immediately, bringing his hand to the front of my neck and loosely gripping me while his mouth moved savagely over mine.

My arms were up, wrapping around his neck, my fingers burrowing into his hair and his free hand moved down to my jeans, pulling the button free. Then his mouth was gone, his chest heaving as he gripped the edge of my sweater and pulled it up over my head. My bra was unclasped and tossed to the ground as his mouth returned to my neck, where he'd been holding me.

Sloppy, desperate kisses landed against my throat, and moved down my body until his eyes were tipped up, watching me as his tongue slowly traced my nipple. I moaned, pushing my fingers through his dark hair as he continued to watch me through his half-lidded gaze. He sucked my nipple, lapping at it slowly as though it was a meal he'd been desperate for. Then with a growl, his hands came to my ribs, and he picked me up and tossed me onto his bed.

"Fuck. The way I've needed you—" He broke off in a rasp before bringing his strong fingers to my jeans and pulling them down my legs. They were tossed behind him, then he was staring down at the lace covering my bare mound.

Our eyes met, and his mouth slowly came down on mine again as he pulled the fabric at my hips until it was ripping. I was insatiable for him, and the way he'd said he needed me kindled a fire inside, forcing it to burst. I moved, getting to my knees and cradling his jaw as we began kissing again.

His hands roamed over my skin, moving down to my ass where he cupped my cheeks, pulling me impossibly closer to him. I wanted him out of his clothes, like he'd done to me, so I pushed his jeans down, and then he fell back onto the bed and I moved down his long, lean body.

"Fuck, Daisy." He breathed, watching as I pulled on the band of his boxers and pulled his erection free. He was long, thick and gloriously veined.

I smiled, while gripping the base of him, then very slowly pulled the tip of his cock into my mouth, swirling my tongue over the metal piercing.

He moaned above me, his hand was digging into my hair, pulling as I took more of him into my mouth. His hips began to thrust, which forced more of his throbbing length down my throat.

I heard him hiss as he pushed my head down, fucking my mouth in steady thrusts.

"Look at how you choke on my cock, Daisy."

I ached for him to fuck me, for him to touch me. As if he could read my mind, he suddenly pulled my mouth free and with a feral gleam in his eye, he sat up and pulled my arm.

"Get your ass over here. I want to taste this pussy while you take me."

On my knees, I moved so that my hips were near his face, and then his hands were on them, pulling me over him so that I was facing the door. My knees went on either side of his face, my toes going to the headboard behind him. His fingers slid through my pussy, spreading me wide for his tongue to sweep in and taste all of me.

So good.

I moaned, placing my hands on his stomach while he expertly devoured me. Hooking his arms over the backs of my thighs, he pulled me, delving deeper with his tongue. I ground down, rotating my hips to fuck his face. Finally, I leaned forward to pull his cock back into my mouth. I sucked and lapped at the tip while he gripped my ass.

Rocking my hips against his face, I bobbed my head, taking his length as deep as I possibly could. The depth made me choke, which he seemed to love. His groans reverberated through my clit, making my climax coil inside me like a lit fuse. The more I took of him, letting the tip of his swollen cock hit the back of my throat, the more he groaned into my sex.

Until finally, I squeezed the base of his shaft and slowly stroked up while lowering my face. Suddenly, his abs constricted, and his hand came down on the back of my head. I was still fastened to his mouth like a fucking meal, but his chest curved inward, which allowed him a better angle for his hand to push against the back of my head, making me take even more of him, and then I felt it.

His hot release shot down my throat as he groaned loudly. His tongue swept over my clit, latching onto it and sucking as hard as he could. I came so hard, I saw stars and tiny lights bursting behind my closed eyelids. My breathing was ragged, and I couldn't help it, my mouth opened on a scream, mid swallow, allowing some of his release to slide back down his length and dribble down my chin. He was breathing hard, and I let up on his length, slowly licking the ribbons of release from his tip.

"Fucking shit, that was the best thing I've ever felt in my life." Killian rasped, falling onto his back.

I smiled, rolling off him because my legs were weak. That orgasm had ripped through me like a tidal wave, stronger than any I'd ever had in my life, and it wasn't enough. I was already craving more of him.

As if he needed it too, he moved with me until he was braced on his forearms. His thumb came down on my bottom lip while he searched my face. I could feel him getting hard again, the tip of him already nudging my entrance.

He was about to say something when suddenly there was someone pounding on the front door. His head dipped in defeat as he waited for who I was sure would prove to be Giles. Because that guy had the worst fucking timing.

Sure enough, the door opened, and we heard him call up.

"Prez?"

I smiled up at Killian with a dopey smile. He returned it, stroking my jaw, pushing strands of hair off my face.

"Prez, it's important. You need to come out here and calm these fuckers down," Giles warned, his voice echoing up through the house.

Killian continued to stare down at me while frustration tugged at his features, and he finally called back, "I'll be down in a second, wait outside!"

A second later, the door had closed, and we were alone again.

"Such a fucking mess for me."

I rocked into his hand, already feeling worked up again, but he only groaned and brought his fingers to his mouth, sucking away the taste.

"Fuck, can't wait." He seized me in his arms and suddenly my chest was on the bed, my ass up. His palm landed against my left cheek, and then he soothingly stroked it before adjusting us so that he was positioned right behind me.

"You need to be reminded of what I said." He pulled my arms back and gripped my wrists as he thrust inside me in one harsh push.

"Oh god." I moaned as he pulled out and then entered me again.

"I don't know how much clearer I can make this, but you will be in my bed tonight, Daisy. Don't make me come find you because no matter where you go, I'll follow."

He began fucking me slowly, pulling on my wrists. The burn in my arms, coupled with the feel of him sliding in and out of me was so good that all I could do was moan and beg for him to take me harder.

Our skin slapped together as he released my wrists and suddenly gripped my hips with force, groaning as he lifted me higher and angled us so his cock slid deeper inside me.

"Prez!" Giles called again from downstairs.

"Scream for me, Daisy. Tell him exactly who's fucking you." He jolted forward, pulling my hips back. "Tell him who you belong to."

I broke, shattering completely with an orgasm so intense that stars edged in along my vision, all while my voice cracked screaming his name.

"That's right." He slowed his thrusts as he groaned, and I knew he was spilling inside me again. My limbs were made of honey and heat, completely loose and lifeless as I worked to catch my breath. He pulled out, cursing as his hands swept through the mess leaking from my slit.

"I'll never get tired of seeing that."

I made some humming sound and stretched out on the bed. I knew I was making a mess of the covers as his release slid from me. He continued to swipe at it and then rub it against my ass, while muttering curses. Then his lips were on my back, his tongue sweeping up my spine.

"Don't leave me again."

His words were a tiny puzzle piece locked away in my chest.

This man had claimed me; patch or not, I belonged to him. I knew it in my marrow, the framework of my bones and my very being were now stained with him. There was no escaping him.

I watched him pull on his boxers and his jeans. His bare back was to me, and I wanted to trace the gorgeous animal that was inked there. The wolf with dazzling blue eyes, not green. Something in my chest seemed to kickstart at the way those blue eyes moved me while I continued to watch him dress. His boots came on next and then his hoodie. His cut came over his shoulders, the back saying his name, The Wolf, then under that, Killian Quinn—President. Stone Riders MC. Virginia.

I had memorized the words but watching him go made me ache in a new way. I didn't want him to. I wanted him to come back to bed to touch and hold me. I wanted more of his secrets and to see more of who he was under that leather that covered his chest, and the stone that resided inside it. It felt like he'd cracked his ribs open for me and showed me inside where his heart lay.

I was greedy enough to want my fingers wrapped around that organ. When he breathed, I wanted to feel it. When he hurt, I wanted to soothe it. When he bled, I wanted to as well.

Shit, I was in love with him. I'd never had these feelings for anyone in my life.

And fuck were they dangerous.

Once Killian left, I decided to head back down to the club and tuck away in the office. The lighting in this room was brilliant, so I'd started bringing in plants to hang out on the window sill. I had been using the office, even after being relieved of shredding information, but it didn't stop me from becoming nosey and trying to see if I could glean any more information about why Killian had taken the job from me.

I looked around, ensuring no one was about to walk in, and I tugged the drawer that held all the off-limit files. It was locked, just as I had suspected, but there were a few loose manila files left on top that caught my attention.

I picked one up, realizing it didn't have any marks. I tilted it so I could read the label, but that was blank too.

With hesitant fingers, I pulled the rubber band from around the file and pressed my thumb on the inside panel to prop it open.

They were drawings.

Picking one up, I inspected the artwork with a bit of a confused expression.

The drawings were done in reverse, the page completely shaded with graphite, but outlined objects were made with what looked like an eraser. It was so detailed and mesmerizing. My finger followed one of the circles around the page and then chased another line that twisted into what looked like a vine. The entire thing looked like something you'd find in an adult coloring book.

Intricate designs, all in shades of gray.

I flipped to the next page and found a similar drawing. Then another, this one of a motorcycle—still utilizing the same medium of pencil and drawing in objects with the eraser. After flipping through a few more, I finally froze when a familiar looking flower appeared.

It matched Killian's tattoo.

Were these his drawings?

"There you are!" Red burst into the room without knocking.

I jumped, letting the page slip from my fingers.

Red's gaze followed the page and then inspected what I was doing.

"He's been doing those since before I can remember."

She shut the door behind her and moved over until she was standing next to me. She saw the flower, and I noticed how her brows pinched as she gathered the drawings into her hands.

"This one was rather special, if I remember right."

Something in my chest tightened. "Why was it special?"

I had stupidly assumed he'd gotten the daisy inked for me...but it was lighter than his other tattoos. Faded as though he'd had it for a long time, so it wasn't done on my behalf.

Her gaze remained on the art. "I can't recall. I just remember it had to do with a really difficult time in his life. He started drawing daisies when he was ten…or maybe it was eleven. Started being the only thing he ever drew. It was around the time his mom left, and then his dad was put away."

Why would a daisy mean so much to him? Seemed like such an odd thing to grow attached to.

"Killian was such a romantic when he was young. Took after his mother in that way. She was always jotting down poems on her wrist and hand, on the back of Jefferson's cuts too." Red giggled, getting lost in her memories.

"What happened to his mother?" My voice was soft, terrified it would be something as horrible as what Jefferson did.

Red let out a gentle sigh when she finally stood up and handed me the drawing.

"No one really knows. She was here…and then one day, she was gone. She left Killian a note, but I wouldn't know what it said. He took it hard, being only nine at the time. He loved his mother, more than anything. Then only a year later, he was abandoned again."

"Then Simon took him in?" I drew my own conclusions based off what I knew.

Red nodded. "Anyway, that's all-ancient history. Simon used to keep these drawings, said they were good for Killian. He had a hard time speaking when he was young, drawing was his outlet."

"But he didn't draw…he—"

"Erased." Red finished for me, spearing me with a look.

We stayed locked in a staring contest for too long before she finally broke away.

"I'd say there was something to that, but I'm no psychologist. A broken boy who likely witnessed atrocious things, who utilized the ability to erase as a form of art. Poetic if you ask me." She lifted her shoulder, then continued staring at me.

"I don't know anything about you, Laura. Except that Callie vouches for you, and what I've seen since you got here. But who you were before that, I don't know."

My mind raced. Was she accusing me of something, or was she just curious?

"Only reason I bring it up is, he's going to give you a property patch. You'll be a part of this club. If you have any skeletons in the closet, you might want to tell him. He doesn't do well with surprises." She let out a sigh, while walking over to the plants. Her fingers brushed over the leaves in a soothing gesture.

"You've started sprucing this office up," she stated.

I looked around, realizing she was right. I hadn't even noticed how many small effects were my touch. The calendar, white monitor and keyboard, wireless mouse and clear pen holder. There was a gold stapler and an organized stack of post-its. On the back wall was a cute bohemian style message board with cute matching pins, and a few reminders in place.

There were the plants, the new speaker, and even the cute chair I had found in the old storage shed that I had reupholstered.

"You suit him. I'm glad that you're here and I'm proud of what you did for those girls last night. No one gives much stock to those girls being here, but they bring life into this place just like the president does, or anyone else."

I knew she was right, but to me it was simply that they were people, not Sweetbutts or property or anything else.

"I just see them as people."

Red walked over and placed her hand on my shoulder, peering down at me. "You'll stop after a while. Not that it'll make you a bad person, but after so many years, you stop having the luxury of seeing beyond the structure we have in place. It keeps us safe and helps bring meaning to what we do."

"He told me to leave these for you. Just wanted to be sure you got them. After an attack like we had, I have a feeling he'll be gone for a bit."

I reached out and accepted the keys to Killian's truck, feeling like someone had just shoved a lit candle into my chest. He left me his truck to drive while he was gone.

I smiled and then took out three of his drawings and set them aside.

TWENTY
KILLIAN

"You really couldn't have handled that without me?" I asked, not looking over at my VP.

Dealing with the members who wanted to fight the Death Raiders took all morning. It was time I didn't have and an argument I shouldn't have had to sort.

The gravel crunched under Giles's feet as he followed me. Before long, we were in the club, heading in through the church doors.

"Sorry Kil, they were insistent."

I spun around, anger piercing my tone. "Then fucking put them in their place, Giles. That is your job as vice president. They will listen to you, or you will make them listen to you. You've been asking me to handle the Laura shit for weeks and I finally do it, and you fucking interrupt me."

Giles paled, a wince working into his features. "Sorry…"

A strange feeling twisted around in my gut—something like exhaustion. The club was all I cared about my whole life, and now all I wanted was my vice president to be capable of dealing with shit so I could fuck my…

Old lady…never had one of those before, it was the only term I'd ever give to any relationship I *would* ever have, and yet the term didn't feel significant enough to describe what I felt for Laura.

I could feel her deeper than that.

But walking around calling her my soulmate might be a little too much.

"So, what's the plan with paying Silas a visit?" Giles asked, pulling me from my thoughts.

I let out a sigh and grabbed my phone. Wes had texted he was on his way.

"We wait for Wes to get here; he'll be going with me."

Giles left his features neutral, but I could tell he was pissed. "I want you here, to make sure things go okay. You need to establish a presence here. Let people ask you what to do, let them know you're in charge. Besides, I have an idea and I'll need your help to pull it off."

He nodded, digging his thumbnail into the wood of the table.

A moment later, the church doors opened, and Callie and Wes walked in.

Callie looked around as if she were looking for Laura, her brows dipped when she didn't see her.

"So nice of you two to join us. Callie, did your husband tell you that your best friend was held at gunpoint last night?"

Callie's face flung sideways, her glare snagging on her husband.

"What?!"

Wes didn't so much as flinch. He just stared at me, crossing his arms over his chest.

"Wes?"

"I didn't fucking do it, Silas did," he argued, and fuck that was the wrong thing to say.

She stepped into his line of sight. "But you didn't tell me!"

"We were on a trip, River. Would have stressed you out." He was calling her by her nickname now, which meant he was trying to correct his fuck up.

"A trip where?"

Callie finally turned and let out a sigh. "I'm still following some leads on that blogger activist stuff. Especially after the incident the other day. I just wanted to look into something, but it was a dead end."

"You need to run that shit by me, Cal," I said, flicking my gaze to her and then to Wes.

He nodded, dipping his head. Callie only glared at me. "You know my response to that, *Kil*. Fuck the club, and fuck you if that's how you're going to treat me." She flipped me her middle finger, then moved around the table. "Now, I am going to go find Laura and check on my friend."

She got as far as the doors when I called out, "Silas made a deal with you, right?"

Wes had told me that was one reason he was off-limits to us, because while Wes was unconscious after Silas helped save his life, he made a deal with her to gain protection.

She slowly spun around; her eyes narrowed. "Yes."

"He broke it by taking Laura. Wes and I are going to him to straighten shit out. Wanted you to know."

She lifted her chin and then let her hands fall. "Our agreement was that Natty would stay safe, but I had no idea I had to clarify that my best friend would also be on that list of keeping safe."

"Wait, you knew about Natty?" I leaned in, a little curious now.

She pursed her lips. "I mean I assumed. She acted too weird when we confronted her all those months ago. He was acting weird too. I just sort of connected the dots. But was it confirmed?"

I nodded. "Last night he threatened Laura because we allowed Natty to talk to Jameson King. Said we put her in harm's way."

"Fuck." Wes groaned, hanging his head.

He understood just how bad this was. Silas had already threatened us once, regarding some mysterious person associated with the club. We had no idea then who he was talking about, but now there was no question.

"Also, just a head's up. We may be taking in a pregnant Chaos Kings' property patch. She's been fucked over by the VP in the club, and the club is trying to force King to remove her."

Callie gasped. "While knocked up with the VP's baby?"

I nodded.

"King said she's been around since she was a teenager, they all knew her. But the VP wants nothing to do with her or becoming a dad. Club is the only home she's ever known. He doesn't mind setting her up somewhere else, but he's worried about her safety. Feels like only another club would actually keep her safe from the Chaos Kings."

"We'll take her!" Callie offered, as though the decision was up to her.

"I said as much, not sure where we're going to put her, but we'll figure it out."

Callie put her hand on her stomach. "So that's why Natty had to talk to Jameson…"

"He wanted to make sure it was safe here," Wes finished for her, looking up and sharing a meaningful look with his wife.

"Do what you have to do with Silas, just be careful, and can I talk to Natty and see if she'll share any more details with me about him? Because if he's secretly important to her then I don't want to kill him or anything."

I stared at the ground for a moment, thinking over why Natty would cover for him. I caught how she looked at him last night, why not just tell us he was a bad guy when we asked about him three months ago?

Didn't make any sense.

"Yeah, go ahead and see what you can find out. Take Laura with you, she's friends with her, and I know Natty has to feel something about Silas taking Laura and holding her hostage."

"Got it." Callie waved us off and left through the church doors.

Wes stared at me. I stared back. We'd had a rocky few weeks as I transitioned into this role. Well longer, because it hurt like hell that Simon Stone had chosen him as President, instead of me. But it wasn't his fault, and I knew I had to stop holding him accountable for it.

"Ready?"

Wes nodded, then pulled on his leather jacket with his patches and colors indicating he was still an active member of the Stone Riders MC. Made me proud as hell to see his name stitched into that leather, knowing his past and how unlikely it was for him that he'd ever join in the first place. Now he was here, with the club, and had the only woman he ever wanted, with a baby on the way. I was happy for him.

So happy it finally helped me put a few things into perspective.

"Let's ride, brother." I slapped his back and we exited the club.

"Do you have the cameras in place?" I asked as Wes drove the old truck down the dirt road. This truck had no plates, and it was one we liked to use when we were doing something we didn't want traced back to us.

Wes nodded. "Callie has no idea though so if it comes back on us, you're taking the blame."

"Noted," I mused, watching the landscape change.

Pyle had less river and more fields, way less foliage, and more power plants. We passed Strings, and I inwardly cringed. Their strip club was shitty and needed a new paint job. I'd honestly considered starting one in Rose Ridge, especially for the girls who were attached to our club, so they weren't in Raider territory, but we were already in enough hot water as it was with the local businesses and I didn't need a reason for the government to come snooping.

"I heard Laura's a bit of a hero…at least to the Sweetbutts."

I glanced over at my best friend, unsure of how much to share. I was still upset he hadn't come back in time, but considering his wife's rig was nearly caught on fire, I decided to give him a pass.

"Apparently she went toe to toe with The Roman on behalf of them."

Wes stared straight ahead, then started laughing.

"You told her how you feel?"

I smiled, shaking my head. "I told her enough."

"I want to know how that went." Wes was still laughing as he turned down another dirt road, which would lead us to the farm.

"She knows to be in my bed every night."

My best friend tossed his head back, laughing loudly. "Well, good for you man, so you're putting your patch on her?"

"Something like that." My gaze returned to the window, needing to steer this conversation somewhere else. The idea still felt like I was placing a spotlight on her, a dinner bell for anyone who wanted to hurt her.

I needed to tell Wes who Laura was.

The longer I kept it to myself the more dangerous the situation was becoming. I would after this, so we could stay focused.

We'd finally passed the city and were approaching a few farms. White fences stretched along the yellow weeds; the deep navy sky above made the farms look practically dead. Sasha and Simon's came up as we curved the road, their small cottage-style house, adjacent to a big red barn, gave the appearance that a happy couple lived here. Not a dying man and the woman he stole from a rival club.

Parking off the shoulder of the driveway, we exited quietly. Wes took his phone out and shot a text to Callie, and I did the same with Giles. Once he got a response back, he waved us forward. Callie was probably going to kill us both for doing this, but if Wes wasn't worried then I wasn't going to either.

Sasha was Silas' mother; they'd both been Death Raiders for years until Simon Stone, the leader of the Stone Riders, stole Sasha from them. They'd been together for nearly five years, until Simon passed...or so we assumed. Turned out, he was just being a devious, calculated prick. A dying one, but not dead. Simon being Callie's dad, and Sasha being Silas's mom, had put the rest of us at the very awkward disadvantage of having Sunday brunch together each week. I was invited because Callie and Simon considered me family. We had a truce each time we gathered; there were no patches or clubs...

Except today.

Today there'd be blood.

We made it around the house and to the back door when Simon met us. He looked tired, his usual hazel eyes were dim, his skin pale and his hair lackluster. His muscle mass was waning too; he nearly looked like a wraith standing in front of us with just a simple t-shirt, his leather cut, and blue jeans too loose on his hips.

"You have ten minutes. I told Sasha I wanted to walk through the greenhouse and check on the peppers we're growing. Once she's in there, I can usually keep her there for a while. Since no one else has arrived yet, I'm assuming Silas will just be on his phone, waiting."

He still assumed his daughter and her friend would be arriving. We were tricking him too, told him we only wanted to scare Silas a little, our old leader had no idea what was actually in store for Sasha's son.

We nodded and waited around the side of the house for a few more minutes until we saw Simon and Sasha walking toward the greenhouse.

Wes pulled up the footage for the camera on his cell and entered the house through the side door. I pulled a Glock out from the waistband of my jeans and kept it pointed down. Slowly making my way through the living room, clearing the dining room, I finally paused when we reached the foyer.

With his back to us, Silas was on the phone facing the door.

His black hair was slicked to the side like some villain from *Peaky Blinders*, and his Death Raider cut was layered over a black hoodie. I lifted my arms, aiming at him, and then pulled the hammer back, letting the click of the gun being armed fill the room.

The leader of the Death Raiders turned, lowering his phone.

I held out my hand for the device while keeping my gun on him.

He was about to lunge, but Wes was there, holding his phone up with the camera footage on it.

"I don't think so." The live feed played, showing Callie crossing her arms while talking to Natty. Laura was there too, and all three women looked pissed. There was no audio, so he had no idea what they were saying. What it looked like though was that we were holding Natty hostage, especially because the girls decided to talk in the cellar.

Silas had pale blue eyes, so pale they reminded me of something supernatural…like a ghost or a wraith. They were looking between Wes and me as though he wanted to rip our throats out.

His gaze slid to the window then back to us.

"Simon?"

"You threatened the Stone Riders, you stupid fuck, of course *Simon*," I said, barely holding my anger in check. I wanted to kill him, but Simon made me swear I wouldn't.

Silas's eyes flicked to the screen.

"If you hurt her, I have ways of enacting revenge from the grave."

"What is your fucked relationship with Natty? She acts like she doesn't even know you. Are you stalking her or something?" I asked, stepping closer.

He merely glared at me.

"Let's get him in the barn before Sasha comes back. We can't get any blood in here."

Wes pushed Silas forward, and he walked out through the front door and kept walking until we were inside the barn.

"You wanted an alliance, and instead of asking me why she was talking with Jameson King, you just attacked us. At our own club. You knew it would brew a war. What I want to know is why." I pushed him one last step, until he was at least ten feet from us, and our weapons were on him again.

Silas left his arms loose, keeping his gaze on the exits.

"I told you that I would bring war to your doorstep on her behalf."

Wes shook his head. "That's not what you said, and you know it. What the fuck is your situation with her?"

"None of your concern. All you need to know is it's my job to ensure she's safe."

Wes gave me a look, and I knew he was wondering the same thing. We needed to talk to Simon about the trade that happened for Natty all those years ago.

"You fucked up, Silas, because while you were protecting your girl, you took mine and put a gun to her head."

I nodded toward Wes. He grabbed his cell phone and made it to where Silas could see what was happening.

The girls were all still talking. Natty looked caged off with her arms crossed, and Laura was throwing her hands around as though she was yelling. In the corner through the door, Giles could be seen holding a gun.

"Fair is fair, right?" Wes asked.

Silas ground his back molars together as he watched then glared at me.

"I didn't hurt yours."

Cutting the space between us, I got nose to nose with him and screamed, "You held a motherfucking gun to her lips, asshole. You scared her."

Silas only scowled, acting completely unshaken.

Then with a sneer and a devilish smile, he said, "I would have gutted her in front of you if it meant you got the message to keep Natty safe."

I lost it. The back of my pistol swiftly flew into his face hard. Then I did it again until a gash opened up in his brow and blood began to pour.

"So then you understand why this little alliance is over." I hit him again, and now that he was on the ground, I kicked him. "And I plan on gutting *you* in front of Natty. Seems like she'll be pleased, considering she doesn't even give two shits about acknowledging your existence."

Wes clicked his tongue. "Maybe we should take one of Natty's fingers. Make it to where she can't bake those scones anymore...or you know what?" He snapped his fingers like he just got a great idea. "Hasn't Rune been watching her and asking about her. Perhaps we can allow him to take her as his old lady."

"Your club doesn't work like that. You fucking wouldn't." Silas seethed.

I got in his face again. "Oh, we would, motherfucker. You didn't just threaten my girl, you touched her. Put her in your lap and held a gun to her head. You have no idea what I'm going to fuck up for you. You want Natty out of the club? Now you're going to have to fight us for her. You just completely fucked all your chances of having her safe and unharmed."

Silas lashed out, getting to his feet and pushing me in the chest. "Your club doesn't fucking do this shit. It's part of your code. It's part of Simon's code."

I screamed in his face again. "That was before you touched what belongs to me. Simon was a fair leader. Wes was a balanced president, but me? I'm a motherfucking mad man, and when it comes to the people I love, I will not stop until you understand that you can't touch what's mine."

I ran a shaky hand through my hair then more calmly explained, "I liked Natty too, but now I know she's important to you. I want to hurt you, Silas. I want you to understand the fear I felt last night."

Silas was finally showing some semblance of emotion. His pale face became flushed, and his jaw looked like it was two seconds from breaking.

"You bet on the kindness of our club. And you just fucking lost."

I tossed a picture at him. I had it printed this morning, while I was waiting on Daisy in the club. It was of Jameson and Natty talking, the two of them laughing and smiling. They looked like a couple in the photo. I had a feeling it would enrage Silas, and sure enough, as he stared down at the image, rage painted his features in vibrant strokes.

He wasn't just angry; he was devastated.

Interesting.

As we turned to leave, I thought I saw a single tear fall from his lash. But I was probably wrong. Our job was to intimidate him and ruin him, so if he was fucked up emotionally then good.

As long as it meant he understood that he could never touch Laura again.

Would we actually hurt Natty? Not a fucking chance, but he didn't know that.

We were about to exit through the barn door when all the sudden Silas spoke up, still staring down at the picture.

"Wait."

Wes and I turned toward him.

"You're right. I led with anger and fucked up. I shouldn't have touched her. I'm sorry, Killian. I didn't know she was yours, but when the girls pushed her forward, I hoped she was important enough to get your attention. I was angry…and I'm willing to offer you intel as a way to make things right, so that *she* stays safe with your club."

I knew the "she" was Natty. He seemed to have a difficult time saying her name for whatever reason.

"What sort of intel?" Wes asked, stepping closer.

Silas crumpled the photo in his hand and squeezed his fist.

"The kind that proves I'm still a worthy ally."

TWENTY-ONE
LAURA

I needed a break.

Natty had initially wanted to clear things up regarding Killian, but the second I wanted an explanation regarding Silas, she froze. Callie and I had tried talking to her, reasonable and nice—we even went somewhere private so her business wouldn't be talked about. We asked Giles to watch the door, which he took really freaking seriously because at one point he walked inside with his gun drawn.

But no matter what, Natty wouldn't budge.

I had asked her about her relationship with Silas, and she played dumb. So I had to break out the big guns.

"I was literally kidnapped by him, set in his lap and held at gunpoint. When he was asked why, he mentioned your name," I had pointed out, but Natty just stared ahead as though we were crazy.

Her responses were: "No idea what you're talking about, and I've never heard that name before."

Callie and I looked at one another in frustration. Why was she protecting him, and if she wasn't then why was she playing into this? We needed more info. Callie mentioned that Sasha might know, so we decided to stop interrogating her and let her leave.

She was pissed, of course, and ran straight up to her room. I felt a tiny bit of guilt, especially because she had tears in her eyes, but at the same time, I was literally held at gunpoint because of her ex. Or her boyfriend…or whatever the fuck he was to her.

"I'm hungry," Callie said, rubbing her stomach.

I smiled, staring down at her hand. "You're starting to kind of show."

"Right?" she exclaimed excitedly. We both stared at her slim figure, moving our hands over the smallest, tiniest bump that was protruding from her stomach.

We walked to the apartment, and I knew Giles was close by, watching over us. That or Harris. Once I shut us inside, I locked the door, knowing Giles could still get in if needed.

"Let's see what Mr. President stocked in the house," I mused, pulling open a cupboard.

Callie took a seat on the stool, looking around.

"Wow, so he really moved in then?"

"He did."

I found dried pasta, bacon and some gouda cheese. "Want me to make some homemade mac n cheese?"

Callie leaned onto her elbows. "You know how to do that?"

Waving her off, I pulled up my phone. "No, but I'm sure there's a TikTok about it."

"How come it's not bothering you that he moved in?"

I laughed and started searching for a pot. "Oh, it did. You missed like a whole big blow up. But he also made a very big dominant show of not wanting me to leave, but then we had oral sex and…." I hesitated, realizing I had to finally come clean about everything.

"Just oral?" Callie's smile turned devious.

I bit my lip. "Not just oral."

Callie searched my face and then rounded the counter.

"Tell me, Laura Witt! Tell me right freaking now!"

Laughing, I pushed at her hands that were two seconds from pinching me.

"We have sort of been hooking up."

Her hazel eyes were round and massive. "When did this start?"

"Night we all had dinner together."

"But you were drunk." She tilted her head, concern tugging at her brows.

My hands came out as if I had any way of explaining.

"He didn't touch me."

"Oh. *Oh.*" Understanding dawned.

"Yeah…I sort of straddled the man and took what I wanted. But after that, he was just all over me, and everywhere. We've had a hard time keeping our hands off each other."

"Okay. Wow. This is a lot to process."

I nodded.

"How was the sex?" she whispered, a sly grin sliding over her features.

"I'll save you the sordid details, but best I've ever had. There was just one thing that sort of threw me off."

Callie went rummaging for a drink. Once she found a bottle of water, she leaned against the fridge. "Does he have a crooked dick?"

Bursting out in laughter, my chest practically vibrated at her random comment. "No. Not even a little, it's perfect and straight and thickkkkkk."

Her hands flew up to her ears. "Ewwww Ohmygosh, he's like my brother. Please stop."

Smiling victoriously, I pushed on, "He had this tattoo…it was very out of place with his others."

I started filling a pot with water, assuming that would get us closer to mac n cheese, when Callie's brows furrowed. "Is it the daisy?"

So it was a daisy then.

"Yes!" I spun to face her. "He wouldn't talk about it." I was fishing for information, and a part of me felt guilty, especially since Red had already given me so much. But I wanted more.

She waved me off. "He's had that forever. It was his first tattoo. I remember because my dad teased him about it."

That lined up with what Red had said. But why did he get it? What did it mean to him?

And if he'd had it for so long then why was it the nickname he'd given to me?

Callie started inspecting her phone, not paying attention.

"Hey Callie?" I was slightly off-kilter, my mind running a million miles a minute. Something told me he was saying something in his weird Killian language. Part of me wanted to curl into the gesture, whatever it was, and respond in kind. The other part of me wanted to keep him at arm's length, as far away from my heart as possible.

The two urges warred inside me, tugging at my entangled heart strings. Killian hadn't confessed anything to me; he hadn't made any promises or any vows. He'd merely told me to stay. But for him, I knew that was nearly as vulnerable as it would be for him to tug the organ out of his chest and then wear it on his sleeve.

Biting my lip, I slammed my eyes shut and blurted, "I want a tattoo."

Callie paused, her gaze sliding up to mine. She would never charge me for using my skin as a canvas, not when I was the first person to sign up when she needed practice. I could pay her; she just wouldn't accept it. No, we'd trade just like always. She smiled, still staring at her phone. "And I want my nursery painted."

Sly bitch. I couldn't help smiling at her cleverness. "Deal."

No questions were asked why I wanted it or what I wanted to get. She likely knew by now that my eagerness for ink was more like an addiction at this point.

She hopped off the counter. "Excellent. Should we ask if Natty would like to join us for an afternoon of ink and dessert?"

"Dessert?"

She tossed the corkscrew pasta aside. "Yes, at this rate, I'm going to starve."

"Touché. I have no idea what I'm doing."

We both laughed and then exited the apartment.

We stood in front of Natty's door, hoping she'd give us another chance. We were frustrated in our own way with how she responded, but we also respected her privacy and knew there had to be a reason she wasn't telling us anything.

Her door swung open after a minute or so. Her eyes held a sorrow that tugged at my chest in a painful way. She'd been crying, her eyes were red rimmed, and her mascara had run.

Callie stepped forward first. "We're sorry, Nat. Let us make it up to you."

Natty's gaze flicked over to me, and then her nose twitched as she sniffed. Her hair was still braided; little strands were frizzy, framing her face, but her raw beauty was still so striking. I often thought of Natty like a fairy-tale character or a Disney Princess. She was pretty in a way that didn't seem real. She didn't have pores, or pimples, or any scars that I could see. She had a few sparsely placed freckles, which only blended beautifully with her dark brows and lashes.

Her bowlike lips pursed as she considered what Callie was offering.

"Where are you going?"

Callie looked over at me, then returned to her. "I'm giving out tattoos, if you want one, of course. Laura is getting one, and we're hungry."

Natty glanced behind her and then let out a sigh.

"Only if Laura agrees to a girls' night at The Hollow and sings a song of our choice."

Callie slowly turned toward me, as my face nearly caught fire.

"What's she talking about?"

Natty looked between us, fresh panic on her face. "Oh my gosh, I'm so sorry. I didn't know—"

I shook my head. "It's fine. I was going to tell her, I just..."

"First, you hold out on details regarding Killian, and now this." Callie held up her hand, her mouth open, irritation leaking into her words.

"Let me grab my jacket and purse." Natty pulled us both inside and then shut the door behind us. Callie continued to stare at me.

"I have a difficult time sharing certain things, I'm sorry. Natty only knows because she showed up. I didn't tell her."

My best friend's hand moved to her slightly swollen stomach and let out a sigh.

"I get it. When I came back and was working through everything, there were tons of things I didn't share right away."

She brought me in for a hug, and then we started inspecting Natty's room.

The space was warm and cozy. With a small counter and sink, her humble kitchen looked similar to something you might find in a college dorm room, but it didn't seem to deter her from cooking. She had a dish rack with two plates, glasses and three pots drying inside.

Her living space had a smaller L-shaped couch with fuzzy cushions, and a small television rested on a white dresser. Her full-sized bed was directly behind her couch, and with several strings of fairy lights lit up, it made the space above her window glow. She had green vines trailing around her frame and up along the upper wall, which, mixed with the lighting, was so relaxing and cute.

I was half tempted to suggest we just hang out in her room, but I also wanted the tattoo.

Natty grabbed a red jacket from a coat rack, and then her small backpack purse came around her shoulders.

We exited the room, and I noticed Natty locked the door behind her. It seemed so odd to me that the club was her home, but also, she had managed to create a safe space for herself that seemed so opposite of the chaotic club below her room. A beautiful life that seemed happy. Like someone had handed her a knife and then given her full rein to carve out a world within these walls.

It made me glad for her and invigorated that maybe I too would carve out my own place here and belong.

Making our way outside and to Callie's car, we stopped first at the Shake Shack. Callie had worked at the small establishment as a teen, so we were regaled with stories and hilarious memories while we waited for our orders.

Once we had a ridiculous number of fries, three different flavors of shakes and burgers, we headed over to Dead Roses, the tattoo parlor. Since it was a slower night, there was only one other artist on shift, who was currently watching Netflix out front, waiting for any walk-ins.

Which left us alone in the back. We knew Harris and Giles were around, watching, but they weren't inside with us, which allowed us some privacy. I was shocked that Giles didn't stay behind and send someone else. When I asked, he merely smiled and said he was right where Killian wanted him. I could tell he was proud of that, and I felt… like I'd somehow become more precious than even his club.

We sat at the table in the break room with our food spread out. Natty got a veggie burger but attacked it with the same ferocity as my pregnant friend did with her beef patty.

"You decide on a name yet?" Natty asked around a bite of her food.

Callie took a sip of her shake then cleared her throat. "We're thinking about Ford."

"Ford Ryan?" I quirked a brow, teasing my friend so she wouldn't catch onto the fact that I had secretly wanted that name. I had left dozens of little post its around her house, in her purse, and in the club. To keep up the ruse, I'd suggest something that started with an L.

Her face flushed. "This is why I didn't want to tell you."

Natty started silently laughing while still chewing.

"What about Logan Ryan or Lee Ryan?"

Her hazel eyes rolled as she crinkled the paper for her burger. She'd already devoured it. "You need to let this L obsession go."

"Just promise me you'll name her after me when she turns out to be a girl."

Callie slid out of her chair and threw her dinner away. "I will do no such thing."

We all laughed, and as soon as Natty and I finished, we moved toward Callie's space.

"What are we designing today?" Callie asked me, while pulling out her sketchbook.

I was suddenly nervous as I considered what this would mean when her and Natty saw it. And more importantly, when Killian saw it.

"Here, let me sketch it." I grabbed her notebook.

Callie's attention went to Natty who was flipping through a book with previous designs.

She stopped and stared at one in particular and then slid it in front of my best friend.

"Can you do this, with the shading?"

Callie's brow furrowed as she studied it.

"Where do you want it?"

Natty drew closer then pointed at her chest. "Over my heart."

Curious, I peered over at the binder where Natty had found her image. The one she'd selected was a myriad of trees. Withered and dying trees, with twisted roots and bare branches. I wondered at its significance when Callie turned back toward me.

"We're going to start with you because it'll take me longer." She pulled on a pair of latex gloves and then started digging through her rolling desk of supplies.

"Between the shoulder blades?" she asked, while pulling on a pair of glasses.

I tugged my sweater off until I was just in a tank top. The back dipped to where my bra strap cut across my back, leaving my upper shoulders bare.

"Yep, right in the middle."

Callie made some sound and then let out a sigh. "Okay, now regarding the lettering..." I could hear the hesitation in her pause. "Are you sure you want it to say...that?"

At war with myself, once again, I had to shove down the fear and just push on.

"I'm positive."

There was no turning back now. This was going to thrust us into new territory, and I had no idea how it would end, but for the first time since meeting Killian, I was completely sure of what I wanted.

I was watching Callie's coworker finish up Natty's tattoo. The original plan was for Callie to do it, but my design took well over an hour to complete, and my beautiful, pregnant friend was tired. Trey, Callie's coworker, was a nice guy with massive arms and a goatee he'd died pink. Natty seemed to warm up to him, considering they'd been chatting peacefully for the past forty-five minutes.

I was scrolling through my phone, trying to ignore the fact that Killian hadn't texted me. I wasn't sure what I had expected. We'd had a moment this morning, and sure, I technically slept in his arms last night, but it wasn't like he offered me a property patch or said we were dating now.

It made me feel foolish, thinking he might reach out to me at some point during the day. I didn't like feeling this way, and the longer I went without hearing from him, the more I realized how unacceptable it was that I was merely waiting on him to be the first to reach out.

So, gathering my bottom lip between my teeth, I texted him.

> Me: Running a little late, did you eat already?

It was already past seven, and part of me wondered why he wasn't curious where I was yet.

I watched the screen, seeing that he'd read the message and was now about to respond. The dots on the screen bounced and then stopped.

When nothing else came through, I decided to navigate over to the tab I still had open for available rentals in Rose Ridge. It was habit now. It was also hard to convince my brain of what Killian had said about following me wherever I went and not letting me out of his bed. I wanted to think that meant relationship, but I was too scared to trust that notion. I browsed through one-bedroom rentals, I was also listening to Natty talk about her tattoo with Trey.

"Why a forest of dead trees?" he asked, while his hand moved in a steady motion over her chest.

Her gaze was up on the ceiling, her ankles crossed, and overall, she looked cozy and comfortable. With a sigh, she quietly answered, "It's sort of complicated. It's the dark woodland, like a cursed forest…but a forest just the same. It represents someone I know…someone that is a part of my life, even if I don't want him to be."

Trey stayed quiet and the buzzing from the gun stayed consistent. Callie was cleaning up her space, and then I heard Trey ask.

"Sounds like maybe it's someone you should forget. They hurt you?"

Natty shook her head. "Never."

Then with a contemplative look, she expanded, "There was this movie when I was a kid that I watched…it was about this man who was in love with this woman, but she was cursed and turned into a hawk every night, and he a wolf. It made it so the two could never be together, even if they only loved each other and all they wanted was a life together. They knew because of the curse it was impossible. That's how it is with him. We have this curse between us, this thing that will always keep us apart."

Trey wiped up the ink as he continued moving his gun over her chest. The dark lines against her fair skin were oddly mesmerizing.

I was so entranced in her story about this person who was her dark forest when my phone vibrated with a text.

> Killian: Something came up. I'll be back in a few days. Giles is going to shadow you whenever you leave. Please use my truck while I'm gone. Don't walk anywhere alone, that includes around the property line.

I stared feeling my heart flutter and my stomach swoop.

Instead of replying, I tucked my phone back into my purse and peeked back over at Natty. Her dead forest was nearly finished when Trey must have asked a new question that I had missed because Natty was still sharing with him more than she ever had with me or Callie.

"He *is* dangerous. I don't pretend he's not; it's part of why we're not together. He would never hurt me, but he would very seriously burn the world down on my behalf. He's all fire and fury. But somewhere, down deep—" She trailed off, flicking her gaze in my direction.

I wasn't fast enough, so I stared back at her. I wanted her to know I was a safe space, but I also knew she was too guarded to trust me. Still, this story she told of this man who loved her…it touched some place inside me that was starved for that sort of obsession. For someone on this planet to love me that way, to want me like that.

A flush crept up my face as embarrassment sunk into my chest. I had assumed that would come from Killian, but my gut told me it wouldn't. Maybe for once I'd be wrong. I had no idea if Natty saw my face or had the sense to know what I was thinking of after the brand I'd put on my back, but her next words felt like they were just for me.

"We write each other letters. We don't add our names or address it to one another. It's just this phantom idea that one day our curse will be lifted. It's been years since I've felt his touch, but he finds other ways of getting through to me. Sometimes it's the lack of words, and the things they don't do that we need to pay attention to. Sometimes these creatures of darkness only know how to show their love by not bringing their demons around us. With him, I understand that. His fire would burn me; all I want is to live in peace, but he's war."

My phone buzzed again, and I pulled it free to see Killian had texted again.

> Killian: I texted you, Daisy. Text me back, that's how this relationship thing goes.

I fought a smile and lost.

> Me: Wasn't aware we were in one.

His text came back almost immediately.

> Killian: Guess I have to convince you again. It's fine really, I enjoy reminding you.

Callie was cleaning up her station, and Natty was finally getting wrapped.

> Killian: You want an official request, or will you just accept wearing my name on your back?

He had no idea. I heaved a sigh.

> Me: So I have to be called an old lady then?

> Killian: You do. You ready for that?

I didn't even have to think about it.

> Me: I've been ready.

His texting stopped after that, but it still left me with a steady warmth cradling my heart, and something I thought I'd lost began to form.

Hope for a future here, to belong somewhere. To belong to him.

Perhaps this time it would actually last.

Something sinister whispered in the back of my mind, *don't bet on it.*

TWENTY-TWO
LAURA
THREE MONTHS AGO

I was standing on a bus platform, watching as people loaded up their bags and suitcases into the undercarriage of the greyhound. Killian had loaded my things without me even asking. Which was fine.

I wasn't going to pretend like the night prior hadn't happened, and by the looks he continued to give me, perhaps he wouldn't either. The way he'd hesitate before saying he just wanted a chance to fuck me before I left…there was something broken in me because why did I want to call his bluff? That desire right there was why I needed to go. It was better this way. I was leaving before getting into some complicated and confusing relationship with this biker who seemed too angry and confused for his own good.

I knew about baggage, and Killian had a ton of it.

When Callie hugged me and said her goodbyes, Killian stepped up.

I was toe to toe with this giant of a man, this larger-than-life person who somehow got under my skin within a matter of days and was now going to be a stain on my memory, and maybe even my heart. He was staring at me like he was thinking the same thing. Like I'd dug too far into his chest, too soon, and without any permission. We didn't go on a date. He hadn't brought me flowers or told me I was beautiful.

He was mean and cold.

And different.

Still, when he handed me the tiny pebble, my heart thundered as swiftly as a racehorse gunning for the winning lap. He didn't have to say anything. I understood the gesture from what he'd told me while we were playing Truth or Dare, but then he did open that gorgeous mouth, those too soft lips parted, and he laughed, pinning his forehead to mine.

"You nearly got me, Daisy. Had me tripping up, and just like my mom always said, it's the smallest acts that can bring a person down. I'm giving you this as a reminder."

I swallowed past the lump in my throat. The feeling that was growing in me, too big, too wide, as though Killian hadn't handed me a tiny rock, but instead a piece of his heart.

"Reminder of what?" I left our foreheads trapped together, my breath coming in and out too quick.

Killian's hand came up around my back, stroking down my spine.

"A reminder of what a single pebble can do. One kiss. A pretty face. Someone who seemed to match me in nearly every way. It's a reminder not to fall. You were a gift, and I'm glad you're leaving because if you stayed, you'd ruin me."

The intercom for the bus came to life, alerting me that my bus was about to depart.

We separated, and Killian took a step back.

I tried to take in his vest, the colors and patches, the way his name was sewn into the soft leather. The howling wolf head that was stitched into the shoulder. The way the dark leather made him look like he was one of Death's agents, here on earth, to distribute life sentences.

Blinking, I turned and climbed onto the bus and took my seat, without looking out my window. The pebble in my hand might as well be gold for how tightly I protected it. Every second that we idled there on the platform made my stomach churn because I knew he hadn't left yet.

Sure enough, right as we began to pull forward, I allowed myself one last look. And there he stood with a look on his face that I'd stash away forever. Jaw clenched tight, eyes narrowed and focused on my window, he looked as though he was about to break into a run and chase after me.

He looked as though he was holding himself back.

He looked like he maybe wanted to love me, and if I stayed...well, maybe I would have learned to love him back.

It was the second day of being back in DC when I received his text.

The one that changed the trajectory of everything. Because while I was back in my apartment, wearing my clothes and working at my various jobs—nothing felt the same. There was this odd feeling in the pit of my stomach that I couldn't shake. It wasn't simply because the city now felt empty without my best friend in it, but it was like there was this echo of something I could have had.

But I'd let it go.

It seemed to scream at me in all different manners that something in my life was missing or gone.

I'd get up, go to work. Eat lunch.

Missing.

Go back to work and try so very hard to fall back into the role I had once played in this life I never seemed to connect with. I'd left home in hopes that I would find somewhere that fit me. A place that would feel like home. DC had never felt that way, not once.

Something was missing.

My mother called me, reminded me I needed to come home soon. I nodded along, like always, but this time I knew I wouldn't be headed over to Callie's house afterward to dish about how unbelievable my parent's demands were. This time I would go back home, hide in my room and stare at a small pebble.

Gone.

The echo worsened with each day, and with every single one, I would open the text thread that sat dormant. The one with the message I hadn't replied to. It sat like an oil stain, smearing every ounce of logic and focus I once had. A secret winding vine among the digital tabs on my phone.

I'd flip over to social media, only to go back to that message and stare. My thumbs would hover over the text, and nothing would happen.

I wanted to say something. Anything but that echo would reverberate and shudder inside my heart, forcing me to close out the thread.

Empty.

Empty.

Empty.

Callie's apartment was a shell. I'd let myself in, desperate to see something that reminded me of her. It was like a fairy tale, where she'd been whisked off to an imaginary kingdom, one I would never be allowed to enter. Pulling open her fridge, I nearly burst into tears at the box of uneaten Go-Gurts. She enjoyed the children's treat; yet, she'd never told me why.

I wished she had. There were so many things I began wishing for. Like this new life my best friend was now starting. My feet moved, and I was suddenly staring at Maxwell, her Great Dane's imprint on her threadbare couch.

My phone came out again, and there in my best friend's apartment, I stared at the message that had been haunting me, and I made a decision.

Justifying that it was for her, my best friend.

Deep down I knew a different truth.

For it wasn't the messages between Callie that had me choosing to move to Rose Ridge. It was the one I'd been avoiding since he'd sent it.

Now I stared at it, smiling with a new lust for adventure.

> Killian: Come back, Daisy…and this time, fucking stay.

TWENTY-THREE
KILLIAN

My phone was dead, and I was getting really sick and tired of sleeping in this shitty hotel. We'd been gone for three days, and with each day, I was starting to feel like my skin was being pulled and stretched. Like I was about to come out of it. While I knew this was important, my mind screamed at me to go back to Laura.

Silas was still with me and Wes, watching as Jameson's vice president had secret meetings without him. I could care less what the fuck his club was doing, but it was too much of a coincidence that Luke Holloway, the vice president of the Chaos Kings, was meeting with my father in Cherrywood Penitentiary.

It started a week ago, according to Silas. Twice in one week and then three times this week. One of which I witnessed myself. I had no idea what they were talking about while they were meeting, but it was too abnormally timed with the fact that Jameson had reached out to the Stone Riders for help with Luke's pregnant old lady. It was also strangely timed with what my dad had learned of Laura's existence in my club.

"We need to get back," Wes said, staring at his watch.

I knew he didn't like being away from Callie this long, but I also knew that we'd told Simon before we left, and he was keeping her company while we were gone. So, Wes felt a modicum of security in that.

I, on the other hand, was restless about leaving Laura after just starting things with her.

"Yeah, I think so too."

Silas gave no reaction, just stared at us with those pale blue eyes. "Our deal stands?"

We mounted our bikes, and I gave him a nod. "She'll be safe with us. Just don't ever do that shit again."

Silas gave me a quick nod, then one to Wes, before putting on a pair of sunglasses and revving his bike to life. Once he was situated, he pulled off and was gone in a plume of dust before we even had a chance to set out.

Two and half hours later, we were entering the city limits of Rose Ridge. Wes gave me a salute as he veered off a side road, which would lead up the butte to his house that overlooked the city. I continued through the main channel of town, slowing down to about twenty miles per hour.

My eyes flicked over The Drip, seeing a few people outside of it holding signs. As I went by, I saw a few pointing at me, others raising their fists, menace straining their faces as they screamed words I couldn't hear.

His sign read, *Bad Bikers—get them out of our town.* Another sign said, *Stone the Riders.* My anger surged as understanding occurred. This was a protest, and the city had gathered to rally against our club. It had a sour feeling stirring in my stomach.

Not having a patch had protected Laura that day.

In response, I revved my bike and then sped past them, making my engine echo through the street, loudly.

Pushing on toward the club, I felt relief tug at me as I edged closer to our road.

I slowed as I came upon a new security system at the edge of the drive, built to keep people out. There was now a keypad along with a metal gate, secured by iron beams sunk into concrete along each side of the entry. The metal entrance stretched along the property, and barbed wire attached to the top, which would prevent anyone from climbing in.

This was good. Especially after the Death Raiders rolled in like they owned the place. Still, I didn't currently have the code, and Giles likely texted me, but I didn't have any way of checking it because my phone had died. There was a button to push, so I went that route, waiting for someone to come on and answer.

Letting my bike idle, I waited by the speaker until I heard someone speak up.

"Hello?"

"Get this gate open. Now."

The line went dead, and then I heard someone yelling from closer down the drive.

Then I heard a click, and the metal gate was swinging open.

Riding down the dirt path and kicking up dust, I noticed the club was packed with bikes in front, which meant most of the members had been called in. I was proud of Giles for making the call, especially if the fucking town was picketing against us.

My legs were sore as I parked my bike in front of the apartment. All I wanted to do was take a shower and see Daisy. Preferably take a shower with her, then fuck her, hard and slow. I'd also like to kiss her. Then maybe just stare at her for a while.

I needed to just be around her, like a fucking solar panel. I wanted to absorb her, to take her in and, as always, greedily inhale every ounce of her sunshine.

"Prez. Finally." Giles jogged down the stairs, exiting from the club. "I fucked up. I'm so sorry…I had it made and wanted to wait for you, but she found it, and I—"

I got off the bike and unclasped my bucket helmet, lowering the skull gaiter from around my mouth.

I was about to ask Giles what he was talking about when there was commotion near the front of the club, and someone was running toward me.

I saw sunshine and leather and my heart nearly burst from my chest.

Laura's lips were spread into the most beautiful smile, and over her tight long sleeved shirt, she wore a black piece of leather around her shoulders. On the front was sewn in white: Daisy.

The bottom of her cut had SRRV for Stone Riders Rose Ridge Virginia.

I knew my name would be on her back. My smile soon matched hers as she threw herself into my arms. My hand went under her ass, and her legs connected at the ankles around my hips.

There was clapping and cheering coming from the porch of the club, but I ignored it.

Even when they yelled, "Prez officially has an old lady!"

I just held her to me, and then I began walking up the apartment steps.

My mouth was on hers as I kicked the front door shut. I set her down on the counter and lifted off her, breathing hard.

"You saw it early." I pinned my forehead to hers.

She smiled, trailing a finger over my chest. "Giles put it in the office."

"Where you work." I shook my head, silently laughing at the way my VP used that brain of his. Of course she'd see it in there.

"I planned to give it to you."

She tipped back and gave me that smile I was weak for. "I liked it this way better."

About to return my mouth to hers, she put her hand up to stop me.

"I have one request."

"Anything." I spread her thighs, so they fit around my hips.

Her lips were at my ear as she whispered, "Fuck me while I wear your patch."

My cock swelled within my jeans as something like a growl came from my throat.

As I carried her upstairs, I thanked whoever was up above, giving out second chances because there was no way I should have this girl in my arms right now.

Not after how I treated her, or what I did to her once she arrived all those months ago. Closing my eyes, I tried to push the memory away and enjoy the feel of her in my arms.

Three Months Ago

It was well past midnight when I finally succumbed to seeing Laura.

She'd just shown up without warning, a car full of suitcases and boxes, and I knew she was inside with Callie. I knew I should leave her alone, but I couldn't.

She came back.

Was it because I asked her to?

Or was it simply because she missed her best friend?

As I walked from the club and toward the back part of the house, I couldn't find a reason why it mattered. I would go to the guest room window and make her let me in. I would tell her that I didn't care why she came back; I was simply grateful she did.

I wanted her…. I couldn't quite work out why or understand all the reasons why I was so willing to lower my defenses, but it didn't matter. She was here, and I wasn't going to overthink it. I wanted her, and I was going to tell her I did until she returned the sentiment.

Nearly to Wesley's back gate, the darkness crowded me as I walked until I froze, hearing my name.

"Killian."

I stared at the man who had been more like a father to me than Jefferson Quinn ever had. The same man who had chosen someone else to lead his club, someone who faked his own death…

"Simon."

Hurt didn't even begin to cover how I felt toward my mentor, my pseudo father. He had trained me for this role. He'd had me under his wing since I was ten years old, and then just like that, he'd replaced me. Without warning, without a conversation first, without any explanation as to why I wasn't enough for the role. The other members all fell into place, accepting that me, the vice president, wasn't asked to take over.

No one questioned it. Or if they did, I wasn't aware of it.

Simon was still sick, and while he'd faked his death, he was still on the brink of it. He walked closer; his leather cut seemingly heavy on his shoulders as he bowed his head. His dark hair was tied back, his white shirt the only color I could make out against the midnight air.

"We need to talk." He was right in front of me now, flicking a quick glance to the gate a few feet off, then behind me to the kitchen door that had a private entrance.

Anger and hurt warred in my chest, making my jaw ache with how hard I was clenching my teeth. "About what exactly? You choosing Wes over me and embarrassing me in front of the entire club?" Tapering my eyes at him, even in the dark, I stepped closer.

"Or how about we talk about you making me bury you, grieve you... What could you possibly need to say to me?"

Simon's face didn't slip into anything other than the same unreadable expression he always held as the leader I knew and grew up with. Not the slightest emotion flitted across his features, and for once, I wished they would. My own father had failed me; I never expected Simon to follow suit.

The wound was so deep, tears burned my eyes. I dipped my face to ensure they'd stay in place. Weakness was the last thing I wanted to show him.

I wasn't sure what else to say, especially with the tight knot forming in my throat.

He pulled me away from the fence back toward the club. "You need to see something. For the sake of the club, and the longevity of our family, you need to know what's coming next."

Simon moved and expected me to move with him. The urgency to discover what exactly he was hiding, or talking about, sat right there at the forefront of my mind, just like club matters always did with him. I never wanted to miss a ride, never wanted to skip a meeting. The club was my life, and he was the person who made it that way.

Glancing back once toward the fence, I let the urge to run to Laura go. Just for one night, I'd let her sleep, and tomorrow, I'd go to her.

I should have realized it then...that regret is just honey-soaked poison.

We consume our choices so easily; they go down with a smile. Good intentions. Only to destroy us with a ticking clock over our heads.

Simon sat me down in his office. The walls were so familiar, but after thinking I'd lost him, it was messing with my mind to see him back in his chair.

"You know it was supposed to be you." Simon started.

I began shaking my head when he spoke again.

"I knew Wes would bring Callie back. I knew about his house, and his plans…I knew he was planning to leave. Call it a dying man's wish to have his wrongs corrected but I owed it to both of them to fix what I had a hand in breaking."

My mouth firmed into a tight line. I had nothing to say to that because it didn't change anything.

Simon leaned over his desk, catching my gaze.

"I saw you break, Killian. When you were ten. Just a cub abandoned by his parents, and raised by his pack. I saw you reshape, reform. You were always meant to take this club."

Finally lifting my head, I tilted it back. "Why?"

Because spouting off some bullshit about my childhood trauma wasn't enough for me.

Simon's eyes sparked as he smiled.

"Because you're without weakness, son. Wesley's was always Callie. He'd do anything for her. You'd do anything for the club. The Stone Riders need you. I am dying, and now that Wes has Callie. You're up. I need to know if you're committed to securing the club and protecting it from what's coming."

"What's coming?" I shifted my feet underneath the desk.

Simon's sorrowful glare cut through me.

"I need to know that you're willing to step into this role first. You'll be with me for the next few months until the transition. You won't be here as often. I need to know you want this."

Laura flashed in my head. A blink.

The club was all I had ever wanted. Wes had just given it up, while Simon said he was never intended to actually keep it. The gamble was still there that Wes decided to. Simon was counting on the fact that Wesley's weakness for Callie would place the club back in my hands.

"This club is all I've ever wanted. I'm committed."

Simon glared for a second longer then shook his head.

"You can't lead this club and be distracted. That's all I'll say on the matter."

He stood and tossed me a set of keys.

I caught them in one hand. "No distractions here."

TWENTY-FOUR
LAURA

I was hiding from Killian.

Well, sort of.

I stood in the guest bathroom downstairs, staring at myself, and smirked. Not ready for him to see the tattoo I'd gotten. I decided I'd be clever and tell him to fuck me in the new property patch. I heard from Callie back when she started wearing hers that it was like catnip to them.

I decided to test the waters and see how it would go.

My hair was curled, and I'd reapplied some gloss on my lips. I'd shaved, showered, and moisturized every single inch of my skin and now as I stared at myself in the mirror, I was excited for what Killian would think.

I flipped the light and sauntered upstairs.

When I had asked for a second to get myself together, he'd been more than willing because he wanted to scrub the remnants of the road and shitty motel off him. Now as I walked upstairs and sauntered into his room, I found him standing by his dresser, completely naked.

His ink was deliciously dark against his pale skin. My gaze flicked to that daisy again, and my curiosity grew talons, needing to rip the answers from him.

I was so focused, I hadn't even registered that Killian had gone completely still, or that his eyes were hooded and fixated on me.

"You're more than I ever dreamed of," he whispered, turning toward me.

"You dreamed of me?"

His smile turned bashful, and it made something crack inside me.

"I dreamed of finding someone…my match." He covered that daisy tattoo with his palm.

I stepped closer, my bare feet silent against the plush carpet under me.

Then I was directly in front of him and leaned in to press a kiss over the tattoo.

"Tell me what it means, and why you call me it."

His gaze searched mine, a frantic sort of panic swirling within those verdant orbs.

"When I was a child, my mother and I bonded over movies, specifically the classics. She loved Cinderella, and I didn't really mind watching it because it meant we spent time together." His bashful smile returned, and my chest swelled.

It allowed me to examine a tiny piece of him and finally understand.

Your eyes are Cinderella Blue.

"I already told you a bit about what she'd said regarding the pebble."

I nodded, stroking his chest.

His gaze was shy as he tucked a strand of hair behind my ear. "When she left…there was a letter with a dried daisy pressed inside."

I stroked the petals of the flower to encourage him to continue. With a slow blink and small inhale, he finally did.

"She told me in that letter that one day I'd be tempted to fall in love. She knew her warning about the pebble would stop me from letting that person in some day. So she told me to think of a daisy. Strong, resilient."

His hand rested on my throat, slowly trailing down over the name printed on my cut.

"Strong enough to push through gravel, grow between rocks. Strong enough to withstand this sediment around my heart. I gave you that pebble that day on the bus platform and said it was a reminder."

I held my breath as tears burned the backs of my eyes. He let out a tiny laugh, shaking his head.

"It wasn't a reminder, Daisy."

Why did it feel like he'd just made an incision in my chest and inserted a piece of himself? My throat felt thick, my voice feeble as I tried to find the words.

"What was it then?" I managed to whisper.

His head was pinned to mine, similarly to that day on the platform. His hand touched the ends of my hair as he confessed.

"It was surrender."

All this time…he'd been calling me Daisy since the second time we met.

"I took that dried flower into a tattoo shop when I was sixteen. Simon wouldn't let me get one any sooner, no matter who I asked in the club. But at sixteen one of the members took pity on me. I handed him the flower, it was all dried, falling apart regardless of how hard I had tried to keep it together. The man, Sly, that was his name…he took one look at the pathetic flower still hanging on by a thread and he inked it over my heart. So I'd always remember my mothers parting words, and last wish for me."

My mouth moved even though I didn't process what I was trying to say.

"She wanted you to find your daisy."

Killian's hand came over mine, where it was pinned to his chest.

"She wanted me to find my match. She wanted me to…" His voice pitched, almost like he couldn't bring himself to say it. That was okay. I would say it for the both of us.

"I love you," I whispered, my voice shaking, eyes watering.

He smiled, lowering his mouth to mine.

"Ditto, Daisy."

My arms came up, and we were lost to our lust as his mouth moved as violently as a storm against mine. He didn't kiss me; he claimed me.

"Get on your hands and knees, Daisy. Let me fuck you while I stare at my name on your back."

My spine arched with the silent need to show him what I had branded into my skin, but I wasn't ready. Even after that confession, I wasn't.

Moving on the bed, I looked behind me as he got into position, and then his hand was stroking the letters of the cut, as he thrust inside me.

"Gonna ruin you," he vowed, and my fists clenched the bedding.

His groan reverberated against the walls as he rocked into me. My hair was wrapped around his fist as he slid out and returned, slamming forward. He was so deep, and the way he pulled at my scalp, the burn was so sensational that I moaned, greedy for him to continue.

"You need more?"

His ruthless grip and intense speed intensified, and with my neck arched, my pussy being stretched, I screamed my release into the room. Instead of letting me go, Killian released my hair and hovered over my back. He was utterly gentle as he slowly pumped out his release and then began whispering words into my skin.

"Perfect for me."

"Mine."

"Heaven."

Kisses landed against my shoulder, and then I was being rolled to my back, and his mouth covered my breasts, his wet kisses covered my nipples and the slope of my tit. He covered my ribs, and with his hands under me, he gently licked my belly button, catching my gaze.

"I like dreaming, Daisy. You give me the best ideas." He kissed around my stomach again. It made me emotional, my head screaming he was telling me something—something that would tie us together forever.

I shut it out and pushed my fingers through his hair.

He laughed and kissed me again. "One thing at a time."

We made love again, this time he slid in through the mess he'd already made, holding my hips while he fucked me slowly. His lips covered mine, and my heart was so swollen with joy, that a few tears slid down the side of my face.

When it was time to sleep, I slipped into a t-shirt, and I smiled, knowing I had my own secret I'd be able to share with him soon enough.

My smile slipped as the lights turned off and Killian's arms came around me. Red's words about my own skeletons came back. I needed to come clean with him. It likely didn't matter, but I owed it to him to explain who I was regardless.

I sat watching Killian click his remote at the new flat screen in the living room with a flustered look on his face. He wore jeans, a pair of white socks and a hunter green long sleeve. His hair was wet from his shower. I'd insisted on taking separate ones because I still wasn't ready for him to see my back. Surprisingly, he agreed but not before he fucked me against the bathroom wall.

Seeing him try to set up all the apps and channels was mildly entertaining, and I'd been content to watch for the past half an hour.

Every now and then, he'd curse and pull up the user manual.

"Don't you have a prospect who can do this for you?" I asked, sipping my coffee again.

"Probably, but I don't want them in here." He looked over at me. "Especially now that you're living here."

I let that go because I'd been here for three months. Four months now.

It was starting to snow outside, marking the end of the month. Thanksgiving was approaching, and I had no idea if my parents wanted me to go home, or what their plans were. We were estranged, but I still wandered back home around the holidays, as theirs was the only home I'd ever really known.

Thinking of them reminded me of what I needed to do.

"Can you take a break?"

Killian glanced over then turned back to the screen. "What for?"

"I need to talk to you about something."

He let out a frustrated sigh and then walked over, placing a kiss on my lips before claiming the seat across from me.

I turned to face him. "You may not remember this, but I actually told you and everyone else in the club that my last name was White."

Something flickered in his gaze, but it was gone just as soon as it arrived.

"Okay." He drawled out.

"Well, I was just trying to cover up my real last name... Witt. As in Senator Witt's daughter."

His dark brows hit his hairline. "No shit...the senator of the state is your dad?"

I nodded, biting my lip.

"I wasn't trying to lie to you...and now that we're together, I wanted to be sure you knew. That way we don't have any secrets between us. My dad's name is Hugh; my mom is Lacy...they might meet you someday."

His face dipped as he toyed with the hem of his shirt.

"I mean you don't have to...I just—the holidays are coming up, and I might..." I trailed off, unsure what energy I was picking up from him.

But my worries were misplaced because he grabbed my face in his hands and kissed me, hard. "I'd love that, if and when. I'll meet them and I'll even act like a proper boyfriend and everything."

I smiled into his kiss. "Really, proper?"

His lips moved against mine again. "Yeah, I'll withhold telling your dad how good your pussy feels around my cock."

"You're horrible." I pushed at his chest.

"What other secrets do you have, my beautiful Daisy?" He kissed the tip of my nose.

"I sing down at The Hollow. I'm pretty good actually...and I've saved up some money doing that, so if we don't work out and you need me to move out, I can."

His grip returned to my face; his fingers splayed into my hair.

"You're mine now, beautiful thing. All mine. I'll share you with the sun, your parents, and I guess the audience you sing to, but that's it."

"I suppose I'll share you with your club," I whispered back.

He stilled and then leaned back.

"Don't. If I had to choose between you, it'd be you. Always you."

I shook my head about to contradict him, but he caught my chin and then made sure I met his eyes. "I'm serious."

I stared back, and for some reason, I chose to believe him.

He kissed me again, and I wished I would have remembered how once upon a time, he'd asked me to move back, told me to be his, and then when I arrived, he never came back to me.

He'd left me.

Because something about his promise felt just as fleeting.

TWENTY-FIVE
LAURA

My skin pebbled with nerves and excitement.

The lights in the room were bright and centered on the stage as I watched from behind the curtain. Callie, Wes, Natty and Giles were seated in the back row, and Killian was at a table right in front of the stage.

Natty and Callie had called in the girls' night promise, and when Killian had found out, he was too excited to hear me sing to let me back out of it. Tonight, I wore a pair of denim jeans that flared over my cowboy boots and a small, cropped tank lay underneath my property patch. It was my first time wearing it in public, and while I was nervous, I was also excited. Callie wore hers, and with Giles, Wes and Killian all in theirs, our little group certainly changed the vibe of the room. Jack was in the back smiling at me, encouraging me to continue.

When the announcer mentioned my stage name, I nearly died of embarrassment. Especially when Killian's head tipped back in laughter. Shit, should have thought about that part.

Oh well.

I walked out, and Killian stood to clap, smiling so wide that I nearly started crying.

I'd never had people who loved me like this before. Never a core group of friends, or people who would show up to something like this on my behalf.

With that in mind, my fingers moved over the keys, and I played "Stand by Me," singing with my lips spread into a smile as I closed my eyes.

The song erupted and came from my chest like a sacrifice, my lungs burning and my insides shaking as I continued to the next song. Jeff Buckley's "Hallelujah," and finally one of the newer songs from Jessie Murph.

By the end, the crowd was a riot, all on their feet, clapping and cheering. Killian jumped on the stage, and I was pulled into his arms with his lips at my ear.

"You were fucking incredible, Daisy. I'm so proud of you. My heart nearly stopped when you started singing 'Hallelujah.'"

Mine did too. He was in my head as I pulled the darkness out of those hidden parts of my soul and left it all in the song.

Natty and Callie were there next, waiting for us as I exited the stage.

We were all on a high. We did two rounds of drinks, tipping extra for my favorite bartender, before we finally scaled those metal steps and exited into the cold November night.

Since there was only street parking, we had to walk down a block to get to our trucks. Giles and Natty rode with us, but Wes and Callie had brought their own vehicle.

The stringed lights from the front of The Hollow aided us against the dark night but once we cleared the yard, we had to navigate with only a few streetlights overhead. I was tucked under Killian's arm listening as Giles prattled on about how dumb he felt, not knowing about The Hollow's existence when all the sudden, there was glass shattering on the road next to us. It seemed to come out of nowhere. We faltered, our eyes darting down to the road, trying to make sense of the broken bottle, and then up.

Where had it come from?

We were standing in a particularly dark patch of street, seeing as the furthest street light wasn't even on. Killian hesitantly continued forward, pulling me with him when suddenly there was another bottle that shattered directly in front of us.

I stepped back right as Killian roared, "Giles, Wes, get them in the center."

I was being pushed into the middle of the street with Callie and Natty as the men surrounded us, facing every direction, each one with a weapon pulled and pointed in the directions they each faced.

The shattering stopped, but peering through the men around us, I saw an orange flicker from the direction of where the bottles came.

"Are those…" I whispered, still unsure if I was seeing correctly.

Another glass bottle flew through the air, this one on fire.

"Fuck!" Killian yelled right as it landed near us. The glass sprayed so close, it hit my jeans.

"Get them in the truck, now!" Wes screamed, and Giles moved.

The torches being held down the road began multiplying and moving. As did the number of glass bottles being thrown at us.

We all piled into Callie's rig, Giles taking the driver's seat.

"Keys are in my purse, just hit the start button!" she yelled, hanging onto the handlebar above her head.

"Everyone down. If they lob something at the car, I don't want you to get hit."

We did as we were told, but I stole one last glance at Killian through the window. He was aiming his firearm straight ahead, while backing up toward his truck before Giles had us turned in the opposite direction and heading to safety.

There was a wildness in Giles's eyes as he continued to check his rearview mirror. I held Callie's hand, and she held Natty's. We were still ducked down low in the seats when all the sudden the sound of another car revving its engine was right next to us.

Natty screamed as they veered the nose of their car directly next to where she was sitting.

"Shit," Giles yelled.

"Hold on, girls." He pulled the car to the side by tilting the steering wheel, forcing the one trying to hit us off the road.

It seemed to work at first, but then someone was driving up next to us on the opposite side where I was sitting. My heart hammered in my chest as I watched the driver, who was wearing a wolf mask, jerk the wheel so their car hit ours.

My eyes slammed shut right as a familiar truck hit that car from behind, forcing it off the road.

I sat up and turned, seeing it was Killian's truck. His headlights made it difficult to make anything out, but I could see Wes was in the passenger seat.

Relief sailed through me as they took the spot next to us on the highway, so no one else could.

We drove like that, all of us breathing heavy while Giles continued to flick his gaze from the rear-view mirror to the road.

The sound of a motorcycle broke the silence. We watched a singular headlight appear on the opposite side of our car, navigating down the middle turn lane. The bike kept pace, so it was directly next to Natty's door.

I looked over, but couldn't make out the rider. Not until he pulled ahead a tiny bit and the back of his leather jacket revealed his affiliation.

Death Raider.

The back didn't reveal his name, but I knew it was Silas.

Natty became motionless when she caught sight of him. She released a shuddery breath when ten more Death Raiders came up behind him, all taking up that middle lane. They rode with us all the way back to the club and then continued past the property when both of our vehicles had made it safely through the gates.

"Daisy, pack a bag, you're sleeping in the main house tonight."

Killian's first words to me in what felt like hours had my frozen limbs moving. When we'd arrived, we huddled inside the main room of the club, ensuring everyone was safe. Killian had a cut on his face, and Wes had one on his arm, but otherwise, there were no casualties.

"Where will you be?" I asked, tugging on the edge of his leather cut. His arm was around me, but his gaze was distant.

When he didn't reply, Natty let out a scoff before standing from the couch she was on.

"They're all going to die tonight."

My head snapped over to where she was standing, so did Callie's.

Natty's somber expression didn't change as she continued, "*He* will kill every single one of them. I'm assuming Wes and Killian will go too. The attack on their women can't go unpunished."

No one said anything. I watched my friend, knowing she was speaking of Silas, but still unsure why she wasn't saying his name.

"Callie, Laura, you can sleep in my room tonight," she finished before walking up the stairs.

Killian pressed a kiss against my temple and then took my hand, guiding me back to the apartment. Before we walked out, I saw Callie and Wes in an argument. I was almost positive she didn't want him to go, and I didn't blame her. I didn't want Killian to either, but I also knew it would go against his nature not to.

"Will you promise me that you'll be careful?" I asked as I packed my things.

He ran a hand through his hair, clearly feeling agitated.

"Killian."

He still didn't respond.

"Promise me."

"Only if you promise me not to go to The Hollow again, and you can't wear your cut in public anymore."

I nearly laughed because the idea of finally having his name on my back, and now having to give it up was ludicrous. "Then you don't wear yours anymore."

"I'm serious, Daisy."

"I'm serious, Killian. I will if you do."

He shook his head. "I don't have time for this. Get your shit, and go over to the main house."

With that, he walked out and slammed the door shut.

TWENTY-SIX
LAURA

I took the floor because Callie was currently pregnant, and I wasn't about to steal Natty's bed. It was nearly seven thirty in the morning, and the November sun was nearly nonexistent as gray seemed to replace any natural light in the room. I stood, stretching my arms above my head, trying not to wake anyone. I snagged my phone off the charger and began to scroll through my notifications.

Killian had texted at three in the morning.

> Killian: You better be sleeping. Just letting you know I won't be back for a while. We're held up in one of our safe houses, and tomorrow I have some meetings. I'm sorry I was an asshole.
> You're my favorite thing about breathing. Please let me kiss you tomorrow.

I smiled at his text and let out a relieved sigh.

Another notification caught my attention, which had me walking out in the hall and padding down to the kitchen, so I could make a call without waking anyone up.

The room was warm because Red had already started baking bread.

I tucked away near the desk at the back and pressed the contact's name and waited.

"Laura?"

"Mom?"

She'd texted me something cryptic and I'd just called her, my name showing up on the caller ID.

"Yes, thank you for calling me."

I heard people talking in the background and knew she was in business mode.

"What can I do for you?"

It would waste my time and hers if I acted hurt or tried to talk to her like a daughter would. When she was focused in this way, she was the senator's wife, not my mother.

"Your father is coming into town today, a very impromptu trip, but he'd like to see you."

I sat up a little straighter as confusion whirled inside me.

"Dad's in Rose Ridge?"

"That is where you're located at the moment, right?" Her tone was bland, but it screamed disapproval.

"Yes."

"Then yes, he was meeting with a local club out there..." She paused, then quietly added, "I hope you haven't had any run-ins with them...I understand they're rather dangerous."

What was she talking about?

I blinked. "Mom, you're not making any sense. Why would Dad..."

"Honey, you're breaking up. Can you meet him for lunch?"

I had my father's personal cell phone number and couldn't fathom why I couldn't just call him myself. Unless...he didn't take it, which would mean he was doing something he didn't want monitored.

"Is Dad in business with a motorcycle club?" My mind raced back to those files...the ones I was abruptly removed from.

"Laura you aren't associated with them, right?" her voice became terse, as if she were worried.

"Mom...just tell me what you know about dad coming here."

There was more talking. "I'm going to have to nail down a solid time with you later, I'm getting called away, but sweetheart... please be careful."

The line went dead.

I lowered my phone and sat there processing for a second.

My gut told me my father was here meeting with the Stone Riders, which meant he was meeting with Killian. But...it just didn't make sense. Had Killian reached out to him, knowing my dad would step in and help if it involved his daughter? Or was there something I was missing?

I bit my nail, peering over my shoulder to where Red's large purse sat. Her keys were right on top.

She was in the pantry, gathering more flour...If I was going to take them...now was the time.

I jumped up and quickly swept her keys into my hand, letting the sleeve of my hoodie drop so they were hidden. I just needed to get into the office and get that file cabinet open. I needed to know if there was a file on my dad, and if so, then I needed to know why Killian was keeping it from me.

I was wrong. I had to be, but...still, I had to be sure.

Bypassing the pantry, and avoiding the main room, I slipped into the hall and then the office and gently shut the door. No one else was up yet, so there wasn't anyone who would be wandering around the club.

I briskly crossed the office floor and navigated to the right key, then slid it into the cabinet. The drawer opened easily, revealing the remaining files. I thumbed through the last names starting with S, then T, until I was nearing W.

Then my hand stilled.

Witt.

No.

My eyes winded with fear as I tentatively tugged the file out.

No x marked on his file, which meant they were still working with him.

With shaking fingers, I stuffed it under my shirt, and then locked the cabinet back up.

Back in the apartment, I sat on Killian's bed cross-legged and stared at the folder.

Then I went back through the timeline in my head.

He'd pulled me off the files weeks ago. It was out of the blue...after that meeting with the Chaos Kings.

Had one of them recognized me and outed me? Why did he act like he didn't know when I told him?

I had to know what was in the file.

I delicately flipped it open. The first thing I saw was a piece of paper with the state seal on it. I read over the paper. It was a way for Simon Stone to bypass certain legal loopholes in obtaining the acres of property that bordered his land. The signature was from fifteen years ago, back when my dad was first elected as mayor of Richland. Dad shouldn't have had the clearance to offer Simon that sort of deal.

Setting that aside, there was another paper, more legal info about certain products that were pushed through state lines with dad's approval during his time as governor. There were several sheets where my father signed off on properties, naming their adjacent businesses as nonprofits, and other highly illegal things.

Then there were images.

A political rally where the Stone Riders were surrounding a group of protestors. My dad was on stage, speaking. One image had someone's face down on the concrete while my dad spoke in the background.

More images came up. These ones were of him with...

Fuck.

A stripper. She had her back to the camera, but he was half-dressed, and you could see my dad clearly about to enjoy whatever she was about to do to him.

Another image was of him in a sexually compromised position with three women in bed.

This was blackmail.

Mutually assured destruction. I flipped through a few more pages when suddenly I stopped.

It was another dated picture of someone shaking my father's hand during that initial election when my dad had won the mayor ticket. I could see my dad's face, but the man's back was to the camera, the only way to identify who he was, was by his leather cut.

My eyes widened as I traced the image of the howling wolf, and then the name etched into the back.

Killian Quinn.

Oh god.

My stomach churned.

He didn't just know of my father; he had worked with him from the start of my dad's political career. He'd likely ran up several of the raids my father put his seal of approval on.

Now they were meeting after those activists attacked us. It was too conveniently timed.

I got up, got dressed and slid my cut on over my hoodie. Tying my hair up, I left the apartment with the file in my purse.

TWENTY-SEVEN
KILLIAN

The tension in the room could be cut with a knife.

I leaned against the wall, staring at the men in front of me, and tried to keep myself from reaching for my Glock. All I wanted to do was shove it in their faces and tell them to fix this.

We were attacked, out in the open, with our women—and by a bunch of fucking keyboard warriors.

"I understand what you're asking of me, but I'm afraid it's not that simple." Senator Witt—*Hugh*—explained in that condescending tone he used in DC. He wore a neatly tailored suit, and for the first time since meeting him all those years ago, I finally registered that his daughter had his eyes. And for some reason that realization enraged me.

Because I knew I owed Daisy an explanation about my connection to her father. I just didn't know how to have that conversation. Not after she opened her delicate heart and shared all her secrets with me. Not after I lied by omission.

But how would I explain that I knew him?

Granted, it's been at least six years since I had any dealings with him, but it didn't change the fact that there was an established connection at some point.

"Make it that simple then," I snapped, desperately trying to control my tone.

His blue eyes narrowed. "I don't have the power to—"

"The mayor of Rose Ridge gave them his blessing to come after us. Our connections at the local PD confirmed it. They were given the green light to attack us in a fucking residential neighborhood. Now, if you can't erase this proposed legislation and make an example out of them, then we'll make one out of you."

His expression was murderous. His assistants cleared their throats.

They looked so out of place in my father's house. We sat at the old, chipped table with the threadbare curtains drawn and the mismatching chairs. The conversation about my mother was sitting too close to my heart, and now being in this house…fuck it hurt.

I sneered, tacking on a little reminder. "That's how this works, in case you forgot. You wanted us in your pocket, to help you when you needed it. That means when we call for favors, you answer. Plain and fucking simple."

Mouth parted; he was about to say something when there was a commotion near the back door. I heard Giles arguing, but seconds later, he tripped backward as if someone had pushed him into the room, and my heart jumped into my throat.

Following Giles was *sunshine and leather.*

"Hello, honey." Daisy's sharp blue eyes bounced from me to the table, and her expression twisted into a scowl. "Father."

She was wearing my property patch over a thick hoodie; her hair was swept up into a messy bun, and she carried herself like she was the queen of the goddamned world.

"Laura, sweetheart." Senator Witt rose from the table; his panicked gaze flew to me before landing on her cut. "What are you wearing…and what are you doing here?"

Had he missed her calling me, Honey?

She smiled and then moved to stand directly in front of me.

"Oh this?" Then she turned around so he could read the back.

An odd mixture of pride and terror swept through me, making my fists clench.

Hugh's face paled.

I reached my hand out to grab her wrist, but she moved too fast.

Her gaze flicked between us. The men with her father exchanged nervous glances, my men didn't even flinch, if anything they'd step in to protect her over me. That made me calm the slightest bit.

"I know everything." A slap echoed through the room as Laura slammed the manila envelope full of her father's secrets down. "And, with all of my heart." She placed her hand over her chest.

"Fuck you both."

Her hurt gaze landed on me painfully hard as she stormed back through the back door.

Hugh's eyes widened as they landed on the folder. He acted like the thing would grow fangs and bite him. So while he stared and tried to ascertain what leverage we had on him, I jumped out of my chair and ran outside.

I went after her, right as the Senator roared my name. That file shouldn't exist, and if any of our other allies knew that we kept tabs on everything they'd done that was illegal, we'd be fucked. Yet, I couldn't keep my feet from moving toward Laura.

"Daisy."

She wouldn't stop. My chest burned like she'd just flung acid at me and didn't want to stick around to watch me burn. My eyes narrowed on the words on the back of her cut.

Property of Killian Quinn bent around the design of our club insignia—a skull with roses blooming from the eyes.

My heart pounded quicker with each step she took.

"Laura!"

She spun around, tears stained her face and clung to her lashes.

"I was honest with you, Killian. I shared my secrets with you, and you sat there—acting surprised. You made a fool of me!"

I stopped far enough away that she didn't feel crowded. I had mentioned being at a safe house, it was an idiot choice to go to the one place she knew about. I had men stationed at the start of the drive, all of which should have stopped her from getting this far. I suppose the cut on her back made it so they didn't question her arrival.

"I know...I didn't know how to—"

She stepped closer, her face getting pink as the cold air clung to the tears on her face. "Was this a big joke? Did everyone know?"

The way her voice shook nearly had mine doing the same.

I was so fucking afraid she wouldn't hear me out. I needed her to hear me out.

"Jameson King first told me when they came to discuss our club taking on one of their pregnant women."

She scoffed, shaking her head. "More secrets."

Yes, more secrets than she even knew what to do with.

"You took the files from me after they came." Her eyes narrowed in understanding, and now it felt like I was about to lose her. I stepped forward as she pulled her arm out of reach.

"You didn't want me to find his file."

I didn't know what to say. She was right, but not for the reasons she assumed.

"At first, yes…it was simply that I didn't want you involved. He's one of our biggest political assets. But it changed…I was falling for you, and I didn't want you to see your father in that light."

Her head was shaking, more tears falling.

"You said I was more important than the club."

Hurt and fear flayed me open, forcing me to close the gap between us.

"You are. This is new…I can't—"

She pulled away from me right as her father slammed the back door to the house and thundered down the weathered steps.

Her gaze remained on me, her arms pulled in tight.

"I'd understand if you hadn't known he was my dad, Killian. But even now…you texted me this morning, but couldn't share that you were meeting with my dad? You know who told me?"

I didn't respond. Her citrus scent was overwhelming my senses, making me want to pull her back into my chest.

"My mother. She was trying to schedule a lunch for me and my dad. She mentioned some sullied biker club that he was meeting with."

An echo of one of my fears reared its head, forcing my patience to snap.

Her father was stopped by Harris, and Riley. Hugh was screaming but we'd begun walking back toward my truck, which she parked further down the drive.

The gravel crunched as she stormed away but I was on her heels.

"Exactly, Laura. You grew up in a world that doesn't even touch mine. Your dad is a sick fuck, but he's still your dad. I wasn't going to ruin that for you. You don't understand the way my world works. This is likely just a passing moment for you. You'll wise up in a few years, go back home and marry some senator's son."

She scoffed, swiping at her nose and eyes, but I knew deep down I was right.

"What are you saying right now, Killian?" She stopped by the hood of my truck.

I couldn't take the look on her face, but it felt like this might be the only chance I had to set her free.

"I'm saying that I think we're having fun...but I have no delusions that it will last. You're going to leave...one phone call from home, and you'll be back at the family mansion, attending parties and playing the role of dutiful daughter."

Watching as she wore every single emotion on her face was breaking me. I just needed her to be safe and not a target anymore... I wanted her to tell me I was wrong and wrap her arms around my neck, vowing to never leave me.

"If that's what you think then there's nothing I can do to change your mind, Killian."

Her steps crunched the gravel under our feet as she gave me her back and walked around to the drivers side door, and then got in.

Fuck. This was all a mess, and I just needed a second to think before anything else happened.

Right as I thought it, my phone buzzed in my pocket.

Jameson King.

"Ya." I stood there watching as the woman I loved backed up and drove away.

Jameson didn't waste a second. "I need to move Penelope tonight. Some shit is going down. I need your help, Quinn."

What else was going to happen on this fucking day?

Rubbing the stress out of my forehead, I tried to think.

"Yeah, okay. Bring her, we'll get her set up." I'd have to tell him about the attack, so he was aware, but that was just one more problem I'd have to solve later.

My gaze lifted to where Laura had driven off.

You said I was more important than the club.

She was; I just didn't know how to prove it.

TWENTY-EIGHT
LAURA

I CIRCLED ROSE RIDGE FOR HALF AN HOUR.

Mostly, I just had to clear my head, but the idea of using all of Killian's gas held some appeal. Now, I was back at the club, needing to talk to Callie and Natty to get some perspective. They both had been in the club in some aspect for a long time; perhaps there was an element to Killian's freak out that I was missing.

I scaled the steps and knocked on Natty's door.

She opened with a huge smile on her face. I envied her and decided I wanted to know how she was always so happy. She was living a separate life from the man she supposedly loved, and yet she seemed completely content.

"We were wondering where you went." She shut the door behind me.

"Killian's been keeping secrets." I heaved a sigh and plopped down onto her couch then began to explain everything that had happened.

I didn't hold anything back, not about my dad or his workings or anything else that was supposed to be secret. I just poured my heart out, and then I waited.

Callie exchanged a look with Natty before both women crowded me. Callie hugged my side, and Natty came over, kneeling in front of me to hug my middle. I froze for a second, unsure how to respond, but the longer they held me, the more I broke.

Tears streamed down my face, and a hiccup got caught in my throat.

"Neither of us are strangers to the pain of the club and how its members can be hyper-focused on the wrong things," Callie said, sitting on the arm of the couch.

I sniffed and looked up, watching her.

She played with my hair, almost like a mother would. Regardless that my own mother never had. Thinking of my mom had the images I'd seen in the folder rushing back. While my relationship with her was frosty, she was still my mom. She deserved to know what was going on.

"They're assholes most of the time. Loyal, hard, and usually overly protective. But they'd lose themselves without us. They'll act like it's not a big deal, like the club is enough."

"But it's not," Natty cut in, locking her soft gaze with Callie's.

"It's why Silas follows me like a wraith. He finally has what he wanted, which makes him similar to Killian in that way. They're both new presidents, and yet, Silas is here, watching me more often than not. I see him on my way to work every morning. He follows me home at night. It makes me wonder when he has time to lead his club."

My heart pinched tight, knowing Killian would likely be the same.

"Killian loves you, Laur. But it's tethered to this place he came from. You have to understand that he is likely terrified of anything happening to you," Callie started, but I shook my head to interrupt her.

"That's so cliché though, and I don't think I can stick around for him to be a distant asshole simply because he's worried about me."

Callie's expression softened. "I wasn't telling you the truth before about his dad and the murder."

My blood felt frozen in my veins as I waited for her to continue. She battled with her words for a few seconds before she finally relented.

"He was there. His dad had him in the car...he was so young, Laura. Ten years old, finally getting to tag along with a dad that was absent and forgetful. Right after his mom left. His dad pulled up to Strings, and Jenny was out back smoking. Killian was right there in the front seat as he watched his father take a life then dump her body. My dad told me it wasn't the first time. He said there were times Jefferson would hurt

Killian's mom. Considering his background...I think he's genuinely traumatized by the idea of anything happening to you."

That sobered me.

Not enough to forgive him, but it did have me reconsidering his motives and reasons. I knew in my bones that Killian didn't just think we were having fun. He wasn't risking everything he had, merely for someone he thought he'd pass the time with.

Especially not after he'd shared the bit about his tattoo and his mother.

Before I could ask any more questions or further our conversation, Natty's phone lit up with a call.

It was close enough that I saw Killian's name flash across the screen.

That old insecurity flashed quick in my chest, and I knew Natty realized it when she gave me an apologetic look before answering. She stayed where she was, so we could both hear what was going on.

"Hey, Killian."

She was quiet, her brows furrowed as she nodded. "Yeah, I can have it ready by then. Callie and Laura are here too. We can prep it together."

Natty's eyes landed on me as she smiled. "She is here. She's fine."

"I can't keep her here, Killian, but I don't think she's exactly eager to leave."

I rolled my eyes.

With another sigh, she hung up and then explained what we'd be doing.

"Penelope is on her way; we need to go prep the cabin."

I stood with the other two. Callie looked at me with the same confused expression that I had.

"Maybe on the way you could explain who she is?"

Natty laughed. "Yeah, guess I could do that."

The cabin was vacuumed, mopped, and aired out. We put fresh sheets on the bed and made sure there was food in the kitchen. I'd even snagged one of Red's bread loaves and some fresh jam she'd bought from a local farm store.

Natty had explained who Penelope was and why she was coming to stay with us.

I was weirdly excited to meet her, although considering the circumstances, I wasn't sure how friendly she would be.

Within the span of an hour, there were two bikes pulling up and a large silver truck between them.

We exited the cabin and waited on the porch. Killian dismounted one bike, and Wes cleared the other.

Then a man I had seen a few weeks ago jumped from the truck. Jameson King.

The president of the Chaos Kings.

He walked around the hood and opened the passenger door. A streak of midnight hair flashed as the woman exited and then held Jameson's hand until her feet were steady on the ground. She cleared the truck, and my eyes immediately dropped to her swollen stomach.

She was really pregnant, likely due within the next several weeks.

I cast a quick glance to Killian to gauge his reaction and noticed his gaze was already on me. My face flushed as I returned my focus to the woman in front of me.

Penelope had long black hair, cute bangs that were styled in a way that made her face look narrow. She had glittering blue eyes and thick black lashes. Porcelain skin and red lips. She was stunning. She wore a blue long-sleeved shirt that stretched tightly over her breasts and stomach, paired with a pair of jeans and brown boots.

Jameson walked with his hand on the small of her back as he helped move her forward.

"Hi." I stepped forward and thrust my hand out. "I'm Laura."

Her gaze flicked to my leather cut, which I realized belatedly that I was still wearing.

"It says Daisy, but I go by Laura."

Penelope took my hand and gently shook it. "I'm Penelope. You can call me Pen if you want."

Callie came up next, making introductions, and then Natty.

We moved into the cabin as Wes and Killian went to the truck to grab a few bags. Only two to be exact.

Penelope took in the cabin, lightly dragging her finger over the table and counter in the kitchen. With emotion glossing her eyes over, she thanked us.

"This is more than I could have imagined. When Jamie said that he had a spot for me over here, I expected to be shoved in the basement or some musty room."

I didn't miss the nickname she'd given the club leader.

Jamie.

We all laughed, and then Natty stepped closer to her.

"This is a good place, Pen. I think you'll love it. If you need friends, we're here." She gestured toward us, and my heart felt the pain of the admission.

Would I be here?

I needed to talk to my mom, and help her through whatever fall out was likely about to happen. I should make a trip home and talk to her. I felt like she deserved to know about her husband's infidelities. I would want to know.

I smiled at Penelope and flicked a quick gaze over to where Killian stood. "I have to get back to the clubhouse, but it was great to meet you. Natty will leave my cell number, feel free to text or call if you need anything."

Penelope smiled and gave me a grateful nod.

Jameson continued watching her as though she was the only thing that mattered in his entire world. I recognized the expression on his face and realized this might be more complicated of a situation than either of them likely let on. She was pregnant with his vice president's baby according to Natty, but the way Jameson watched her made me think…

He looked at her the way Killian sometimes watched me.

Pushing away the thought, I cleared the door and began walking back to the club.

I knew Killian would follow, so I just continued walking. The cabin was about half a mile from the main clubhouse, so the walk helped clear my head.

As I reached the back gate to the apartment, Killian was crowding my back.

As soon as we were through, his hand was around mine, his fingers intertwining.

I let him lead us up the porch steps and into the house.

Part of me wanted to push the reality of our fight away, and just stay blissfully ignorant to what he'd said. I kept thinking over what Callie had said and tried to piece together a resolution regarding the man in front of me.

He kept pulling me until we were upstairs, and then once we were in the bedroom, he finally let me go.

"You goin' somewhere?"

I laughed; it sounded pitiful and weak.

"You tell me you think we're just having fun after I tell you that I love you and that's the first thing you have to say to me?"

His jaw clenched; his eyes found the floor…but he didn't respond.

Whatever. I folded my arms across my chest. "I was thinking of going to see my mom, tell her what my dad did. She deserves to know."

I slid the cut from my shoulders and set it on the bed. He watched my every move with fierce precision.

"She knows." Killian's intense gaze captured mine, leaving me speechless. "Simon had the photos of him with other women anonymously shown to her. She wasn't given a copy, so it wasn't like she could show him, but she had enough information to leave him."

"She just never did," I muttered, sinking to the bed.

My hoodie was making me itch, so I stripped it over my head. Suddenly, I just wanted a shower and to restart the entire day.

Walking away from the man at my back, I padded toward the bathroom, tugging the button on my jeans.

I heard a gasp behind me.

Turning to look over my shoulder, I saw Killian's gaze was fastened on my back.

The tattoo.

I'd never shown him. Between everything that had happened, I had never found the right time to reveal it.

His feet carried him closer, and with the dark circles under his eyes and the jacket covering his arms, he looked like a dark angel.

Surprisingly warm fingers traced over the design between my

shoulder blades.

"You have a wolf in the middle of your back," he whispered, then brought his finger down along the words. "It has green eyes and –" His voice cracked.

I kept my chin on my shoulder, watching him.

"You got this done before I gave you your patch." Frenzied green eyes met mine.

I nodded. "Yes, Killian. I had *Property of the Wolf* inked into my skin, so I'd forever be branded as *yours*."

His face shuddered as his fingers trembled at my back, making emotion clog my throat.

I turned fully, so I was facing him.

"Even if you think this is a passing phase of mine…Wherever I end up, Killian, I'll always carry this on my back. I've made you a permanent part of my life, whether you want to be a part of it or not."

His Adam's apple bobbed. His eyes glittered, and then his voice hitched once more.

"I was a coward…I said 'ditto' before, when really what I wanted to say was, I love you."

He stepped closer, cradling my jaw. "I love you so much it's painful to breathe because I wonder what will happen to me if you ever leave me. I love your voice, and that night when you sang, and I sat there, watching you like an idiot, all I could think was how beautiful your voice would sound to our children as we rocked them to sleep. I want to hear your voice echoing through our house that we live in together. I love you, Laura Witt. I am in love with you, and I don't ever want a way out."

His lips crashed against mine like a wave caught in the torrent of a storm. His kiss branded my lips, a promise of forever as he moved his mouth over mine. I let his hands drift down my body, taking my clothes and depositing them on the floor. I did the same with him, until we were naked in front of one another.

Killian's kiss landed on my neck as he rasped against my skin.

"Gonna need you to face the wall, hold on to the trim of the doorway." He guided me toward the bathroom door. I did as he said, facing the wall and gripping the wood border for the door.

My breasts hung free as Killian pulled my hips back.

His mouth landed on my tattoo, his tongue tracing a line as he guided his cock into my pussy from behind.

With one hand covering the tattoo, he thrust his hips forward *hard*. The jolt sent me into the wall; my breasts mashed against it as my nails dug into the wood frame.

He was ruthless as he slid out of me and then hammered his length back in through my slickness. Just when I thought he was going to move fast, he brought his hand around my hip and pressed the pad of his fingers to my clit, as he continued to slowly fuck me from behind.

His chest was aligned with my back as he moved his hips. My head fell back against his shoulder as he continued to rub circles into my clit while guiding his cock into my pussy. Over and over, he hit somewhere deep inside me until I was moaning for more.

That had his pace increasing as he pulled my ass against him, his hips thrusting forward.

"That's it, Daisy. Come for me." He rasped against my shoulder as his hips frantically drove into me, making my hand nearly slip from the wood in front of me.

I couldn't think. I couldn't breathe. He was everywhere as he brought the fingers he'd buried in my cunt up to my mouth.

"Suck them clean, beautiful."

I lapped at his fingers. My chest was still smashed against the wall, and my breathing was ragged as my orgasm built. With a harsh squeeze of my ass, I fell apart.

His name was on my tongue as I screamed; he was shouting too as he emptied himself into me.

I sagged against the wall, but he pulled me back into his arms.

A gentle kiss landed on my neck and then the side of my head.

"Let's go to bed, Daisy. I got shit sleep last night."

I nodded, still too numb to speak. He carried me to bed, and when I curled under his arm, I shut my eyes, and I didn't think.

I didn't remember.

I just felt, and I loved.

More importantly, I allowed myself to be loved.

TWENTY-NINE
KILLIAN

Daisy and I stayed in bed for the rest of the day.

We watched movies, ate junk food, and fucked. It was the best day I'd had in...probably ever. I wasn't eager to let her go or to get back to real life where I had to deal with the shit from the attack, and the senator who had been blowing up my phone for the span of an entire day.

I suppose seeing that his daughter was the property of the president of the biker club that handled his dirty business was likely not the best news he'd received.

I smiled at the memory.

"What are you smiling at?" Laura swiped her thumb over my mouth.

My dick twitched under the sheet, already hungry for her again. Just half an hour ago, she'd straddled my face and then took my cock. We needed a break. I knew we did, but when she touched me, it was difficult to keep my hands to myself.

"The look on your dad's face when he saw your property patch."

She let out a small laugh, snuggling into my side.

"He keeps calling," I mused quietly.

She hummed. "You should talk to him; he's an important asset. Don't burn your bridge."

She was right, but the connection with him nearly ruined what I had with Daisy. She swatted my stomach.

"Call him."

Relenting, I raised my phone to my ear and did just that.

It rang a few times before he picked up.

"Mr. Quinn, it's nice of you to return my call. I need to speak with you."

I pulled Laura closer to my side. "So speak."

He made a sound of frustration.

"In person…and I'd appreciate it if you brought my daughter, so I can explain myself to her. She won't answer my calls, and I don't need her mother hearing anything that's been blown out of proportion."

I was about to tell him to fuck off, but Laura tapped my chin, and when I looked down at her, she nodded. Likely being able to hear everything we were saying.

I could see it in her eyes: she wanted…or maybe needed this closure with him.

"Fine, we'll be there within the hour."

We met at one of our other locations, a steakhouse that had been closed for nearly a year. Near the front of the restaurant where the daylight still offered enough light to see by, we slipped inside. I'd told Wes and Giles about my meeting, and since Jameson was still on the premises with Penelope, he'd gotten a text as well.

Laura was wearing a simple long-sleeved shirt with her property patch over it and a pair of clean denim jeans. Her hair was dried, and curled down her back, her face clear of any makeup. I was eager to take her back home, and stay there.

I heard her quick intake of breath and felt when she froze in place.

I slid my hand up her back to calm her down, while guiding her forward.

Senator Witt was in the middle of the room as we entered. The people with him yesterday were no longer present. It was the first thing that had my teeth on edge. I scoped out the place, looking over the shadows and other exit points. But then I stopped. This was the senator and Laura's dad. A prideful prick but not a dangerous one. His discretions were never bloody or had anyone being hurt, it was all just to cover what he did with his dick.

Laura held onto my wrist as she stared off with her dad.

"Thank you for coming. We need to discuss a few things."

Laura looked up at me, and then her dad clicked his tongue as if he were suddenly emotional. His arms opened, and he beckoned Laura forward.

"Can you give your old man a hug? It's been too long, sweetie."

Laura took one step forward, but I pulled her back to my side.

My phone was out, held down in my other hand, pressing on Wesley's number.

It was the burner phone we took with us on raids, it connected to only one number and the other party understood what it meant if a call came through in the middle of a deal.

"You're going to prevent her from hugging her father?" Hugh's silver suit accented his graying hair and his sharp blue eyes. But something sinister seemed to lurk in their depths. Which had my stomach churning. *Had I been wrong, was he dangerous?*

"No, you don't usually hug me." Laura tipped her head back and looked at me, as if she were connecting the dots of what was happening.

Fuck. He was planning something.

"Cut to the point, Witt. What the fuck do you want?"

That's when everything in my stomach felt like it'd been diced and shredded because a familiar pair of eyes that matched my own stepped out from one of the corners.

My breath stalled in my lungs as I pulled Daisy closer.

"Hello, Son." My dad smiled as he drew closer.

He was in civilian clothes, a dark shirt and jeans. His face had a few days' worth of growth, and his eyes glimmered with the destruction he had promised when I last saw him.

My father was going to kill me, and if he was successful, then he'd kill Daisy too.

"What he offer you?" I asked my dad, moving to tuck the phone away, so I could grab my gun.

Laura moved with me and wisely started to slide behind me.

"I offered clemency," Hugh said with a twisted sneer.

My eyes focused on him instead of my dad for a brief second. "You owed that to our club."

My dad laughed.

Hugh narrowed his focus. "I fulfilled my end of the deal, seeing as Jefferson will now be taking over as president."

Daisy gasped.

"And what of your daughter?"

My heart slammed against my ribs with hope that the senator would take pity on her. Have mercy. Take her out of here and get her to safety.

"She would have ruined me if anyone caught wind that she was fucking the president of a biker gang. She'll be taken care of as well. I'll tell her mother it was an unfortunate accident."

The door behind us opened as someone new joined the fray.

Daisy turned to look, but I wouldn't take my eyes off the men in front of me.

That was until I heard a click, the sound of a gun being prepped.

I spun around in time to see Luke Holloway, the vice president of the Chaos Kings holding a gun to Laura's head.

Her hand found mine as she shuddered. "I love you."

My eyes widened, processing what was about to happen, and then right as my mouth parted on a scream, someone's gun went off and all I could see was red.

THIRTY
LAURA

My eyes were slammed shut, my fingers gripping Killian's, and then the gun went off.

I expected a bullet to burrow into my skull.

But there was a scream, and it didn't belong to me.

My eyes popped open, and my father was gasping for air while staring at his chest and the red spot that was covering his white dress shirt. He'd been shot.

Then the sound of the gun falling to the floor echoed, along with the arrival of several motorcycles. The man who'd had me at gunpoint had dropped his firearm, and turned to look through the doors he'd just come through.

"Holloway, the back!" Killian's father yelled, while waving his arm and frantically eyeing the doors at my back.

"Dad. Fuck!" Killian roared, darting forward only to drop down when a warning shot came from around the corner, where his dad had disappeared.

The shot missed Killian, but not my father. A second wound opened in his stomach, making him drop to his knees.

My eyes drifted from my father to the woman standing in the back corner who had fired the first shot.

"Mom?"

Her face was stricken; her hands shaking.

"I knew he was evil," she cried, falling to the floor, "but to have his own daughter killed." She choked on a sob, and I moved.

Killian was on his feet, moving with me.

My knees landed in front of my mother's, my father was bleeding out behind me, and I couldn't muster a single tear for him.

"I followed him. I wanted to tip you off, which is why I called. I knew there was something going on after that biker showed me those photos all those years ago. I kept ignoring it but something told me this meeting was going to be an illegal one. I followed him so I had my own proof that he was still doing this shit."

Her eyes were wild.

I rocked her in my arms as she cried.

"Thank you, Mom. You saved my life."

She sobbed harder, clutching my arms. "He was going to kill you, Laura. How was I married to that?"

Finally, a tear did slip free, but it was for her.

I ached for her, that she had married and put up with such a monster for so long.

We rocked back and forth, until Killian and Jameson appeared in front of us and helped us up.

"Giles is going to take you to the club."

I nodded deftly.

Then as Killian was about to turn, I gripped his hand. "Your dad?"

Killian searched my face, his jaw clenching.

"I'll find him."

I had no other choice but to believe him.

My mom sipped her tea while she relaxed on the couch. She was in loose-fitting sweats, a baggy shirt, and a pair of socks that belonged to me.

"What's going to happen? Will I go to jail?" Her blue eyes slid over the rim of her mug.

I shook my head.

"The Stone Riders will take care of it."

She nodded then sipped again before offering me a smile.

"You're one of them now, aren't you?"

Warm honey melted in my chest. "I am."

"You never really seemed to belong in our world, sweetheart. You've been going against the grain since you were a young girl. It always broke my heart because I worried about you. I had no idea where to put you."

I let the silence grow as she continued to sip.

"Then you moved to DC, and you didn't have any roots, and I settled, thinking perhaps you'd just fly and only ever have wings. But I can see it now. You have roots here; this is it for you."

Just then the front door opened, and Killian walked in.

He slipped out of his boots and cut, then wandered over to where we sat.

"Hello Mrs. Witt, can I make up the guest room for you?"

I blushed at his polite attitude toward her. I had no idea he had it in him.

"It's just Lacy, and yes, that would be wonderful. Thank you."

Killian placed a kiss on the top of my head and then moved toward the hall closet where we had clean sheets. He'd moved a new bed into the room as well.

She smirked at me from over her mug again, and you'd think she hadn't just killed her husband in cold blood a few hours earlier. Somehow, it made me glad.

I wanted my mom to be free, even if it meant she had to do the unimaginable to get there.

My mom stayed for three days before departing for Richland.

Killian was the sweetest I'd ever seen him be while she was with us.

He was polite, kind, and extremely chivalrous. But I also saw worry hanging over him.

We still hadn't found Jefferson.

To distract him, I decided to show him something.

"Where are we going?"

I pulled his hand until he was following behind me.

"Just a few more steps."

We cleared the main floor of the club and were headed down the hallway.

Then I was pushing open the office door.

"Open them."

Killian did as I said, slowly taking in the room until his gaze landed on the far wall.

"Are those?" he started, and I walked closer with him.

"Your drawings." I'd framed as many as I could find. It included some rummaging through his room in the club and a few of his old boxes. Now at least ten pieces of his art graced the walls, and a new desk sat perched on the opposite side of mine.

"I also added a framed photo of us." I touched the four by six image of us together. It was the day he'd gotten back and I had run at him wearing his property patch. Someone had taken a photo of when he scooped me up into his arms. The smile he gave while stroking the glass of the photo undid me.

His eyes bounced up, landing back on the walls. "What is this, Daisy?"

I turned toward him and placed my hands on his chest.

"Where we belong." I smiled. "I help run things from here, but it's your club, so I wanted you to have your own desk, your own space. I wanted you to know you're not alone. I'm in this with you. I'm here. Standing next to you or waiting at home while you deal with things in the club that I can't witness. Whatever and wherever this club takes you, I'm in it with you. I'll hold things down while you're gone and help carry them while you're here."

His eyes glittered as he tucked a piece of hair behind my ear.

Then, so soft it nearly broke me, he whispered, "you belong and forever will be in here." He moved my hand over his heart. "No matter where we go or what we do. You're it for me, Laura Witt. One day that will change to Laura Quinn, and then we're going to have kids."

"Yeah?" A tear slid down my cheek.

His lips lightly brushed against mine. "Yeah."

I sank into the feeling of hope, and I chose to cling to it.

"Tell me why you erase them instead of drawing."

His soft chuckle reverberated through my chest.

Eyeing one of his pieces of art that resembled a daisy, he let out a sigh.

"You can't fuck up something you erase, you can only fuck up something you create. I learned how to perfect the skill of avoidance."

I swatted his chest playfully because that's exactly what he'd done with us.

"Why didn't you come to me after you told me to come back?"

We settled in one of the chairs, Killian pulled me into his lap.

"Similar reason. I hadn't started anything with you officially, no matter how badly I wanted you. Didn't want to create something and fuck it up. Simon wanted me to focus on taking the club over, and had explained I needed to make sure I was without distraction. You became a piece of paper covered in graphite in my mind. I'd slowly erase pieces of you as I could, until I was able to see the entire picture."

I thought that over. "You were afraid."

He hummed, kissing my back where that tattoo rested, under my shirt.

"I was fucking terrified, Daisy. Nearly lost you too…but once it was time to step into this role, I was sure I could just toss you out of my mind. Not peel back any layers at all and discover what could have been. But then you got drunk that night in my truck, and you revealed your cards when you asked to touch me. I realized it was what I'd been waiting for."

"For me to jump you?" I scoffed, shaking my head. Streaks of light poured in through the glass, making the plants and the glowing lights I had strewn up on my side of the room glow.

Killian stroked a hand up my back. "For you to claim me."

I bent in for a kiss, but our mouths were hungry and our hands desperate.

Before long, Killian had slammed the office door shut and bent me over his desk.

With the sounds of our unraveling, I smiled, clenching the edge.

I was going to enjoy my life with Killian Quinn.

Every single day I'd push to remind him and myself of exactly where we belonged.

THIRTY-ONE
KILLIAN
ONE WEEK LATER

Church was too crowded.

Our club wasn't being very welcoming, and I didn't entirely blame them, but they'd have to acclimate.

"We have a common enemy," I said, standing at the front of the room. Jameson King was standing next to me.

"Jefferson Quinn and Luke Holloway are forming a new club. They took over half of the club from Chaos Kings, Mayhem Riot and even a few members from the Death Raiders have joined."

Silas wasn't pleased to learn this, but he'd declined on attending this little meeting. When he learned that we'd be inviting Jameson to live on our club property, he was less than thrilled and even delivered a warning that he might be popping in from time to time.

Whatever the fuck that meant.

I stared out at the group of men in front of me. Their cuts had skulls wearing crowns, ours had the skulls with roses blooming from the eye sockets. Most men wore grimaces and anger laced each and every word that anyone muttered.

"For the time being, we're allies." Jameson spoke up next to me.

"Where is our club going to go? We can't both be here in Rose Ridge," one of his members asked. I saw a few others nodding their heads. A few of mine shook their heads, almost as if to silently say they weren't welcome here.

"We have a large house on the back of the property. It's big enough for the ones who need a place to live. For the rest, you can drive back and forth. There's a separate entrance, so you won't even have to drive by our club, or even be a part of it. You'll be on your own."

Someone scoffed, and a few others grumbled.

"We understand this isn't perfect—" Jameson started.

"But it will work," I cut in.

"Just until we find Jefferson and Luke," Wes added, and there was a sound of agreement finally coming from both clubs.

Then Jameson leaned over the table and leveled each of his members with a glare.

"While you're here, you will be respectful of the town, the club, and its women. And I can't stress this enough..." His glare turned glacial. "If any one of you tries any shit with Penelope, I will kill you on the spot."

His members nodded their understanding.

I gave the same speech to my men. "Penelope is under Stone Rider protection. She isn't to be touched, talked to, or even smiled at. Everyone understand?"

Everyone agreed.

I could tell Jameson's shoulders relaxed a bit.

"While we have so much manpower, maybe we should take care of those fucking activists." I smiled at the room, and a chorus of agreement went up. While Silas indeed had gone back to enact revenge on the bloggers, they'd seemed to disappear entirely. Then it became difficult to nail down who had been a part of it. We couldn't kill fifty people and have it go unnoticed by the feds. So, we came up with a better idea.

I held up a file and slapped it down on the table.

"We were able to grab a print from the Zippo lighter one of the assholes dropped that tried to start Callie's car on fire. The rest of the bloggers have been meeting at the local coffee shop. We're going to begin collecting their prints. One by one."

"And do what with them?" someone called.

I smiled at Wes, who smiled at Jameson.

"We're going to plant their records on open investigations—specifically ones that could tie back to either of our clubs. These fuckers will go down for crimes we committed."

The laughter in the room made my heart soar.

I wanted to brag and tell them this was Laura's idea. My evil little genius. She had asked me a few days ago whatever happened with the lighter she'd grabbed. She'd also told me about their meetings in the coffee shop, and it clicked. Plant evidence, framing them for crimes we committed.

Shut them the fuck up.

I was president now, and with half the Chaos Kings here, it wasn't going to be easy, but we'd make it work.

Honestly not much was phasing me, not as long as I had Daisy.

I couldn't believe how worried I was about her being my pebble, not when she ended up being my entire world.

Funny how perspective can shift everything.

I concluded the meeting, allowing the members to disperse. Something told me Silas was going to be watching over our club a little more carefully now that all these new members were roaming about.

And with Wes and Jameson now by my side, I felt like we'd get my dad.

It was only a matter of time.

EPILOGUE
PENELOPE

Two Months Later

I tried to smile with everyone else as Laura took the stage. She was glowing from how happy she was. I wasn't assuming, I knew she was happy. She'd come over to the cabin with a tub of ice cream in tow the other night, crying over what Killian had done for her.

He'd paid to renovate this place for her.

New stage, lights, the piano was top of the line. The space was larger, the bar in the back extended, with new appliances. The entire place looked new.

There were even comfortable seats to sit in after Laura had heard me whine about my back. She was in regular demand at The Hollow, which was fun for Natty, Callie and me and the girls nights we consistently required.

Although this chair wasn't nearly as comfortable as it seemed last week.

No matter how I sat, my back seemed to throb in pain. I hissed, trying to adjust again only to have Callie glance over.

"What's wrong?"

I adjusted again. "Nothing, just can't get comfortable."

"Here," she stood, trying to help me, "stand up, I'll find you a pillow."

"Where are you—" she'd already walked off, and the house lights were dimmed indicating that Laura was about to start singing.

I stood, as Callie rushed back, a small pillow in hand but froze, her eyes going wide…and dropping to my feet.

I spilled water or…

"Your water broke!"

Oh shit.

My water… "Laura!" Callie cupped her hands, yelling over the heads of all the people sitting at tables to hear Laura sing.

My face flushed. Callie's filter was non-existent these days, not that I had known her long enough to know if she used to have one.

Laura rushed off the stage, right as Natty made her way from the bar.

Harris, Riley and Brick hurried over, all watching for danger.

"She's in labor!" Callie urged, and gripped my hand.

Harris seemed to panic, his eyes went wide as he looked down at my stomach. My blue jeans were soaked, and to think I was feeling prideful just yesterday about how I could still fit in them as long as I folded them down.

"Jameson will need to know." Riley said, carefully guiding me up the stairs.

Fuck, why did this place have such steep stairs?

Each step felt like daggers were being dragged over my stomach.

"Want me to carry you, Penny?" Harris asked hesitantly. I'd grown close to the older biker, to the point he felt almost like a father to me. More so than anyone else.

But still, I couldn't fathom the idea of—

A burning pain seared across my abdomen, making me moan in pain.

"Yes, fuck. Please carry me. Get me the fuck out of here."

I slammed my eyes closed as Harris picked me up and began to run. I held onto my stomach, not watching as he tucked me into the car, or to even see where my friends went. I was focusing on breathing.

The next thing I knew we were pulling into the hospital.

My eyes wouldn't open because the pain was so intense.

"Where is he?" Harris asked gruffly. I knew he was asking about Jamie.

I wanted to know too. It was rare he left me alone these days, especially with Luke trying to come back around.

"On his way." That was Riley.

When had I made it into this room?

"You'll need to get into a gown, Penelope." Doctor Beckett informed me, calmly. I opened my eyes, seeing her confident smile.

She ushered the men out of the room, but allowed me to have one friend. I chose Natty, as her and I had become closer than I was with Laura or Callie.

"Here." Natty helped me into the god-awful gown, it was gray with blue stripes.

"It's completely open in the front." I gaped.

A nurse walked in, carrying something. I wasn't paying attention.

"Yep, not much privacy from here on out."

Okay…

"You can tie these strings over your breast to keep them somewhat covered."

I fumbled with the strings, awkwardly arched as pain continued to rip through my middle.

"Just get into bed, Pen. I'll do all this for you." Natty stroked my back, and urged me toward the bed. I did as she said, awkwardly crawling in. A friend of mine used a midwife to have her baby and was in a bathtub after her water broke. The idea freaked me out, so I'd opted for anything but that when I started my care with Dr. Beckett.

"We're going to get you hooked up to an IV, and all situated so you start to feel comfortable, okay?"

I nodded at the nurse and continued to breathe.

Right as she left the room, I could hear someone screaming from the hall.

I craned my neck trying to see, but Natty moved first.

"We're being guarded, don't worry."

I wasn't but, still I absently touched the plain gold band on my ring finger.

"What if…" I started when the door burst open.

"That's my fucking baby!" Luke shouted, pointing at me. His neck was straining, veins on the brink of popping.

I took in his disheveled look, his closely cropped chestnut hair and hazel eyes. The way his handsome face still tugged at the abandonment, and rejection he'd left me with. The life we'd nearly built together.

Jameson barreled through the door a second later after Luke's gaze fell on me, but it didn't go to my stomach.

It went to the finger I was touching and the ring resting there. I wanted to say something, explain myself and tell him why I'd done it. How there was no other option for me. It wasn't real, but I didn't owe him that. My mouth clamped shut, even as I registered his reaction.

Pain and hurt flashed in his eyes as Jameson pushed past him, "Yeah, well that's *my* fucking wife."

Book Three will follow Penelope's story.
(Yes, Silas is getting a book- it will be the fourth and final book in the series.)

Click Here for Bonus Material
Including an extended epilogue for Killian and Laura, spicy scenes, and a moment between Natty and Silas.

ALSO BY ASHLEY MUÑOZ

Mount Macon Series

Resisting the Grump

Tempting the Neighbor

Saving the Single Dad

Stone Riders

Where We Started

Where We Belong

WWP

WWE

Standalone

Only Once

The Rest of Me

Tennessee Truths

Rake Forge University Series

Wild Card

King of Hearts

The Joker

Finding Home Series

Glimmer

Fade

Anthology & Co Writes

What Are the Chances

Vicious Vet

ACKNOWLEDGMENTS

This book wouldn't have happened without the help of my beta readers, Melissa Mcgovern, Amy Elizabeth, and Kelly Drudy.

I mean that very seriously.

Ocassionally there are overwhelming odds that are difficult to push through and overcome. Christmas came with extra company, and more stress than I knew what to do with—these amazing beta readers worked tirelessly to help push me to finish this story.

Thanks to Amanda Anderson who worked effortlessly to nail down the branding concept for this series, and cover. Who helped sort through photo after photo for the perfect cover image. Who helps me stay focused, encouraged, and on target. I can't wait to smash the goals I boldly set for the year and see this series soar.

To Tiffany Hernandez, my PA. Still my ride or die, still in my corner, and still keeping me organized, while also proofing all my projects. I am so eternally grateful to have you.

To my agent, Savannah Greenwell. Thank you so much for pushing this book and snagging such an incredible deal with Dreamscape to get this into audio so quickly.

Thanks to my amazing editor, Becky Barney who was such a huge help in not only a quick turnaround time with this project but being so helpful with rounding out the final story.

Echo Grace, thank you for nailing the concept for this series and once again delivering such an incredible cover. Your talent is out of this world.

Thank you to my book beauties, and all the new readers who constantly recommend my books.

Last but certainly not least, thank you to my family and my eternal support system who love me and help me through every challenge and new aspect of this growing business. A huge thank you to my husband, Jose who jumps in to help with shipments, branding content for PR Boxes, and so much more. I couldn't do this without you.

ABOUT THE AUTHOR

Ashley is an Amazon Top 50 bestselling romance author who is best known for her small-town, second-chance romances. She resides in the Pacific Northwest, where she lives with her four children, husband, and pets. She loves coffee, reading fantasy, and writing about people who kiss and cuss.

www.ashleymunozbooks.com